KEEPERS of the Heart

With tender memories of Missy, Sandee, and Bippy—
my floppy-eared, big-hearted friends who bounded through life
with perfect joy and no regrets. Keepers all.

OTHER BOOKS AND BOOKS ON CASSETTE
BY JOANN JOLLEY:

Secrets of the Heart

Promises of the Heart

Legacy of Love
(with Lucile Johnson)

KEEPERS of the Heart

a novel

JoAnn Jolley

Covenant Communications, Inc.

Covenant

Cover painting by Steve McGinty

Published by Covenant Communications, Inc.
American Fork, Utah

This is a work of fiction. The characters, names, incidents, places, and dialogue are products of the author's imagination, and are not to be construed as real.

Printed in the United States of America
First Printing: October 2001

08 07 06 05 04 03 02 01 10 9 8 7 6 5 4 3 2 1

ISBN 1-57734-960-1

Library of Congress Cataloging-in-Publication Data

Jolley, JoAnn, 1945-
Keepers of the heart: a novel/JoAnn Jolley
p. cm.
ISBN 1-57734-960-1
1.Mormon families--Fiction. 2. Pregnant women--Fiction. 3. Mormon women--fiction. I. Title.
PS3560.O436 K44 2001
13'.548--dc21

2001042542

Prologue

Somewhere along the line, it had all come down to this: one pale, puffy-eyed, scraggly-haired woman squinting into a small patch of bathroom mirror rubbed clean of fog after a hot shower. "You are pathetic," she moaned, firmly pinching one sallow cheek to coax a bit of color into her face. "How did this happen, anyway?"

"I think I can answer that," a cheerful male voice said close to the bathroom door, which was slightly ajar. He waited for her to quickly shrug into a light terry cloth robe, then pushed the door open and waved away some of the steam. "It was a joint venture, you know, Mrs. Barstow." He nuzzled her damp neck. "And, like everything else we do together, it'll be a huge success."

"Huge is right," she grumped, turning so he could see her profile. "Who would have guessed? Paula Enfield Morrison Donroe Barstow, Type A advertising mogul, mother of grown children, now forty-two, pregnant, and sick as a myopic mosquito in a catsup bottle." She shook her head incredulously. "I thought it was supposed to get better after the third month or so. It's been almost seven—but who's counting?"

Ted grinned down at her. "Yeah; it seems like only yesterday that we found out."

"Speak for yourself, buddy," Paula rejoined, though she couldn't help warming to his smile. She could never get enough of that smile. Impulsively she reached up to touch his cheek, still rough with overnight stubble. "It really is pretty amazing, isn't it?"

He wrapped his arms around her. "Like a fairy tale. Only this is even better—instead of just happily ever after, it's happily *forever* after. I like the sound of that." His blue eyes sparkled.

"Me too," she agreed. "Although I wouldn't mind snapping my fingers and having the next couple of months disappear in a blur of unparalleled speed." She patted the prominent curve just below her waist. "The sooner this child makes an appearance, the better."

"You mean makes *her* appearance," Ted corrected.

The word sent a flutter of delight rippling through Paula's body, and even the baby seemed to respond with a playful swishing movement. After giving birth to three sons, she could hardly wait to have a daughter. The words of her dear friend, Karti Richland, crackled into her memory: "There's nothing quite like having a little girl. I was thrilled with my boys, of course. But when Andrea and Ruthie came along, they made me feel . . . whole, somehow." Paula smiled as she thought of Karti, who had died eighteen months earlier following a plucky battle with cancer. *Are you up there now,* she wondered silently, *choreographing the delivery of this little spirit to our home? It wouldn't surprise me a bit. Take care of her, will you? And see that she gets here safely. Oh, and tell her that as long as she'll be arriving before summer, she ought to be glad she's coming to sunny California instead of your lovely but rather chilly home state of Idaho.* The baby's foot or knee or elbow firmly nudged her in the side. *Okay, so she already knows that.*

A sudden wave of lightheadedness and nausea caused her to lean heavily against Ted. "I think I'll just go lie down for a bit," she murmured after a moment, then shuffled toward the bed.

"Sure thing," he called after her, his voice tender and solicitous. "Can I get you any of your favorites—chicken and sauerkraut? Mushrooms and blueberry yogurt? Hot caramel over scrambled eggs?" He grimaced as he mentioned the last concoction. "I could ask Millie to whip something up."

"No thanks," she replied, her lips fading to white as she positioned herself carefully among the rumpled covers of their king-sized bed. "I'll get something later." She glanced at the small clock on her nightstand. "You go ahead; you're already late for work."

"Spoken like a true boss-lady. On my way," he quipped, saluting smartly before he marched in to turn on the shower. The bathroom door closed, leaving Paula alone with her thoughts and a churning stomach. She had never forfeited a meal to this pregnancy, but the nausea and weakness were unrelenting, and her own appearances at the offices of Donroe & Associates had been curtailed to one or two days a week, a few hours at a time. In reality, she was perfectly content to have her husband running the show for the time being; she simply wasn't up to it. Besides, they were equal partners, and he kept her up to date on business matters. For now, it was all she could do to be a marginally chipper lady-in-waiting.

She nibbled on a wheat cracker taken from her nightstand drawer, then closed her eyes and took several long, deep breaths, exhaling each one slowly. The actions seemed to diminish her queasiness, and she rolled gingerly onto her side, resting her cheek against one of several crisp white pillows. Before long her body relaxed, and she slipped into a pleasant state of abstraction somewhere between dreaming and wakefulness. She loved these peaceful interludes and welcomed the familiar, satisfying impressions they revealed.

Today, an ethereal image of the San Diego Temple shimmered at the edges of Paula's consciousness. Her lips curved into a delicate smile as she recalled her marriage to Ted in that sacred house, two days after an extraordinary temple session during which they had each (along with Millie, Paula's faithful housekeeper and friend) received their endowments. "Can we do this?" Ted had whispered close to her ear following the sealing ceremony. "I mean, can we really stay this happy—forever?" One glance into his brimming eyes, the azure of a thousand summer skies mirrored in their depths, had convinced her that he would spend the rest of his days trying.

"It's definitely something I'd be willing to work on," she had whispered back, her countenance alive with more love and passion than she had ever felt for another human soul.

Now, nearly a year later, she could barely remember not sharing her life, her bed, her breath and being with him. "What took us so long?" she murmured softly, shifting ever so slightly beneath the rose-colored comforter. A tiny grin flickered across her mouth at the next thought. *I suppose it could have had something to do with his wife.*

Paula and Ted had been business associates for nearly a decade; she had hired him to write promotional copy for her advertising agency after her dismal marriage ended and his career as an award-winning investigative journalist went down in the flames of political intrigue. Their collaboration, for the most part, had been a happy, intense, and productive one; his extraordinary creative gifts, together with her business sense, had eventually widened the gap between her company and the rest of the industry. From her high-rise office in downtown Los Angeles, Paula Donroe had built and superintended an advertising dynasty to be reckoned with. And she couldn't have done it without Ted Barstow.

It had been a little more than two years since the parallel unraveling of their lives had set into motion a chain of events that finally brought them to the altar. Ted's second marriage had disintegrated. Paula's youngest son, twelve-year-old TJ, had been gunned down in a senseless act of violence. Then each of them, in their own roundabout way, had become connected to the Mormon Church—she by conversion and baptism in the wake of her tragic loss, he by reactivation after more than twenty-five years of bitter recriminations against the religion that he blamed for his parents' breakup. In the end, having nearly lost each other in the fallout, they had come together in an astonishing moment of revelation and pure joy. Three months later, in a sealing room crowded to the doorjambs with those—both seen and unseen—who loved them most, they had commenced the journey of their lives.

"And now . . . a baby. A daughter," Paula breathed with a contented sigh, opening her eyes to gaze at a tall aspen just outside the window, its medallion-shaped leaves vibrating slightly in a cool early-January breeze. "It doesn't get much better than this." Her face scrunched up as a new tide of sickness lapped at her insides. "Hold that thought," she mumbled. "At least for another couple of months." She turned slowly onto her back, closed her eyes again, and spread her arms out to either side, trying to relax. *Dr. Parkin warned me that some women are sick for the whole nine months,* she reflected. *Especially those who are—how did she put it?—"more mature." An obvious euphemism for "over the hill and out of shape." But what does she know? I've still got plenty of time. Why, when this little darling graduates from high school, I'll only be—*

"Sixty!" Paula wheezed, her lips suddenly feeling like two halves of an enormous dried apricot. The exclamation was followed by a low, disembodied moan.

She felt the mattress shift slightly as someone sat down beside her. "No doubt about that, my love," Ted's adoring voice whispered.

Paula felt his warm breath against her face and peeked out at him from beneath half-closed eyelids. "About what?" she asked warily.

"You said it yourself—sexy!" He chuckled gruffly, brushing a strand of dark hair away from her forehead. "Quite simply, I find you to be," he lifted her hand and pressed his lips intimately against the soft, smooth flesh of her palm, "the most alluring woman on the planet." His eyes held hers for a long moment, then he raised an eyebrow. "I trust you were dreaming about me."

She swallowed a giggle. "Whatever you say, dear," she cooed.

"Good. Then I'll be on my way. New year, new week, all that sort of thing. Gotta hit the ground running." He stood, still clinging to her hand, squeezing it tenderly. "We'll miss you at the office." His eyes moved to her midsection. "Both of you. Have any exciting plans for the day?"

"Mmm," Paula replied, her face momentarily clouded by a faraway expression. "I need to get started on the nursery. The shower is Saturday, and I'd like to have a place to put everything. Besides, this little girl is going to be here in just a few weeks, whether or not her room is ready." She looked up at Ted, her dark eyes large and uncertain. "Can you believe I've put it off this long? I haven't meant to; I know we've had the new wallpaper and furniture picked out for months. It's just that I couldn't quite bring myself to . . ." Her voice trailed off as she rested a graceful hand against one side of her stomach.

"I know, sweetheart," he soothed. "And I'm sorry. Would you like to wait until tonight? We could do it together."

She smiled warmly at him. "Thanks, but this one is mine. It'll be good for me, I suppose; it's quite possible that on some level I still need to come to terms. I'll be all right. Just don't be late, okay? Millie's making your favorite—lamb chops. And Scotty doesn't work tonight, so maybe the two of you can shoot a few baskets or something." She smirked endearingly. "Our lovable anti-Mormon will never even know he's been to a family home evening."

"Then it's a date," Ted grinned, bending over to kiss her lightly on the forehead. "I'll call you later."

Paula nodded and closed her eyes as his large hand slipped tenderly away from hers, and she felt the mattress relax slightly as he stood. She listened to his firm footfalls against the carpeted stairs, and a few moments later heard him chatting easily with Millie downstairs in the kitchen. Within a minute or two the garage door chugged open, and his Jeep Cherokee's motor came to life with a guttural roar. The vehicle moved quickly out of the driveway, its brakes squeaking a little as Ted stopped for an instant before proceeding down Valley View Drive toward the interstate. These were all sounds and sensations that had become familiar and dear to her over the past several months, and this morning she listened carefully until the last vibration of the Cherokee's motor was beyond earshot.

She slowly nibbled another cracker, waited for a few minutes, then sat up and swung her legs gingerly over the side of the bed. "Okay," she murmured resolutely, "this is it." She cinched her terry robe more closely about her body. "Today, the past meets the present and makes way for the future." Sighing deeply, she glanced heavenward. "But I don't think there's any way I'll be able to do it alone, Father. I'm going to need some help on this. Please."

Paula bowed her head briefly, then slowly stood and shuffled through the open bedroom door. A few hesitant steps brought her to the closed door of her youngest son's room. Today was the day she would put away his life.

Chapter 1

The brass knob felt smooth and cool to Paula's touch as she turned it and pushed against the heavy oak door. As it swung silently open, she felt an anxious flutter rise in her stomach. *Why am I so nervous?* she wondered. *I've been here dozens, maybe hundreds of times over the past two years, but I've never felt so . . .*

Two years. The thought stopped her halfway into the room. Had it really been that long—two years since she had last seen her sandy-haired, freckle-cheeked, relentlessly energetic twelve-year-old son cavorting around their driveway basketball court? Romping with his best friend, their golden retriever Rudy? Hiding beneath the bedcovers late at night, a penlight tucked behind his ear, reading one of those Western novels he loved so much? Regaling her with endless stories from his new favorite, the Book of Mormon? *Two years. TJ would've been fourteen now—a teenager. What does a teenager do in heaven, anyway?* A familiar ache settled in the back of her throat as she reached for the light switch. *Whatever it is, he's not doing it with me. Not doing it with us.*

A basketball-shaped lamp blinked on beside the bed, illuminating the room with cool white light. Like a small island of time left undisturbed by life's ebb and flow around it, this space was still TJ's—the high-energy red, white, and blue polished cotton bedspread; basketball posters adorning the walls; photos of Paula, Scott, and TJ at the beach and on a ski vacation at Lake Tahoe; rows of dog-eared paperback books crowded tightly into a double-wide bookcase by a small study desk; a silver boom box tucked beneath one corner of the bed. His clothes still hung in the closet, his socks and underwear and T-shirts nestled together inside a bright red chest of drawers against one wall.

Millie faithfully cleaned and dusted here regularly, leaving nothing untouched but everything in its place. It was as though she caressed the room spotless every week.

Paula sat down heavily on the bed and stared silently at the floor for a long while. Finally, she rubbed an unsteady hand across her forehead. "How can I do this?" she whispered. She spread both hands against the colorful spread and hunched over as though in pain. "It's like throwing him away—throwing it all away. My precious boy." A sudden rush of emotion seemed to press her backward against TJ's pillow, and she covered her eyes with one arm as tears threatened. How could she possibly relegate the remains of her son's life to some dusky, uninviting corner of the storage room? They needed this space, of course; she and Ted had talked about it months earlier and agreed that it would make a perfect nursery. Besides, it was high time she made peace with the past and tucked most of these tender memories into a special corner of her heart for permanent safekeeping. But it was one thing to think about it, talk about it, even plan for it, and quite another to actually step across the hall and begin sorting pieces of her son's life into small, conveniently labeled packages. TJ's Books. TJ's Collection of Old Movies. TJ's Report Cards. TJ's Basketball. TJ's Pajamas. Paula moaned and pressed her lips together as a large knot of grief constricted her chest and erupted into her throat. *Two years, and it seems like yesterday when I held him in my arms for the last time.*

A light knock at the open door told Paula she wasn't alone. Lifting her arm away from her eyes, she wiped at her damp cheeks and turned her head toward the sound. Millie stood in the doorway, her short round figure silhouetted against the hall light. When she spoke, her voice was soft and infinitely gentle. "Ted mentioned that if you were up to it, you might be going through some of TJ's things today. Do you need some help, dear? I brought a few storage boxes." She carefully lowered three plastic containers to the floor. "We can do it together, if you like."

"Thanks, Millie," Paula said gratefully, sitting up and swinging her legs over the edge of the bed. "I thought I'd rather do it alone, but now that I'm here, I . . . I just don't seem to be able to think of what to do first." She gazed mournfully at her friend and shook her head. "It's like my brain is mush, you know?"

Millie sat beside her on the bed. "I understand," she said, patting the younger woman's hand. "I felt that way for a long time when I came to clean; then I got to talking to TJ a little every week, and it seemed to make things easier. Still, I never had to put anything away permanently, so this is different somehow—like saying good-bye once and for all, not just 'Hi, how are you today, kiddo?' like I've done for the past hundred weeks or so." She sighed deeply, and Paula knew this would not be easy for either of them. "But if I might make a suggestion . . ." Millie's voice trailed off.

"Yes, of course," Paula said quickly. "What did you have in mind?"

"Well, there's a family in the ward . . . Ruth Gardner and I have been visiting teaching them for about a year now. The Tiltons."

"Oh, I think I've heard you mention them—a big family," Paula responded. "He's a construction worker or something. They live a ways out of town, don't they?" The image of a large, humble man bearing fervent testimony the previous fast Sunday flickered across her mind. She couldn't recall his wife.

"That's right," Millie smiled. "The thing is, Brother Tilton has been out of work quite a bit lately; he hurt his back, and he can't do the heavy jobs he used to. His wife never complains, but we can see the worry in her eyes every time we visit. They have four boys and two girls, and finances are awfully tight in their family right now. We fixed them a nice dinner for Christmas last month, and the bishop helped us get a few little gifts for under the tree, but they're not exactly having a prosperous new year so far. So I was just wondering . . ." She hesitated, and began twisting the slender gold and topaz ring on one of her fingers.

Paula's brows knit together as she gently prompted her friend to continue. "Well, I don't know quite what that has to do with this," she made a sweeping gesture around TJ's room, "but I'm sure you have something up your sleeve. Please go on."

"All right, then," Millie said, seemingly relieved by Paula's encouragement. "The Tiltons have twin boys, Mark and Clark—sweet young men, but very shy. They'll be eleven next month, and they're growing like weeds. At the same time, TJ's closet and drawers are bursting with nice things—perfectly good clothes that could maybe be put to better use than just being stashed away in boxes. The twins have a couple of younger brothers who could grow into them, too." She looked directly into Paula's wide, dark eyes. "I believe TJ would have liked the idea."

Millie's words hung in the warm air for long moments as Paula closed her eyes and tried to imagine what it would be like to see the Tilton twins decked out in her son's wardrobe. The thought was almost too intimate, too painful to bear, and her shoulders sagged under a new burden of grief. Two thin streams of tears moistened her cheeks, and she shook her head laboriously, as though moving in slow motion against a current of regret. Finally she cradled her face in her hands and bent as far forward as her pregnancy would allow.

Two minutes passed, then five, then more. Millie's blue-gray eyes widened in alarm, and she put an arm around Paula's shoulders. "Oh, my sweet girl," she murmured, her voice heavy with emotion, "I'm terribly sorry—didn't mean to upset you so. It's hard enough to deal with the heartbreak of going through his things, but to give them away . . . whatever was I thinking? Of course we'll just pack everything up, save it so you'll have something to remember—"

"Not a chance," Paula interrupted firmly, raising her head to flash Millie a resolute if watery smile. "I'll admit the idea put me off at first—tore at my heart, in fact, thinking of giving such personal things away to strangers. But then," she sniffed a little, "all of a sudden it was like this Book of Mormon video started playing through my mind. I saw King Benjamin on top of that awesome tower of his, reminding the people to feed the hungry, clothe the naked, take care of one another so everyone had enough. Then there was the prophet Alma and his little band of refugees, looking out for each other under the most terrible circumstances, trying to keep body and spirit together in the middle of an unforgiving wilderness, hiding out for weeks at a time, all the while looking over their shoulders for that horrid King Noah and his thugs—all of it for the sake of bringing souls to the truth." She paused for a moment to brush a hand across the bedspread. "That was one of TJ's favorite stories, you know. Those folks might have started out as strangers, but I could almost see the love grow in their eyes as they kept the faith and shared whatever burdens came along."

"I see," Millie said, her hands folded serenely in her lap. Her eyes glistened as she studied Paula's face.

"And then . . . then I had the strongest impression. It was like a moving picture with all kinds of colors and intensity, but just slightly out of focus. I saw TJ holding his favorite shirt—the blue one with the alligator on the pocket—then reaching out to put it around the shoulders of a light-haired boy about his size. And I swear, the smile on my son's face could have lit up New York City on Christmas Eve."

"The boy had a big heart," Millie stated quietly.

"Still does," Paula added. "In a matter of seconds, and without words—only the look in his eyes and that crazy, gypsy-free smile of his—he taught me a world of truth about living the gospel. That's really the key, isn't it? Helping. Serving. Rescuing. Making friends out of strangers. Healing oneself by taking care of somebody else. It makes sense—and I do agree with you, Millie."

"About what?"

"No doubt in my mind—TJ thinks giving his stuff away is the coolest thing since basketball. Maybe cooler." Paula looked at Millie, her brown eyes luminous. "How can we *not* do this?"

The older woman beamed. "I'll get some more boxes."

"And I'll get dressed," Paula grinned, loosening the belt of her robe. "I'll meet you back here in ten minutes."

Millie nodded, raised herself slowly from the bed, and moved almost to the door. Then she stopped and turned back toward Paula. "By the way," she said, "there is something you should probably know."

"Hmm?" Paula was already padding toward the door herself.

"The Tilton twins. They're blonde."

"What a surprise," Paula chuckled softly.

Several hours later, the two women again sat side by side on the bed, this time to survey the results of their labors. "I guess that about does it," Millie puffed, her gaze roving about the room with more than a trace of nostalgia. "I never dreamed there were so many things to be . . . decided on," she added, glancing briefly at Paula's wan but satisfied expression.

"I know," Paula said, rubbing the back of her neck. "But now that it's done, we can relax and get on with putting together a world-class nursery." She smiled and patted her stomach. "Nothing but the best for my daughter."

The smile faded as she considered three piles of boxes standing in the room like solemn sentinels, nearly filling the open space between TJ's bed and the door. Each group was labeled by a small piece of masking tape on which a single word was written. The pile marked CLOTHING was the largest—six long, deep boxes of neatly folded apparel that would easily dress two youngsters comfortably, even stylishly, from the skin out for several days at a stretch. "I hardly ever saw him in most of these things," Paula had murmured during the packing. "His tastes were utterly predictable—baggy brown pants, the blue shirt, gray socks, Air Jordan sneakers. Anything else could just stay in the closet." She had hesitated while folding the shirt, thinking she might keep it; but the vivid memory of TJ's joyful expression while giving it to his golden-haired friend had made her reconsider. In the end, she had simply pressed a lingering kiss to the jaunty-looking reptile on its pocket and carefully laid it at the very top of the box.

The second pile, labeled MISCELLANEOUS, was comprised of four smaller boxes filled with books, rolled-up sports posters, CDs, the boom box, a few videos, whatever was usable from his desk drawers, and three or four hand-held computer games. Seeing that the last box was not quite full, Paula had carefully unscrewed a miniature basketball hoop from the wall above TJ's desk, retrieved a small red foam ball from a corner of his closet, and tucked them into the box. *A perfect fit,* she had smiled to herself.

Her gaze moved to the smallest pile. It sat close to the bed—a plastic Albertson's grocery bag leaning against two heavier plastic storage containers. On top of one of the opaque white boxes was a strip of tape marked SAVE. Here Paula had stored a few carefully selected treasures reclaimed from this space that had once been her youngest son's sanctuary—small pieces of him that she would keep forever. A dog-eared Zane Grey novel; his Michael Jordan T-shirt; several small framed snapshots of the family on vacation; his seventh-grade class photo—each one would remind her of his unruly hair, playful brown eyes, exuberant smile, and sturdy physique when the precise images began to fade from her mind as she knew they would, and in fact, as they already had. His Book of Mormon, signed by the elders who had taught him the gospel, and a small dark-blue journal with Jesus' picture on the cover, given to him by a loving Sunday School teacher not more than three weeks before he died, would never let her forget that his life—and his death—were woven inextricably into the fabric of her own testimony. She had resisted his conversion, forbidden his baptism, and ultimately driven him to tag along with Scott, his sixteen-year-old brother, to the gang-infested streets of downtown Los Angeles one sultry November afternoon. It was there a sniper's bullet had put an end to TJ's shining young life before it had hardly begun. Later, when grief and longing opened her heart to the reality of spiritual things, she had listened to the elders' message and become a Latter-day Saint. To her dying day, she would bless and curse the events that had brought her to the waters of baptism.

Paula reached out to pull the rounded grocery bag onto her lap. Through its thin plastic she could feel the rough-grained surface of a basketball. Opening the bag, she rotated the ball with her hand until the initials TJD, scrawled in large black permanent-marker letters, came into view. She ran her fingertips deliberately across the homemade monogram, feeling, memorizing the same grooves and ridges he had touched thousands of times before, then hugged the ball to her swollen midsection and rocked gently back and forth. *If there's basketball in heaven,* she mused silently, *my boy will have 'em cheering in the bleachers.* The impression brought a small, reluctant smile to her lips.

Millie's kind hand rested on her shoulder. "You must be awfully tired, dear," she said. "So many memories and things to sort through—enough to wear on a body from the inside out. You need to rest yourself and gather strength for the little one. Why don't you go lie down for a bit? I'll finish up here."

Paula glanced at her watch: nearly four o'clock. No wonder she felt like a wrung-out mop. "I think I'll take you up on that, my friend; old pregnant ladies don't have much steam left by this time in the afternoon." She reached up to pat Millie's hand, which still lay lightly against her shoulder. "And thanks for your help. There's no way I could have done it without you. If TJ had been here, he'd have given you a noisy peck on the cheek and shouted 'Nice job, Milleee!' loud enough to raise the rafters."

"Wouldn't surprise me if he's been here all the time," Millie said with a tiny catch in her voice. "'Specially after you had that little intuition earlier. I suppose he's just keeping a low profile, spiritually speaking. Maybe helping us to let go a little."

"Probably so," Paula agreed. "Anyway, I get the feeling he's happy at the way things have turned out. Now, I think I'm ready for that little nap." She yawned and stretched, mentally comparing the size of her stomach to that of the plastic-clad ball. They were about the same, she thought. Or at least they felt like it. Setting the ball beside the SAVE pile, she urged her heavy body away from the bed. Once she was upright, a sudden wave of lightheadedness caused her to sway in place for a moment. Millie took the cue instantly and circled an arm firmly around Paula's back, then walked her slowly across the hall to her room and helped her to lie down on the large bed.

"You're an angel," Paula murmured, closing her eyes and relaxing against the pillows. She felt Millie gently tugging the sneakers from her feet and covering her with a soft blanket. "The mother I never really had."

"Oh, pooh," Millie replied lightly, but Paula could hear the warmth in her voice. "Just doing what I can to help. Besides, anybody'd be proud as punch to be your mother. I mean that, girl. You're a keeper." She bent to brush a gnarled hand lightly across Paula's cheek. "Now, I think I'd better go see what I can do about that lamb chop dinner we promised your husband." Without another word, she turned and shuffled from the room.

Left alone, Paula willingly gave in to exhaustion and expected to fall asleep right away. Instead, while her body lay pleasantly oblivious, her mind began a delicate game of cat-and-mouse with Millie's words, going back to them again and again. "Anybody'd be proud as punch to be your mother. You're a keeper." *Millie's such a dear,* she mused. *Sometimes I think she knows me better than I know myself.*

Without warning, Paula's mind raced back across the better part of four decades, straight to the sprawling Enfield estate in Connecticut. Her early childhood there had played itself out on idyllic spring and summer afternoons spent reading or daydreaming in the gazebo; early on sparkling fall mornings, when she sneaked outside to dance, tracing nimble swirls in the dew across a broad expanse of lawn behind the family mansion; and in the deep, cold winter, when her sizeable doll collection, arranged neatly in three semi-circles on her large canopied bed, would serve as an appreciative audience for her twice-weekly dramatic presentations. As the only child of upper-crust parents, she had all the comforts and toys and opportunities she needed to be happy. Through elementary school, she was at the center of a large circle of energetic, bubbly-faced youngsters. By the time she reached ninth grade, every girl in school wanted to be Paula Enfield—and every boy would have given up three months' allowance to spend one hour in her shadow.

The only cracks in her contentment, it seemed, were at home. It wasn't a bad life, she thought—just a bit lonely. Her father, a tall, severe man who had more money than he knew what to do with, was rarely home and never in the mood for diversion. Paula understood, even from her earliest years, that he was extremely busy running a business and teaching part-time at Yale University, so she adored him from a distance. An occasional pat on the head from his large, cultured hand could keep her going for weeks.

Marjorie Enfield, Paula's mother, was slightly more accessible but perpetually distracted by her bridge club, garden club, book club, charity events, and a continual succession of migraine headaches. Occasionally she would send her daughter on a "special outing"—usually to a local museum or art gallery—with one of the servants. Paula always thanked her mother politely and pressed a light kiss to Marjorie's smooth cheek. *You're so beautiful. I love you so much,* the young girl would think, her gaze taking in her mother's rich brown hair, luminous dark eyes, full lips, and slender, elegant figure. *I hope one day you'll be proud of me.* The thought always caused her a little pain, but she would quickly shrug it off and go to her room to practice smiling saucily into the mirror.

These days, Paula rarely stopped to consider what her life would have been like if she had actually finished growing up in the tolerable but detached family setting of her youth. Her father, of course, had expected her to follow in his footsteps at Yale, while her mother had always been busy . . . well, having a headache. In the end, it didn't really matter much what anyone thought. By the time Paula was sixteen, she had fallen deeply in love with Gregory Morrison, a passionate, gifted young artist who promised her the world and an unending supply of adoration (not necessarily in that order). Ignoring their parents' fierce objections, she took him up on the offer, and they eloped. For Paula, this overt act of rebellion meant the end of her relationship—however good or flawed it might have been—with Howard and Marjorie Enfield. There was simply nothing left of it—only a bitter silence that echoed in her mind every time she recalled the sudden "click" on the phone line seconds after she told them of her marriage. Still, with Greg she finally had someone to belong to, the freedom of unconditional, no-holds-barred, soul-satisfying love. With any luck at all, they would be able to make it last the rest of their lives.

It was over in less than a year—not for lack of love, but for lack of time. Greg's life ended one dark February night beneath a crumpled motorcycle on a rain-slick highway, and Paula found herself utterly alone and desolate. Three weeks later, she discovered she was pregnant. She couldn't go home, so she worked as a waitress until the baby came. Then, her heart breaking into a million shards of misery, she placed her precious son for adoption, determined to give him a better life than what she could provide. Under the circumstances, it was the right thing to do; but it left her feeling unworthy. Definitely not a keeper.

Years passed, and Paula made an enviable life for herself. Her second marriage, to Richard Donroe, was a disaster; but she rose from its ashes with a thriving advertising business and two sons, Scott and TJ. Then TJ died—but not before hooking up with two young Mormon missionaries who taught him the gospel, and who later helped Paula find her way into the fold. What she didn't know at the time was that Elder Mark Richland, who personally escorted her into the waters of baptism, was the son she had bathed with her own solemn tears twenty-two years earlier, just before giving him up to be delivered into the arms of his new adoptive parents. The revelation of his identity came quite by accident, but it changed both of their lives forever. His mother, Karti, and Paula became fast friends in the months before Karti's death, and her bond with Mark grew deeper and stronger. She had given him away once, but she would never let him out of her life again—never.

A graceful smile settled on Paula's lips as she snuggled against a pillow and her thoughts returned to this day, this hour, this moment. *I've done it,* she reflected. *I've made a good life, and Ted has made it even better.* Indeed, their married life had not been without its adjustments—she'd had to make room for his things in her closet, for example, and there was the ongoing debate, in deference to his bachelor days, about whether leftover pizza was an appropriate breakfast food. But the important things were in place: family prayer, activity in the Church, mutual respect, something chocolate at every meal. And oh, the love! She saw it in his vivid blue eyes every morning, and felt it in the gentle touch of his hand against her cheek when she so much as sighed at some real or imagined dilemma. If this past year was any predictor of the future, she knew she had the best of all possible worlds to look forward to. And, as an added blessing, their new child would only make it better. *Yes,* she reasoned, *it's a fine time to be a mother again. What's more, this little girl will know with absolute certainty, no doubt about it, that she's a keeper. I guarantee it.* This firm resolve welled in Paula's heart like a fountain of unexpected delight, because she instinctively knew that she could make it so. In some miraculous way, her own astringent upbringing had given her the power.

Once again, her thoughts turned to the mother who had virtually disowned her when she was little more than a child. Now a widow in her late sixties, Marjorie Enfield still lived on the Connecticut estate and filled her time with bridge parties, gardening, and an occasional outing to a theater matinee in New Haven. But there was a difference these days, Paula thought—a softening that had begun two years earlier, across the hall in this very home. Prior to that, except for a one-day trip to Connecticut to attend her father's memorial service, Paula had not seen or spoken to her mother for over twenty-three years. But when TJ died, Millie made a call, and Marjorie appeared for her grandson's funeral. She was reserved, dignified, austere as usual—until Paula went looking for her late that afternoon and found her in TJ's room, crumpled on the bed, brokenhearted over the fact that she had never even known the boy. They sat side by side, then held each other, weeping for the loss of a tender young life, and somehow beginning to heal their own divided hearts in the process. Marjorie stayed the weekend, and when it was over they had at least started to come to terms with themselves and each other. When Paula kissed her mother's cheek at the airport, it was just as soft and smooth as she had remembered. Maybe more.

"Oh, Mother, you must come when the baby arrives," Paula murmured. "It'll be like a new beginning for all of us. And you'll love Ted. He's the best." Marjorie had been ill with pneumonia at the time of their wedding, but had sent her best wishes with a set of monogrammed sterling silver napkin rings and an ornate card. "Be happy," she had written in a delicate, flowing hand above her signature.

"Absolutely the best," a male voice drawled as Paula felt someone sitting beside her on the bed. She opened her eyes to see Ted smiling down at her.

"There you go again," she protested lightly, resting her hand on his arm, "catching me talking to myself. Couldn't you at least cough or something when you come into a room?"

"What, and miss the best conversations of the day? I don't think so." He bent to press his lips against hers, then pulled back and studied her face for a moment. "You okay?"

"Of course. Why wouldn't I be? My absolutely-best husband is here, after all."

"You have a point." He grinned, then his expression sobered a little. "I understand you completed 'Mission: Impossible' today. Millie said it took an unexpected turn."

Paula nodded. "Millie is an angel."

"Among other things," he added, sniffing appreciatively. "I can smell dinner now."

"Uh-huh . . . followed by a trip to the gym, perhaps," she smirked, pinching a tiny bulge at his midsection. "Married life and Millie's cooking . . . double jeopardy, my friend."

"Hey," he rejoined, straightening up quickly, "I was just slouching."

Paula smiled impishly and waggled her eyebrows. "I knew that," she said.

"Anyway," he continued, loosening his tie, "I think your compassion and generosity are, as Carmine would say, 'totally awesome . . . bad, girl, baaad!'" They both chuckled as an image of their fiery-haired office manager came to mind.

"It wasn't the easiest thing I've ever done," Paula admitted, her countenance darkening a bit as the feel and smell and texture of TJ's things teased her memory. "But I do believe it's one of the best. Millie—and TJ—helped me to understand that." She gazed up at him with glistening eyes. "I kept his basketball."

"Good for you," Ted breathed, grasping her hand. "Now, let me be the first to offer my own private delivery service, at your disposal. I can do that, you know; I'm the elders quorum president. You just say the word, and it's done."

"Any time, Mr. President. Millie has taken the few things I'm saving down to storage, and the rest is all packed and ready to go." She paused for a moment. "It's in . . . his room."

"Perfect," he said. "I'll get Scott to help me load it into the Cherokee tonight after home evening, then we can take it over to the Tiltons when I get home tomorrow."

A look of alarm rose in Paula's eyes. "We? Oh, I'm not sure I could . . . it's one thing to pack TJ's things for somebody else, but I really don't know if I'm up to—"

"It's all right, sweetness," he interjected. "Whatever you decide to do is fine. We'll just wing it tomorrow, okay?"

"Okay," she replied, clearly relieved. Perhaps she would be able to gather up a little more courage in the next twenty-four hours.

"But however we do it, there's one thing for sure," Ted added, his eyes twinkling.

"Oh, and what might that be?" She somehow knew his response would bring a smile to her face.

"Well, you gotta know that tomorrow night, the Tiltons won't be just Tilton . . . they're gonna be *rockin'!*"

She was right. It was the widest smile of her day.

Late that evening, securely nestled in her husband's arms, Paula ventured to ask the question that had been dancing at the edges of her mind since mid-afternoon. "Ted?" she whispered, hoping he was still awake, though his even breathing told her he could have drifted off.

"Hmm?" he murmured against her cheek. The subtle rush of his breath made her heart beat faster.

"Ted, can I ask you something?"

"Sure," he replied, stroking her hair. "Can I get you some chicken and sauerkraut or something? I could run out to the all-night deli and—"

"No, I'm fine," she insisted. "But I do need to know something."

He yawned. "Anything, my love."

"All right, here goes." She leaned up on her elbow and laid one hand on his chest. "Ted, do you think . . . do you think I'm a keeper?" Then she held her breath.

"A keeper," he repeated slowly. "A keeper? Gee, I'm not sure exactly what you—"

"Millie brought it up earlier today, just after we'd finished cleaning out TJ's room. 'Anybody'd be proud to have you for a daughter,' she said. 'You're a keeper.' Is that what you think, Ted?"

He let out a long, slow breath. "Dunno. It's probably still too early to tell."

Her throat tightened. This wasn't exactly the answer she had expected. "Excuse me?" she questioned.

"Well, you know what they say," he murmured.

"No, I don't believe I do," she replied cautiously. "What do 'they' say?"

"The first million years are always the hardest. If things are still going okay after that, the rest of eternity is gravy." He snorted softly. "So give me a little space here, will ya? Check back with me in, say, a million five, and we'll figure it out from there."

The beginnings of a smile tugged at her lips as she contemplated his statement. Without moving a muscle, she asked, "And in the meantime?"

Ted lay quietly for a few moments, then carefully shifted himself in the bed until they were lying almost nose to nose. "In the meantime," he began in a voice edged with quiet intensity, "I believe that if I were to keep you for a million trillion years, it wouldn't be long enough. If it wasn't forever, I'd be getting the short end of the deal. Millie was right, as usual: anybody would be proud to have you. Especially me. You're definitely a keeper, Paula Barstow. Definitely a keeper. And in a million five, that will still be my answer."

He pulled her close and held her in a long embrace, until his muscles relaxed and she felt his chest rise and fall in the measured cadence of sleep. But she lay awake for a long time, staring into the cool, dark air above them, savoring the truth of his words, feeling them illuminate her soul.

She had been mistaken earlier. *This* was the widest smile of her day.

Chapter 2

Ted had slipped silently out of bed, showered, dressed, and left for the office before Paula even lifted an eyelid the next morning. *It must be the pregnancy,* she mused, stretching slowly until her muscles felt deliciously taut, then relaxing back into the pillows with a contented sigh. *I used to be up before dawn, ready to take on the world.* She patted her rounded stomach. *Now all I'm doing is taking on cargo.* "Not that I'm complaining, you understand," she whispered, gently rubbing one side of her belly where she felt an insistent flutter of activity. "It's just that things are, well, a little different now." Something sharp jabbed at her rib. "But better," she added quickly. "Definitely better." *This kid is not afraid to speak her mind, even before she's born. Heaven help us when she's a teenager . . . I'll have to keep a close eye on her from my rocking chair.*

The room felt stuffy. Paula rolled onto her side and sat up inch meal, swinging her legs carefully over the side of the bed so as to keep any sudden waves of nausea at bay. Pleasantly surprised when no illness materialized, she took it a step further by standing, then paused to allow a brief moment of lightheadedness to pass. "C'mon, wild thing," she said, patting her stomach again, "let's get a little ventilation in here." A few seconds later, she stood at the large bedroom window overlooking their front yard. Pushing aside one panel of drapes, she slid open the window, closed her eyes, and breathed in deeply as a burst of cool, light air freshened her senses. "That's more like it," she smiled. This January morning was beautiful, she thought. Not much smog, a playful breeze, and—

CLANK! The sound of steel hitting cement jangled her eyes open, and her gaze traveled quickly to the driveway below. In an instant, the source of the noise became clear. "The Viper," she sighed. "Won't he ever leave it alone?"

As she watched, two long legs in jeans emerged from beneath the front end of a low-slung, dark-green vehicle, followed by a muscular T-shirted torso and a head of dark, wavy hair. The young man reached for a heavy, oversized wrench or tool of some kind on the cement beside him, then proceeded to wipe the greasy instrument across the front of his shirt. "That's my Scotty," she murmured, shaking her head as she surveyed several more broad swaths of grease next to the new one. But as he came to his feet and his lean, hard body moved easily, even gracefully around to the other side of the car, she couldn't ignore the sudden rush of pride that rose in her chest.

This isn't the same Scott Eric Donroe I knew a year and a half ago, Paula reflected gratefully. Her mind flashed back to the ugly insolence, the seething fury, the outright rebellion she and Millie had endured for several months after they lost TJ, when she had despaired that her older son would ever find his way out of high school, much less make a place for himself in the world. But all that had changed one dark night, when Paula had been viciously attacked by an intruder in her own home. Scott had rescued her from grave injury, possibly even death, and in those life-defining moments their relationship had shifted dramatically. Later, they had talked—really talked—about TJ's violent death for the first time, and Scott had spilled out his anguished belief that he was responsible for it. No one, not even Paula, could have guessed at the depth of his guilt and remorse. Finally, they had clung to each other and wept for their lost son and brother.

That was the beginning, she thought, *and it couldn't have turned out better. Well, maybe a little better,* she conceded with the trace of a smile. *He could have joined the Church. But time will tell; he can't hold out indefinitely. One step at a time.*

Now eighteen, Scott was an energetic, self-assured young man. Shortly after the intruder episode, Paula had taken him to visit the Ninja Academy of Martial Arts, owned and operated by her friend, Bonnie Solomon. Like the proverbial duck to water, Scott had taken to karate and kick boxing with a near-missionary zeal, and within a short time had earned the coveted black belt—along with nearly every member of his gang, the Crawlers, to whom he had given the ultimatum of "Join the class or join the Scabs (a rival gang)." Paula herself had taken lessons, becoming moderately proficient by the time her pregnancy and illness had forced her to the sidelines. But she intended to take it up again once the baby arrived.

Bonnie had declared Scott her best student ever, and upon his graduation from high school had offered him a full-time position as assistant instructor at the Academy. The pay wasn't great, but it was enough, and he poured enormous energy into the job. His work with the students exceeded even Ms. Solomon's rigorous expectations, and Paula was sure that Bonnie would keep him on as long as he wanted to stay. *Possibly forever,* Paula mused, *or at least until his Dodge Viper is paid for. Whichever comes first.* He had worked countless hours of overtime to save up a down payment on the nine-year-old car, and now he spent as much time as he could restoring it to mint condition. Occasionally he escaped to the mountains for a day, where he created wonderful pen-and-ink drawings on a worn sketch pad.

"Hi, Mom," Scott called out when he noticed her at the window. He was one of the best-looking kids in the world, if she said so herself: tall and athletic, with dark, wavy hair, vibrant hazel eyes, and a smile that had already sent the hearts of dozens of girls into meltdown. *And nice, too—at least most of the time,* she added to herself as she smiled and waved at him. *Still a hothead on occasion, but a far cry from the sullen, angry-eyed adolescent I was trying to slap into submission a couple of years ago. Has he grown up, or have I? Probably a little of both.*

Paula had never stopped hoping, praying for Scott's spiritual awakening. He'd become friends with Mark Richland, and had spent a fair amount of time with the Richland family in Idaho, accompanying Paula and Ted on occasional weekend visits. At first he had been charmed by Mark's beautiful younger sister, Andrea, who was close to his age and shared his love for drawing. But since she had made it abundantly clear, during one of their moonlight strolls beside a gentle stream near the family's property, that she was not interested in a serious relationship with anyone but an active Latter-day Saint, he had shrugged off their friendship and distanced himself from her family. He and Ted got along reasonably well, and he had willingly helped load TJ's things into the Cherokee the night before—even flashed Paula one of his bedeviling smiles as she watched. "Way to go,

Mom," he'd said, giving her a quick peck on the cheek between trips upstairs. "This is a good thing you're doing. That family will appreciate it." He had a good heart; she knew it. Now, if only he would open it to the gospel . . .

Give the boy a little room here, Paula reminded herself sternly. *He's had a rocky life, but he'll come around. Besides, he's got contrariness in his genes; if you remember correctly, you didn't exactly take a flying leap into that baptismal font yourself. It took more than just a smidgen of divine intervention to get you there.* She shuddered involuntarily as she recalled TJ's innocent, energetic pleading with her to read the Book of Mormon—a request she promptly ignored. By the time she finally got around to it, he was already gone. In the end, losing him had opened her spiritual eyes to what was really important in life. But the price had been almost too high. She squeezed her eyes tightly shut and breathed a short, silent prayer. *Please don't make Scotty go through something like that, Father. It would break my heart—our hearts—all over again. Please, dear Lord . . . don't. I can wait.*

Feeling a sudden chill, Paula turned away from the window and crawled back under the thick down comforter on the bed, where she lay until late morning, memorizing the myriad sensations of a tiny body exploring its own limited world inside her. *Like a story within a story,* she thought. *What will your story be, little lady? A happy one would be nice. Born under the covenant . . . a great beginning, at least.* "I hope I'm up to this," she said, moaning softly. Something like a judicious head-butt clattered against her spine. "All right, I'll give it my top priority," she promised with a resigned sigh. Then both mother and daughter settled down for a little nap.

Ted was home by six-thirty, full of news about their latest coup on the advertising front. "Some hotshot writer at *Time* wants to do a story about the company," he announced over dinner. "Seems we've developed a reputation for, shall we say, *selective* advertising." He glanced slyly at Paula in between spearing green beans with his fork. "Now, I wonder how a rumor like that could've gotten started."

"Not a clue," she returned with a straight face, but the light in her eyes was unmistakable. Two years earlier, several months after her baptism, she had come face to face with her own conscience in a battle of wills over whether she should agree to create and launch a multi-million-dollar advertising campaign for Green Pointe, one of the country's most prestigious liquor companies. She had made the deal, but abruptly changed her mind on the very morning she found a bottle of Green Pointe bourbon in Scott's high school backpack. The incident had pricked her heart as a mother and her scruples as a new Mormon enough to prompt a revised company policy at Donroe & Associates: no advertising deals that would compromise or conflict with gospel standards. If revenues suffered for it, Paula would deal with the consequences.

Fortunately, it hadn't come to that. In fact, their business had skyrocketed over the next few months, surpassing even the prodigious income they would have realized from the Green Pointe deal. No one seemed able to account for the phenomenon, but Paula had a pretty good idea of what was going on. "According to the Book of Mormon," she would explain patiently to anyone willing to listen, "it's the law of the harvest. You reap what you sow. Do good and prosper; that sort of thing." Her employees just nodded, smiled, and went on about their business, grateful that the winds seemed to be shifting in their favor. But now, even the national press seemed to be taking note of the situation. Two other news magazines had already done articles on Donroe, and the prospect of a third was utterly exhilarating.

Ted's voice broke into her thoughts. "This reporter wants to interview us next week. Think you'll be up to it, Chief?" The confident expression on his face belied the exaggerated concern she heard in his voice.

"Well, gee whiz, I don't know," she responded in a high, nasal voice while nudging a piece of baked halibut around the perimeter of her plate. "I don't have a thing to wear, and besides, I've got this appointment for a manicure, and I don't think my hair will be exactly the right length, and I'm feeling a little chubby lately, and—"

"Terrific," he said, beaming across the table at her. "Wednesday morning, ten o'clock."

"Wouldn't miss it," she laughed. "You know me so well, Barstow."

"Not nearly well enough, my dear," he said smoothly. "But give me another hundred years or so, and I'll have a decent start." He paused and regarded her closely. "You look better today—not so pale and exhausted. With all you did yesterday, not to mention the emotional implications, I thought you would've been down for the count, at least for a couple of days. Instead, you seem . . . relieved, or something. Certainly in good spirits."

"Guilty as charged," Paula replied lightly. "I suppose it did me good to finally tie up some loose ends, put things in order. Get ready for happier days to come. Or maybe this pregnancy has just taken a natural turn for the better. Whatever it is, I'm content to go with the flow."

Ted leaned back in his chair. "So, does this mean you'd like to 'flow' on over to the Tiltons' with me this evening to make our special delivery? We could go out for ice cream afterwards, and—" The sudden shadow in her eyes stopped him in mid-sentence. "On the other hand," he added quickly, "it's perfectly fine if you'd rather not—"

"I'd rather not," she stated flatly, then reached out to touch his hand. "But I've been thinking about it all day, and there's something I'd like you to do for me, if you don't mind."

"Name it." He stared at her with a question in his eyes.

When she spoke, there was an obvious tenderness in her voice that told him more than her words alone could express. "I've written them a note explaining everything—telling them a little bit about TJ, about us, even about Millie's suggestion and the spiritual nudge that prompted me to go along with it. I—I felt like it would be easier on all of us if I wrote it, instead of trying to tell them in person and risking an emotional outburst. Something like that might make them reluctant to accept what we have to give."

Ted nodded his understanding and turned his hand to clasp hers tightly. "I would be honored to deliver it," he said. "And I would be doubly honored to take you out for ice cream afterwards."

"Ah, Mr. Barstow, you are *so cool,"* she replied, batting her eyelashes as she wiped one small tear from her cheek, where it had strayed earlier. "I'll be waiting."

"Then it's a date," he grinned. "Just give me a couple of hours, and I'll be back on your doorstep." They finished their meal in peaceable silence. Half an hour later, upstairs in their room, Paula smiled as she heard the Cherokee pull out of their driveway on its errand of compassion.

"For some reason, this is darned near the best ice cream I've ever tasted," Ted observed as he and Paula sat close together in a red Naugahyde booth at Trixie's Sundae Shoppe. It was late—nearly eleven o'clock—and they were the only customers, which suited them perfectly.

"It must be like Nephi said when he described the fruit of that wonderful tree," she observed. "'It was most sweet, above all that I ever before tasted.' Tell me again what happened," she urged for the second time. This was worth hearing more than once.

"Well," he began, chuckling a little as he tried to put a slightly different spin on his experience, "remember before we were married—or even thinking about it, for that matter—when we were smack in the middle of developing a huge ad campaign, and you called some of the copy I'd written 'pure magic'?"

"Indeed I do," Paula replied. "It was way beyond excellent—more like 'superb to the hundredth power.' Made me feel like I absolutely couldn't exist for another moment without having that product in my life."

"And you told me so, too," Ted reminded her. "For me, *that* was the pure magic—knowing how you valued and appreciated my work. So, in a sense, we both got what we wanted: you loved the ad copy, and I loved the way you loved the ad copy." He flashed her a quirky little smile. "Am I making any sense at all here?"

"Just keep talking," she said genially. "I'm sure I'll catch on sooner or later."

"Okay. The thing is, that's exactly what happened tonight—everybody got what they wanted . . . what they needed. When I knocked on the Tiltons' door, they had no idea what I was doing there, although they graciously invited me in. But when I handed Sister Tilton your note and she began to read it, I literally saw her countenance light up from the inside out. Then she started to cry. It was kind of like Niagara Falls being lit from behind by a thousand mega-power floodlights—the most beautiful thing I've ever seen. Except, of course, for your face on our wedding day."

Paula felt a slight flush rise to her cheeks. "Go on," she said.

"Pretty much the same thing happened when Brother Tilton read the note. That crisp little hundred-dollar bill you tucked into the envelope didn't hurt any, either. They gathered their children into the living room, and he read your message out loud to them. I'd been a little nervous, you know—afraid they might not be in a receptive frame of mind. I'll tell you, I'm not sure I'd be humble enough if it came to that in my own life. But talk about 'pure magic' . . . nothing could have been sweeter than watching that family hugging and kissing one another—then having them hug and kiss me until I thought I'd died and gone to heaven." His voice broke a little as he added, "There's no doubt . . . absolutely no doubt in my mind that your note was inspired." He riveted his gaze on her for a long moment. "But then you knew that, didn't you?"

"I believe I did," she answered quietly. "Please . . . finish the story."

"Gladly. The twins helped me unload the Cherokee. They were quiet at first; I guess they didn't know quite what to think. Clark was the shy one, almost painfully polite, and Mark kept shaking his head like he couldn't quite believe what was happening. But after a few minutes of opening boxes and stuff, they both really loosened up. You'd have thought it was Christmas morning on the richest side of town. They're good kids—wanted to share everything with the rest of the family. Tall, too; I can definitely see a future for them on the ward basketball team." He smiled warmly at Paula. "TJ's things have found an awfully good home."

"I'm so glad," she breathed, then searched his eyes for a confirmation. "It really was the right thing to do, wasn't it?"

"The right, the best, the only thing to do," he replied without hesitation. "And like I said before, it was pure magic—everybody got what they needed and wanted. The Tiltons got a lot of temporal help, as well as—thanks to your note—a sense of belonging to something larger than themselves, a feeling of being cared for. And I got the kind of indescribable spiritual rush that comes with being in the right place at the right time, doing the right thing. It doesn't get any better than this, my love. I just hope I've been able to give you the sense that something incredible happened tonight. And all because of you."

"Whoa," Paula chuckled demurely, "I can't take all the credit, and you know it. Millie started the ball rolling, after all, then TJ and the Lord put in their two cents' worth. And your personalized delivery service brought it all together. A rather well-orchestrated group effort, I'd say." She leaned comfortably against his shoulder.

"Yep," Ted agreed. "Pure magic." He tenderly kissed the top of her head. "I love you, Mrs. Barstow, you know that?"

"Actually, I do," she grinned. "But somehow I never get tired of hearing it."

"Then I'll keep on saying it. In fact, let's go home, and I'll *show* you how much I love you by rubbing those beautiful feet."

"Ah, the end of a perfect day," she sighed. They had never been closer.

The next morning, Millie was just setting out a late breakfast when the doorbell rang. "I'll get it, dear," she said to Paula, who was sitting at the table in a deep-pink velour robe, nibbling a piece of dry toast. She was feeling tolerably good at the moment, and was entertaining thoughts of putting in an appearance at the office later that afternoon. Or maybe she'd stay home and work at the computer in her den. In any case, with the *Time* interview coming up in just a week, she needed to bring herself up to speed on a number of new company innovations Ted had masterminded. *He's so good at what he does,* she mused, then smiled to herself. *And so cute, too—my blonde-haired, blue-eyed Casanova. Or studmuffin, as Scotty would say. Can't argue on that account.*

Her meandering train of thought was interrupted by Millie's childlike squeal of delight. "Why, Nora!" she exclaimed. "What a nice surprise . . . won't you come in?"

Nora . . . Nora. Paula mulled the name over in her mind, but couldn't place it. *Must be a friend of Millie's. Everybody in the ward thinks she's their best friend—and everybody in the ward is probably right. Bless her heart, she draws people to her like the warm earth welcoming a new planting of spring flowers.*

She heard the door close, footfalls in the entryway, then Millie came into view with her sturdy hand at the elbow of a small, rather fragile-looking woman with light brown hair and enormous blue-black eyes. The woman, who looked to be in her early to mid-thirties and was dressed in jeans and a large flannel shirt, cradled a covered oblong basket in her arms. She looked vaguely familiar, but Paula was fairly certain they had never met. She turned in her chair and offered their visitor a thin smile as she waited for an introduction.

"Paula, dear, look who's come," Millie beamed. Seeing a slightly vacant look in Paula's eyes, she hurried on. "Oh, I guess the two of you haven't really . . . well, then, let's see what we can do about that. Paula, this is Nora. Nora Tilton."

Nora Tilton. It took a second or two for the name to burn itself into Paula's mind, but when the recognition came, her eyes grew wide and instantly filled with tears as an unseen power beyond her understanding urged her to her feet. Before Nora could even shift her basket to the crook of one arm and extend her hand, Paula had closed the small distance between them and enfolded the woman's slight body in a warm embrace. "Sister Tilton . . . Nora," she heard herself whisper against the delicate ear. "Welcome to our home. Thank you for coming."

When they pulled apart, Nora's expression was slightly bemused, and she was the first to speak. "I—I thought *I* would be the one saying thank you," she said in a full, musical voice that belied her small stature.

"Believe me, the feeling goes both ways," Paula assured her. "It's not every day that things work out so perfectly." She glanced over at Millie. "And we have this dear lady to thank for it. She came up with the idea." The older woman's face flushed crimson, and her gaze dropped to the floor. But when she looked up again, her delight was unmistakable.

"Well, I just wanted to make sure you knew how very much we all appreciate what you did . . . what happened last night," Nora said. Her grateful smile was an appealing blend of self-consciousness and rekindled hope. "The children seem to have new life to them this morning, and Robert and I couldn't sleep last night for talking about what a blessing this is to our family. You simply . . . can't know. The boy you lost—TJ—must be looking down on us this very minute, so proud of what you've done. We'll take special care of his things, and not a day'll go by that we won't think of him. He's a part of us now," she finished in a tremulous voice. By this time, all three women were wiping at their eyes.

"Won't you sit down for a bit, Nora?" Millie asked. "I've just made a little breakfast, and maybe you'd like to—"

"Oh, thank you so much," she broke in, "but I left the two babies with a neighbor, and I've got to get back to them. Little Zachary has an ear infection, and if I leave him with Madge too long, his fussing will send her into orbit." She suddenly glanced down at the basket in her arms and laughed a little—a slow, delicious sound that Paula thought would be a soothing balm to any child's ears, infected or not. "Uh-oh, I nearly forgot." She held out the basket to Paula. "Croissants. I made them this morning; it's an old family recipe. My one claim to fame in the baking department. I hope you like them."

Paula lifted the yellow cloth cover and breathed in a warm, yeasty aroma. "Mmm, heavenly," she crooned. "We'll enjoy these to the last scrumptious morsel."

"I'll be on my way then," Nora said, moving toward the entryway. Then she suddenly stopped, pivoted in place, and hurried back to Paula, where she planted a firm kiss on her new friend's cheek. "Thanks again—so much," she said with deep feeling. After doing the same for Millie, she had turned again toward the door when she stopped for a second time. "Oh," she murmured, her tone almost apologetic, "one more thing." Reaching deep into her jeans pocket, she brought out a small object and held it out to Paula, who opened her hand to receive it. "Clark found this in the back pocket of TJ's Dockers," Nora explained. "We thought you'd want to have it."

Paula looked down at a small, copper-colored ring. The letters "CTR" were clearly visible where they rested against her palm. "I didn't know TJ had one of these," she said, grasping the ring with her fingers to hold it up for closer inspection. It was not an expensive ring, but the burnished letters seemed to glow with a life of their own. "I don't think I've ever seen it before."

"I believe he got it in Sunday School," Millie offered. "His class had a scripture chase, and the reward for winning was a CTR ring. Imagine that—not even a member yet, and he did better than everyone else. When he showed it to me after church, he was proud as a peacock. He never took it off after that, except to shower or play basketball. But it all happened less than a week before we lost him, so you probably never saw the ring. He must have tucked it in his trousers pocket that Saturday morning before he . . ." Her voice trailed off, and she gazed out the window.

"It's lovely," Paula said, a small knot of regret tightening in her throat. "Funny, isn't it? Two years ago, I wouldn't have known or even cared what those three little letters meant—'Choose The Right.' But now," she chuckled a little, "they've become part of my life, like a latter-day mantra. Words to live by." *I'm trying, kiddo,* she declared silently to her son as she slipped the ring onto the little finger of her right hand. *I'm really trying.* "It's a perfect fit," she smiled. "Thank you, Nora."

"You bet," the slight woman said. "I'll be going now—really. Have a nice day." She lifted her hand in a half-wave, then turned and quickly disappeared into the entryway. Moments later, the front door opened and closed softly.

"Such a lovely person," Millie said. "Sometimes she's not quite sure of herself, and she's certainly seen her share of adversity, but her testimony is solid as a rock. That family will get by, even if it's not so easy. They've got the will. And now, thanks to you," she grinned at Paula, "they've got at least part of the way."

"Oh, pooh," Paula laughed, mimicking her friend's pet expression. "Anything for a batch of fresh croissants." She made a mental note to keep tabs on the Tiltons and help where she could. They were now connected, after all. The thought sent a pleasant rush of warmth through her body as she slowly turned TJ's ring on her finger.

Chapter 3

"It's about the shower on Saturday. There's been a slight change of plans." Meg O'Brien sounded even more energetic than usual, and Paula could hear the anticipation in her rich voice. Visiting teaching partners for nearly two years now, they had become close friends. And if it was possible, Paula thought, Meg was even more excited about the new baby than she was. Indeed, it wouldn't have surprised her to discover that Meg had been planning this shower long before the child had even been conceived. "You may be forty-one," she had joked at the wedding reception, "but there's still gotta be an egg or two in there that's up to going the distance." As it turned out, she was right.

"What's up?" Paula laughed into the phone. "Don't tell me; you've just kept adding to the guest list until they couldn't possibly all fit into your house. So you've rented the L.A. Coliseum for the afternoon."

"Hmm, I didn't think of that. Maybe for the next one."

"The *next* one?" Paula gasped. "Good grief, this old body has endured enough stretch marks for a lifetime. Let's just take it one trimester at a time, shall we?"

"Oh, all right," Meg grumped dramatically. "But you never know."

"Well, I think I do," Paula rejoined. "Anyhow, what's this big change in plans?"

"You'll love it, especially now that you're feeling a little better," Meg replied. "Here's the deal. As part of the festivities, Eloise Martin and I have decided to treat you to an utterly extravagant prelude to the party—beginning with an early lunch, then a trip to the spa for a facial, massage, manicure, pedicure, and whatever else strikes your fancy. After that, we can do a little shopping if you're up to it; then we'll mosey on out to Eloise's family cabin near Wildwood Canyon, where the rest of the guests will join us about six o'clock for dinner and all the other shower stuff. We girls can stay as late as we please, nibbling on cheese and chocolate and roasting marshmallows in their huge fireplace. Then, when it's all over, we'll deposit you and your booty—no pun intended—in the middle of your front lawn and make our getaway. Sounds like a dream come true, doesn't it?" Meg sounded very pleased with herself. "What do you think?"

Paula could only stare wide-eyed at her bedroom wall. She felt her heart quicken with joy at the thought of spending time with two of her best friends. Eloise, recently released as the ward Relief Society president, had tenderly taken Paula under her wing at the time of TJ's death, and they had been close ever since.

"Halloo," Meg prompted after several seconds. "Anybody home?"

"Y—yes," Paula finally said. "It just sounds like such an . . . *event.*"

"And that it will be," her friend gushed. "Hey, when Meg O'Brien is in charge of something—especially such an auspicious occasion—you just step out of the way and let the good times roll. S'mores and all."

The mention of this campfire delicacy actually set Paula's mouth to watering. How many years had it been since she and the boys had cracked out the marshmallows, chocolate bars, and graham crackers around a roaring blaze during one of their weekend excursions to the mountains? TJ couldn't have been more than three or four the first time; he had tried so hard to assemble the gooey confection perfectly, but had ended up accidentally dropping it into a small heap of ashes near the fire, then collapsing into dismal sobs. Scotty, so much older and wiser at the time—all of seven or eight, as she recalled—had immediately taken charge and carefully instructed his younger brother in the cultivated art of making the best S'mores in recorded history. Somewhere, she had a photo of their chocolate-smeared faces and triumphant grins. She'd have to dig it out one of these days—maybe have it enlarged and framed. Where had she stashed all of those old albums?

Meg's insistent voice pulled her back to the present. "Excuse me . . . earth to Paula . . . are we still connected?"

"At the most basic level—the taste buds," Paula laughed. "You've got me hooked, my friend; I'd do anything for S'mores. They're an entire food group by themselves, you know."

"Then it's a done deal," Meg exulted. "Eloise and I will pick you up at eleven A.M. on Saturday. Come casual."

"You got it," Paula said, an unmistakable note of anticipation energizing her voice. This day, she thought, would be one to remember.

"Well, you're looking chipper, my girl," Ted observed over dinner that evening. "Has our daughter been tickling you again?"

"Not exactly," Paula smiled. "But in a way, she is responsible for my exceptionally good mood."

"How so?" he asked, his vivid blue eyes alive with interest.

"It's the shower," she explained.

"Ah, yes, the shower," he repeated, leaning back in his chair. "A lovely daily ritual of bonding. She must love it when you scrub all over with that tantalizing lavender soap you use."

Paula reached across the table to punch him playfully on the arm. "Not *that* kind of shower, silly. I'm talking about the *baby* shower—you know, Meg's big production this weekend."

"Oh, *that* shower," Ted grinned. "You mean when the girls all get together to play games, have a few laughs, take turns feeling the baby kick, snarf cookies and fruit punch, and you come home with a carload of presents. It's Saturday night, isn't it?"

"Yes," she said, "but Meg and Eloise and I are making a day of it." At his look of mild surprise, she continued. "They're treating me to lunch and a whole-body makeover at the spa. The shower will be, as they say, the icing on the cake."

"Wal, yew little partee animall," Ted drawled. "I suppose this means I'll have to find something else to do with my day besides spending it with my beautiful wife." He shook his head and sighed dramatically.

"Puttering in the yard comes to mind," she suggested with a little smirk.

"Spoken like a true lawn Mormon," he rejoined, and they both laughed as one of their favorite memories surfaced. Shortly after Paula had been introduced to the Church and argued with Ted about it, he had been writing advertising copy for a commercial lawn mower account, and, in one of his more distracted moods, had mistakenly typed "Lawn Mormon" in one of the ad's headlines. She had never let him forget it, and the phrase had occasionally cropped up in their conversations since. When it did, they always enjoyed the moment.

"Seriously," she said when their laughter had subsided into peaceful silence, "you might want to take Rudy out for a little excursion. As golden retrievers go, he's definitely a senior citizen, and his old joints seem to be getting stiffer every day. Isn't that right, pal?" She reached beneath the table to scratch the wide, furry head near her feet, and was rewarded by a few contented thumps of the dog's feathered tail. "I try to take him out two or three times a week, but he could use even more exercise. Millie said the vet recommends it."

"Then I'll see what I can do," Ted declared agreeably. "But you have to promise that the night belongs to me."

"Deal. It'll be just you, me," Paula rubbed her belly indulgently, "and little Griselda here."

"Cute name. Really adorable," he grinned.

"I thought you'd like it," she returned. "Now, don't you have some home teaching to do or something?"

"What? It's not even the middle of the month yet! But, yes, I suppose I could force myself, especially since my companion is picking me up in," he glanced at his watch, "yikes! Four minutes. Just time to brush my teeth." He stood abruptly and leaned over to kiss her lightly on the lips. "Later, sweetness."

"I'll be here," she said. "Waiting to tell you about the little chat I had with Nora Tilton this morning." He hesitated, clearly anxious to know more. "Go!" she urged. "I'll tell you everything when you get home." He flashed her a quick, expectant smile, then disappeared into the entryway.

Later, they lay awake far into the night as Paula related the details of Nora's visit. Finally, Ted pressed a kiss to the CTR ring on her finger and sighed with obvious satisfaction. "We did good, woman," he said, and she could hear the smile in his tone. "It's great to be able to help out." He was silent for a long moment. "Now, if we could just do the same for the twenty or so other families in the ward who are struggling . . ." His voice faded into the darkness.

"There are that many?" Paula asked in amazement. Her casual dealings with the sisters of the ward had not revealed such widespread neediness. Sylvie Randolph, whom she and Meg visit taught, had seemed to be one of only a few who had financial troubles. But as elders quorum president, Ted would know.

"At least," he clarified. "Most are single mothers, and most of those aren't active, so they're not high-profile. If we're not careful, they tend to slip through the cracks and get lost."

Paula wasn't sure where her next words came from, but they escaped her lips before she could stop them. "Is that what happened to your mother?"

She felt him stiffen slightly beside her. "Why do you ask?" he said.

"No particular reason," she replied carefully, sensing that he was not altogether comfortable at this turn of the conversation. "We've never really talked about it, and I just wondered."

He drew in a deep breath and took his time letting it out. "All I really know," he finally said, "is that we moved to another neighborhood, a much poorer one, after my father and that woman in our ward . . . well, after my parents split up. It was tough, and as far as I knew, no one from the Church ever offered to help."

"Maybe they did," Paula suggested gently. "Maybe she just wouldn't accept it."

"Possible," he admitted. "But if it happened I never knew anything about it. She was awfully bitter."

"And so were you."

He chuckled without humor. "You could say that."

She leaned up on one elbow and laid her hand on his shoulder. "Don't you ever wonder where she is now, what she's doing, or how your brothers and sisters have turned out?" She thought she remembered there had been four or five children in the family.

"Not really," he sighed. "It wasn't exactly an Ozzie and Harriet childhood, if you want to know the truth, and I'd prefer to leave the past right where it is—in the past. Besides, I wouldn't know where to begin. Can't we just—"

"Not a problem," Paula interjected cheerfully, warming to the subject. "It shouldn't be all that hard to track them down, using Church records or the Internet. For purely personal reasons," she squeezed his shoulder, "I'd kind of like to show off my extraordinary husband to the rest of his family. And if we could find your father, we could—"

"I don't think so." He paused, then took in a breath and blew it out with an impatient puff.

"Well, all right," Paula agreed gently, rubbing his arm until she felt the muscles relax a little. "Maybe it's better left in the past—at least for the time being."

"Sounds good to me," he mumbled. She could hear the relief in his voice.

"On the other hand," she added, "maybe he's changed, turned his life around, come back to the Church and all that. Could be your mom isn't quite so bitter these days, either. You'll never know unless you—"

Ted grunted softly. "Hey, I know the gospel teaches us the importance of loving and forgiving others. As far as my family is concerned, I'm working on the forgiveness thing, but it may take some time. Can't we just leave it at that?"

"I suppose," Paula murmured. "It's just that—"

"Good. Then let's get some sleep. Morning comes too early." Without another word he rolled away from her, punched his pillow, and settled in for the night. Within a few minutes he was snoring softly.

"Good night, my love," she whispered against his neck. "One day we'll figure this out. You'll see." She smiled into the darkness.

By morning, their conversation had seemingly been forgotten, and Ted was his usual amiable self. Paula was slicing fresh bananas and strawberries onto a large bowl of Wheaties when he came downstairs. "Millie's day off," she stated matter-of-factly when she saw his bemused expression. "You love the breakfast of champions, so I knew I couldn't go very far wrong."

He picked up the cereal box and gave it two firm shakes. "Just making sure you left some for Scott. That kid can eat half a box at one sitting."

"He's a growing boy," she smiled, pouring milk over her own bowl of raisin bran. "Six foot three, two hundred thirty pounds of pure muscle, pecs, and buns of steel. Those baggy martial arts uniforms really don't do him justice." As she set the pitcher down, her eyes grew pensive. "I miss sharing meals with him. Seems like he's never around."

Ted settled back in his chair. "At least he's outgrown the Crawlers, except for a couple of friends who hang out in his shadow. And we generally have a pretty good idea of where he is—either at work or tinkering with his car. Seems content to stay under our roof for the time being. No known girlfriends, drug addictions, or other bad habits. It could be a lot worse."

"Or a lot better," Paula added. "He could be saving his money, thinking about college, learning the family business. Going to church."

"All in good time. I was twenty-one before I even started thinking seriously about a career. So far, Scott's just testing the waters of adulthood. With any luck at all, he'll become one of us before we've frittered away his inheritance. That way he can take care of us in our old age. Personally, I think he's just sticking around to see how little Griselda turns out." He reached over and gave Paula's stomach a friendly pat. "Now, I'd better get going. If I'm late to work two days in a row, Carmine will have my head."

"Fine by me," Paula joked, "as long as I have your heart."

"No doubt about that," he said, straightening his tie as he bent to kiss her. "Will we be seeing you at the office today?"

"Actually, no," she replied. "Carmine e-mailed me everything I need to bone up for our reporter friend's visit, so I think I'll stay at home and conserve my energy for Saturday. But count on me next week; if I'm feeling as good then as I am now, I'll be there every day to crack the whip and snap you poor fools into shape."

"Something to look forward to," Ted grinned. "In the meantime, I could bring some takeout home for dinner. Delaney's has a special on their famous Irish stew."

"I'd love that," she called after him, seeing that he was halfway to the garage. She was already anticipating the rich stew's slow-cooked, full-bodied taste. "In fact, get two or three orders; we can freeze some."

"For Millie's next day off, eh? " he called back over his shoulder.

"I'm not sure it'll last that long," she laughed. "Besides, there's always Wheaties if we run out."

Delaney's stew did not settle peaceably upon her pregnant digestive system that evening, and by morning she was back to the queasy, lightheaded state she had become accustomed to over the past several months. "Only a few more weeks," she moaned, leaning her forehead against the cool tile of her shower stall as steaming pellets of water kneaded her aching muscles. Afterward a long nap refreshed her to a degree, and she was grateful to feel a little of her strength returning through the afternoon and evening. With any luck at all, she'd be smiling again by the next day—just in time for Meg's All-American Spa Adventure and Baby Shower.

Chapter 4

Saturday arrived in a cloudless blue haze, cooler than usual but still warmer than most parts of the country in January. Paula was waiting at the front door when Meg O'Brien's Taurus wagon swung into the driveway promptly at eleven o'clock. "Don't ask," Paula said quickly when Meg and Eloise eyed their friend's pale, drawn complexion. Even a double shot of makeup hadn't quite camouflaged it. "Just know that today I'm much, much better."

"Then I'd hate to have seen you yesterday," Meg chuckled nervously. "Are you sure you're up to this?"

Paula smiled gamely. "If a manicure and S'mores are involved, I'm good to go."

"Well then," Meg declared, "let's get this show on the road." She shifted jauntily into reverse, backed out of the driveway, and pointed the Taurus downtown.

A light lunch of oriental chicken salad, flaky dinner rolls, and iced ginger ale seemed to calm Paula's stomach, after which the threesome headed off to Spa Magnifique for an afternoon of indulgence. From head to toe—scalp massage to pedicure, with minute attention to the refreshment and rejuvenation of all the weary muscles and sagging skin between—they relished these pampered moments, quickly abandoning any idea of shopping so they could spend another hour or two in this gracious cocoon of comfort. By the time they left the spa just after four-thirty P.M., Paula felt deliciously renewed in both mind and body.

Several cars were already crowded into the small parking area by the time Meg and her company arrived at the Martins' cabin an hour later. A light dusting of snow had fallen during the day, leaving the early-evening air fresh and bracing. Stepping from the car, Paula was glad for the warmth of her royal-blue velour maternity sweat suit. Even though the cabin was nestled close to the mouth of the canyon, the temperature here was much cooler than what she was used to in Woodland Hills.

Gathered inside the spacious, elegant cabin were about fifteen women of varying age and heritage. Some were getting comfortable in front of a welcoming blaze in the massive stone fireplace; a few were milling about in the kitchen, setting out a tempting dinner buffet. Two or three huddled together outside against the deck railing, mesmerized by a small group of deer nibbling on some foliage.

"We're here!" Meg trumpeted as she and Paula entered the front hall with Eloise close behind.

"Reason enough to eat!" someone shouted as the three were swept into the vaulted great room on a wave of celebration. Smiles and hugs seemed to be the order of the day, and Paula wasn't complaining. Instead, she savored the feeling of delight bubbling inside her.

Picking up a plate to take her place in the dinner line, Paula inadvertently bumped against the elbow of a small woman in front of her. "Oh, excuse me," she murmured. "I hope I didn't make you spill—"

The woman turned around, and Paula saw a smile to rival any she had yet seen that evening. "Nora!" she exclaimed, feeling her own face come alive with elation. "How wonderful to see you!" She hadn't expected to see this new friend so soon again; they had barely met, after all.

"Millie invited me," Nora explained. "She asked me to bring some of my croissants. How could I refuse?" Her radiant expression reminded Paula of exactly the way she had felt in high school gym class, when she'd been first to be chosen by the team captain.

She curled an arm around Nora's slim shoulders. "I'm so glad you're here," she said warmly.

After dinner, sipping hot cocoa from a ceramic mug shaped like a baby bottle (where did they come up with this stuff, anyway?), Paula glanced over the diverse group of women who had come to share in her anticipation of a life-transforming event. They were, in a sense, unlikely strangers who had become friends by virtue of their common sisterhood in the Church. Among them were full-time mothers, single career women, business owners, affluent socialites like Caroline Wintersweet and struggling young divorcees like Sylvie Randolph, both of whom

Paula had come to know and cherish as their visiting teacher. There were a Vietnamese acupuncturist and a saucy black college professor in the bunch, as well. And who could have calculated the impact of Bonnie Solomon on her life? This amazing martial arts instructor, another of Paula and Meg's teachees, had singlehandedly pulled Scott back from the brink of destruction by teaching him, among other things, the fine art of self-appreciation. *You'd never know it to look at her,* Paula mused, *standing there in her tight-tight bellbottoms beside the Relief Society president, chatting about her latest—is it fourth or fifth?—husband's fetish for previously owned Elvis Presley impersonator memorabilia.* Paula was proud—and frankly amazed—to call these women her friends. *The sisters I never had,* she reasoned. It was the gospel, pure and simple—such an extraordinary way of bringing people together.

"All right, girlfriends," Meg called out like a good-natured drill sergeant, "listen up! We've come here to have a good time, and it all begins right here." She gestured dramatically toward a round oak table in the center of the room, now supporting a large pile of colorfully wrapped gifts. Several additional presents were tucked beneath and around the table.

Paula tried to glance inconspicuously at the collection. *Good grief,* she thought, *are all these for the baby? I'm not sure there'll be nearly enough space to put them all in TJ's . . .* A small lump of sadness formed in her throat, but it was quickly replaced by a sense of urgency. *It's not ready yet. TJ's room is still only an empty space with four blank walls and a basketball light switch, certainly not a nursery. So much to do: paint, carpeting, wallpaper, special lighting, new furniture—a hundred little details that we've already talked about and planned for, but have never really put together.* She made a mental note to talk with Ted that very night about getting the project finished. In the meantime, they'd have to keep all of these new things in storage.

Bonnie Solomon's hearty voice cut into Paula's thoughts. "Well, I don't know about everybody else, but I figure there's no time like the *present.*" When the laughter died down, Bonnie herself traipsed over to the table, rummaged through the gifts until she found a small white box decorated with teddy-bear stickers, and shoved it decisively into Paula's hands. "Here's a beginning," she said, smiling broadly and reaching out a slim, muscled hand to pat her friend's shoulder.

The gift was—predictably enough—a miniature martial arts uniform, complete with a tiny black belt attached to a bright pink rattle. "You can't start kids out early enough these days," Bonnie declared eagerly. "Look inside." Tucked into one arm of the little suit was a rolled-up certificate, good for one year's worth of lessons. "Soon as this little charmer is potty trained, you bring her on over to the Academy," Bonnie ordered. "We'll see what we can do." She winked at Paula. "There's a martial arts competition at the Olympics, you know."

"I'll remember that," Paula laughed. "Thank you, Bonnie. This is a great start."

As the evening rolled on, this shower took on the free-wheeling, relaxed mood of a do-it-yourself party. After a few gifts had been opened, the women took turns telling jokes, reminiscing about the births of their own babies, putting together impromptu skits about the more hilarious aspects of motherhood, even offering advice based on their own experiences. Listening to them, Paula calculated that the bright-faced, steady-eyed women in this room had been responsible for bringing nearly a hundred children into the world. A few, like herself, were pregnant now, and would soon make new contributions to the ward population. And the single sisters in the group, far from appearing lonely or intimidated, seemed to drink in this lively atmosphere as a cheerful toast to their own auspicious futures. Paula thought she had never seen such a happy gathering.

When perhaps a third of the gifts had been opened, Paula chose a small green and yellow package from the pile. It was from Sylvie Randolph—two lovely hand-sewn baby bibs with the letters "ABC" expertly embroidered in bright colors on their fronts. "I didn't know if you'd decided on a name yet," she said, smiling shyly at Paula, "so I just went with the alphabet."

"They're perfect," Paula said, her heart swelling with love for this sweet but determined young woman who struggled so courageously to raise two young daughters on her own. "And no, we haven't come up with a name yet . . . haven't even talked about it, really."

"Well, then, it's high time you did," a throaty and somewhat imperious voice called out from one corner of the room. It belonged to Evelyn Jeffries, a stout woman in her mid-forties who had joined the Church at about the same time as Paula. She and her husband, James, and their four children had moved into the ward some six months earlier. Evelyn was an amazing woman—taught philosophy and political science at UCLA, and regarded Prokofiev as easy listening music. She also had a smile that could have lit up even those infamous three days of darkness in Nephite times . . . and now it was shining in Paula's direction.

"I agree," Meg chimed in. "What say we try to come up with a few options? If anyone can do it, we can." Half an hour later Paula had a list of dozens of names—from the ridiculous to the sublime, Agora to Zanzibar—safely tucked inside one of the gift boxes. The final decision, of course, would be up to her and Ted, with a little help (not to mention lobbying) from their friends.

As Paula unwrapped the remaining packages, she decided to give up all pretense of formality and just let her mouth hang open permanently. These were not simply baby gifts; they were pure expressions of love and support and absolute joy from every woman in the room, from the smallest pair of pink and white booties, to a handmade "quiet book" featuring gospel themes, to the elegant wooden cradle finished and painted in soft green and cream colors by three of the sisters. But perhaps what touched Paula most were the unexpected gifts for her: a lovely nightgown; perfumed bath items; the latest book on child-rearing by a popular Latter-day Saint author; a gift certificate for a month of weekly massages. "My goodness, I should have a baby more often," she joked, but tears were very near the surface. "How can I ever thank you all?"

"Just be happy, and enjoy being a mom," Nora Tilton said quietly. "It's the best job in the world."

"Even when it's the worst job in the world," Meg added with a theatrical sigh. A round of knowing laughter and applause followed her statement. "But then, you already know that, having raised two great kids already."

"I suppose," Paula replied, "although this is quite . . . different. A daughter—and she'll have the Church, where the others didn't."

"And she'll have US," Bonnie sang out gleefully from where she was standing near the fireplace. "It takes a village, you know. Or, in our case, a ward."

"Do you think this means she'll actually show up in church one of these days?" Meg whispered close to Paula's ear. To their knowledge, Bonnie Solomon had not seen the inside of a Mormon chapel (or the outside, for that matter) in at least a dozen years.

"Stranger things have happened," Paula replied lightly. "Although none comes to mind at the moment."

As the women chatted while the last of the wrappings were being cleared away, Meg stood and raised her hands to quiet the group. "There is one more gift," she said with a mysterious smile. "We thought we'd save it until last." Without further explanation, she reached behind her leather wing chair and pulled out a rather large, elegantly decorated package. "It's from your mother," she murmured, laying it carefully on Paula's lap.

Paula stared at her friend with wide, doe-like eyes. "Wh—what? I don't understand. How did she know . . . when did she . . . well, I'm speechless."

"A first," someone observed, and a gentle tide of laughter rippled through the group.

Paula fingered the wide pink satin ribbon tied around the white box, not knowing quite how to proceed. A small knot of undefined emotion—was it confusion, longing, cynicism, hope?—formed in her throat and constricted her chest. What had the wealthy, cultured, terminally distant Marjorie Enfield sent for her granddaughter-to-be? A silver spoon? Monogrammed diapers? A custom-made teething ring with solid-gold letters spelling "Keeper" floating inside? The irony of such an image brought a tiny smile to her lips.

"Just open it," Meg urged. "I think there's a note inside."

Paula's fingers were trembling slightly as she carefully undid the bow and slipped the box out of its ornate gold-and-white wrapping paper. Lifting the lid, she noticed that the gift—whatever it was—lay blanketed in the most delicate, palest pink tissue paper she had ever seen. It was fine and almost translucent, though its muted coloring kept the contents from showing through. Lying on top of the tissue was a small ivory envelope, addressed to Paula in Marjorie's well-bred, flowing hand.

She picked up the envelope, slowly ran a fingernail beneath its sealed flap, and drew out a folded note paper embossed with her mother's initials. Then she silently began to read the brief message.

My dear Paula,
I consulted a member of your church about the formalities and such of welcoming a new child. She was most helpful, and a member of the Mormon congregation in Hartford offered to make this. It is so very lovely, don't you think? May this precious child bring you as much joy as I felt when you were born.

Affectionately,
Your Mother

The words blurred, and Paula felt tears coursing down her cheeks. *"Precious child . . . as much joy as I felt when you were born." Oh, Mother . . . Mother.* She sat quietly for long moments, her head bowed, as the words played in her mind again and again, detouring through her heart in an endless procession of regret and thanksgiving. *At least now I know. She felt* joy *when I was born.*

"What is it?" someone whispered respectfully, urging Paula back to the moment.

"Oh, sorry," she sniffed, wiping at her face. "The note from my mother—it caught me a little by surprise. We aren't exactly what you'd call . . . close." *But she felt joy when I was born. That counts for something, doesn't it?* Somewhere in the deepest part of her, she believed it did.

"But what *is* it?" another voice repeated, this time a bit more insistently.

Paula tenderly pulled back the paper. Inside, nestled on a second cloud of pastel tissue, lay a white silk blessing gown, long and graceful and perfect. Just perfect. Its tiny neckline and sleeves were bordered with hand-sewn miniature pink and yellow rosebuds; a few of the exquisite little flowers trailed down the skirt to a bit of lace at the hem. Paula touched the sumptuous fabric, rolled it smoothly between her fingers, felt its softness against her skin. *Like the temple garment,* she mused reverently. *I can feel the innocence, the holiness of it. My little girl will be an angel on her blessing day.* With a rush of emotion, she lifted the hem to her lips. *An angel straight from heaven.*

By this time, several women had gathered around Paula's chair to admire the dress. "Oooh, your mother is so sweet," one of them cooed.

"Yes, . . . yes, she is," Paula murmured. "This was a very sweet thing to do." She made a mental note to call Marjorie first thing in the morning and tell her so.

"And speaking of sweet," Meg broke in, "it's time for dessert. Whoever gets their coat hanger ready first wins a cozy place by the fire, and—"

"S'mores!" they volleyed back in unison.

An hour later, a barely glowing fire cast flickering shadows into a still, darkened room where women sprawled against fat cushions on the hardwood floor or lounged on couches, chairs, or huge beanbags. Some were dozing in perfect contentment; others were staring into the coals or chatting quietly with those nearest them. Paula sat off to one side in a comfortable recliner, contemplating the events of this day as she gently rubbed the side of her stomach where the baby seemed to be settling in for a little nap. *Sweet dreams, Gris,* she smiled, *or whoever you are.* She tucked one last morsel of chocolate-and-marshmallow-covered graham cracker beneath her tongue. *One day I'll tell you all about this terrific party.* She felt a delicate little jab next to her navel. *Of* course *we'll have pictures.*

Sylvie Randolph was the first to stand and stretch luxuriantly. "Sorry to break things up," she said, "but Sister Mecham is watching my girls, and it's past their bedtime." One by one, the others followed her lead with hugs all around, while Meg and Millie helped Eloise clean up in the kitchen. The miniature grandfather clock on the mantel was chiming nine-thirty by the time the station wagon was packed and ready to go. Meg would drive Paula and Millie home, while Eloise would spend the night at the cabin. At the door, Eloise folded her ample arms around Paula and kissed her tenderly on the cheek. "We all love you, my dear," she smiled. "That little girl is awfully lucky to be coming to your home."

"Thank you," Paula said warmly. "This has been a wonderful day."

"And it gets better," Meg stated casually as the women donned their heavy sweaters.

Paula cast her a sideways glance. "How do you figure? I mean, I can't imagine how—"

"Nothing, my friend. I just meant there's nothing like a good night's sleep after an indescribably delicious day like this. That's all."

"Point taken," Paula agreed, suddenly feeling the weight of exhaustion settling in her bones, wondering how she could possibly walk the ten thousand miles to Meg's car. Somehow she made it, but drifted off at almost the same moment the Taurus's engine sprang to life.

"Home sweet home," Meg announced as they pulled into the Barstows' driveway. No sound or movement from the backseat, where Paula had stretched herself lengthwise during the hour-long ride.

"She must be out cold," Millie whispered. "Should I wake her?"

"Not just yet," Meg advised in a conspiratorial tone. "Let's get all these gifts into the house, then we'll be ready for the grand entrance."

"Okey-dokey," the older woman chirped. She retrieved a garage door opener remote from her purse, and they pulled into a small space next to Paula's red Jaguar convertible. Ted had heard them coming and met them just inside the door. In fifteen minutes they had noiselessly unloaded the Taurus and taken the gifts upstairs—all while Paula lay oblivious to their stealthy comings and goings.

Finally, Ted discreetly opened the car door and leaned in to kiss the top of his wife's head. "Hmm, smells like a campfire," he chuckled against her dark hair. She stirred a little, then slipped back into never-never land. Next he tickled the tender area behind her ear, and she brushed off his hand as if shooing away an annoying mosquito before rolling over and burying her face in the seat. Within seconds, she was making a feeble sound that vaguely reminded him of someone sawing on a gourd. When he grabbed one arm and pulled her slowly to a sitting position, her even breathing told him it was a lost cause. "I always knew she was a sound sleeper," he mumbled, "but this is ridiculous."

Turning back to Meg and Millie, who were waiting anxiously outside the Taurus, he broke the bad news. "I'm afraid it's out of the question tonight; the lady is beyond reviving. I'll just have to carry her up to bed now, and we'll do the rest of it in the morning."

"Rats," Meg grumped good-naturedly. "I wanted to see the look on her face when . . . well, you know."

"Tough break, Sister O," Ted grinned. "I guess you just plain tuckered her out today."

"Yeah, but it was one of the best days in recorded history." Meg's eyes glistened as she returned his smile. "Have her call me tomorrow, will you? I want to hear every last detail."

"Yes, ma'am," he replied. "And thanks again." He leaned over and pressed a light kiss to Meg's cheek. "We couldn't have done it without you. Now go on home to your brood." He stepped away from the Taurus and motioned for her to get behind the wheel.

Millie tugged firmly on his shirt sleeve. "Uh, haven't you forgotten something?"

Ted stared at her blankly for a second or two, then his blue eyes lit up as he caught her drift. "Ah, yes . . . my wife." Millie thought she saw his cheeks flush a little as he opened the back door again and leaned inside. "Come to Papa, dear," he murmured as he tugged, turned, and maneuvered her limp form into his arms. Once they had cleared the car's interior, he shoved the door closed with one foot and nodded to Meg, who quickly waved and backed her Taurus into the star-filled night as Millie punched the garage door button.

Halfway up the stairs, Ted leaned heavily against the banister to balance Paula's weight and catch his breath. "And Clark Gable made it look so easy," he muttered.

"Mmm?" Her neck muscles tensed a little and she lifted an eyebrow, but her lids remained closed.

"Never mind, Scarlett," he breathed against her forehead as she relaxed again. "Let's get you to bed." Later, lying beside her, he smoothed a few locks of dark hair away from her face. "So, you had a good time today, did you? Well, just wait until tomorrow." He fell asleep with a bone-weary but satisfied smile touching his lips.

Paula's nose twitched before anything else moved. As her body gradually roused into wakefulness, she began sniffing in earnest. What was that smell? It was faint but pungent, reminding her of the ubiquitous traces of paint and sawdust in the atmosphere during the months her offices were being remodeled some years earlier. *Must be my pregnant mind playing tricks on me*, she surmised. *Or maybe one too many S'mores*. Still, it seemed very real, even down to the slightly acrid taste of the air when she breathed.

She rolled over and nudged Ted's shoulder. When he didn't move, she tugged on his earlobe until a deep, playful growl erupted from his throat. "Give a guy a chance to sleep, will ya?" he whined, keeping his eyelids sealed against the morning sunlight streaming through their bedroom window.

"Ted, something smells funny," she said, sniffing again loudly to prove her point. "I can't quite place it, but I think it's coming from the hall." She swung her legs over the side of the bed and began to pull on her robe. "I think I'll just go see what—"

"Oh, no you don't." Ted, now fully awake, had grabbed her arm and was pulling her firmly back toward him. Seeing the startled question in her eyes, he broke into a sudden grin as he tried to explain himself. "I mean, if there's something to be investigated, we'll do it together. All for one and one for all, right?" With his free hand, he reached for his own robe.

"Okay," she said warily. "But I really think I can do this by myself. I'm pregnant, not comatose."

"And you are *so beautiful.*" He kissed the back of her hand with a great flourish, then bolted from the bed and made sure he was the first one to the door. Swinging it open, he motioned her into the hall. "Shall we?" he said gallantly.

"Sure, I guess so," she replied, her voice edged with friendly suspicion. It occurred to her that he was entirely too alert for such an early-morning hour. Ordinarily, his eyes would begin to focus only after a brisk shower and a shot of V-8 juice. She decided to play along.

Hand in hand, they walked a few steps down the hall to TJ's room, where they stopped in front of the closed door. Ted turned and clasped her shoulders firmly in his hands, staring down into her eyes with such tenderness that she felt her knees weaken. "We wanted to do this last night," he said calmly, "but you were—to put it in your own words—comatose."

Paula giggled endearingly. "I guess you're right about that. I don't remember a thing after I collided with the backseat of Meg's car." Her expression clouded a bit. "But what does that have to do with—"

"Everything," Ted smiled, pushing TJ's door open. "Absolutely everything." With a gentle hand to her back, he guided her into the darkened room. "To the future," he whispered next to her ear. Then he flipped the light switch.

For an instant, Paula couldn't respond to what she saw. There was too much energy, too much beauty, too much love in this room to make it believable, and she stood transfixed with surprise and wonder. But little by little, as she began to comprehend the transformation, a crescendo of emotion rose in her chest and welled in her eyes. "I can't believe it," she murmured with almost no voice at all. "It's incredible."

The empty space that had been a somber memorial to her lost son less than twenty-four hours earlier had now been expertly recast into a cheerful, animated room that would soon welcome the newest member of their family. Every detail that Paula and Ted had planned and chosen months before, floor to ceiling, had come to life virtually overnight, from the luxuriant forest-green carpeting beneath their feet to the recessed ceiling lights that washed the space in a subdued, peaceful ambience. Above a smooth, light-green wainscoting around the bottom half of the room, playful animal babies of every color and description frolicked across a background of ivory wallpaper. A charming antique bassinet graced one corner, and nearby stood a pink-and-white changing table, stocked with diapers and ready for action. In the opposite corner, a comfortable gliding rocker, upholstered in soft burgundy fabric, sat beside a graceful mahogany table topped by a Tiffany reading lamp. Within easy reach of the rocker, a built-in wall cabinet housed a miniature CD system; an album of "Mozart's Greatest Hits" was propped against its Lucite cover. The shower gifts were neatly stacked on and around a glass-topped white wicker bureau outside the small attached bathroom.

Paula's hand moved instinctively to her heart. "Oh, my," she breathed. "It's . . . it's everything we wanted. And then some."

"Then I take it that you approve?" Ted's arm was around her shoulders, and he gazed at her expectantly.

To his surprise, she shook her head emphatically. "Not the right word," she declared. "Definitely not the right word."

"Oh?" A hint of alarm rose in his eyes.

"I'd say 'adore' is a more apt description," she clarified. "To be closely followed by 'relish,' 'savor,' 'appreciate,' 'admire,' and 'applaud.'"

"Oh, well," he chuckled, "as long as I know how you feel. So you like it?"

She wrapped her arms around him. "I love it, sweetheart. But how in the world did you pull it off? A project of this kind usually takes weeks, and I was only gone for a little tiny day."

"A method to the madness," he smiled. "We were wondering how to get you out of the house long enough when Meg came up with her fantastic spa-and-shower idea. Since I'd already ordered the furniture and had it delivered to the office, it was just a matter of getting some guys from the ward to make like weekend carpenters, then help get everything set up. Hey, when the elders quorum president speaks, they listen." His eyes shone with pride as he continued. "Meg said she could keep you busy until nine o'clock or so, and we were absolutely determined to make it work. With several of us on the job, the whole thing was actually finished with a whopping thirty seconds to spare." He winked at her. "Of course, we needn't have worried; you were out for the count anyway. I'm just glad everything turned out all right."

"It's perfect," Paula said, leaning against him and taking a long, slow whiff of the lingering paint and varnish fragrance. "This has been the best weekend of my entire life."

"Better than the weekend we were married?" he questioned.

"On second thought," she said after a moment of contemplation, "this has been the *second* best weekend of my entire life."

That afternoon following church, Paula spent hours in the nursery, patiently arranging and rearranging drawers, closets, baby wipes, and all the other tiny details of a newborn's life. It would be several weeks yet before the baby came, but it never hurt to be prepared—especially now that there was room for everything. She left the blessing gown in its sturdy white box and carefully laid it in the bottom drawer of the wicker bureau, but not before reading her mother's note several times.

When she was satisfied that the nursery was impeccably organized, Paula sauntered into the hall and closed the door behind her. Ted was meeting with the bishop, Millie had been invited to a friend's house for supper, and Scott was out taking the Viper for a spin, so she had the house to herself. Glancing at her watch, she made up her mind. *It's still early enough in Connecticut—the perfect time to call Mother.* She hurried downstairs to her study, and was soon flipping through her brown leather address book for Marjorie's number. Finding it, she wavered for only a moment before lifting the telephone to her ear. "Can't wait to tell you about the shower," she murmured as the phone rang once, then twice. "Can't wait to thank you."

The third ring was interrupted by a small click, and Paula knew her mother was on the line. "Hello," a mature woman's voice began, then paused for a few moments.

Paula didn't hesitate, though her throat was unexpectedly swollen with emotion. "Oh, Mother," she blurted out, "you can't possibly know how much I—"

"This is the Enfield residence. Please leave a message." Three beeps, then silence.

Paula's whole body slumped in disappointment as she replaced the receiver without saying a word. "The miracle of modern technology," she muttered. "Canned Mother." But this message was too important, too intimate to be stashed away in some impersonal answering device. She would have to try again, and maybe again, until she could finally connect with the real Marjorie Enfield. Until she could be sure that her mother knew how very much her gift—and her priceless words—had been appreciated. In the meantime, for some reason Paula felt like she was ten years old again, in the middle of a major sulk. Where was her mother, anyway? Why hadn't she answered? It was after nine P.M. in Connecticut, and probably snowing, to boot. What could an elderly woman possibly be doing away from home, driving through a winter blizzard at this hour? A nagging uneasiness began to form in the back of Paula's mind, and she ran the fingers of one hand through her dark hair. *No reason to go ballistic here,* she reasoned. *Mother is absolutely, perfectly fine. She can certainly take care of herself, just like she's been doing for the last sixty-five-plus years. She probably just turned the phone off before she went to bed.* Sinking into a large overstuffed chair next to her desk, Paula closed her eyes and concentrated on draining such unproductive ruminations from her consciousness. *I should call her every week,* she thought with a twinge of regret. *Well, maybe every other week.*

A warm, furry pressure against her ankle brought an instant smile to her lips. Without opening her eyes, she reached down to scratch the broad golden head resting comfortably on top of her foot. "Rudy, my man," she sighed. "Looks like it's just the two of us here tonight." The dog responded with a low moan of pleasure, and she heard his heavy tail thump against the carpet.

After a few minutes of companionable silence, Paula reached down to give one of Rudy's ears a friendly tweak. "Hey, buddy, I'm feeling a little restless, and I get the feeling this child craves some exercise. She's been doing trampoline stunts against my rib cage for the last couple of hours. What do you say . . . would you be up for a little stroll through the neighborhood?"

A gentle "woof" answered her question, and the two old friends were soon ambling down the sidewalk at a decent clip. Halfway to their favorite park, however, Rudy's pace slowed to barely a walk, and his flanks heaved as though he was utterly winded. Finally he simply stopped and sat back on his haunches, panting heavily.

Paula knelt beside him, stroking the thick hair on his back, whispering words of encouragement and affection. After a minute or two, the big dog seemed to be fine. She breathed a sigh of relief, wrapped her arms around his massive neck, and planted a firm kiss on the top of his head. "Old age catching up to you a little, eh boy?" she said lightly. "Well, we're not taking any chances. Let's call it a day." She picked up the lead, and he walked contentedly by her side as they made their way slowly back to Valley View Drive. Once home, she settled him on his favorite blanket in a corner of the TV room, making a mental note to call the vet first thing in the morning.

Later, lying alone in bed and waiting for her husband to come home, Paula reflected on the intriguing cycles of life. Since her conversion to the Church, she had come to understand and appreciate the eternal nature of the human (and, she trusted, the canine) spirit. Departed friends, furry or otherwise, and family would never really be lost to her; she knew that. They had simply been relocated for the moment, having used up their time on earth, and were now traveling happily along in some parallel universe that she could imagine but couldn't quite discern. Meanwhile, in another subdivision of this heavenly metropolis, the latest crop of unproven spirits—eager, enthusiastic ones, she assumed—were jogging in place at some celestial intersection, impatient for the green light to signal their long-awaited entrance into mortality. Paula fancied that among them was her own daughter, undoubtedly one of the pushy ones who insisted on balancing for the takeoff with one sneaker pushing against the curb. Or against Paula's backbone, as the case may be.

So where, exactly, did that leave any of them—premortal, earthbound, or, as the prophet Alma described the exiting pilgrims, those who had been "taken home to that God who gave them life"? Clearly, Paula thought, in order to comprehend it, a person would have to view the plan of salvation as a whole, not simply define its individual parts. This one grand idea—that life, whatever its sphere, was a close-knit tapestry of spirit and intelligence and never-ending progression—could catch hold of a person's very soul and transform the nonbeliever into a passionate member of God's army. That, she decided, was what it felt like to be a Mormon—to understand the beginning, the middle, and the end of it all. Except there was no end; there was only forever. It was the essence of the heavenly gift.

Paula closed her eyes and pressed her fingers against both temples. "Good grief," she murmured aloud, "where did that come from? The only time I used to think that deeply was after a couple of double martinis. Or triple, if I really wanted to plumb the meaning of existence." She smiled at the memory. "On the other hand, I suppose I wasn't really thinking at all—just flirting with the endless vagaries of my life. But this . . . this feels good. This feels right. It's like the missionaries said when I challenged them two years ago: the gospel has all the answers. You just have to look for them."

Her head began to throb, and she reached over to switch off the lamp beside her. "Perhaps I'll continue the search tomorrow."

Chapter 5

Early Wednesday morning, Ted and Paula stared at each other across the breakfast table. Both were dressed in their most impeccable business attire, which seemed to lend a certain air of formality to their meal. He buttered his toast with deliberate care; she lifted a forkful of scrambled eggs to her lips with the precision of a diamond cutter.

"Nervous?" he asked, reaching for the small glass of cranberry-apple juice near his plate.

"A little." She dabbed at one corner of her mouth with a napkin. "No reason to be, really; we've been interviewed by business and news magazines before, and we know our company better than anyone. Still, when a reporter from *Time* is doing the interviewing, it seems like something above and beyond 'business as usual.'"

Ted nodded. "We'll give him a good show." He reached out to pat the bulge beneath Paula's waist. "Listen and learn, missy. Your mama will knock this guy out with her brainpower. Not to mention her incredible charm and beauty."

Paula flushed slightly, then rested her hand lightly on top of his. "Just make sure you keep me on track today," she said with quiet intensity. "I've been boning up for the past few days, but you're the one who's been running the company since we, uh, commenced growing a family."

"No problem," Ted declared. "Besides, I'm sure our reporter friend will be intrigued to know that one of America's most savvy businesswomen is also about to become a mother—for the fourth time. It'll be a great sidebar to his story."

"Maybe so," she conceded. A glance at the kitchen clock told her they still had plenty of time. "And speaking of mothers . . . I finally made contact with mine yesterday afternoon. You were late getting home last night, and I didn't have a chance to tell you. I'd been trying to reach her for two days, but she never answered."

"Oh?" He raised an eyebrow. "How's she doing? All right, I guess, if you were able to get through to her."

"That's just it," Paula responded. "I'm not sure I actually *did* get through to her."

"How so? I thought you just said—"

"Oh, I spoke with her all right. But she didn't really sound like . . . herself."

Ted couldn't resist chuckling a little. "And just what does Marjorie Enfield 'sound' like?"

Paula ignored the light sarcasm in his voice. "I couldn't quite put a finger on it. She just seemed vague or something. Distracted. I thanked her profusely for the blessing gown and her lovely note, but she didn't have much to say. And when I asked her where she'd been since Sunday afternoon, she just coughed and said 'Away, I believe' in a kind of small, strangled-sounding voice. It was odd—certainly not what I'd expected."

He took another sip of juice, then gazed at her intently. "Since when has your mother *ever* been what you expected? From what you've told me about your childhood and the difficult circumstances of your first marriage, I wouldn't say she was exactly a shining role model for mothers everywhere. I know you've been a little closer since TJ's death, but I can't imagine you'll ever be—"

"I know. I know," Paula interjected, holding up a hand to quiet him. "We've still got some issues to work out, and it may never happen, at least in this life. I guess I was just hoping that with the baby coming and her gift and all, she'd be a little warmer when I called. Instead, she was just . . . different. That's all." She shrugged. "Chalk it up to old age and Connecticut winters. I'm sure when I call her again, she'll be fine." *Next week . . . I'll call her next week,* she vowed silently. Picking up her fork, she scooped up the last of her eggs and ate them quickly. At least she was feeling good this morning—better than usual, in fact.

"Okay then," Ted declared, glancing at his watch. "We'd better get going; I've still got a couple of fact sheets to print out for our guest, and we need to be totally collected before he arrives. Your chariot or mine?"

"Yours, I think," she replied, picturing her snappy red Jaguar convertible. "You know I love the wind in my hair, but I believe it would be best to save the wild-woman look for another day."

"Then the Cherokee it is," he said gallantly, pulling out her chair as she stood. "Shall I check on Rudy before we leave?"

"No need," she said. "I gave him his meds and let him outside for a few minutes earlier, so he should be all right until Millie gets back from the temple around noon. The vet gave him some pretty powerful antibiotics on Monday, and told me he shouldn't be allowed to go out in the smog for more than ten minutes or operate heavy machinery for a few days." The big dog now rested quietly on his blanket in a warm, dark corner of the TV room. Their trip to Dr. MacKenzie's Creature Comforts Animal Clinic had revealed a slight respiratory infection, and Rudy was responding well to his medication. But it made him drowsy, and he seemed content to stay downstairs by himself.

Ted and Paula quickly relaxed as the Jeep sped along the interstate toward Los Angeles. They chatted happily—more like a couple of teenagers heading for a day at the beach, she reflected, than two high-powered advertising executives on their way to meet with a representative of one of America's most prestigious news magazines. Deep down, she had a good feeling about this interview; it would give them a chance to crow a little about their successes, perhaps make a few salient points about the importance of having integrity in one's business dealings. Despite her initial case of nerves, Paula always enjoyed a lively interaction with the media; and Ted, who was more reserved in these kinds of encounters, provided the perfect complement to her dramatic flair. Together, they would make a friend of this reporter and admirers of all who read his article.

A light drizzle had begun, then intensified by the time they exited the freeway, but traffic was lighter than usual and their vehicle moved quickly down the off-ramp. "I love a rainy morning," Paula chirped as they merged into a larger four-lane street. "It settles the smog, and makes everything look fresh and a little fuzzy around the edges—kind of like an impressionist painting." She smiled. "A watercolor." Visions of splashing merrily through mud puddles, an umbrella in one hand and her little girl's delicate fingers clasped firmly in the other, flashed through her mind. It was definitely something to look forward to.

"I know what you mean," Ted observed. "It never rained much when I was growing up in Utah, but an occasional summer thunderstorm would blow through, and afterwards you could actually see the steam rising from the grass and sidewalks. I loved the smell of it."

She glanced at him, raising an eyebrow. "So, then . . . life wasn't *all* bad when you were a kid."

He shrugged and offered her a wry smile. "It had its redeeming moments."

They settled into a comfortable silence for the last few minutes of their drive. Approaching a wide intersection about a mile from their office building, Ted shook his head as he braked to a stop, having barely missed a green light. "I should've taken the yellow," he muttered, glancing at his watch. "This is the longest red light in the history of civilization. The rain has slowed us down, and I've still got some things to do at the office before that reporter comes." He hunched his shoulders and stared long and intently at the crimson globe suspended above them in the gray sky, as if he could turn it to green by the sheer force of his will.

Paula patted his knee. "Just relax and enjoy the scenery," she soothed. "It'll be our turn soon enough. Besides, we've still got more than an hour before the interview, and I'm sure you can get everything—"

"Finally!" Ted's exasperated voice cut into her sentence as the light changed to a brilliant emerald-green color. "It's about time!" He punched the gas pedal with his foot, and the Cherokee shot forward into the intersection.

Suddenly, something big and moving flashed at the periphery of Paula's vision. She turned her head to the right, and at that moment events slowed to a fraction of their normal speed. A large white truck was lumbering straight toward the Cherokee, its massive front end aimed directly at the passenger-side door like a heat-seeking missile. In her altered state of movement and perception, Paula could see every detail clearly, from the broad-beamed floodlights mounted on the vehicle's roof all the way down to the bright beads of rain clinging to its polished chrome grille and bumper. She even saw the driver, a dark-haired young man whose face was contorted with terror and disbelief.

He must have run the red light, she thought as her arms moved instinctively to cover her belly. What seemed like hours later, there was a sharp grinding of metal, and she felt pressure where her arms had been.

It was the last thing she remembered.

* * * * * * * * *

"It doesn't look good," the doctor announced. She removed her glasses and rubbed her fingers wearily along the bridge of her nose and up between her eyebrows. "I'm going up to surgery with her now, and we'll do everything humanly possible. But I need to ask . . ." Her voice trailed off uncertainly, and the steady look in her kind eyes wavered.

Ted set his teeth and grimaced as he struggled to sit up on the emergency-room gurney. The wrenching impact of the crash had dislocated his shoulder and broken three ribs, and there was a deep gash above his left temple where his head had collided with the Cherokee's steel door frame. He'd be fine, but at the moment he felt like a fire had been set in the center of his chest and was burning out of control. He pushed the pain aside and looked squarely at the white-coated woman in front of him. "Just say it, Dr. Parkin. Whatever you need, you've got it. I could give blood, or a kidney, or anything else, up to and including my heart." He gave her a quirky little smile. "Although, in a manner of speaking, she already has that. Just let me know."

The doctor smiled thinly at his attempt to ease the tension. "I'm afraid it's not quite that straightforward," she explained gently. "What I need to ask you is . . . to make a very personal decision. A very tough one."

"Go on," he said, swallowing awkwardly as a steel band of dread tightened around his throat.

"All right," she agreed, her voice almost apologetic. "Hopefully, this will have a positive outcome. But we still need to face the fact that even in this day of medical miracles we may not be able to save both of them. If it comes down to a choice, we need to have your permission one way or the other. Mother or baby."

Ted stared at her, his jaw slack. "You mean you want me to tell you which one I'd rather keep?" A brief memory of his and Paula's recent "Am I a keeper?" conversation flashed through his mind.

"Essentially, yes."

His sigh was deep and ragged. "You know," he said, barely able to speak around the knot of grief and fear in his throat, "we've loved this child from the day she was conceived. It would be utterly heart-breaking to lose her. But my wife is . . . well, there will never, ever be another Paula, and I refuse to finish the rest of my life without her. It took me too long to find her in the first place." He swallowed hard and gazed intently at the doctor. "Am I making myself perfectly clear?"

"I believe so," she replied. "As I said, I hope it won't come to that, and we can make this a success story for both mother and daughter." She paused. "Paula's my friend too, you know."

"Yes, I know," Ted replied. "She's in good hands."

"We'll do our best," Dr. Parkin said. "Cross your fingers for us." She squeezed his hand, then turned and strode briskly from the room.

"You can do better than that," a gruff voice said beside him. Startled, he turned to see Scott leaning against a wall near the room's back entrance.

"Hey kid," Ted offered with a wan smile.

"How you doing?" Scott approached the gurney and examined the thick bandage on his stepfather's head. "The hospital called me at work and I dropped everything. I've been here for a few minutes." He stuffed his hands into the pockets of his jeans. "I heard what the doc said about Mom and the baby."

Ted's shoulders slumped. "Yeah, it's pretty bad. We're all pulling for them. What was that you said a minute ago, when you nearly surprised me out of my skin?"

"I said," Scott replied, his jaw set in a determined line, "you can do better than that."

"Better than what?" Ted shook his head vigorously, wishing the massive shot of Demerol they'd given him hadn't muddled his brain.

"Better than just crossing your fingers. Or 'pulling' for them." A glimmer of impatience rose in the boy's eyes. "Think about it."

"Okay, okay," Ted conceded, pressing a hand to his throbbing temple. "I give. What are you talking about?"

A deep, condescending sigh rose from Scott's chest. "A blessing, Ted. Mom needs a *blessing.* And so does the baby." He smiled crookedly. "Matter of fact, you could probably do with one yourself."

"A blessing." Ted stared blankly at the young man. He'd heard the words, but they seemed to be coming from a stranger's mouth. Was this the same kid who had spent the majority of his teenage years rebelling against every form of structure or authority in sight—especially the Mormon Church? The same obstinate malcontent who, for at least two years now, had steadfastly refused to go to church, couldn't bring himself to sit through a single home evening, wouldn't give any missionary the time of day, even turned down repeated invitations to play a friendly game of *Celestial Pursuit?* Paula had tried again and again to energize his spiritual batteries, but thus far she had prodded in vain. And now here he was, standing in this sterile, impersonal hospital emergency room, reminding a dazed Ted in no uncertain terms of his priesthood responsibility. Go figure.

He decided not to press his luck. "You're right, of course," he said meekly. "I haven't been thinking all that clearly. Thanks for bringing me back, Scott."

"Hey, what's a wayward son for?" the boy grinned.

Since Scott had brought it up, Ted gave in to his growing curiosity. "But I can't help wondering why you would think to . . . how you knew . . . didn't have a clue that you even believed . . ." His fuzzy brain and drug-dry mouth couldn't quite form the words.

Scott picked up where he left off. "Well, maybe I don't exactly *believe,* but I figure a few extra prayers can't hurt. They're for my mom and my little sister, after all. You have to do what you can." He coughed a little and stared at the floor. When he lifted his head, there was a definite twinkle in his warm hazel eyes. "Besides, Millie made me come and tell you what to do. She's rounding up the bishop and maybe a couple of other guys to come over here and help."

"That's our Millie," Ted chuckled. A few seconds later his expression changed dramatically. "Uh-oh," he said, "we've got to get up to surgery—now! Dr. Parkin said they were going to start operating right away . . . but there still has to be time for that blessing. Let's go!" Steeling himself against the pain in his chest, he draped a thin hospital robe around his shoulders with one arm, then slid sideways off the gurney. As his feet hit the floor, the room began to spin and the muscles in his legs turned to liquid.

In an instant, two strong arms were around him, supporting him, guiding him to a wheelchair in the corner. "There you go," Scott said when the furniture finally stopped gyrating. "Free ride to the fourth floor, coming up. Hang on." He released the brake, and they hurried toward the nearest elevator.

Outside the surgical suites, a soft-spoken young woman at the nurses' station shook her head. "I'm sorry, I really am. They took Mrs. Barstow into surgery about ten minutes ago." She pointed to a small carpeted area across the aisle. "It'll be a while until we know anything. You're welcome to wait, if you like."

"Yes, thank you," Ted responded hoarsely. Scott wheeled him into the waiting room, where he slumped down in the wheelchair and covered his face with his hands. "We're too late," he moaned. "I should have been here. Should have given her the blessing."

Scott lowered himself onto a swaybacked pea-green sofa next to Ted's chair. "We can't think about that now," he said matter-of-factly. "We just have to hold on and keep her in our thoughts until this is over. Like we always say at the Ninja Academy—'To Think Is To Be.' It's helped me through a lot of tough martial arts competitions. If I can see it in my mind, feel it in my heart, I can do it. So maybe if you just close your eyes and see yourself blessing Mom, feel the power flowing from your hands into her body . . . well, it could help, don't you think?"

Ted slowly lifted his head, and his eyes met Scott's. "I like your style, son," he said, and couldn't help smiling in spite of the circumstances. "What you suggest is not exactly your traditional priesthood approach—you know, the laying on of hands and such—but I get the feeling that Somebody up there is more than willing to take all comers. Especially when the stakes are so high; when our prayers are so important." He swallowed hard, clasping and unclasping his hands several times, then nodded firmly. "Let's do that, Scott . . . let's focus all the love and good thoughts and energy we have on what's happening right now in that operating room. It'll help; I'm sure of it."

"You bet," Scott grinned. "I'm with you all the way." Without another word, the two men bowed their heads, each in his own way appealing to a higher power for the deliverance of a loved one. The prayers might have been very different in structure and content, but no one could doubt that they flowed from the deepest chambers of two anguished hearts. And when they finally looked up, first Scott and then Ted a few minutes later, the tears on their cheeks confirmed the fervency of their supplications.

"Whoa," Scott whispered, "it was awesome—like somebody was really listening."

"Yeah, I know," Ted agreed. He propped an elbow on one of the wheelchair's arms and rested his head against his hand.

Scott took a closer look at his stepfather. "Hey, you're as pale as my friend Twinkie was the first time we went skydiving. Seems like you ought to be taking it easy. Would you like to lie down? We could find an empty room somewhere, or—"

"No," Ted replied firmly. "I need to be here—in case there's any news. But I wouldn't mind stretching out on one of these couches for a while."

"Say no more." Scott came to his feet and stretched out a hand. Ted clasped it weakly, then Scott curled an arm around his shoulders to steady him. They made their way slowly to a long, orange-colored sofa in a more secluded area of the waiting room, where Ted lay down with a grateful, weary sigh. "Hold on for just a sec," Scott said as an idea occurred to him. "I'll be right back."

"I'm not going anywhere," Ted mumbled through a haze of exhaustion as he watched Scott disappear across the hall. Minutes later he was back, two pillows under one arm and a bright-green thermal blanket draped across the other. "Hey, not exactly color coordinated," he grinned, "but it'll have to do." He carefully placed one pillow under Ted's neck and the other beneath his knees, then spread the blanket from his chin to his toes.

"That feels good," Ted sighed. "Where did you learn to . . . take care of people so well?"

"You can thank Ms. Solomon for that," he explained. "I had to take a week's worth of first-aid training when I started working at the Academy. It comes in handy every once in a while; we get our share of sprained ankles and stuff."

"Hmmm. It sure does feel . . ." Ted's words faded as he slipped into comfortable oblivion.

Through the afternoon, as Ted lay sleeping and waking and sleeping again, the tiny waiting room filled then overflowed with ward members and others who'd been apprised of the catastrophe: Millie, Bishop Peters, Eloise Martin, Meg O'Brien and her husband Kevin, who was Ted's good friend and one of his counselors in the elders quorum presidency, Bonnie Solomon (who had heard the news from Scott), even Nora Tilton, who had been visiting teaching at Eloise's house when the telephone rang. In deference to Ted's needs, they situated themselves as far from his couch as possible, communicating quietly in whispers and frequent hugs. Even though several hours had passed without news, the prevailing mood seemed to be concerned but optimistic.

Paula's assistant, Carmine Brough, had been at the hospital since late morning. Now she stood disconsolately a little ways apart from the group, speaking to no one, her sturdy frame barely able to hold up the wall she leaned heavily against. She constantly dabbed at her eyes and hiccupped occasionally, her attention riveted on the nurses' station across the hall, waiting, hoping for any sign of activity that might bring news. Eloise brought her a small cup of water, and she accepted it gratefully. "Are you all right, dear?" Eloise inquired.

Carmine shook her head and yanked distractedly at her tightly-permed red hair. "Paula's my best friend," she wailed in a small, thin voice, "and now she's dying."

"Oh, now don't you go thinking like that, my dear," the older woman scolded gently. "She's a strong woman, feisty as the day is long, and she's surely not going to give up that easily. I believe Someone is watching over her, and her little one as well. We'll be giving her a priesthood blessing as soon as she's out of surgery. If it's the Lord's will, they'll both be fine."

"And what if it isn't His will? What then?" Carmine bit down hard on her lip. "Oh, I can't even think about that." After a moment she lifted her chin and looked Eloise straight in the eye, her expression almost defiant. "You know, I've been hearing a lot about the Mormons ever since Paula became one—never put much stock in God or religion myself, but she's seemed happy enough, so I haven't been one to complain, just listened politely whenever she got off on the subject. But now I'll tell you what. If this blessing thing works out and she pulls through, I'm willing to listen—missionaries and the whole enchilada. I'd even think of getting dunked, if that's what it takes. Not that I'm promising anything right now, y'understand; she'd have to be totally out of the woods before I'd agree to it." She paused, not quite certain how to proceed. "But I suppose now's as good a time as any to let your God know what my intentions are—or could be, depending on how things turn out." She lowered her voice. "Do you think He'd take that into account?"

Eloise's softly powdered face lit up. "I'm sure He would, Carmine. And your prayers will be greatly appreciated. Now, would you like to meet Bishop Peters?"

She put a gentle hand to Carmine's back, and was just guiding her into the waiting area when a sudden hush fell over the group.

"It's Dr. Parkin," someone whispered. "At the nurses' station."

Bending over the counter to speak with a nurse, the slim doctor looked like a teenager in her green scrub suit and close-fitting surgical cap. But when she straightened up, even from a distance one could see the shadows of fatigue circling her eyes, the deep wrinkles cleaving her forehead, the parched look of her colorless lips. As Paula's friends and family stared at her in respectful silence, she squared her shoulders and forced a half-smile to her lips. Within seconds, she had cleared the few yards between the nurses' station and the waiting room.

Pulling off her cap, the doctor sighed deeply. "This was a tough one—quite a few internal injuries," she said. "I wasn't the surgeon, of course . . . I just assisted and gave my input concerning the pregnancy. Dr. Iman is the best thoracic surgeon in the business." Seeing their eyes, she responded to the next question without being asked. "We won't know anything for a while yet."

"And the baby?" Ted had managed to get himself up from the couch, and was leaning heavily on a nearby chair in order to remain upright. His expression looked pinched and exhausted.

"Mr. Barstow," the doctor said, moving quickly to his side, "you really should be under observation, at least for the next twenty-four hours or so. I'll see about getting you admitted right away, and—"

"I asked about the baby," he interrupted in a gravelly voice. "Please . . . tell me."

"She's alive. There was some bleeding into the uterus, but she still seems viable, and there's no sign of premature labor. That's about all we know at this point. We'll keep you informed." Dr. Parkin spoke with a curious detachment, and Ted found no comfort in her words.

"I'd like to be in the same room with my wife," he said.

"I'm afraid that's not possible," the doctor responded, this time with a little more warmth and genuine regret in her tone. "No one is allowed to visit intensive care patients except for five minutes every hour." She offered him a conciliatory smile. "But I'll see what I can do about finding you a room three or four doors down the hall."

"Thanks," he murmured. "And right about now, I think I could use—"

"A lift," Scott said behind him, nudging the backs of his knees with the seat of the wheelchair. Ted collapsed into it and looked up at the boy gratefully.

The tiny waiting room seemed to bulge under the burden of a thousand unanswered questions, but Dr. Parkin raised a hand before anyone else could speak. "Now, I know you're all anxious for every bit of news, and determined to be here for Paula," she said. "But the truth is, we just won't know anything for several hours yet, and you'd all be better off at home, getting some rest. So please, go back to your families now, and try to be patient. I'll let Ted know everything as it happens, and he'll pass the word along." Her gaze scanned their reluctant faces. "Please trust me . . . I've been through these kinds of things before. It's better this way."

"But she needs a blessing," Nora Tilton called out. "Can't someone at least do that?" Instantly Dr. Parkin felt the intensity of more than a dozen pairs of pleading eyes focused on her.

After a long pause, she nodded slowly. "Well, all right. Paula has often spoken to me about her religious faith, and I can't help thinking that such a—what was it? Yes, a blessing—could work in her favor." Expressions of relief and thanks rippled through the group. "But only two of you will be allowed in the room, and only for a couple of minutes. She's still in recovery."

"Yes!" Ted exclaimed, albeit feebly. "Let's do it!" He tried to bolt from his chair, but immediately toppled into the arms of the two people nearest him, gasping in pain and barely hanging on to consciousness. They lowered him carefully back to the chair, his face pasty and covered with sweat.

"I'm afraid that doesn't include you, Mr. Barstow," the doctor said, her voice warm with sympathy. "You're in no shape to be anywhere but horizontal right now, and there's a bed with your name on it just down the hall. I'm sure one of your friends here can pinch-hit for you."

Ted could barely speak through his pain and vertigo. "Okay . . . couldn't think straight enough to do it anyway," he whispered. Turning his eyes toward the circle of friends around him, he inclined his head first toward the bishop, then toward Kevin O'Brien. Both men nodded soberly in response. "Thanks, guys," Ted murmured. "I trust you to help her."

"It won't be us doing the helping, brother," the bishop said. "We're just the instruments."

"But we'll be the best darned instruments we know how to be," Kevin assured him earnestly. "Then we'll be in to do the same for you." He rested a hand lightly on Ted's drooping shoulder. "Now get out of here, and let us go do our job."

"That's right, Ted dear," Millie said, leaning over to kiss his forehead and press her cheek firmly against his. "We need you to be well and strong—for Paula. And for all of us, too." Her lips trembled as she straightened up, and he could see tears glimmering in her eyes. "I'll take care of everything at home." He barely had time to flash her a weak grin and mouth "thank you" before Scott commandeered the wheelchair and pushed him briskly down the hall.

"Now, ma'am," Bishop Peters said, addressing the doctor, "if you'll be kind enough to take us to Paula, we'll give her that blessing."

"Of course," she replied. "Please follow me." Turning to the others, she smiled with genuine warmth. "Thank you all for coming, and for waiting so patiently. Paula is extremely fortunate . . ." Her voice caught, and she paused for a moment before continuing. "So very fortunate to have you as friends. If anyone can help pull her through this, you can." She cleared her throat. "Now, if you'll excuse me, I'll show these gentlemen to her room. Please go home and get some rest; it's the best thing you can do under the circumstances. We'll keep you updated on her condition."

"Thank you, Dr. Parkin," someone said. "And bless you." A murmur of assent filtered through the group, and she raised her hand in quiet acknowledgment as she escorted Kevin and the bishop out of the waiting area.

Half an hour later, after seeing most of Paula's friends and family on their way, the two men slipped noiselessly into Ted's room, where they waited several minutes until his eyes fluttered open. Seeing them, he tried to lean up on his elbow, but grimaced with pain and lay back down again. "How'd it go?" he questioned, studying their faces for any clue.

"Pretty well, I think," Kevin said. "We could definitely feel the Spirit."

"And?" he pressed. "Is she going to be okay? Will the baby make it?"

The bishop reached out to touch Ted's arm. "We left it in the Lord's hands," he replied softly. "Sometimes, when the Spirit doesn't give you specific words, that's all you can do. But we had a good feeling about it."

Despite, or perhaps because of their words, Ted felt a large knot of grief and terror forming in his throat. *The elders left TJ in the Lord's hands,* he reflected silently, *and he died. What am I supposed to think?* The room suddenly seemed cold as his hands gripped and twisted the thin sheet covering his body. "A good feeling," he repeated in a stiff, unnatural tone. "What's that supposed to mean?"

"It means," Kevin said gently, "that we wait, and hope, and pray, and exercise as much faith as we can possibly muster. It means that in the end, everything will turn out all right. It has to, because God knows the plan perfectly, and eventually it will be executed perfectly. In the meantime, it's up to us to reconcile our will to His. I believe that sometimes, under intense circumstances, He actually withholds information from us for a time. It's His way of testing our faith and acceptance of His will, I suppose—not an easy thing to go through, but it makes us stronger. 'More fit for the kingdom,' as the old hymn goes."

Ted smiled grimly. "Now I know why you're my counselor in the elders quorum . . . you're so much smarter than I am." He sighed in weary resignation. "What you say makes absolute sense. But the trick is just to hold on to that 'perfect plan' idea, and then maybe I'll find a little peace. It's the waiting that's so darn hard, you know? I just can't imagine life without . . . without . . ." His voice trailed off as the muscles in his jaw began to quiver.

"Don't even go there," Kevin urged. "Just let the doctors and the Lord do their work."

Ted closed his eyes and let out a long, tortuous moan. "Okay. Okay . . . I'll try."

"Fair enough," Bishop Peters said. "Now, we'd like to give you a blessing. Goodness knows you're going to need a little something extra to get you through these next few days."

"Appreciate that," Ted breathed, his eyes still closed. He tried to say something more, but his pale lips couldn't quite form the words.

The men positioned themselves on either side of the bed and rested their hands lightly above their friend's brow. Uttering words of comfort, healing, and recovery, they closed their administration with a second humble appeal on Paula's behalf. By the time they had carefully lifted their hands and wiped the tears from their own cheeks, Ted had slipped into a safe haven of sleep. They clasped each other in a firm embrace before moving silently from the room to join their wives for the solemn ride home.

"Mr. Barstow . . . Mr Barstow." The words penetrated Ted's brain through a haze of exhaustion and Demerol. "Mr. Barstow . . . may I speak with you? It's important." A firm hand was squeezing his arm, shaking it a little.

"Mmm?" He screwed one eye open and looked up at a shadowy figure leaning over his bed. "What time is it?"

"Four A.M.," the voice said, and the gentle shaking continued. "Please, Mr. Barstow, could you wake up now?" Whoever it was, they meant business.

Ted opened his other eye, and the figure began to take shape. Dr. Parkin's dark, curly shoulder-length hair was haloed by a shaft of dim light from the hospital corridor. Relief flooded her countenance when she finally saw the recognition in his eyes. "How are you doing?" she asked.

Ted's hand moved to his bandaged head. "Not too bad, actually," he reported. "I guess I needed some sleep, and I was out like a—" His expression suddenly darkened, and he gripped the sleeve of her blue lab coat. "Wait a minute . . . what is it, doctor? You wouldn't be here at this hour if something weren't going on. It's Paula, isn't it?" She didn't reply immediately. *"Isn't it?"* he pressed.

"Yes," she conceded. "It's Paula. And we need your help."

"My help?" Ted couldn't resist a low chuckle. "I'm afraid you've lost me there. I don't know anything about—"

"I realize that," she broke in. "But sometimes medicine isn't everything—and you may just be our last hope." Her eyes virtually glowed with intensity as she stared at him.

"What are you saying?" he asked gruffly. He felt his heart thudding against his ribs, sending waves of pain coursing through his chest.

Dr. Parkin sat beside him on the bed and began to speak in low, urgent tones. "A little while after your friends gave Paula that blessing, she started doing better. Her vital signs improved, she was breathing more easily, and everything looked good. Even the baby seemed to be doing well. Until . . ." She rubbed her forehead nervously.

"Until?" Ted prompted.

"Until about half an hour ago, when things started going terribly wrong. I—I can't understand it; she's just failing, and there doesn't seem to be anything we can do."

"Oh, my Lord," Ted moaned, covering his eyes. "Please don't let it come to this."

"That's why I'm here," Dr. Parkin continued. She gently took hold of his hands and pulled them away from his face, then looked into the depths of his moist eyes. "To ask you to give her another blessing."

He gaped at her incredulously. "But I—"

"Please." She squeezed both of his hands between hers. "I may not know much about organized religion, and I'm certainly in the dark when it comes to your Mormon priesthood. But over the years, I've seen enough miracles in the delivery room to be convinced of the reality of a higher power than medical skill alone. And at the moment, your wife needs a heck of a lot more help than what we mortals have to offer. I've spoken with Dr. Iman, and he agrees that we're just about out of options." She stood and motioned toward one corner of the room. "I brought a wheelchair. Will you do it?"

He was already sitting up on the side of the bed. "Of course," he said, mentally blocking out his pain and focusing on the task before him. At least he was feeling a bit stronger than he had been several hours earlier. "If you'll hand me the phone, I'll call one of my friends to come and assist, then we'll—"

"No time for that," the doctor interjected. "We've got only minutes before . . . well, it's just too tight. It's you or nothing."

Ted gulped. "Then I guess it's me." As she wheeled him down the hall, he bowed his head and offered the most fervent thirty-second prayer he had uttered in his life.

Paula's ICU chamber was cold as a meat locker and busy as a construction site when they arrived. Almost as if according to some prearranged signal, the small cadre of doctors, nurses, and technicians bending over Paula stopped what they were doing, lined up close together against a side wall, and watched Ted almost reverently. Dr. Iman, Paula's surgeon, leaned over the wheelchair. "You have about two minutes before we have to start working again," he whispered. "Maybe less if her vitals start going crazy again."

"I understand," Ted responded quietly. His hands were ice-cold as he braced them against the arms of the wheelchair and tried to raise himself to his feet. When he wavered, Dr. Parkin curled an arm about his waist, walked him to Paula's bed, and stayed with him.

She lay perfectly still on her back, unconscious, pale as death, beautiful even in this bizarre setting. The swell of her abdomen was barely discernible beneath the pastel green sheet draped across her body. Moving as if in slow motion, Ted bent over to brush a kiss across her brow. "Sorry about the cold hands," he whispered. "I'll make it up to you later. But right now you and I have got to work together on this healing thing. Do your best, okay?" Wincing in pain as he stretched out both arms toward the crown of her head, he nestled his hands firmly in her thick, dark hair.

From the moment of contact, warmth began to flow into his chest, into his upper arms, into his wrists, his palms, his fingers—so much warmth that he felt it radiate into the room's chilly atmosphere. Words beyond his own came to him then, and he heard himself calling to his wife from somewhere beyond the mortal dimension, entreating her to be healed, begging her to remember the home and family she adored, willing her to come back to him. Finally, he reminded her in the words of an early Christian apostle that "'all things work together for good to them that love God.' We both love Him," he added, "and there is still so much good to be done. I bless you to know that your life is in His care, and we will see this through . . . together. In the name of Jesus Christ, amen."

A round of subdued "amens" rippled around the room as Ted lifted his hands from Paula's head and leaned over to press one last kiss to her lips, this time noticing a bit of color in her sallow cheeks. He raised his head to smile at the earnest little makeshift congregation around him, but a sudden wave of lightheadedness buckled his knees and sent him reeling backward. Dr. Parkin, who had never left his side, grasped his waist firmly and guided him expertly into the wheelchair. "Time to get you back to bed," she declared, bending over to release the brake. As they left Paula's cubicle, the hospital workers gradually returned to monitoring her condition, but now without the frantic sense of urgency that had driven them earlier.

"That was extraordinary," Dr. Parkin said as she helped Ted get settled back in his room. "I could feel the power . . . everyone could."

"I just hope it's enough," he sighed. "She's in pretty bad shape, isn't she?"

"I'm afraid so. But with all that good energy on your side, I wouldn't be at all surprised if she totally, completely beats the odds. In fact, I'd be willing to bet on it." She smiled down at him. "Now get some rest, young man; you deserve it. I'll let you know how she's doing. And thank you . . . so much." She wiped at something near the corner of her eye, then turned and hurried from the room.

Ted leaned back against his cool, welcoming pillow. "And thank *You,*" he breathed, gazing toward the ceiling. Never had he been so content, so filled with peace, so assured of divine intervention on his behalf. He had felt the power, too . . . and now he had every reason to believe it was enough. A smile of gratitude touched his lips as he dozed off.

An hour later, his eyes flew open when the hospital PA system suddenly came to life and blared shrilly through the hallways.

"Dr. Parkin and Dr. Iman to ICU. Doctors Parkin and Iman to ICU. *STAT!*"

Chapter 6

Ted was exhausted. Millie, Scott, and several others had come and gone many times, but he had not left Paula's bedside for nearly two days straight. She'd probably come out of it, they said, but her body had to begin the healing process first. Waiting, it seemed, was the only option. And hoping. And praying. He squeezed her hand one more time, trying to force vitality back into her limbs with an infusion of his own strength. "Dear Lord," he murmured, "please bring her back to me. Please." Sighing heavily, he let his head drop to his chest and sat quietly, half-dozing, for a long while.

A gentle hand on his shoulder roused him. "Ted," Millie's kind voice said behind him, "I've come to send you home for some supper and a good night's sleep." She began to tenderly massage the tops of his shoulders and the back of his neck, and he moaned softly. "There's plenty of food in the fridge, and I'll bet a nice hot shower sounds pretty good right about now. I'll look after our girl here."

His shoulders drooped. "Thanks, Millie, but I—I really couldn't sleep in our bed . . . not without her there. It'd just remind me of—"

"Oh, pooh," she broke in, still kneading his shoulders. "A bed's a bed, and you're so tuckered that even a she-wolf howling right next to your ear couldn't keep you awake for more than ten seconds. Besides, you need to keep yourself strong for Paula and the family. There's no way you can do that if you're so sick and tired you can't see straight. You're still recovering from your own injuries, you know."

He smiled ruefully. "You're right, as usual. I just don't know if I can leave her."

Millie plunked her hands on her broad hips and huffed good-naturedly. "What, you don't trust me to watch over her? That girl's like my own flesh and blood, if you want to know, and I've known her—"

"Yeah, yeah," he said, rolling his eyes. "You've known her a lot longer than I have." His gaze softened. "And you do have a point. I guess I could go home for a shower and a bite to eat, but I'll be back in a couple of hours. Promise you'll call if anything happens."

"Cross my heart. You'll be the first to know."

"Okay," he said. "But give me a minute alone with her first, would you?"

Millie smiled and patted his cheek. "Always the hopeless romantic. I like that in a man—and so does our Paula. I'll be right outside." She turned and shuffled from the room.

Ted sat down next to the bed and took Paula's right hand in both of his. "Well, sweetness," he said, caressing the back of her hand gently with his thumb, "I guess I'll take off for a little while. I hate to desert you like this, but Millie will be right here, and I promise I'll come back smelling a whole lot better than I do now. Can I bring you a hot dog or anything?" Recalling the baby shower only a week earlier, he smiled. "Or maybe a nice, ooey-gooey S'more would hit the spot. I'll see what I can do. Now get some rest, you hear? And remember—no fooling around with that swarthy Dr. Iman while I'm gone."

He stood, and still clasping her right hand in one of his, he reached out to smooth a lock of dark hair away from her brow. "I love you," he whispered, then closed his eyes and leaned forward to press his mouth firmly against her forehead for long, exquisitely drawn-out moments, almost as if he could emboss the message on her brain in lip-shaped letters. Then he straightened up, turned, and strode quickly from the room.

He was back less than two hours later, freshly fed and scrubbed, ready to continue his vigil. After giving Millie a grateful hug and sending her home to rest her arthritic bones and look after Scott, he settled in for the night, lying beside Paula on the narrow hospital bed, one arm draped across her waist, her head resting near his shoulder so he could hear any sound she might make. A nurse brought an extra blanket and pillow, then dimmed the room's lights until they barely cast thin shadows against the walls. The muted hum of hospital activity in the hall quickly lulled Ted into relaxation.

Sometime before dawn, Paula opened her eyes. She lay perfectly still for a long while, listening to a dull, throbbing sound close to her ear. When she realized that it was her husband's heart, she paid even closer attention to its regular cadence. He was sleeping soundly, and she saw no reason to wake him right away.

Ever so slowly and with infinite care, she began to flex every muscle in her body, one at a time, making sure each was alive and receptive to her mental commands. Finally, when she was ready, she lifted a trembling hand and laid her palm against Ted's cheek. "Good morning, my love," she whispered.

He smiled and stirred a little, then snuggled his cheek against her hand. "Am I in the middle of an exquisite dream," he murmured, "or is this really the voice of my better half?"

"One and the same." She spoke through a haze of pain and exhaustion, but there was no mistaking the love he felt in every word.

He opened his eyes just as they filled and overflowed with moisture. "Welcome back, Mrs. Barstow," he said close to her ear. "Welcome home."

They lay quietly together, reveling in these moments of silent, secret reunion, until a nurse appeared to check Paula's vital signs. "If you could just roll her over a bit, Mr. Barstow," she whispered agreeably, "I'll be able to reach her arm and—"

"Here, let me do that," Paula said. She turned slowly, carefully from her side to her back, wincing at the sharp pain in her abdomen.

The nurse's hand flew to her chest. "Mercy! You're awake!"

Paula smiled wanly, exhausted by her small effort. "And I intend to stay that way." She turned to Ted. "How long was I out?"

"Way too long." He switched on a small lamp mounted above the bed and studied her face in the dim light. She looked wonderful to him—pale and bedraggled, with pain etched in her features, but beautiful nevertheless. If she lived to be a hundred, she would never stop being beautiful to him.

The nurse scurried away to report this development to her superior while Ted and Paula chatted quietly. Not many minutes passed before Paula's energy began to wane, and she lay back against her pillow with a sigh of exhaustion. "Guess I can't expect to do everything at once," she murmured. "Need to keep my strength up for the . . ." Her hand moved to her stomach, then down a bit farther. Alarm rose in her eyes when she felt a much flatter, smoother surface than she had remembered. And now that she thought about it, she hadn't felt any life moving inside her since she'd awakened. *What has happened?* She wasn't sure if she could take the news—but it couldn't wait.

Ted was watching her intently. When she looked up at him, he spoke first in slow, measured tones. "The baby," he said, reading her mind.

"Yes. Please . . . tell me," she moaned, closing her eyes as a hedge against the fear.

He quickly moved his hand to her chin. "Look at me," he urged gently. When she did, he continued. "The baby is beautiful, Paula. She's absolutely beautiful." His face broke into a wide grin.

Paula rubbed her temples. "You mean . . . you mean she's all right? She's still here, still with us?"

"Exactamento, my dear," he said with a flourish. "She's a fighter . . . just like her mother. Dr. Parkin said she came out hollering."

"But how . . ." She couldn't even think of the rest of the question, so she just stared at him, waiting for more information.

"Okay—I'll fill you in," Ted announced. "What's the last thing you remember?"

She bit her lip and scowled. "A monster white truck, coming at me like it wanted to eat me for breakfast."

"That was the day before yesterday," he explained. "The guy ran a red light and creamed the Cherokee. He walked away with some scratches and bruises, I broke a few ribs and got banged up a little, but you got the worst of it. They rushed you into surgery as soon as they got you to the hospital. There were some pretty nasty internal injuries; they had to remove your spleen and reconnect a few things."

"No wonder I'm so sore," she said, rubbing her midsection. "What happened to the baby?"

"She was all right at first; the bishop and Kevin gave you a blessing right after the surgery, and everything looked good." He gave her an apologetic half-smile. "I would've done it myself, except I was nursing my own mementos of the incident."

He patted his chest, and Paula felt the heavy tape beneath his shirt. "Poor baby," she murmured, imagining his pain.

"Anyway, a few hours later things started going seriously wrong, and Dr. Parkin actually came to my room and asked if I'd give you another blessing. She was pretty upset, and they were running out of time." He shrugged. "So I did."

"And obviously it worked," Paula smiled.

"Yeah," Ted continued. "Although I thought for sure we'd lost you when I heard them call both of your doctors to ICU a couple of hours later. As it turned out, the baby was in trouble—the placenta was torn or something—so they decided to take you back into surgery for an emergency C-section." He stopped and looked at her earnestly. "Now, this is where it *really* gets interesting. Once they'd removed the baby, they had a clearer view of your delicate little insides, so they decided to check and see how the earlier repairs were holding. Believe it or not, they discovered a tiny but dangerous tear in one of your abdominal arteries, and were able to fix it right away. Dr. Iman told me later that if they hadn't taken the baby, they never would have found it, and eventually the artery would've ruptured—probably while you were giving birth. You would have bled to death before anyone even knew what was happening."

"Whoa," Paula breathed. "It's like . . . Someone was up there looking out for us, putting all the right pieces together."

"No doubt about it," he concurred. "Especially after that blessing."

"How so?"

"Well, everyone in your room felt the power, and they told me so afterward. But the most amazing part was what I heard myself say—quoting the Apostle Paul when he taught the early Christians that everything works together for good in the lives of those who believe. Funny . . . I don't ever remember seeing or hearing that scripture, yet there it was, rolling off my tongue like I'd just read it yesterday. And it all came true in the end—things *did* work in our favor, even when it looked hopeless. Even when you took a mini-vacation from consciousness." He kissed her lightly. "We have a lot to be grateful for—including an adorable little daughter."

"Speaking of whom," Paula said, "I'd kind of like to introduce myself. Is she all right? Can we go see her—now?" She tried to sit up, but her severed stomach muscles responded with a surge of intense pain, and she sank back to a horizontal position. "Or, on the other hand, maybe she could come and visit me."

Ted smoothed the blanket across her body. "All in good time, Mommy. She's still in the newborn ICU. Dr. Parkin thinks she'll be just fine, but she's a tiny one—barely three pounds. They'll have to keep a close eye on her for a while. When she's gained a little weight she'll be ready to go home. Until then, you need to concentrate on getting yourself well."

Paula's mouth formed a small pout. "But when can I see her? She doesn't even know who her mother is."

"As soon as you're up to it and the doctors have checked you over, I'll wheel you down to the nursery myself," he promised. "Besides, it's not as if the little beauty hasn't gotten pretty darn close to you already. They, uh," he glanced at her with a hint of self-consciousness, "they've been giving her your milk, pumped fresh around the clock. She loves the stuff." A thin streak of crimson inched its way up his neck and settled along his jaw.

"I see," Paula said demurely. "Kind of like maternal Wonder bread. Builds strong bodies twelve ways—while you sleep."

He cleared his throat. "Something like that. Anyway, I suppose you'll want to be nursing her yourself from now on, and—"

"An excellent idea," Dr. Parkin said, striding purposefully into the room. "I see you've rejoined us, Paula. Welcome back." Her smile was almost as wide as Ted's. "Mind if I check your vitals? We need to make sure things are progressing smoothly."

"Hey, if it'll get me down to the nursery any faster, you can play dominoes on my incision," Paula joked, extending her arm for the blood pressure cuff.

"I think we can arrange that," the doctor said amiably. "The nursery, not the dominoes."

Late in the afternoon, after several doctors had examined her and declared her travel worthy, Ted helped Paula out of bed, settled her carefully in a wheechair, and escorted her to the newborn intensive care unit. They checked with the attending nurse, then Ted pushed his wife through double doors into a large, well-lit room. Her eyes widened in amazement as they rolled past several incubators housing the smallest human beings she had ever seen. A few were convulsively flailing their pencil-thin arms and legs; most of the others lay still and quiet, their birdlike hearts fluttering rapidly inside their tiny chests, tangles of wires and tubes monitoring and assisting their intuitive struggles for survival. "They're so eensy," she murmured, reaching for her husband's hand as her gaze traveled from one cubicle to the next. When they approached the end of a row, she glanced up at Ted. "Which one is ours?"

"Over here," he said, pointing to his right. He maneuvered the chair close to an incubator with a bright pink card taped to one of its Lucite partitions. The words on the card confirmed their destination: *Baby Girl Barstow.* "The nurses call her Chiclet," he observed as he set the chair's brake. "She has this pretty little mouth, and when she opens it a certain way—especially when she yawns—it's shaped exactly like . . . well, like a Chiclet. It's kind of hard to explain, but you'll see."

Paula stared at him. "Like a piece of *gum?*"

"Like an *adorable* piece of gum," he grinned. "It's a mark of character. But don't take my word on it; let me introduce you to your daughter." He extended his hand and helped her to her feet.

Supported by one of Ted's arms around her shoulders and the other at her elbow, Paula gazed down at the infant for a full minute before speaking. Finally she looked up at him, her eyes brimming. "Beautiful," she said. "So beautiful."

"We do good work," he murmured.

She leaned over the incubator to get a better look. The baby lay peacefully on her back, clad only in a tiny diaper cheerfully decorated with pink bunnies. The soft white knit cap on her head was slightly askew, covering one ear and revealing a small tangle of dark, curly hair at the opposite temple. A few wires were taped to her chest and a feeding tube was in place, but unlike most of the other infants Paula had seen here, there were no other paraphernalia attached to the child's minuscule body.

"She's doing well," Ted whispered, as if sensing Paula's observation. "She had a little respiratory problem yesterday, but the catheter and breathing tube came out this morning. As soon as she gets a little more meat on her bones they'll move her to the regular nursery."

Paula nodded and continued to study this miniature person. Everything about the baby seemed perfectly formed, though incredibly small and fragile, from her wizened little face to the creased bottoms of her Lilliputian feet. Even in repose, her arms and legs appeared strong and agile, and her tiny hands, with long, slim fingers curving gracefully inward toward her palms, were the most exquisite things Paula had ever seen. *Her entire little body could fit easily into my two hands,* she thought uneasily. *How can I ever take care of something—someone—so small? So completely, utterly dependent?* The memory of TJ's birth flitted through her mind. *He was nine pounds, two ounces—more than three times what she weighs. She looks so—so breakable.*

Ted's voice cut into her thoughts like he was reading them. "Pretty amazing, isn't she? Want to touch her?" He lifted a small sliding panel on the side of the incubator. "Go ahead—she won't break."

"I knew that," she lied with an uncertain little laugh. Slowly, almost timidly, she maneuvered her hand and arm through the opening until the tip of her pinkie finger made contact with the baby's palm. Instinctively the delicate fingers curled around Paula's fingertip, which registered the sensation as if it had been barely brushed with a feather. Nothing had ever touched her so deeply. In that moment, as tears welled in her eyes, she felt an undeniable connection with this fragile new life. Whatever lay ahead, they would face it with love and joy . . . together. The thought swelled her heart with anticipation.

"There—there it is!" Ted whispered eagerly. "Look at her mouth!"

As Paula watched, the baby's lips, formerly curled together like tiny deep-pink rosebuds, stretched open into the most perfect mini-rectangle she had ever seen, then slowly broadened into a wide, luxuriant yawn. It was, as Ted had insisted earlier, adorable.

"Okay . . . Chiclet. I can see that," Paula agreed as she carefully withdrew her hand, already missing the feel of her daughter's skin. "And she is a charmer." She lowered herself to the chair and looked up at him coyly. "Any thoughts on a *real* name?"

"Hey, that's your gig," he smiled. "Although Chiclet does have a nice ring."

"For a puppy or a parakeet," she rejoined, thumping his leg with the back of her hand.

"I thought you had a list of names or something," he said. "From the shower."

"You're right. I'd almost forgotten." The memory of that extraordinary day washed over her like a warm, jasmine-scented bath. "I think I left it in one of the drawers in the baby's room. Would you bring it to me? That will at least give us a place to start."

"Sure thing." Ted reached down to release the wheelchair's brake. "But right now, you're probably way overdue for a nap." He glanced at his watch. "In fact, it's not all that long until bedtime. What say we have a nice romantic dinner back in your room, then I'll go home and sack out for the night. First thing in the morning I'll be back with the list, and we can get down to business."

"Can't think of a thing I'd rather do," she said, suddenly overtaken by bone-deep exhaustion. With some effort, she kissed her fingertips and pressed them to the side of the incubator. "I'll see you tomorrow, little Chiclet," she murmured, smiling at this innocent term of endearment. "Mommy loves you." She glanced at Ted. "And Daddy loves you, too."

Paula was nearly asleep by the time they reached her room. Ted lifted her onto the bed and tucked a blanket around her. "Can I get you anything?" he asked. "A pain pill? The *Wall Street Journal?* Pizza?" She was out cold. "Okay, then—pizza it is. Three full slices will be consumed in your honor, and the rest will be donated to the Theodore Barstow Home for Starving Husbands."

He leaned over to kiss her forehead, then lingered to breathe in her slightly musky scent. "This time last night," he whispered, taking her hand in both of his, "I was actually afraid you'd never wake up. Never open those gorgeous brown eyes and look into mine. Never see Chiclet do that cute little thing with her mouth. Never be whole again." He smoothed a stray lock of hair at her temple. "What a difference a day makes, eh? Now we have it all, and the future is whatever we make it. As I said before, we have a whole lot to be grateful for. I suppose I'll spend the rest of my life showing the Lord how much I appreciate His help. And showing you how much I love you. Shouldn't be all that hard on either count." With a final brush of his lips against hers, he turned and moved soundlessly from the room.

As the door closed softly behind him, Paula stirred a little in her sleep, and a contented smile flickered across her countenance. This was a dream worth savoring.

Chapter 7

"Hey Mom, how's it going?" Scott's voice boomed as he strode into her hospital room early the next morning. He leaned over to press his lips to her cheek, then plopped himself down in a chair next to the bed. "I stopped by a couple of times yesterday, but you were sound asleep. I figured things were going okay though, since Ted was grinning like a live turkey the day after Thanksgiving when he got home last night."

Paula smiled at her son, who looked handsome and relaxed in brown cords and an intense lime-green T-shirt that set off his dark hair and hazel eyes dramatically. There was no grease on his shirt or under his fingernails; that was a good sign. "I'm doing great—just terrific," she said. "Still a little sore after the two cut-and-paste jobs they did on my tummy, but I can't complain. I'm awake and alive, and you've got a brand-new little sister in the bargain."

"Yeah, that's pretty much what Ted said." Scott's tone was a study in nonchalance, but she saw the glimmer in his eyes. "A little sister, huh?"

"A beautiful little sister," Paula confirmed. "Would you like to see her?"

His casual facade cracked for a moment, and she could see through it to his boyish eagerness. Then he pulled back again and spoke in his Mr. Mellow voice. "Yeah, sure, I guess that'd be fine. I cleaned up and everything." So that was it; he'd actually torn himself away from the Viper long enough to shower, shave, and make himself presentable for the baby. Paula was impressed. They had never really discussed her impending motherhood, and Scott had seemed rather detached through the months of her pregnancy. But now that the child had arrived, he was clearly intrigued by the idea of being a big brother.

"I'd kind of like to see her myself," Paula said. "If you'll be my chauffeur," she gestured toward the wheelchair in the corner, "we can go down right now."

"Then let's do it," he replied, coming to his feet and reaching for the chair in one long-limbed motion. Paula was taken aback by the gentleness and care with which he helped her into her robe and settled her in for the ride, but she said nothing.

A few minutes later, they stood beside the baby's incubator. "So this is baby Chiclet," Scott murmured, staring down at the infant with a bemused look on his face. "I gotta tell you, this is just about the teeniest thing I've ever seen. I mean, even my buddy Twinkie's Chihuahua dog Hickey has this kid beat all to—" He broke off suddenly, and a slight blush crept into his cheeks. "Well, little Hickey is a lot bigger." His gaze shifted from the baby to Paula's face. "Is she, like, all there?"

"I believe so," Paula smiled. "She's actually in much better shape than most of the babies here. We can take her home as soon as she's gained some weight."

Scott nodded. "It just seems like not everything could possibly fit into that little body . . . it's a miracle that she's even alive, you know?" He bent over the incubator to study her more closely.

"I know, Scotty. We've been very blessed." Paula felt the truth of her words even as she spoke them.

"Would you like to feed her?" a pleasant voice said behind them.

Paula turned in her chair and saw the round, cheery face of a middle-aged nurse. "Who, me?" she questioned.

"Well, I'm not talking to this handsome young man here," the nurse chuckled. "It's just about feeding time, and I thought as long as you're here, you might want to give it a shot. We've been tube-feeding her, and she's used to your milk by now . . . just not used to *you* yet. I'll get her for you." She hurried around to the other side of the incubator and began tinkering with some of the wires connecting the baby to a monitor.

Scott quickly bent over the chair and spoke in a strained whisper. "Mom, does this mean you're going to . . . uh . . . you'll be holding her and, um . . ." He seemed to be at a loss for words.

"Yes, sweetie," Paula replied, trying not to giggle at his obvious discomfort. "I'll be nursing the baby."

"Sheesh," he muttered under his breath, then glanced at his watch. "Hey, you know what? I think Bonnie's expecting me to help out at the Academy this morning. She's starting some kiddie classes, and I need to move some furniture and stuff." He looked at her semi-apologetically. "Gotta run. Will you be okay here with Chiclet?"

"I'll be fine," she smiled. "You go. Have a great day."

He breathed out an enormous sigh of relief, then leaned over to squeeze her hand. "Okay. Thanks. See you later. Ted'll be here as soon as he can. He's spent hours on the phone last night and this morning, calling lots of people to tell them you're awake and doing okay. You wouldn't believe how many calls we've had, asking about you. I swear, we can expect to hear from someone in the Richland family at least every couple of hours, not to mention your mom and all your friends in the ward. Now that they know you're on the mend, I'm sure the phone in your room will never stop ringing."

Seeing the nurse approach with a small bundle in her arms, he spun around and hurried toward the room's automated double doors, but stopped abruptly after a few steps and returned to Paula's side. "Almost forgot," he said, pulling a folded sheet of yellow paper from his pocket while keeping a wary eye on the nurse. "Ted asked me to give you this—said you'd know what to do with it."

Paula recognized it immediately as the list of baby names from her shower, and eagerly took it from him. "Thanks, Scotty," she said warmly, noticing that Ted had scrawled "Chiclet" at the top of the list. "Now, I'm sure Bonnie's waiting, so get out of here." Chuckling, she blew him a kiss as he quickly disappeared—or was that escaped?—through the doors.

"Are we ready?" the nurse asked as Paula stuffed the paper into a side pocket of her robe.

"I think so," Paula replied, reaching for some antiseptic wipes on a nearby counter. When her hands were clean, she held out her arms to hold her daughter for the first time.

The baby had been carefully wrapped in an ultra-soft cream-colored blanket, and only her tiny, scrunched-up face was visible between the top of the blanket and the knit cap swathing her head. The complete bundle was little more than a foot long, its fragile weight barely noticeable as Paula cradled it in the crook of one elbow. She pulled the blanket down a little, and could see the baby's pulse throbbing energetically at the side of her thin neck. Brushing the back of her index finger delicately across the infant's cheek, she marveled at its silky texture. At the same moment, she noticed the little girl's partially open mouth straining toward the pressure on her face. *I know that look*, she thought, smiling at an earlier memory of her sons' mealtime antics. *Time to give her what she wants.*

With the nurse's help, Paula untied her gown and urged the baby to her breast. To her surprise, the child began nursing eagerly. "So, I guess we've been properly introduced," Paula whispered when it was over, watching the baby fall into a deep, satisfied sleep. She carefully pressed a kiss to the tiny forehead. "Remind me to tell Millie you'll be having your first steak in a couple of weeks. Medium rare."

"Mercy," the nurse observed as she retrieved the bundle and moved back toward the incubator, "I've rarely seen a newborn nurse quite so heartily."

Paula laughed out loud. "Me neither. And if she keeps it up, that's exactly what I'm going to be pleading for—mercy."

Late-morning sunlight was streaming through Paula's window, bathing everything in a buoyant glow, by the time Ted sauntered into the room with his hands behind his back. "I've been to visit our daughter," he said with a knowing smirk. "I understand she ordered in from Taco Bell for brunch."

"What can I say?" Paula returned, pulling his face down to hers for a warm kiss. "She's a snacker."

"Like another lovely woman I know. And speaking of snacks . . ." He brought his arms around in front of him, revealing a large bouquet of vibrant yellow roses in one hand and a two-pound box of See's chocolates in the other. "These might not be awfully original, but I figure it's the thought that counts. And the taste."

"And oh, I do love the taste of yellow roses," she said, breathing in their fragrance and pretending to nibble on one of the elegant petals. She winked at him. "The chocolates are nice, too."

"Well, if you can't quite finish them off," he observed, "we can always give 'em to Chiclet."

She leaned back against her pillow with a satisfied look. "Either way, she'll get some. Personally, I think she'd prefer chocolate milk."

He sat beside her on the bed and took her hand, pausing for a moment to let the mood settle. "You look beautiful this morning," he said. "How are you feeling?"

"Like a new woman," she reported, then smiled demurely. "Like a new mother."

"It certainly seems to agree with you."

"Thank you, my love," she said sweetly. "Both Dr. Parkin and Dr. Iman have been in to see me. They say if there are no more glitches, I'll be good to go in a couple of days. Three at the most."

"Terrific!" he exclaimed. "I thought you'd be stuck here for longer than that."

"Not if I can help it. Of course I'll have to take it easy for a few weeks, but they're amazed that I've done so well."

"Miracles do happen," he said as though he had believed it for a hundred years. He glanced at the yellow paper lying on her nightstand. "Been going over the list?"

"I have," she stated, picking up the paper. "So many names, and some of them were actually pretty good. I narrowed the field by closing my eyes, visualizing the baby, and trying to match a name with the face. I even went down to look at her again, just to be sure."

He raised an eyebrow. "Does that mean you've made up your mind?"

"Yes. Definitely."

"And what if I don't like it?"

She smiled mysteriously. "Oh, but you will."

"Well then, don't keep me in suspense."

"Okay," she said—a little smugly, he thought. "I think she looks like Alexis."

His jaw dropped. "Like what?"

"Like Alexis," she repeated. "It fits, don't you think? Besides, it—"

Ted's face folded into an exaggerated scowl. "Hey, wait a minute. You thought Chiclet was a weird name, and now you're saying our daughter looks like a *car?* I mean, it's an awesome set of wheels and everything, but who in the world would name their child Lexus—much less think she *looks* like one?"

Now it was Paula's turn to stare open-mouthed at her husband, and stunned silence hung thickly in the air for long, awkward moments—until she caught the glint of humor in his eye, the slight upward curve of his lips. Then she proceeded to toss one of her extra pillows at his chest, giggling like a teenager, holding her stomach to cushion the pain it caused.

"Gotcha," he laughed. "Let's just hope that even with braces, Alexis will never look like a Lexus. Personally, I'm hoping she'll take after her mother—who, by the way, bears absolutely no resemblance to any motor vehicle, living or dead. Except, of course, if you count being the grandmother to a Viper."

After several seconds, Paula caught her breath and slowly relaxed into a slightly more serious demeanor. "Then you like it?" she asked hopefully. "The name, not the car."

"Actually," he grinned, "I like both of them—but the name, definitely. Alexis it is." He winked at her. "In the crib, not the driveway." Paula rolled her eyes at the jokes, but Ted continued. "When she graduates from college, maybe we can spring for the wheels."

"Whew," Paula sighed. "There's a special reason I picked it, you know—in addition to the fact that she looks like Alex—" He smiled benignly. "She looks like, uh, her name." She pointed to a line on the yellow paper. "Whoever suggested the name wrote something else in parentheses. See right there? It's from the Greek word meaning 'helper of mankind.' When I saw that, I couldn't get the doctors' words out of my mind: if this baby hadn't come ahead of schedule, they never would have found that damaged artery, and I wouldn't have survived. She helped me live, Ted. No matter what else she does with her life, she's already saved her mother."

Ted ran the fingers of one hand through his hair. "Whoa," he breathed, "that sure puts things into perspective, doesn't it? It's a perfect name—and even more perfect now that I understand its meaning. Our little helper." He smiled slyly at his wife. "She deserves a Lexus. Or at least another taco."

Paula swatted him lightly on the shoulder. "With my luck, she'll have your sense of humor." Her hand lingered to caress his arm. "Seriously though, I believe this new little life has brought us more blessings than we'll ever be able to calculate. Since the very day we found out about her, it seems like we've enjoyed life more, had more to look forward to, spent more time planning for the future and less time reliving the past." She pressed her fingers to his cheek. "It's like a new beginning, so full of hope and promise that I can hardly—"

"That's it!" Ted blurted out suddenly. "You've done it again!"

Her eyes narrowed, and she looked at him suspiciously. "Done what again?"

"Found another perfect name. Listen to this." He grabbed both of her hands and squeezed them tightly, his eyes glowing with perfect anticipation. "Alexis Hope Barstow." Studying her face for a reaction, he leaned forward until their noses almost touched.

"Alexis Hope Barstow," Paula repeated, rolling the words across her tongue as though tasting them.

"What do you think?" he prompted. "It fits, doesn't it?"

Her smile seemed to eclipse the rays of sunlight filtering into the room. "Like a hand in a kid glove. And right now," she added, "I think I'd like to trundle on down and update that little pink card in the nursery."

"The nurses will love it," Ted predicted as he pulled the wheelchair close to her bed. "Although I won't be surprised if they still call her Chiclet."

"Better a piece of gum than a *car,"* she smirked.

* * * * * * * *

Two weeks later, Paula sat at the breakfast table, stirring her second cup of hot cocoa with half a toasted cinnamon breadstick. "This sure beats hospital food," she observed with a contented sigh. "I can hardly wait to introduce little Lexi to Millie Hampton's famous home cooking."

"In a way, you already have," Millie smiled. "In liquid form, of course."

Paula fingered the lapel of her thick blue terry cloth robe. "No doubt," she said in a slightly whimsical tone. "But you have to admit that it probably loses something in the translation. Once she's tasted the real thing—like your spring lamb with homemade mint jelly for instance—there'll be no turning back." She closed her eyes and smacked her lips, remembering the previous evening's meal.

"Oh, I expect she can wait a week or two for that," the older woman laughed. "Let's just get her home from the hospital, shall we?" Her eyes glittered with anticipation.

"Yes, Granny Hampton," Paula grinned. "Today's the big day. I was up in her room earlier, making sure everything's ready." She glanced at her watch. "Ted went in to the office before dawn this morning; he should be here in about half an hour. Then we'll go and bring our baby home." The words caused her throat to pulse with unquenchable joy, and she couldn't speak for a moment.

"It'll be wonderful to have the whole family here," Millie said softly.

Paula felt a warm, familiar pressure against her ankle. "Rudy thinks so too," she sniffed, reaching under the table to pat the big dog's head. "He needs a brand-new best friend."

"A second-generation best friend," Millie observed. "He hasn't been quite the same since we lost TJ, you know."

Paula nodded, rubbing the bridge of Rudy's nose affectionately. "Maybe having a new little person around will breathe some life back into these old bones." A smile crinkled the corners of her mouth. "Rudy's *and* mine." She stood carefully, wincing a little at the tug of pain in her still-tender abdomen. "I'd better go get ready; we don't want to keep our daughter waiting."

"She's done so well," Millie said. "Moved real quick out of intensive care, with a wonderful healthy squeal that makes the nurses giggle every time. I'm sure your visits morning, noon, and night to feed and cuddle her didn't hurt any."

Paula smiled. "What's a mother to do? I'm sure I made a nuisance of myself." She brushed a twist of dark hair away from her forehead. "And I absolutely don't care. Besides, I made friends with a lot of the other mothers while I was there. Most of their babies had some pretty serious problems, and those poor women were just beside themselves with worry and exhaustion. I helped where I could; sometimes I just sat and held a baby while its mother went to get a bite to eat or took a little nap. You'd think I'd given her the moon." A rush of warmth flooded her heart at the memory. "The moms seemed to trust me, knowing that I had a child there too. One of the nurses asked if I'd consider visiting on a volunteer basis, maybe a couple of times a week; she said it really helped to have me there. I think I'd like that."

"They'd be blessed to have you," Millie beamed.

The homecoming was low-key and uncomplicated. Baby Alexis eagerly drank lunch in the new rocker, then settled into her bassinet with a tiny grunt of contentment. Leaning against the cheerful wallpaper to watch her daughter sleep, Paula felt the room vibrate with joy.

"Pretty incredible, isn't it?" Ted whispered beside her.

She smiled into his eyes, as though seeing him for the first time. "I'd say so . . . Daddy."

"Whoa," he breathed softly, a distinct catch in his voice. "It's official, then—I'm a daddy." He shrugged. "What now?"

"Remember the Alamo," she replied.

He regarded her quizzically. "That's a rental car place, isn't it?"

"Oboy," she sighed, rolling her eyes. "So much for building family solidarity."

"Hey, I get it," he grinned after a few seconds. "Those guys down in Texas during the war with Mexico . . . they stuck together through thick and thin, keeping each other going to the very end. That's what we'll be doing, isn't it?"

"Uh-huh," she conceded, breaking into a little smirk. "On a smaller scale, of course—not so many horses and cannons. But we'll definitely stick together."

"Gotcha," he said, his arm circling her shoulders. "Adeste fidelis, and all that sort of thing."

"More or less," she giggled, pressing her face against his chest. "Now let's get out of here and let the poor little tike get some rest. She'll need all the strength she can muster to deal with her crazy old parents."

"By all means." Ted took her hand and they crept noiselessly across the hall to their own room, where he loosened his tie, kicked off his shoes, and stretched out on the bed. Paula lay down beside him and rested her cheek against his shoulder. "Comfortable?" he asked after a few moments, but she was already gone. Within minutes, his breathing was also deep and regular.

The baby's insistent squalling awakened them precisely two hours later, and they shuffled into the hall to find both Millie and Scott waiting anxiously outside the nursery door. "We didn't want to disturb you," Millie whispered loudly, "but it seems like she's . . . she's . . ."

"Either hungry, or needs a change, or both," Paula supplied. "Come on," she motioned for all three to follow her, "let's go see what we can do to make this little girl a happy camper again."

It didn't take much; in fact, Lexi's cries had faded to soft gurgles by the time the four of them had surrounded the bassinet. "She knows she's outnumbered," Ted murmured as the baby's fingers curled around the tip of his thumb.

"She's still so little," Scott said, his voice slightly awestruck. "Do you think she'll ever grow up?"

"It's only a matter of time, big guy," Paula replied. "This time next year she'll be walking and jabbering and beating on your kneecaps to get your attention. You'll be her hero."

"Yeah, right," he sputtered, scuffing the carpet with one sneaker. "I don't know what to do with a baby." He glanced at the tiny figure flexing its arms and legs in the bassinet. "But maybe I could learn."

"No time like the present," Paula beamed. "She needs a fresh diaper before I feed her."

Scott groaned, but to his mother's surprise, he actually picked up a diaper from the changing table and unfolded it while Paula discarded the old one and did the necessary wiping. In his wide, sinewy hand the diaper looked like a small cotton square, and he held it gingerly between his thumb and forefinger as he slipped it carefully beneath the baby. Paula secured the plastic stays, then smiled up at her son. "Good job," she said with as much pride as if he had just earned an Olympic medal.

"No big deal," he grinned. "I can do this." He tugged gently on one of Lexi's tiny feet. "You're okay, kid." Then he quickly cleared his throat and moved toward the door. "Gotta go to work now," he said. "Bonnie's expecting me. See you later."

"Next time you can hold her," Paula called out as he disappeared into the hallway. She thought she heard a low whistle as the front door closed behind him.

Over the next few weeks, a comfortable routine of feeding, changing, and baby-watching settled over the household. "I never thought I'd see it," Millie remarked as she set out Paula's breakfast one tranquil spring morning. "Ted and Scotty, fighting day and night over who gets to hold little Lexi. Landsakes, girl, you'd never get a turn yourself if you didn't have a corner on the child's food supply."

"Yes, I know," Paula laughed. "Two grown men, completely at the mercy of a mini-human being with a toothless grin, lungs of steel, and no discernible fascination with football. Go figure."

"It must be because she takes after her mother," Millie suggested.

"What—the toothless grin or the football part?" Paula spread a wide swath of apricot preserves across a thick piece of wheat toast.

"I mean the pretty part," her old friend chuckled. "She's got your dark curly hair, your perfect skin, even the lovable little pout around your mouth that happens when you get frustrated. Put that all together with her daddy's breathtakingly blue eyes, and you've got an irresistible little doll."

"No argument there," Paula smiled, her eyes glowing. "She is adorable, isn't she? I guess Ted and I do pretty good work."

"Spectacular work," Millie agreed. "And it's more than just her looks, too. She's—well, she's made you a family."

Paula gazed out the window for a moment, her eyes resting on the cool green leaves of a large maple tree in the yard. "I do believe you're right, Millie," she said. "I simply can't remember ever being quite this happy." Her face took on a slightly pensive expression. "Raising Scotty and TJ was a joy, of course; but after Richard left I was on my own." She smiled wryly. "Not that Richard was any help in the first place; he acted like babies were aliens from another planet. Ted, on the other hand, is extraordinary; he never seems to tire of holding Lexi, talking to her, even pacing the floor with her when she's cranky, singing those silly little baby songs for hours on end. It's like he was born to be a father."

"And I'd say Scotty's not far behind," Millie observed.

Paula leaned back in her chair and licked a few crumbs of toast from her fingers. "That might just be the greatest miracle of all. For someone as strong as an ox who routinely tosses large bodies over his shoulder for a living, he has the gentlest touch I've ever seen. When he's holding or changing or just making some kind of physical contact with Lexi, he lets his gruff guard down and I see a subtle change in him—a tender, sensitive side that seems drawn to all the weak and helpless things of the world. His language has improved since her arrival, too; he wouldn't be caught dead cussing in her presence. My favorite thing is when he lumbers into the room, gives her tiny ear or hand or foot a little tug, and booms out, 'Hey there, little sister, how's tricks?' in his deepest voice. I swear she smiles every time." Paula shook her head thoughtfully. "Miracles, Millie . . . we're seeing them every day. Scotty's life seems to be moving in a good direction. At least for now."

Millie carefully lowered herself into a chair across the table and gazed meekly at Paula. "TJ would've loved that little girl," she said quietly.

"I know," Paula agreed, feeling a tiny catch in her throat. "I've thought about that a lot." In time, she knew, the anguish of losing her son and the joy of welcoming a new child would be able to coexist peaceably in her heart. She could sense it happening already, though moments like these were still bittersweet. "I can't help believing he knows her and is watching over her right now. Like a guardian angel."

"A guardian angel," Millie repeated. "Yes, I'm sure of it. And your friend Karti, too—don't forget how anxious she was to meet TJ once she got to the other side. I'd say Lexi has quite a few folks looking out for her—both here and there."

Paula nodded. "And speaking of here, do we have things under control for weekend after next?"

Millie's face broke into a wide smile. "All set," she beamed. "This will be a wonderful occasion, and we'll do it up right—a wing-ding to remember. When I called your mother, she sounded pleased as punch to be invited. Most of the Richlands will be here, too; Sam said he'd come, but with Jake on his mission, Alex will have to stay home to mind the farm. Mark and Andrea are coming from BYU—said they wouldn't miss it. And I thought Ruthie would bubble right through the phone when I told her. She's been wanting to come for a visit, you know. I've already started making the food."

"Then it's a guaranteed success," Paula smiled.

Later, after the baby had been fed and put down for a nap, Paula poured herself a glass of lemonade and ambled out into the warm, tree-shaded backyard, where she relaxed on a comfortable chaise lounge and listened to the mellow trickle of a miniature waterfall Ted had built near the patio. Mentally counting the days, she reflected that very soon one of the more extraordinary occurrences of her life would take place: the gathering of her far-flung family to celebrate the naming and blessing of Alexis Hope Barstow. The event had been put off several weeks to allow Paula to recover fully from her surgeries and the baby to gain strength following her premature arrival. But now that both of them were robust and thriving, they could go ahead with their plans.

For Paula, this would most certainly be far more than just a family get-together. It would, indeed, be a joyful mingling of interrelated lives. As she thought back on it, the unique blending had begun with her discovery of Mark Richland's true identity, then had deepened with her closeness to his adoptive family, broadened as she knelt at a temple altar to begin her own eternal connection with Ted, and had now expanded to include a precious new addition to their circle of love. Another thought sweetened the anticipation: in a few short days, for the first time in her life, Marjorie Enfield would understand what it felt like to be the matriarch of a truly remarkable family—one which had begun under difficult circumstances at best, but which had simply refused to give up or give in. It had taken a while—nearly a quarter of a century, in fact—but it was finally coming together. And Paula Enfield Morrison Donroe Barstow could hardly wait.

Chapter 8

Mark Richland and his sister Andrea were the first to arrive for the long blessing weekend. They had driven through the night from Provo, Utah, and rang Paula's doorbell just after nine o'clock on Friday morning. Flinging open the door, she gathered them both into a lavish embrace, then pulled back to look at them, her eyes shining. "You're so beautiful!" she exclaimed.

"Whoa . . . it must be sleep deprivation with the new baby and all," Mark observed wryly. "If we're beautiful after fourteen hours or so behind the wheel, with leftover Cheetos stuck between our teeth and our eyeballs floating in Coke, then I'd say someone's hallucinating."

Paula tugged playfully on the sleeve of his gray sweatshirt. "You know what I mean," she grinned, stepping back to usher them through the door. "Come on in, you two. I think Millie has whipped up some of her world-famous scones, so you're just in time for breakfast."

"Mmm . . . did you hear that?" Mark chimed in, cupping a hand around one ear. "It's my stomach, growling with appreciation." He patted his midsection. "This little guy's waited a long time for some of Millie's cooking."

"Then don't dilly-dally around about it," a cheerful voice said behind him. Almost before he could turn around, Millie had folded him into a warm hug. "I've made enough for a small army," she twittered, next pulling Andrea into her arms. "Judging from the hungry looks of you, I'd say it's just about right."

"It's awfully good to see you, Millie," the girl said warmly. Her deep-green eyes looked heavy with fatigue, but there was no mistaking the excitement in them as she quickly surveyed the entryway and nodded toward the stairs. "Is, uh, Scott around?" She said the words almost shyly.

Millie and Paula exchanged a glance. "He worked until all hours last night—they're doing some remodeling at the Academy or something," Paula explained after a moment. "With any luck at all, he'll be conscious by noon."

"I see," Andrea said with studied nonchalance. "Well, maybe I'll catch him later."

They all moved toward the kitchen—but not before Mark dropped to his knees and wrapped his arms around Rudy, who had padded into the entry and was waiting patiently, his long tail waving in slow, sedate ovals in the air. "How you been, old buddy?" Mark said, smoothing the tawny hair along the dog's back, then thumping his flanks affectionately. Rudy panted with delight and flicked his broad, warm tongue against Mark's stubbled chin.

"He's slowing down a little," Paula said, reaching down herself to pat Rudy's head. "The vet says it's old age, but he still should have a few good years left if we make sure he eats right and gets his exercise."

"He's so pretty," Andrea observed, running her long, slender fingers down the silky hair on the dog's ears. Rudy closed his eyes as though savoring the moment, then followed the others into the kitchen and curled up in his customary place beneath the table.

As they chatted between bites of scone, scrambled eggs, and fresh fruit, Paula observed the two young people with unrestrained admiration. Mark, now a few months shy of twenty-five, had not changed appreciably since she had first met him during his service as an enthusiastic Mormon elder nearly three years earlier. If anything, he was even more handsome now that he had settled into young manhood with a certain comfortable, focused sense of himself—not to mention a little added meat on his tall frame and fuller, more luxuriant dark hair than a missionary cut had once allowed. And those teasing, soulful chocolate-brown eyes . . . one day a very fortunate young woman would fall into them and never even want to come up for air. Then too, there was the fact that Mark Richland was Paula's firstborn son—a delicious reality that she had discovered by the gift and grace of God and would cherish forever. Little shivers of anticipation rippled down her spine at the prospect of introducing him to her mother.

Her gaze moved to Andrea, who was laughing at one of Mark's jokes in a low, melodious voice that instantly reminded her of Karti, the mother who had been called home before she had been able to completely raise her two young daughters. A wave of longing washed over Paula at the memory of her friend—Mark's vibrant adoptive mother whom Paula had known for only a few short months before cancer took her. Andrea had been a high-spirited, appealing sixteen-year-old at the time of Karti's death; but now, in her nineteenth year, a subtle maturity had crept into her demeanor that seemed to enliven her natural beauty and enhance the charismatic quality of those luminescent green eyes. She had her father's thick mane of chestnut-colored hair, swirling in lush disarray about her shoulders, and her mother's lithe, voluptuous figure. The result was stunning, and Paula's mind wandered to the kind of man she might someday marry. *BYU football star, returned missionary, top of the dean's list, studying to be a neurosurgeon or something. She'll finish law school, then they'll have seventeen adorable children, and—*

"Paula?" Millie's voice stopped her just short of Andrea's receiving the Nobel Peace Prize. "These young folks are well nigh asleep on their feet, especially now that their tummies are full."

"I can see that," Paula responded, for the first time noticing their contented but haggard expressions. She smiled at them. "You two could probably do with a nice, long nap right about now. Millie, if you would—"

"I've made up the sofa sleeper downstairs and put out the big inflatable mattress on the floor," the older woman reported. She pointed across the entryway. "Bathroom's down that hall, with plenty of clean towels and things. Make yourselves at home, dears." She sounded as pleased as a well-prepared squirrel settling in for the winter. "The others won't be arriving until late tonight or tomorrow."

"Thanks so much, Millie," Andrea yawned. "I think I'll take you up on that."

"Me too," Mark chimed in. "I'll get a few things from the car." He pushed his chair back and stood, stretched his arms toward the ceiling for a few seconds, then ambled into the entryway.

Andrea twisted a heavy lock of hair around one finger and turned to Paula. "Will Scott be working tonight?" she asked casually.

"I believe so," Paula replied, then watched as the girl's shoulders slumped ever so slightly. "But he'll be here until about six o'clock, and I expect he'll be taking the day off tomorrow." A look of hopeful anticipation flashed across Andrea's face. "I know he'll be anxious to see you," she added.

"You think?" Andrea questioned. "I wasn't all that nice to him . . . before." Paula knew she was referring to their disagreement nearly two years earlier over his lack of interest in the Church. In fact, she had dumped him. Or had it been the other way around?

"He'll still be glad to see you," Paula declared with complete confidence. "But you probably should know," she added by way of warning, "that he hasn't exactly blossomed when it's come to spiritual matters; and with everything else happening in our lives, I haven't felt like I should push him. We've had several discussions, and I've encouraged him where I could, but our conversations usually end in an impasse. The bottom line is that he's a good boy, but he's *so* not interested in the Church. Says he never will be." The words sounded harsh, even to her own ears, and she wished she'd said it differently—more diplomatically. Still, it was the truth.

Andrea squeezed Paula's arm. "Thanks," she said quietly, with neither hope nor disappointment in her eyes. "I needed to know."

She's a trooper, Paula thought warmly. *She'll find someone who's truly worthy of her.* A tiny grin lifted one corner of her mouth. *Someone who's trooperly worthy of her.*

Less than twenty minutes later, the pair was settled downstairs on the couch and mattress. "They look good," Millie whispered as Paula helped her clear the breakfast dishes. "Especially Mark—it certainly becomes him."

"Excuse me?" Paula said, her brow furrowing as though she hadn't quite understood the words. "What becomes him?"

Millie stopped loading the dishwasher and looked directly at Paula. "You mean you didn't see it? Why, it's as plain as the nose on his face." She paused to smile. "And quite a fine nose it is, I might add."

Paula plopped her hands on her hips and huffed good-naturedly. "Let me in on this, Millie Hampton. What do you know that I don't? Did he say something while I was upstairs checking on the baby, or—"

"Oh, no, he hasn't said a thing. At least not about *that.*"

"And just what might *that* be?" Paula's curiosity was definitely piqued.

"Oh, my dear," Millie said in a conspiratorial tone. "I believe the boy's in love."

"In love." Paula folded her arms and leaned against the breakfast bar. "Mark Richland in love. And just how do you know this?"

"It's all in the eyes," Millie pointed out. "It wasn't there before—not the last time I saw him, anyway. That would have been at your wedding; he looked wonderful, just like the Elder Richland we'd always known. But this time, his eyes are all lit up somehow . . . it's hard to explain. You just wait and see; he'll spill the beans soon enough."

"I don't know," Paula said, biting her lower lip. "I think he would have told me right off."

"Some things need to wait until the time is just right," Millie said with the voice of wisdom. "If I were you, I'd let him choose the moment."

"Hmm . . . we'll see." Paula silently vowed to keep this intriguing bit of speculation to herself. Unless, of course, the subject should just *happen* to come up—at lunch, for example, where the conversation could so easily turn (or be turned) from Millie's delectable caesar salad to the subject of romance. Or dinner. Surely he couldn't be expected to keep the secret longer than that. Whenever he felt the urge, she'd be there for him. If Millie was right, then—

A long, high wail interrupted Paula's train of thought. She hurried upstairs and into the nursery, where Lexi was taking no prisoners on her way to brunch. "All right, munchkin," she soothed, settling into the rocker with the baby at her breast, "before you chug-a-lug this keg and get all sleepy on me, let me tell you the latest scuttlebutt concerning the life and times of your big brother."

By mid-afternoon, Mark and Andrea had roused from their naps and were ready to get on with the weekend. Mark showered and shaved quickly, pulled on a clean pair of jeans and a white BYU T-shirt, and finished unloading his car. Then he strolled into the backyard, where Paula was bending intently over one of her rosebushes, pruning off a few scraggly twigs. Moving behind her and a little to one side, he watched for several moments as her slim hands moved gracefully from branch to branch, snipping off a bit of bark here, trimming a few leaves there. "I thought you hired someone to do this," he finally said in a low voice.

Paula's back suddenly stiffened, and she spun around to face Mark as her garden shears clattered to the ground. "Good grief!" she blurted out, pressing one hand against the base of her throat, where her pulse raced wildly. "Do you make a habit of lurking around people's yards, scaring them spitless?" Her eyes were flashing, her tone sharp and not at all playful.

He stepped backward a pace or two and held up both hands in an attitude of surrender. "Hey, sorry. Didn't think you'd be so bummed. My fault. Sorry . . . really." He shrugged and tried to smile at her, but she saw the confusion in his eyes.

Paula was suddenly weak and out of breath, and her head was throbbing. Then her whole body began to tremble, and she swayed uncertainly on her feet. Seeing the color evaporate from her face, Mark took a firm hold on her elbow and guided her to a nearby lawn chair. "Are you all right?" he asked, his own complexion paling a little. What in the world had he done?

She closed her eyes and drew in several long, deep breaths, exhaling slowly after each one. Finally she bent forward a little and covered her face with her hands.

Mark knelt by her chair and began to rub her back with one hand. "Can I do something? Call someone? What's wrong, Paula? Talk to me." His request seemed to hang in the still, warm air like a bit of gauze suspended over an open wound.

Long moments passed before she raised her head and squeezed out a tepid smile. "I'm okay," she sighed. "Fine, really." She patted his warm hand with her clammy one. "I'd like to say that I don't know what came over me . . . but I'm afraid I do."

He stared at her silently without comprehension, so she continued in a slightly breathless voice. "Here's the thing. When you came up behind me and I didn't know who it was, I just flipped out. It was like everything came crashing back on me all at once—flashbacks of the attack here at my home not long before your mother died, then that kid who ran a red light and nearly killed Ted and me and the baby. Both times, I never saw it coming—and both times I almost paid with my life." She shook her head and wiped a few beads of perspiration from her forehead. "I—I felt like it was happening all over again. And I couldn't stop it." She looked at him sheepishly. "Pretty silly, huh?"

"Not at all," he said gruffly, emotion clogging his throat. "I can't imagine the horror you went through, and it's only reasonable that you would . . . remember sometimes. I'm just so sorry to be the cause of it this time. I should've been more sensitive . . . more careful . . . wasn't thinking. Please forgive me."

"Of course," Paula said, lifting a still-trembling hand to his cheek. "I know you'd never have done it on purpose; you're too much of a gentleman for that. Just give me a few minutes to collect myself, would you? Millie's fixing a late lunch; she could probably use some help setting the table. I'll be there in a bit."

"Okay," he agreed, though seeming reluctant to leave her. "Can I get you a glass of water or something?"

"Tequila would be nice," she grinned, relaxing a little. "But I suppose that would be out of the question."

Mark returned her smile and added a sigh of relief, glad to see her wry sense of humor resurfacing. "Speaking as the missionary who dunked you in the first place," he said lightly, "I'd have to agree. But maybe I could spring for some snappy pink lemonade."

"I think I'll pass," she replied, lifting her chin a little to feel the trace of a breeze against her moist skin. "You go on in; I'll practically be right behind you."

Paula watched his tall, muscular frame move through the sliding glass doors into the house, then closed her eyes and leaned far back in her chair. She spent the next several minutes conjuring up mental images of every happy, peaceful, rejuvenating moment in her life that she could think of—her baptism; an unhurried stroll through the neighborhood with Rudy; Ted's kiss across the marriage altar; the first time she'd held Lexi in her arms. All of these and a hundred more flowed through her consciousness like a spring of healing water, finally washing away the darker memories, banishing them to an obscure corner of her mind where she hoped they would leave her alone, give her some peace. With focus, patience, and determination, perhaps one day she would be able to obliterate them entirely.

Andrea stepped into the hall and closed the bathroom door behind her. She felt refreshed, energetic, anxious to see what might come of this weekend. Not that she was expecting anything at all, she reminded herself, especially since Paula had brought her up to date on what was happening—or not happening, as far as the Church was concerned—in Scott's life. But it certainly couldn't hurt to renew the warm, playful friendship they had enjoyed during his occasional visits to the Richland farm the summer following Karti's death. He might not have been interested in becoming a Mormon, but their shared passion for art and his endless thirst for exploring the geography of Idaho's countryside had gone a long way toward helping her cope with the loss of her mother. Silly as it sounded, it had happened over and over again: when he started in on a string of those lame jokes of his ("What do you get when you cross an elephant and a fish? Swimming trunks. Why do fluorescent lights always hum? Because they don't know the words. How do you find a lost rabbit? Make a noise like a carrot. Ha-ha-ha!") as they hiked up a mountain or ambled through a fragrant meadow, the engaging sparkle in his extraordinary hazel eyes could almost make her forget the somber pall of grief and emptiness that awaited her back at the house. It was wonderful while it lasted; but as it turned out, any hope for a future to their relationship had evaporated in the wake of their disagreement over the need for religion in their lives, and they had both moved on after finishing high school—he to his martial arts instruction at the Ninja Academy, she to a liberal arts education at BYU. At the moment, Provo's masculine elite were taking numbers and standing in line for the beautiful Andrea Richland's attentions, so there was no problem with her social life. Still, it would be awfully nice to see Scott again—just to catch up.

She tucked the hem of her burgundy silk pullover shirt into the slim waist of her gray wool slacks, ran the fingers of one hand through her slightly damp hair, and moved toward the voices she heard in the kitchen. Her nose twitched, followed almost immediately by a low rumble in the vicinity of her stomach. If that was baked beans she smelled, the rest of the meal couldn't be far behind.

"Hey, Andy!"

The voice was a bit deeper than she had remembered, but there was no mistaking it. Andrea spun around just in time to see Scott vault off the third stair from the bottom and land squarely beside her in the entryway, the rubber soles of his Nikes squeaking loudly against the smooth tiles. His next move was to grab her around the middle and lift her high off the floor until she gripped his shoulders to steady herself. Then he set her down and smacked his lips brashly against her forehead.

She caught her breath and laughed at the same time—a mellow, tinkling sound that seemed to catch him off guard, as if he'd just come upon a long-forgotten treasure. He held her at arm's length and gazed into her clear green eyes. "You . . . look . . . *mah*velous," he said in exaggerated tones. "When did you get to be such a babe?"

A deep blush flooded her cheeks. "Just grew up, I guess," she replied. "You don't look so bad yourself . . . been working out, I see." Her fingers instinctively squeezed the tight, bulging muscles in his upper arms.

"Hey," he grinned, flexing beneath his oversized yellow T-shirt. "I get all the exercise I need—and more—at the Academy. Life is just one long karate and kick boxing tournament." He paused. "And I spend a lot of time working on my wheels, too. Wanna see the Viper?" He looked at her expectantly. When she glanced toward the kitchen, he nodded. "But first things first, right? Come to think of it, I'm starving too. Shall we?" He clicked his heels together and bowed solicitously.

"An offer no lady would refuse," Andrea said, threading her arm through the crook of his elbow. "It's nice to be here," she added. "Such a special occasion."

"Oh, yeah. The blessing thing," Scott replied. She thought she noticed a slight shrug of his shoulders. "I guess it's the Mormon thing to do."

"I guess," she murmured as they made their way to the kitchen.

Halfway through Millie's late-lunch extravaganza of chicken caesar salad, honey-sweetened baked beans, hot buttered cornbread, and cherry cobbler, Paula laid her napkin beside her plate and raised a finger to silence the high-spirited group. "I heard that," she declared, raising an eyebrow.

"Heard what?" Scott asked around a mouthful of cornbread.

"Your little sister," his mother clarified. "I think she wants to join the party."

"Ooh!" Andrea exclaimed. "I was wondering when we'd get to meet her." Now that everyone had stopped talking, she could hear the baby upstairs, stretching her lungs in what sounded like a high falsetto.

"No time like the present," Paula said, sliding her chair back. "I'll just run up and—"

"No problem," Scott broke in. "I'll go get Chiclet while the rest of you—"

"Chiclet?" Andrea stared at him as if she hadn't quite heard correctly.

"Long story," he whispered with a knowing wink.

"That would be sweet of you, Scotty," Paula smiled. She was perfectly fine, but on the inside she still felt a tiny bit shaken after her recent encounter with Mark in the rose garden. For the moment, she'd rather not go anywhere—even up to the nursery—alone.

Scott nudged Andrea as he pushed away from the table. "Wanna come?"

"Sure!" She double-stepped to keep up with his long strides as he quickly moved across the entryway, took the stairs two at a time, and navigated the hallway in two or three seconds. By the time they stopped in front of the partly open nursery door, the baby was hollering with a vengeance.

They tiptoed into the room. "Hey, little sister, how's tricks?" Scott whispered as he bent over the bassinet to tug gently on one of Lexi's miniature feet. At his touch she stopped crying, hiccupped a few times, and focused her wide blue eyes on his face. He brushed the side of her neck with his little finger and she gurgled a welcome, trying to burrow her cheek into her shoulder.

"She's adorable—so tiny," Andrea breathed. "And she seems to know you."

"Well, she'd better," he chuckled. "I do most of the diaper-changing around here. Next to feeding, that's the most important thing. In one end and out the other, you know."

She watched in fascination as he slipped his wide, agile fingers beneath the infant and carefully lifted her from the bassinet to the changing table. There he performed the necessary and well-ordered routine of cleaning, wiping, powdering, and re-covering with all the grace and attentiveness of a ministering angel, Andrea thought. When he was finished, he cradled the baby protectively against his shoulder and patted her back, his large hand completely covering the entire upper half of her body. Smoothly moving from one foot to the other, he created a gentle rocking motion that quickly lulled her into sleepy contentment. And the look on his face made it clear that Lexi wasn't the only one enjoying this tranquil moment.

"She's something, you know that?" Andrea whispered. "And you're a wonderful big brother."

"Shucks, all the women tell me that," Scott murmured, brushing his lips across the baby's dark hair. "Let's take her downstairs, shall we? Mark'll get a kick out of seeing her—him being sort of her other big brother an' all."

Dessert was being devoured when Scott, Andrea, and Alexis made their grand entrance into the kitchen. "We saved some for you," Millie smiled. She had already cleared away their other dishes and set out two helpings of hot cherry cobbler smothered with vanilla ice cream. "Sit. Eat. It's melting." Paula held out her arms, and Scott carefully lowered the relaxed baby into them before he and Andrea took their seats.

"And what have we here?" Mark said, leaning toward Paula to take a closer look at this small person, who at the moment seemed quite oblivious to the attention she had generated. Lying quietly in her mother's arms, she gurgled sweetly and regarded this stranger through heavy-lidded eyes. He reached out tentatively to touch her delicate hand, but drew back at the last moment. "Uh, we Richlands come from a family of big babies," he murmured self-consciously. "Even the smallest, Ruthie, was about twice this big when she was born. I—I guess I'm just not used to . . . don't know quite how to . . ."

"Oh, stuff it, bro," Scott laughed. "'Big babies' is right. What are you afraid of, anyway—that she'll break into a million pieces like one of those china dolls they put under glass in some museum? It won't happen, I tell you. She may be little, but she's tough." He smirked endearingly. "I ought to know. I toss her around like a football every chance I get."

"Yeah, right," Andrea chuckled next to him.

Paula couldn't help enjoying the irony of this moment, and it occurred to her that now might be a good time to set the record straight. "Actually, Mark," she began, smiling at him indulgently, "I seem to recall that you yourself weren't all that much of a he-man when you first arrived on the scene. Unless, of course, a birth weight of six pounds, seven ounces qualifies one for the Paul Bunyan Hall of

Fame." When he winced a little, she quickly went on. "Fortunately, you snapped out of it and grew into a magnificent specimen of manhood." His shoulders squared at her words, and she knew she was on the right track. "See? Sometimes very *big* things are delivered in very *little* packages." She glanced down at the smidgen of humanity nestled against the inside of her elbow. "Just give Lexi some time. She'll be playing beach volleyball in a couple of years."

"Which is a whole lot more fun than playing potato-field volleyball in Idaho," Scott needled, glancing at Mark. He felt the sharp toe of Andrea's shoe against his shin under the table. "All right," he whispered. "He's just a dork sometimes."

"Meanwhile," Paula continued, ignoring their banter, "would you like to hold her, Mark?"

"Sure . . . I guess," he replied, casting Scott a sideways glance. "I can do this. I'll be careful." He turned toward her and shifted his weight to the edge of his chair.

I'll be careful, Scott mouthed toward Andrea, rolling his eyes.

"I know you will," Paula said. She rose from the table and expertly settled the baby into Mark's arms, which were extended and stiffly positioned like the thick metal tines of a forklift. "Just relax," she said close to his ear. She gently pushed on his hands, causing his elbows to flex and move closer to his body. "That's it," she smiled as his long fingers slowly, deliberately curled around the tiny body. "Enjoy the moment."

He looked up at her with a self-effacing grin. "I'm better with older kids," he admitted. "On the basketball court."

"You're doing just fine," she said. "Letting her breathe would be nice," she added calmly a few moments later, noticing that his grip had tightened around the baby's middle.

"Oh . . . sorry," he mumbled, quickly rearranging his hands so they were supporting rather than squeezing the small bundle.

"Gimme a break," Scott muttered in between spoonfuls of ice cream and cobbler.

"Shh," Andrea cautioned. "He hasn't been around a baby since Ruthie was born, and that was a dozen years ago."

"It's a miracle she survived." He turned toward her abruptly. "Would you like to see my Viper now?"

"Absolutely," she said.

"Great! I have a couple of hours before I have to go to work. Maybe we could take a drive up the canyon."

"I'd like that." Andrea was beginning to enjoy this weekend already.

"And I think I'd like a little nap," Millie said, removing the cheerful yellow apron she'd worn since early that morning. She smiled, gave Paula a little wink, and quickly disappeared into the entryway.

Within moments, Paula found herself alone with Mark, who was studying one of Lexi's tiny hands with an almost scientific scrutiny. The baby's palm barely covered his thumbnail, and her delicate fingers curled around his thumb but did not meet. "She's something, isn't she?" Paula whispered, reaching out to smooth one of the dark, curly locks on her daughter's head.

"I'll say. Like a miracle." Mark continued to stare at the miniature hand grasping his thumb.

Remembering her earlier conversation with Millie, Paula decided to test the waters of her son's romantic involvement. "Something to look forward to, don't you think?" she asked sweetly.

"Mmm." He stroked the baby's tiny arm with the side of his little finger.

Okay. Dig a little deeper. She allowed a bit of time to pass, then began again in a soft voice. "I mean, once you've found the right woman, it's only a matter of—"

His head shot up like a periscope, and his open gaze met hers for a second or two before moving quickly back to the child in his arms. But in those few telling moments, Paula had seen everything—the vibrating light that seemed to transform his dark eyes into liquid pools; the burnished flashes of hope and yearning; the eager rush of love and loyalty beyond any sense or reason. The signs were unmistakable; she had seen them in her own husband's eyes only . . . when was it? This morning. She knew a man in love when she saw one.

"Then it's true," she said quietly. "There *is* someone."

"Excuse me?" He looked at her then, his eyes wide with innocence, yet playful as he caught her implication. "Would you care to elaborate?"

"I think that's your job," she gloated, leaning back in her chair and folding her arms. "Millie told me she thought something was up, but I had to see it for myself. Talk to me, Mark. Tell me all about her."

He glanced up at the ceiling, then down at Lexi, then out the window for a moment as his complexion took on the color of a full-bodied red wine. A quixotic smile was hovering about his lips by the time his eyes finally met hers again. "It was that easy to spot, huh?"

"Nothing gets past Millie," Paula chuckled dryly. "And as my loyal employee, she's duty-bound to clue me in on all the good stuff." She grinned self-effacingly. "Even though I would have figured it out soon enough on my own. So come on now—give it up. I want *details.* What's her name? How did you meet her? Where's she from? What does she look like? How long have you—"

"All right already!" he laughed. "You're starting to sound like my . . . my . . ." The smile faded slightly, and a shadow flickered briefly across his eyes. "My mother."

Paula swallowed the sudden lump in her throat. The fact that she was Mark's birth mother had no real bearing on this occasion. His *real* mother, the exquisitely beautiful, vibrant woman who had loved and reared and nurtured him through a lifetime of skinned knees and small victories, was not here to share this moment of revelation with him. At best, Paula was a distant second. She didn't mind, really; but for both of their sakes, she couldn't help wishing that Karti Richland hadn't been taken so soon. What was the point? Tendrils of grief and longing for her friend tugged at her heart. All that was left to them now, it seemed, was to comfort each other.

She reached out to touch his arm. "I'm so sorry, Mark. I know this is something you would have wanted to share with Karti first, and you must be missing her terribly right now. It was awfully presumptuous of me to—"

"Hey," he broke in, shaking off the momentary pall that had settled on his features, "it's okay. You were right about one thing: I do miss her—maybe more than ever at this moment. But look at it this way." The grin returned, along with the sparkle in his eyes. "Who else in the world has the advantage of a totally awesome backup mom? A guy would have to be in a coma not to appreciate that kind of a blessing." He glanced down at Lexi, who was beginning to stir in his arms. "And a new little sister to boot."

Paula's smile confirmed her relief. "Speaking of little sisters, I think this one's getting restless. Millie left some apple juice for her on the counter. Could you get it for me?" She held out her arms for the baby. Mark carefully handed her over, then retrieved the small bottle and watched as Lexi snuggled cozily against her mother's body. Feeling the nipple in her mouth, the infant began to suck eagerly at the sweet nectar.

Paula looked at Mark and raised an eyebrow. "Now, where were we? Ah, yes—I believe we were talking about a certain young man who has lately become smitten, and about a certain young woman who has lately done the smiting. I'm well acquainted with the gentleman in question, and have no doubt that he's the biggest catch of the season. Perhaps he would like to enlighten me concerning the lady?" She paused expectantly, and Mark knew there was no turning back.

"Well, since you put it that way," he began, "I guess you're right. 'Smitten' is a good word to describe it." The glow in his eyes intensified. "She's incredible, Paula. You've got to meet her."

"I'd love to," Paula smiled. "But in the meantime, could you give me some idea of what to expect?"

His cheeks dimpled as he flashed her a wide, infectious grin. "Sure. I thought you'd never ask."

"I'm asking."

"Okay. Kelsey. Her name is Kel-sey." He seemed to relish saying the word, rolling it around on his tongue like a half-melted M&M, savoring each new burst of sweetness. "Kelsey Taggart. She's from Illinois, an honors student at BYU, majoring in music performance."

An interesting course of study, Paula mused. "And what does she, uh, perform?"

"She plays the harp." He closed his eyes and sighed deeply, as though calling up the precious image of his absent love. "You've never heard anything so beautiful." He sighed again.

"I see," Paula said evenly, keeping a straight face despite the visions of winged, haloed, string-plucking heavenly beings dancing through her brain. "Like an angel."

"Exactly!" Mark sat up straight in his chair. "I go to hear her practice all the time. When I'm listening, it's a feeling like—like I'm not in my body anymore."

"Uh-huh." Paula bit her lip. *Isn't there a stronger word than "smitten"?* "You don't often meet an honest-to-goodness harp player."

"Harpist," he corrected.

"Harpist. And how did she get started on such an unusual instrument?"

"That's the best part," he gushed. "It really saved her life."

Now Paula felt curiosity bubble to the surface. "Oh?"

"It's kind of a long story," he explained, "but I'll give you the *Reader's Digest* condensed version. Kelsey and her younger brother grew up in a terrible home environment; their mother was bitter and withdrawn, and their dad beat on them quite a bit. In junior high, most of her friends were doing drugs and stuff, and she almost went along with them, thinking it might help her escape from all the pain at home. Just about that time, someone in the community donated an old harp to the school, and one of the music teachers played a short solo at an assembly. Kelsey had never studied music, but she fell in love with the instrument and started taking lessons at school, practicing every chance she could get. And that's not all." Mark's eyes gleamed. "Her teacher, Isabel Norton, was a really nice woman—who just *happened* to be a Mormon."

"Whoa," Paula breathed, now beginning to see how the puzzle pieces had fit together in this girl's life.

"Kind of reminds you of someone else you know, doesn't it?" he grinned. "With me and TJ, it was basketball. With Kelsey and Sister Norton, it was the harp."

"Amen," Paula murmured. How well she knew that nothing happened by accident or mere coincidence where the gospel was concerned. "Please, go on."

"Well, one thing led to another, and by the time Kelsey was in high school she was a star. She had poured her whole heart into her music, and it showed. When word of her talent got around, she was in constant demand to play at weddings, banquets, and other elegant occasions. Sister Norton even arranged for her to play a solo in sacrament meeting, which was her first formal introduction to the Church. She totally charmed the ward members, and they welcomed her with open arms."

"Then she joined right away?" Paula's interest was riveted on this unique story.

His short, sharp laugh had a grinding edge. "Hardly. When she approached her parents about taking the missionary discussions, it wasn't pretty. Her mother went ballistic; apparently she'd had a bad experience with the Church many years earlier, and she couldn't stand the idea of letting her daughter get involved. Her father was drunk at the time, and smacked her across the face. Kelsey didn't mention it again, but started hanging out with some LDS girls at school. They gave her a Book of Mormon, and basically taught her everything she needed to do to get a testimony. Meanwhile, she and Sister Norton had become close friends, and things gradually fell into place. Almost two years ago, on the day Kelsey turned eighteen, she was baptized."

"Did her parents ever come around?"

"No, but her brother eventually joined, and he'll be going on a mission as soon as he finishes a stint in the military. She's so beautiful, Paula . . . inside and out. I can't believe she'd even give me a second glance."

"Well, I can," Paula declared with utter confidence. "How did you meet her, anyway?"

"Andrea introduced us a few months ago. They'd met at some kind of musical event, hit it off, and before they knew it people were asking them to play harp and flute duets all over Utah. I went to a wedding reception where they played, and once I saw Kelsey, everyone else in the room just seemed to fade into the background. I guess Andrea noticed the effect she had on me, so she introduced us while the bride and groom were cutting the cake." He grinned. "Have I ever told you how much I love my sister?"

"A noble sentiment," Paula observed, her eyes shining. "Am I correct to infer that this is a serious relationship?"

"I haven't asked her to marry me yet, if that's what you mean," he replied. "But I think we both know where it's going."

"To the temple, I presume."

He nodded and leaned back in his chair. "I'm a lucky guy, you know that?"

"Yes, indeed," Paula smiled. "To find the love of one's life is a joy beyond expression."

They sat shoulder to shoulder, the silence broken only by an occasional gurgle from Lexi, who had long since abandoned the bottle and was sleeping contentedly in her mother's arms. Paula turned her head to gaze at Mark's appealing face, then looked down to contemplate the innocent slumber of her precious daughter. No matter how you looked at it, life just couldn't get any better than this.

It would be a weekend to remember.

Chapter 9

"This is gorgeous," Andrea said as she and Scott made their way up a small ravine off one side of a lush canyon overgrown with evergreens and wildflowers. They had parked the Viper in a clearing well off the highway, then hiked up to this oasis of color and refreshment.

"A far cry from life in the city," Scott observed. "I found this place a couple of years ago, when I needed somewhere to get my head together. Rode my bike up the canyon one Saturday morning, and here it was."

"Aha . . . the perfect respite for a tortured artist's soul," she declared. The tiny thread of irony in her voice intrigued him.

"Nothing tortured about it. I just needed to be away from civilization for a while. But now that you mention the artist part, I guess that worked out, too. I started bringing my sketch pad along, and I think I've done some pretty good work. Come on, I'll show you." He easily hopped a two-foot-wide stream, then reached for her hand. She didn't pull away after he had helped her across, so he held her hand until they reached their destination.

They hiked upward for a time, then stopped beside a wide, flat rock. It was perched horizontally on a massive boulder that seemed to have been scooped halfway out of the mountain beneath them by a mighty giant's unseen hands. In fact, it looked almost as if this superbeing had, perhaps as an afterthought, pressed his enormous palms into the earth to fashion the six perfect steps leading up to the rock.

"Cool, huh?" Scott grinned. They had climbed the steps, and now stood side by side on the huge rock's flat surface. Because of the outcropping's unique configuration, they appeared to be suspended in air, hanging without support over the vast green valley below. The intense illusion sucked Andrea's breath away, and she clung tightly to Scott's arm, trying to regain her equilibrium. Curling his free arm around her shoulders, he carefully guided her to the back edge of the rock, where it intersected with the granite face of the mountain and formed the floor of a shallow cave. Then he helped her sit on a small natural stone bench just outside the cave. "You okay?" he asked, kneeling in front of her.

"Yes . . . sure," she responded. "It's just that I didn't expect it to be quite so . . . spectacular." She brushed a long lock of chestnut-colored hair away from her face and secured it behind her ear.

"Yeah, I know," Scott beamed. "It kind of bummed me out at first, too—in a good way, of course. Just me and the mighty mountain. After I got used to it, I'd go out and sit on the edge, dangle my legs over, and take huge breaths until I got real dizzy."

She looked at him sharply. "What, to indulge some kind of crazy death wish?"

"Naw . . . not anything so 'tortured,' as you put it. If you'll go out there with me, I'll show you what it's really like." He stood and offered her his hand.

"Thanks, I think I'll pass," she said without apology. What was she doing up here with this adolescent thrill-seeker, anyway?

He shook his head slowly. "Okey-dokey, but you're really missing something. I'll show you what I mean." He rose as gracefully as a muscled feline, stretched his arms in front of him for a little extra flair, and sauntered the ten or twelve paces out to the edge of the rock. The *very* edge.

"Be careful," Andrea whimpered from her seat on the stone bench.

As if taunting her, Scott positioned his right foot parallel to the rock's edge, with about one inch between his Nike and the drop-off to oblivion. Next he extended his arms out to either side for balance, then launched his left leg out into open space, where he swung it back and forth like a pendulum. "See?" he called back to her. "Nothing to it."

"Don't!" she gasped, her eyes wide with terror.

"Why not? I've done this hundreds of times. And now I've got an audience." He began to swing his left leg faster, higher. His right ankle started to wobble under the strain.

"Please!" she wailed. "I don't care how often you've done it! All it takes is one—"

Her plea ended in a strangled scream as Scott's ankle buckled and he struggled furiously to right himself, but nothing helped. A fraction of a second later, with a yelp that sounded like a hurt puppy, he had disappeared over the edge and out of sight. Out of time. Out of life.

* * * * * * * *

Ted met Sam and Ruthie at the airport on his way home from the office. "Four down, one to go," he quipped as they all piled into his new cobalt-blue Jeep Cherokee. "Paula's mother is coming tomorrow evening. We've never had a houseful like this."

"Are you sure it's not too much of an inconvenience?" Sam asked. "We could always stay at a motel, or—"

"Are you kidding? Paula wouldn't hear of it," Ted broke in. "*I* wouldn't hear of it. Besides, we've got it all figured out. You can share the king-size inflatable mattress downstairs with Mark, and Ruthie can snuggle with Andrea on the sofa sleeper. It'll give you all a chance to get caught up on each other's lives. A couple of nights of togetherness shouldn't be all that stressful. Although I must admit that Paula and I have discussed the matter, and we're thinking that if we plan to have these little family get-togethers on a regular basis, we might just go ahead and build a larger house—one with a few more bedrooms and a lot more bathrooms. We've actually been talking about it since before we were married. But for now we'll just have to make do."

"Will all four of us be in the same room?" Ruthie questioned.

"You bet," Ted replied. "Gotta keep our families together."

She folded her arms resolutely across her chest. "Then if Daddy and Mark snore too loud, I get to go sleep with the baby."

"Fair enough," Ted chuckled.

Back at the house, Paula was waiting outside when the Cherokee pulled into the driveway and parked near the open garage door, just behind Paula's red Jaguar. Ruthie flew out of the vehicle and into her arms with a squeal of delight. "Oh, Sister Paula, I've missed you! With Andrea, Mark, and Alex away at school, and Jake on his mission, all I ever see is Daddy Potato-Head." She rolled her eyes. "Can we talk about girl stuff this weekend?"

"Whatever your little heart desires. It's been too long, sweetie," Paula murmured against the girl's fragrant auburn hair. "Since before Ted and I got married." She pulled back a little and held Ruthie at arm's length. "My, but you've turned into quite the beauty." She couldn't help noticing that this winsome girl was not a child anymore. Her physical contours had begun to change in subtle ways, and while she was not yet a young woman, the rounder, fuller shape of her body was apparent. Ruthie's eyes seemed even larger and blacker than she had remembered, too—deep, dark pools that seemed to pulse with vitality and intellect. In another year or two, when the boys finally figured it out, she would be turning heads just like her older sister. These Richland girls had clearly come out on top in the gene-pool Olympics.

Ruthie flushed at Paula's compliment, then flashed her an eager smile. "This is gonna be awesome! Can I see the baby? Is she asleep? I totally love her name! My first little girl will be named Alexis, too! Do you think I could feed her sometime? Maybe I could even help give her a bath and change her. I could baby-sit if you wanted me to, and—"

"Okay, okay," Paula laughed. "We'll see what we can do. But one thing's for sure: ever since I told her you were coming, little Lexi has been dying to meet you. She's probably lying upstairs in her crib right now, wondering why in the world it's taking you so long to get up there. Let's not keep the little princess waiting any longer, shall we? She tends to get colicky when she doesn't get her way." Paula slipped an arm around the girl's shoulders, and Ruthie's arm circled Paula's waist. The two walked together toward the house, chatting like old friends.

"This weekend will be good for Ruthie," Sam said as he helped Ted with the suitcases. "She has lots of friends at school, but at the end of the day she pretty much finds herself knocking around in an empty house with no one to talk to. We read together at night, and I do my best to be attentive, but it's definitely not like when her mother and sister were there. I've been thinking of hiring a full-time nanny, but Ruthie won't have any part of it. Thinks she's too grown-up for such a thing. But really, it would just be for the company." He shook his head and sighed wearily.

"Andrea will be home from BYU soon, won't she?" Ted asked. "They'll have a good time this summer. Maybe you could wait until fall to bring up the subject of a nanny again—and then it might be best to refer to her as a housekeeper."

Sam nodded. "You're probably right. Where is Andrea, anyway? I thought she and Mark would be here by now. Both of them are long overdue for one of my papa-bear hugs."

"I spoke with Paula just before I left work," Ted reported. "Mark ran to the store with Millie; he volunteered to help her with some last-minute shopping. Andrea apparently took a little spin with Scott in his Viper. That car is his pride and joy. They drove up to the canyon, I think; Paula said Scott had to work tonight, so they should be home any time now. Millie got dinner started before she left." He sniffed the air as they entered the garage. "Yep, my favorite—oven-baked lamb chops. With rice pilaf, steamed vegetables, and a little dab of mint jelly on the side, there's nothing better."

"I hear ya," Sam agreed. "Karti used to make a rack of lamb that could bring you to tears. She always told me the recipe was from her secret source in the celestial kingdom. Andrea's tried it a couple of times, but it's just not . . . the same." He smiled sadly. "I guess those heavenly spices have lost their zing." After a brief pause, he looked out toward the street. "It sure will be good to see Andy. She looks more like her mother every day."

Ted was hauling one of the larger suitcases through the door. "I'm sure they'll be back any minute now," he said. "Leave it to the kids to have a good time, huh?"

* * * * * * * *

Andrea couldn't move from the stone bench. She sat frozen in horror for an infinity of seconds, her frightened eyes riveted to the overhang where Scott had disappeared into the thin mountain air. Now there was only silence, and that couldn't be a good sign. One moment she wanted to rush to the edge, scream his name over and over again, scour the valley below for any sign of him. In the next instant she knew she would probably cower on this icy perch forever, terrified of what she would see if she looked beyond the ledge. Would she discover his body far below, impaled on one of the stately evergreens that had broken his fall? Or would he still be alive, clinging frantically to a branch or boulder halfway down the cliff, out of reach, his grasp weakening rapidly, the wild look in his eyes telling her that in a few more seconds . . .

She squeezed her eyes tightly shut, praying for the courage to do what she had to—to find out what had happened. No matter what, she couldn't leave Scott alone on this mountain. There had to be a way to get help. To get him out. A sudden gust of canyon wind fluttered across the rock, chilling her to the bone.

"You have to do this," she said aloud in as firm a voice as she could muster. "Just sitting here isn't going to solve anything." Glancing out at the ledge, she called up a sliver of courage. "I'm coming, Scott. Don't give up. Please be alive." Her voice sounded hollow, unnatural to her own ears, and she felt dampness on her cheeks. A violent trembling shook her body as she came slowly to her feet. Trying to ignore it, she started taking tiny steps toward the edge of the rock.

Five feet from the drop-off, Andrea knew she couldn't walk any farther. Heights had always made her nervous, but this sheer precipice, together with the prospect of what she might discover below, magnified her terror exponentially. She dropped to her hands and knees, then to her stomach, and wriggled the rest of the way. When she was close enough, she stretched out her arms and curled her fingers tightly around the sharp outer edge of the rock. "You can do this," she rasped, willing the taut muscles in her hands and arms to pull her body forward.

Finally, her chin was only inches from the edge. She pressed her eyelids together, took in a huge gulp of air, and shoved her head out into space. It would be just a moment before she could bear to open her eyes, and then who knew what she would—

"GOTCHA!!"

The deep-voiced, gleeful shout came from just below Andrea's chin, and it had the effect of hurtling her into hysteria. Her head snapped back, then forward, and her bulging eyes took in Scott's grinning face but could not comprehend it. Her heart slammed against her rib cage so violently that she could almost hear a bone or two cracking. She tried, but couldn't take in a breath. Then, as if overwired, every nerve in her body short-circuited, and she fell into a dead faint. As her head dangled over the rock's edge, a thin cascade of blood trickled across the side of her neck where it had scraped against the jagged shelf.

The smirk evaporated from Scott's face as he scrambled onto the rock and knelt beside Andrea, pulling her away from the edge and turning her carefully onto her back. He squeezed one of her hands between both of his and pumped it up and down. "Andy . . . Andy, are you all right?" His face was so close to hers that their lips were almost touching, but he couldn't detect any breath or movement in her slim body. "It was a *joke*, Andy. I—I didn't mean to . . . I just thought . . . I only wanted to . . . A stupid joke, Andy. That's all it was." His eyes closed, and he groaned like a wounded animal. If she came out of this, how could he ever make it up to her?

"A joke?" Her voice was feeble and her lips barely moved, but her clear green eyes were raking his face like industrial-strength steel wool.

He looked down at her with remorse and uncertainty brimming in his eyes. "Hey, you're back. Thank goodness! You gave me quite a scare for a minute—thought you were a goner for sure. Heh-heh. Can I get you anything, or—"

"A *joke?"* Andrea's voice was stronger now. Much stronger. Bordering on dangerous. And those eyes—like they were spitting jalapeño peppers.

He decided to retreat into boyish charm. "Yeah," he replied with the most sheepish grin he could manage. "There's a long, flat shelf a couple feet below the rock. I just rolled over onto it and waited. I thought sure you'd catch on right away, but I guess I . . . I guess"—another grin, this time accompanied by a humble shrug—"I was just too doggone convincing."

With some effort, Andrea raised herself until she and Scott were sitting face to face. "Let me get this straight," she said in glacial tones, her eyes never leaving his. "You pretended to fall off a cliff to your death, then hid out until I got around to searching for your remains, at which point you popped out of your little bunker and scared the beejeebies out of me—all so we could both have a good laugh?"

Scott cleared his throat awkwardly and blushed to his follicles. "I guess that's, uh, pretty much it, yeah." His gaze fell to the floor of their rocky perch.

"Well, then," she said, her voice laced with venom, "you were half right. *One* of us was amused."

"Yeah," he muttered. "I blew it. Sorry."

"Take . . . me . . . home," she ordered through clenched teeth.

"Gotcha," he said compliantly. "Uh-oh. Sorry again."

He slunk behind her down the mountain path, and they rode in dismal silence to Paula's home. Once there, Scott parked in front of the house and turned to Andrea. "Hey, I'm running a little late—gotta be at work in twenty minutes, so I think I'll head on out. I'll see you later, okay?" She responded by opening the car door and swinging her legs out. "And Andy?" She turned partially back toward him and met his pleading stare with an icy one of her own. "I'm sorry, okay? Really, really sorry." She continued to regard him with all the warmth of liquid nitrogen. He pointed toward her bruised neck. "Put some antiseptic or something on that scrape, will you? Rock cuts can be nasty." Without a word, she moved more of her body outside the car. "Okay, then. I guess I'll see you . . ." His voice trailed off as she slammed the door and hurried toward the house. "Later." The word seemed to bounce off the dashboard and pummel him between the eyes as he pulled away from the curb. "Stupid joke," he groaned.

Andrea tried to slip into the house and downstairs without anyone noticing her, but Paula happened to be coming down from the baby's room, and they saw each other across the entryway. "Oh, hi!" Paula sang out as she cleared the bottom stair and walked cheerfully toward the girl. "We were wondering when you'd be home. Sam and Ruthie arrived about an hour ago; they're out back with Mark, sizing up my gardening expertise. Millie's just putting dinner on, and we're all . . ." Both her mouth and her feet stopped when she got close enough to see Andrea's face. "Good grief, you're white as a lily! Are you ill, sweetie?" Andrea shook her head and tried to smile, but the effort failed miserably, and tears started from her eyes. She wiped at them furiously.

Paula's eyes moved to the angry red slash on Andrea's neck. "What in the . . ." Her eyes narrowed as she grasped Andrea's shoulders and lowered her voice. "What's going on here?"

"Just an accident," Andrea sniffed, avoiding eye contact with Paula. "I'm fine. But I'd like to lie down for a little while, if I could. Is there somewhere I could go, or—" Her body began to tremble again, though not as violently as on the mountain.

"Of course. Come up to my room, where you won't be disturbed. I'll show you." Paula linked her elbow with Andrea's and escorted her upstairs, then sat beside her on the king-sized bed. "I can tell you're upset," she said gently. "Want to talk about it?"

"It's nothing, really," Andrea protested, though Paula knew better. "I—I was with Scott, and he . . . well, he did this crazy thing, and—"

"He did this to you?" Paula gasped. Her hand reached out to touch Andrea's lacerated neck, but pulled back at the last moment. How could this have happened? She was appalled, furious. Devastated. "Tell me, Andrea," she said as evenly as she could. "If Scott has hurt you, I'll see to it that—"

She felt a firm hand on her arm. "No, no . . . it wasn't like that at all," Andrea said. "He didn't hurt me. Not physically, anyway." She motioned to the scrape on her neck. "This just happened when I fell against a cliff."

"I see," Paula said, rubbing Andrea's hand. This was getting more interesting by the moment. "Are you feeling a little better now?"

The girl nodded. A bit of color had returned to her cheeks.

"Better enough to tell me the whole story?"

"I suppose. It was just a dumb joke, but it was so awful that I—I lost it. Big time."

"I'm listening," Paula said warmly.

Andrea spilled out the story then, pausing every so often to snort, wince, shudder, or wipe away a few tears. At the end, she shook her head dolefully. "I can't believe he'd do that to me," she said. "Doesn't he know how much I care about him? How I'd die if something like that ever really happened?" She searched Paula's face for an answer as her eyes brimmed and overflowed for what seemed like the millionth time.

"I'm not sure he does know," Paula said softly. "After our last visit to Idaho you weren't exactly best buddies, as I recall."

"I know. We argued about the Church," Andrea conceded. "But that didn't mean I didn't care what happened to him." She looked intently at Paula. "You can still love someone even if you disagree with them, can't you?"

"Oh, yes, sweetie," Paula smiled. "If we stopped loving people just because we didn't see eye to eye with them on every little thing, this would be a pretty lonely world. Nobody would have anyone to love. Besides, sometimes making up is the best part of a disagreement."

"I see what you're saying," Andrea agreed. "But I still think some things are too important to disagree about. Like the Church, for instance. I can't ever see myself marrying someone who doesn't share my commitment to the gospel. Some people could do that—I have an aunt who's been happily married to a nonmember for thirty-five years, and she's still hoping that someday he'll join. But for me, that would just be too hard."

"And I agree with you one thousand percent, because we're talking eternity here." Paula's mind raced back over the years since her baptism. "If Ted hadn't come around and gotten active again, we wouldn't be together today. I might have loved him, but knowing what I had just learned about the eternal nature of things, marrying him wouldn't have been an option." She sighed. "Thank the Lord I didn't have to make that decision."

"Which brings us back to your friend and mine, *homus jerkus,* Scott Donroe." Andrea couldn't help smiling a little.

"That was a pretty rotten thing he did to you," Paula observed. *And he and I will have a little chat about it sometime soon,* she vowed silently.

"No argument there," Andrea said. "I don't know what he was thinking. Maybe that was the problem—he *wasn't* thinking. But I can't help remembering the good times we had that summer in Idaho. He was full of it on the outside, but I could tell that deep down he was a genuine, caring human being, gifted with artistic abilities and a sense of humor that never dried up. After Mom died, he got me through some of the toughest times of my life. Which is why . . ." Her words faded, and she cast Paula a bemused glance.

"Which is why . . . ," she prompted.

"Which is why I care about him so much. Still do. Always will, whether or not he decides to fish in Mormon waters—although a certain momentum on his part toward the baptismal font would make my feelings for him easier to deal with. And today, when I thought I'd lost him, it nearly killed me." Indignation flashed in her eyes. "So I may never speak to him again."

"Well, that should solve everything," Paula smirked.

"Does it ever get any easier?" Andrea asked after a brief silence.

Paula looked at her with perfect innocence. "Does what ever get any easier, sweetheart?"

"Trying to understand them. Men, I mean."

"Oh, that. Goodness no! You just get used to it, learn how to 'go with the flow,' as they say, and after a while you kind of start enjoying the mystery of it all. Then you die."

"Something to look forward to." Andrea grimaced, but Paula could see a giggle bubbling to the surface. When it arrived, they laughed until their sides ached.

When Scott crept noiselessly upstairs and into his room past midnight, he found a terse note on his pillow.

I heard you miraculously came back from the dead this afternoon. We'll talk later. Mom.

"Oboy," he moaned as he buried his head under two thick pillows. "You're in big trouble now, Donroe."

Chapter 10

Saturday morning and afternoon passed in a flurry of joyful activity. To Paula, who moved contentedly from room to room, chatting and laughing and reminiscing with her guests, this exquisite spring day seemed a delicious mixture of all the loveliest occasions she could remember or imagine—Thanksgiving, Christmas, birthdays, Valentine's, her baptism, her wedding day, and the birth of her daughter, all rolled into one. Growing up as the only child of wealthy, austere parents, she had never had much sense of family. The gifts had always been plentiful on every birthday and holiday, but somehow the toys seemed to lose their shine long before the day was over. Now, however, she understood that the best things in life weren't things, and gifts of the heart and spirit would never lose their luster. Her home was vibrantly alive with the people she loved most, gathered to celebrate the birth and blessing of Alexis Hope Barstow. Nothing could be better.

The prospect of introducing both Mark and Lexi to their maternal grandmother filled Paula with anticipation and delight. It could be years before they saw Marjorie Enfield again—or maybe never. Connecticut was clear across the country, after all, and Marjorie wasn't getting any younger. Paula wanted their time together to count for something, and she was determined to make it happen, starting tonight. Lexi wouldn't remember, of course, and Mark wasn't exactly an official link in the family chain. But it certainly couldn't hurt to make introductions.

That evening, Andrea helped Millie and Paula set out a dinner buffet. "I notice Scott has made himself scarce today," Andrea observed casually as they arranged serving dishes of hot and cold food along the length of the kitchen bar.

"He always works on Saturdays," Paula replied. "It's his busiest day at the Academy—all kinds of kids hitting the mats from early morning till late at night." She gave Andrea a little smirk. "Lucky for him I'm so out of shape, or I'd go down there myself and toss him around a little."

"And I'd go with you." Andrea popped an olive into her mouth. "I still can't believe what he did to me yesterday. I'm not really mad anymore, but I can't seem to get the horrifying picture of him disappearing over that cliff out of my—" She tossed her mane of chestnut hair and speared a meatball with a small fork. "Well, maybe I'm still a little bit mad."

"I don't blame you," Paula said. "I wasn't even there, and I'm doing a slow burn over it. But if I might offer a bit of, uh, motherly advice . . ." She looked at the girl with an expression that seemed almost shy but infinitely hopeful.

"Anything," Andrea said. "I do care about him, you know."

"I know. So try to talk it through with him before the weekend's over, would you? I'd hate to see something like this cause a serious rift in your friendship; and if you let it go now, there might never be another chance to"—she smiled a little—"let him apologize."

"I hear you," Andrea grinned. "And I'll see what I can do."

"Good," Paula declared firmly. "Now, let's get everyone fed, shall we? Ted and I need to pick Mother up at the airport in a couple of hours."

Paula clung to Ted's arm as they watched Marjorie Enfield emerge from the Delta gate amidst a throng of other passengers. "She looks good," Paula whispered, noticing her mother's erect bearing, elegant slim figure, and firm stride. She wore a tailored steel-gray wool pantsuit with a deep rose-colored scarf at her throat, setting off her gray-blue eyes and the short waves of nearly white hair framing her face. Low-heeled black patent leather shoes and a matching purse completed the ensemble.

"Now I know where you get your fashion sense," Ted murmured appreciatively. "Not to mention your good looks."

Paula felt herself flush, but as she glanced at the patrician, slightly more weathered version of herself moving toward them with an indefinable grace that set her apart from the crush of humanity around her, Paula had to admit that he had a point. "Well, maybe," she rejoined. "But she wouldn't be caught dead in a jogging suit."

"Different strokes," he chuckled.

Different planets, she countered silently as she smiled in greeting and opened her arms. Marjorie didn't come into them immediately, so Paula closed the small distance between them and wrapped her mother in a careful hug. *She used to be taller. And not quite so thin.* "Mother, how nice to see you," she heard herself say as she pulled back from the embrace. "How was your trip?"

"Quite wearing, thank you," she reported, and Paula could see lines of fatigue around the older woman's eyes. "In Connecticut," she glanced at her platinum and diamond wristwatch, "it would be well past midnight." Then she glanced up at Ted, as though seeing him for the first time. "And this is your husband. I recognize him from the wedding photographs you sent." The two had been introduced very briefly at TJ's funeral nearly three years earlier, but her memory of the meeting had all but disappeared.

"That would be me. Ted Barstow, at your service," he grinned. "Very nice to see you, ma'am." He extended his hand, and she responded with a surprisingly firm grip of her own.

The three walked in silence for a few minutes. "Now, you two lovely ladies just have a seat right here," he ordered cheerfully when they reached a cluster of chairs adjacent to the entrance. "I'll be back with the Cherokee in a New York instant." Turning smartly on one heel, he disappeared through the automatic sliding glass doors leading to the parking area.

"Ted is a wonderful man, Mother," Paula said as they lowered themselves into side-by-side orange plastic chairs. "He's certainly been good for me."

"I can see that." Marjorie was staring straight ahead, the black purse perched on her knees, her words spoken in perfectly even, unrevealing tones. Long moments ticked by. Finally, she spoke again. "I've been reading your book."

Paula stared at her blankly. "My book?"

"The Book of Mormon."

"Oh, *that* book." Paula's heart was pounding in her chest, beating so loudly in her ears that she could hardly hear her own voice. "I—I didn't know you had a copy." *I don't believe I gave her one . . . although now that I think about it, I certainly should have.*

"Millie sent me one last Christmas. Said she thought I'd like to know what you believe."

So that's it. The woman must spend a third of her monthly wages buying those books and giving them away. Bless you, Millie. Paula took a deep breath to calm her thumping heart. "And what do you think of it?"

"I'm finding it rather . . . tedious," Marjorie replied, her cool, cultured voice never wavering for an instant.

Paula bit her lip; this was definitely not the time for levity. "And why is that?" she asked innocuously.

She thought she heard a tiny, well-mannered snort escape her mother's lips. "Whoever wrote it could have done with considerably fewer 'and it came to passes.'"

Paula's face broke into a wide smile as she recalled her own first experience with the book. *Like mother, like daughter.* "I know exactly what you mean, Mother. When I read it the first time, I commented to the missionaries that whoever wrote it could've used a good editor. 'A waste of perfectly good golden plates,' I said. 'I've read cereal boxes that were more interesting.'"

Marjorie turned to face Paula, and there was a glimmer of mirth in her eyes. "An accurate description—so far, at least," she said. Then her gaze softened, and it seemed to Paula that her next question begged to be answered. "But what changed your mind?"

Paula leaned back in her seat and thought for a moment. "Frankly," she said, "it took me another reading or two before all the pieces started to fall into place. But trust me, once you start finding the gems of insight and inspiration in that book, all the other stuff will just melt into the background. It teaches about a way of life—a plan of happiness devised by Heavenly Father and Jesus Christ before any of us ever came to earth. If we follow it, it'll lead us right back to Them once we're finished with this life. It's that simple—but you've got to be looking for it as you read." She reached over to pat her mother's hand. "Just don't give up, okay?"

Marjorie sat up a little straighter and cleared her throat. "We'll see," she declared, turning once again to stare into the distance.

Okay . . . fair enough, Paula thought. *Who knew she would deign to read even the first paragraph? May the Force be with you, Mother.*

Ted collected them a few minutes later, and in less than an hour they were pulling into the spacious garage of their Woodland Hills home. Paula had noticed Scott's Viper parked at the curb. "My goodness, it's much warmer here than in . . . than where I live," Marjorie commented as she alighted from the Cherokee. "There's still a bit of snow on the foothills north of the estate." She pulled the rose-colored scarf from around her neck and fanned her face with it.

As they entered the kitchen, a wave of laughter and good-natured bantering drifted up from the TV room. Even Millie had joined in; her rich voice was mingled with the others. "They were just setting up the *Monopoly* game when we left," Paula explained. "Sounds like everyone's having a good time." She grasped her mother's elbow and steered her toward the entryway. "Come on. Ted will put your luggage in your room while I introduce you to the troops."

The muscles in Marjorie's arm suddenly stiffened, and she pressed her elbow against her body. "I don't know," she said uncertainly. "We should leave the youngsters to their fun . . . wouldn't want to impose or—"

"Nonsense," Paula chided. "They're all anxious to meet you. Besides, Sam Richland is no youngster; he'll be sidling up to sixty in a couple of years. The grandson you've never met is a grown man, too—twenty-five on his next birthday. Scotty's nearly nineteen now, and Sam's girls are—"

"Oh, my," the older woman breathed, a slightly panicked expression rising in her eyes. "There are so many of them. I don't know if I could—"

"Of course you can," Paula insisted. "You're where it all started, you know. In a manner of speaking." She tugged on Marjorie's elbow again, feeling an unexpected surge of excitement well in her chest. "You deserve to be introduced as the queen of this family." Her own words stunned her—for most of her life, after all, she had hardly even thought of her mother as a parent, much less a queen—but she was glad she'd said it.

"Queen?" A trace of color snaked up Marjorie's neck and into her pale cheeks as she regarded Paula curiously, then allowed herself to be led downstairs.

"That's more like it," Paula murmured. "This'll be great." They paused at the bottom of the stairs, and she cleared her throat loudly.

Instant silence descended on the room as six pairs of eyes turned to focus on the slim, refined, white-haired woman standing beside Paula. Then, one by one, beginning with Sam, they each rose from where they sat around a large antique wooden game table. "Mrs. Enfield," Sam said warmly, covering the distance between them in two or three easy strides. "It's an honor to meet you." He extended his hand, and when she offered hers he bent to kiss the back of it. She smiled demurely, her expression registering mild surprise.

"He may be an Idaho farm boy," Paula murmured close to her ear, "but he's got manners. His wife taught him everything he knows."

Marjorie cricked her neck to look way, way up into Sam's congenial face, then turned back to Paula with a subtle glint of playfulness in her eye. "So this is the man who raised my grandson," she said reflectively. "He's very . . . big."

The room erupted into laughter as the tension evaporated. Everyone gathered around Marjorie, and Paula made the introductions. She lifted an eyebrow and smiled slyly at Scott, who was standing slightly apart from the rest of the group, eyeing his mother uncertainly. "Come say hello to your grandmother, Scotty," she urged, her voice dripping with contrived sweetness. "She'll be *so* glad to know that you're alive and well."

"Hi, Gran," he muttered, moving close enough to bend over and peck Marjorie quickly on the cheek, all the while keeping a wary eye on his mother, as though she might suddenly grab him by the scruff of the neck and shake him senseless. He managed to escape without incident and hurried to cower behind Andrea, who was struggling to suppress a fit of giggles. Apparently, Paula thought as she watched Andrea smile up at her son, they had made their peace. But he still had his mother to deal with, and if he thought he was going to—

"Mark?" Marjorie was pointing at him, her graceful fingers trembling slightly as she asked. He nodded and approached her, his generous smile revealing a set of even white teeth, and she laid her hand on his arm as she looked up into his face. "I knew you," she said without preamble. "You have your grandfather's eyes." She paused, then lifted her hand to touch his cheek. "I thought I'd never see those eyes again in my life."

Paula shifted uncomfortably from one foot to the other. *I never really noticed,* she mused silently. *It's not like they have anything else in common.*

"And his chin," Marjorie added. "So strong and determined. Even his hairline." She touched a small, slightly v-shaped tuft of dark hair just above his temple.

For some reason, Paula was vaguely annoyed by these comparisons. *Mark isn't anything like my father,* she reasoned. *He's a good, warm, caring man, not detached and aloof like Howard Enfield. Not distracted and consumed by pride and ambition. Not—*

She checked herself in mid-thought. *That was a quarter of a century ago, Paula. This is a new generation, a new hope for the future, a reaffirmation of life. Who knows? If Daddy were still alive, he might be a changed man—maybe even a member of the Church by now. You might as well give him the benefit of the doubt. That's part of the gospel, isn't it—forgiving and forgetting? Let him rest in peace, and just get on with the celebration.*

Ted's hands on her shoulders brought her back to the moment. "Hello—earth to Paula," he whispered teasingly into her ear from behind. "This party would be even better if you were here."

"Sorry," she laughed, turning to face him. "I was just thinking . . ."

"A dangerous pastime," he grinned. "Especially when the goal is to enjoy oneself."

"You're right, as usual." She glanced toward Marjorie, who was now seated at the table, chatting quietly with Mark and Sam. Andrea and Ruthie stood nearby, clearly fascinated by this stylish, austere woman who had suddenly materialized out of their brother's distant past. "Mother certainly seems to be having a good time."

"As well she should," Ted commented. "This is probably the closest thing to a family reunion she's ever seen. Now, shall we join the rest of these happy campers? I see that Ruthie has pretty much commandeered everyone's attention."

They moved closer to the group surrounding Marjorie, where Sam's youngest daughter had just begun a spirited monologue—something about Alex outskiing an avalanche on the mountain last winter. Paula's arm happened to brush lightly against her mother's shoulder, and the older woman turned partway around in her chair. "Oh, hello," she said, not looking directly at Paula but just slightly to one side of her face. "Have you been waiting long? The children are ready, and I . . . I . . ." Words seemed to elude her, and she lapsed into silence.

"Waiting? Children?" Paula studied Marjorie's bemused expression for a moment. "Mother, I don't know what you're—"

"The thing is," Ted interjected quickly, squeezing Paula's arm, "what with the flight and all, it's been a very long day for your mother, and she must be bone-tired. Besides, church comes early in the morning." His hand moved to Marjorie's shoulder, and he spoke to her. "What do you say we call it a night? Everything's all set out in your room, and a good night's sleep will do wonders for the ol' constitution, don't you think?" He glanced around at the others, and they all began to nod and stretch. Millie began to clear away cookie dishes and empty milk glasses, while Scott and Andrea busied themselves boxing up the *Monopoly* game. "We've moved a small bed into Paula's study off the entryway; you'll find it quiet and comfortable there."

Marjorie sighed deeply, pressed a graceful hand briefly over her eyes, then looked up at Ted with a hint of mischief in her features. "Constitution," she said thoughtfully. "I seem to recall an old World War II battleship by that name. It's still in service, I believe . . . but it's seen better days." She raised an eyebrow. "We could be related."

Ted laughed out loud. "I doubt it," he said. "Although you're both national treasures."

Marjorie turned to her daughter and offered a small, elegant chuckle. "I like this man," she said. "He's a keeper."

Paula couldn't help smiling at the words, which warmed her heart like a pleasant memory. "Yes, I know," she replied. "He's definitely a keeper."

"That was weird," Paula observed as she and Ted lay together, enjoying the calm silence of a sleeping household.

"Mmm . . . weird what?" Ted murmured, barely awake.

"The way my mother starting talking about keeping me waiting, and the children being ready. It didn't make any sense."

He yawned. "Well, nothing makes sense when you're exhausted, and Marge had been belted into a cramped plane seat, with bad food and worse ventilation, since this morning. You can't hardly blame her for wigging out a little. Besides, she came back like a boomerang with that 'constitution' comment." Paula could feel him smiling beside her. "Good one. She's a classy lady."

"You're calling her 'Marge' now?" In her entire forty-two years, Paula had never once heard her mother called by anything but her given name. Not even by her father—*especially* not by her father.

"Sure . . . why not? It's a lot less stuffy than 'Marjorie.' Hey, we could even go one better and call her 'Margie.' It'd bring her right into the twenty-first century! What do you think?" He was mostly awake now, and sounded like he had just come up with the sure-fire cure for aging.

Paula made a little choking sound. "I think 'Marge' would be . . . just fine."

"Great," he said, plumping his pillow and settling down beside her. "And don't you worry about her brief little sojourn into the twilight zone. I'm sure it happens all the time as people . . . mature."

"Uh-huh," she responded as he snuggled his head into the soft crook of her neck. "You're probably right. As usual." She smiled into the darkness as he relaxed against her and his breathing became more even. From the marrow of her bones, she could feel it: no two people had ever been so good together. There was absolutely nothing they couldn't do or envision or figure out or make right. They were, after all, Mr. and Mrs. Keeper.

* * * * * * * *

The blessing went off without a hitch as family, friends, home teachers, and other miscellaneous priesthood bearers gathered about the infant Alexis to usher her into the ward and Church family. "Does it take that many to make it official?" Marjorie questioned in a whisper as close to a dozen men took their places in the circle. "Usually a priest or minister just sprinkles on a little water, and it's done." Her brow creased in puzzlement.

"In Mormon land, the more the merrier," Paula whispered back. "No one wants to be left out—in case the child makes good, I guess. Then everyone can claim they had a part in it." Indeed, there would be good reason for pride and satisfaction if even half of Ted's promises came true in Lexi's lifetime: she would be the brightest, wisest, most competent, compassionate, and spiritually attuned young woman of her generation. Not to mention the greatest athlete, if the words "quick," "coordinated," "agile," "vigorous," and "determined" were to have any future bearing on the matter. Ted positively beamed as he took the traditional priesthood holder's stance behind the podium following the blessing, his daughter held high in the air so each member of the congregation could take appropriate note of this extraordinary child and reverently record the occasion in their journals after church. "I'd say you've gotten her off to a rather auspicious start," Paula whispered as Ted returned Lexi to her arms once the ordinance had been completed. The baby cooed contentedly, and Paula tried to remember if her husband had mentioned anything about an angelic singing voice. No matter; it must have at least been implied.

After church, the families loaded into two cars. Ruthie begged to sit next to Lexi during the drive home, and Marjorie sat on the other side of the baby carrier in the backseat of the Cherokee. They rode in comfortable silence for a few minutes; no one seemed anxious to dispel the gracious aura of this exquisite Sabbath day. There would be time enough for reminiscence, laughter, and socializing at the open-house buffet Millie and Paula had planned for mid-afternoon. They had invited dozens of ward members and all of the Donroe office staff, as well as a few neighbors who had brought food and good wishes while Ted and Paula were recuperating from their injuries.

About halfway home, Marjorie reached out to smooth the long, silky folds of the baby's dress. "This is a beautiful christening gown," she said, turning toward Ruthie. "Paula must have had it made especially for this lovely occasion." She fingered a cluster of tiny pink rosebuds sewn into the white fabric at Lexi's delicate wrist.

Ruthie stared at the older woman for a moment, her brows knit together curiously. "I—I thought . . . Sister Paula said *you* had it made. You sent it to her for the shower. Don't you remember?"

The pale color seemed to drain from Marjorie's cheeks. She pressed her fingers to her lips and shook her head, as though trying to clear her mind. She didn't respond to the girl's question.

Ruthie's dark, expressive eyes grew wide with bafflement and concern. "Well, you know me—just a dumb kid," she insisted. "Maybe I didn't hear right when she said it, or—"

"Of course you heard right. Exactly right," Marjorie interrupted, her eyes snapping open. "It was me all the time. Yes, I had it made, then I sent it to her . . . for the shower. Just teasing, my dear young girl." She smiled a bit too brightly and reached across the baby to pat Ruthie's shoulder. "It really is a lovely little dress, isn't it? I knew Paula would love it."

"Yeah . . . it's awesome," Ruthie said with a tone of guarded relief. "I'm going to learn how to sew, so I can make one just like it for my own little girl's blessing someday."

"And you will," Marjorie said decisively. "I'm sure you will." Then she turned her head and stared vacantly out the window for the rest of the drive.

In the front seat, Paula reached over to touch Ted's hand. He shrugged, saying nothing, but she could see the muscles working in his jaw.

"This is going to be a fabulous party—uh, open house. On Sunday, I guess you call it an open house," Carmine Brough observed as she set a large bowl of fruit salad at one end of a long table covered with a lemon-colored linen cloth. The table spanned nearly the entire length of one side of Paula's canopied patio, and it was rapidly being filled by a lavish assortment of hors d'oeuvres, salads, main dishes, vegetables, hot rolls, desserts, and iced crystal champagne glasses filled with sparkling apple juice. Carmine, Paula's assistant and office manager at Donroe, whose stocky figure bulged a little over the low-slung bodice of her lime-green silk pantsuit, had come early to help, and was clearly looking forward to enjoying herself.

Paula, who was standing nearby, couldn't help laughing a little at her red-haired friend's enthusiasm. "I never thought I'd see you so excited about a non-alcoholic gathering," she said, putting an arm around Carmine's sturdy waist. The two had seen little of each other since Lexi's birth, as Paula worked at home these days.

The young woman shrugged and looked at Paula almost shyly. "Hey, it took me a while, but I finally figured out that being snockered doesn't necessarily equate to having a good time." She glanced at the table. "I do appreciate the champagne glasses, though. They give everything sort of a nice, classy touch."

"They're left over from my pre-temperance days," Paula smiled. "Even Kool-Aid tastes better in crystal."

"I hear ya," Carmine agreed. She paused, regarding Paula thoughtfully for a moment, then spoke in an earnest voice. "Being a Mormon has really made a difference in your life, hasn't it?"

"No question," Paula said. "I know everyone at the office thought I was kind of crazy when I decided to join the Church, but it was the best thing that ever happened to me." She looked out across the patio to her beloved rose bushes, nestled against the fence in an explosion of spring colors.

"How do you figure?" Carmine asked.

Paula lifted a goblet and held it up to the light, where its shimmering amber contents sparkled and fizzed. "Well, it's a little like this," she explained. "On the outside, it's still pretty much a champagne glass—cool and smooth as ever, and not too bad-looking." She smiled a little, and her eyes danced. "But on the inside, *everything* has changed. What used to pass for enjoyment is now the real thing, bubbling with reasons to live and love and be happy. Because I now understand that life didn't actually begin with birth, and that it won't end with death, I'm free to absolutely relish everything in between. Even the tough times—"

"Like when you lost TJ and your friend Karti, and then that horrible accident," Carmine interjected thoughtfully.

"Exactly. Even the really awful moments seem more bearable when I have a power outside of this world to lean on, when I remind myself that it's all part of a greater plan. And the good times are so much sweeter." Smiling, she lifted the glass to her lips, tilted her head back slightly, and allowed some of the flavorsome, tingly liquid to drizzle down her throat. "Mmm. Infinitely sweeter."

Carmine picked up a glass for herself. "Makes sense. In fact, I guess that's what the sisters have been telling me all along—although," she chuckled roundly, "they didn't exactly use the champagne comparison. More scriptures than anything else." She took a swallow and smacked her lips. "You may be right about the 'sweeter' part."

Paula's mind was just beginning to register Carmine's words as she returned her glass to the table. "Excuse me," she said slowly, cautiously, "but if I'm not mistaken, I think I just heard you use the words 'sisters' and 'scriptures' in the same sentence with 'champagne.' Am I hallucinating, or would you like to clarify that?" She stared at Carmine, her dark eyes alive with a curious mixture of hope and disbelief.

"My pleasure," Carmine said, her face splitting into a Cheshire-like grin. "See, when you were so bad in the hospital a couple months back, and we thought you might not make it, I . . . well, I kind of made a deal with God. Told Him if He'd let you pull through—'Puleeeze, Sir,' I said—I'd look into the Mormon thing. I already had a copy of the book; Millie sent me one last Christmas, you know."

Paula nodded. *Of course.*

"Well, wouldn't you know it? A few weeks later, these two nice ladies from the Church dropped by to see me—not exactly fashion-plate dressers, but they seemed to know their stuff when it came to religion. Anyhoo, one thing led to another, I took the lessons, and—"

"You joined the Church!" Paula exulted. "What wonderful news!" She opened her arms to embrace Carmine, then pulled back for a moment as the next thought hit her. "But why didn't you say something? Ted and I would have loved to come to your baptism, and—"

"Whoa, hold on a sec, Miz Ell-Dee-Ess," Carmine laughed. "I said I took the lessons, not the plunge."

"Oh," Paula said in a deflated tone, her arms falling limply to her sides as her face clouded over. "I see."

"No, you don't," Carmine insisted. "There's disappointment swimming around in those big brown eyes of yours."

Paula forced a limp smile to her lips. "Well, what did you expect? You had me all pumped up, and now I feel like a volleyball that's been spiked one too many times." She shook her head.

Carmine studied Paula's face. "It would've meant that much to you if I'd joined, huh?"

"Of course. We've been friends for years now, and nothing could have made me happier."

Carmine swigged the rest of her juice and set down the glass. "Then you might as well know that I've pretty much made up my mind to be baptized. Just . . . not right now. Maybe when I get my life straightened up a little more. I'm still working on a testimony, too."

The light in Paula's eyes took up where it had left off a minute earlier, and this time she hugged Carmine fiercely. "I knew it! You'll be a fantastic Mormon!"

"Not to mention a poor one," Carmine added with a little smirk. "Any chance you could give me, say, a ten percent raise? The tithing thing could be a stretch."

"We'll see," Paula laughed. "In the meantime, be sure to take a huge doggie bag home today. There'll be plenty left over. And don't you *dare* leave us out of the loop for your baptism. Millie will want to come, too."

"You'll be the first to know," the chunky redhead promised. Her eyes glowed, and Paula felt sure the day would come sooner rather than later. "Now, let's get this party into gear." She winked at Paula and squeezed her hand, then turned once again to helping Millie stack plates and napkin-wrapped silverware at one end of the long table.

As the backyard filled with friends and family, Paula thought she had never been happier. With the possible exceptions of her wedding and baptism days, she couldn't remember a more joyful occasion. Even baby Lexi seemed caught up in the moment as she was trundled from one guest to another, gurgling with innocent delight. "It's like she was foreordained to be the center of attention," Ted chuckled just before he popped a deviled egg lengthwise into his mouth, followed by a bacon-wrapped water chestnut.

"That too," Paula giggled as she elbowed him gently in the ribs. "Along with every other conceivable gift, talent, intuition, and ability known to man. And probably a few that haven't yet been discovered, if that blessing was any indication."

"So," he responded, licking his fingers with slow, measured passes of his tongue, "you think I laid it on a bit thick, huh?"

"Not at all. I just think you'd better be prepared to deal with the consequences of your promises. It's not going to be easy being the father of the world's first genuine Wonder Woman. For starters, you'll be almost sixty by the time she hits her stride. Probably over seventy when she takes her first flight to Mars, and maybe eighty or so when she discovers the cure for cancer and pioneers the first brain transplant."

"Aw, shucks, I can always baby-sit her husband and seven kids while she does it," he said humbly. "Or fill in for her as Relief Society president when her work as Secretary of State takes her out of town."

"That's the spirit," Paula laughed. "But first, of course, comes potty training."

"Gimme a week or two," he grinned.

"That long?" She waved at Sam over the crowd.

"Hey, we're talking perfection here."

"I'm sure it won't be a problem." She pressed a lingering kiss against his cheek. "Seriously, that was an incredible blessing you gave our daughter." Her voice turned pensive. "Makes me wish I'd had such a start in life."

He put his arm around her. "I'd say you've done all right, blessing or no. Besides, don't you think each of us had our turn before we even came to earth?"

She looked up at him. "What do you mean?"

"Well, it may not be official Church doctrine, but I can't imagine that a loving Father in Heaven would have sent us off on such a precarious journey without giving every single one of His children a personal, individual Father's blessing, can you? I dunno . . . we all had our agency, and maybe some of us wouldn't have wanted one, but if such a thing were available, I'm pretty sure you and I wouldn't have left home without them. On a spiritual level, they could have been what saw us through the tough times and dysfunctional families in our lives and brought us to the point where we found the gospel and each other. Makes sense to me—a Parent wanting the best start for His children, and all that."

"Me too," Paula smiled, "although I really hadn't thought about it exactly that way before." She paused. "And speaking of parents, I wonder where Mother is. I saw her when the guests were arriving, but . . . I think I'll just find her and make sure she's having a good time. Excuse me, would you?" She pulled away from the circle of his arm.

"Sure thing. I'll circulate for a while. Maybe Lexi could teach me a card trick or two." He squeezed her shoulder and turned toward a nearby cluster of ward members.

Marjorie was nowhere to be found in the backyard, so Paula sauntered into the house and through the kitchen. When she reached the entryway, she noticed that the door to the den—her mother's makeshift room—was closed. Pausing for a moment near the door, she thought she heard movement in the room, so she knocked. After a few seconds with no response, she knocked again. "Mother? Mother, are you in there? It's Paula."

The door swung slowly inward a few inches. Marjorie's face appeared in the crack, then she opened the door farther. "Mother, are you all right?" Paula asked quickly, noticing the older woman's wan complexion, rendered even paler by the peach-colored pantsuit she wore. "I didn't see you outside, and I thought maybe you—" She glanced over Marjorie's shoulder to the bed, where a small suitcase lay open, partially filled. "What's that, Mother? Your plane doesn't leave until later tonight, and there'll be plenty of time to pack after everyone leaves. I thought you'd want to be with the others." Marjorie moved aside to let Paula enter, then sat daintily on the bed while her daughter sank into an overstuffed chair next to the small closet. Paula waited silently for an explanation.

"It's a lovely party, dear. Really it is," Marjorie said in a thin voice, her long hands clasping and unclasping in her lap. "It's just that I . . . I hardly know anyone, and it makes me so confu—" She checked herself, then tried to smile. "It makes me uncomfortable. I'm afraid I'm not quite the social butterfly you knew in years past." Her gaze fell to the floor, and her shoulders slumped ever so slightly. "I'm just not quite up to all of this."

Paula moved to sit beside Marjorie on the bed. "Are you ill, Mother? Maybe you should stay with us for a few days. You could see a doctor, and—"

"Goodness, no!" Marjorie huffed. "I'm perfectly fine—a little tired lately, and on occasion a bit forgetful, but nothing out of the ordinary, I assure you." Her back straightened, and she looked at Paula almost defiantly. "I'm simply more at ease in familiar surroundings, and I prefer my own home to anyone else's." Her voice softened, and she touched Paula's arm placatingly. "I do appreciate the offer, but I think it best for all concerned if I leave as scheduled this evening. Now, if you don't mind, I'll just pack my things, then have a little rest." She stood resolutely and began to rearrange the few items in her suitcase.

"Yes . . . of course," Paula murmured, shaking her head a little. "In the meantime, can I get you anything? A cool drink, or—"

"No, thank you," Marjorie said firmly, concentrating on opening a zipper at one end of the case, her back to Paula. "Howard will see to it later."

Howard? Her dead father's name blazed a trail of red flags across Paula's brain. She couldn't help herself; she had to say something. "Mother, you just said that *Howard* will see to it."

Marjorie's hands grasped the sides of the suitcase for a long moment, then she slowly stood erect and turned to face her daughter. "Yes, I did," she said calmly, her eyes riveted on Paula's face. "But I was wrong. Howard is gone."

A breath of relief escaped Paula's lips. "That's right," she smiled. "He's gone. And we're your family now. So you just lie down and have your rest, and I'll be back to get you in time to have a little snack before you leave. You know how you hate airplane food."

"Very well, dear," Marjorie said. Closing the door behind her daughter, she leaned heavily against it and sighed from the depths of her graceful frame. "Of course Howard is gone," she murmured. "How could I have forgotten? He won't be back until next Tuesday."

Chapter 11

"I managed to avoid Mom all day yesterday," Scott said as he loaded the last of Andrea's suitcases into Mark's car early Monday morning. "She was busy with Gran, and all the open house stuff. I bet she's pretty well cooled off—and by the time I get home from work tonight, it'll all be forgotten." He smiled mischievously. "But I'll apologize if I have to."

Andrea wasn't sure a simple apology would be enough. "You may need to tell her what you told me to avoid getting pulverized," she observed.

"No way," he vowed. "That's just between you and me, at least for now." He looked at her severely. "Promise me you won't say anything."

"My lips are sealed. But I'm awfully glad you told me. It'll work out; I know it will." She reached up, curled her arms about his neck, and lifted her lips to kiss his cheek. "Don't look now," she whispered, "but the mother in question just walked out the front door."

"Uh-oh," he grunted, turning slightly to see for himself. "I guess this is it, then, Andy. Have a safe trip and I'll talk to you soon, okay?" He hugged her tightly.

"Mmmpf," she said, her face pressed into the thick sweatshirt covering his chest. Pulling back a little, she smiled up at him. "You're quite a guy, Scott Donroe. You know that?"

"I know," he said hurriedly, "that if I don't get a move on, I might not live until dinnertime. See ya, kid." He ruffled her chestnut hair, then turned to race down the driveway. With a final wave, he jumped into the Viper, and almost instantly its motor roared loudly to life. Within seconds, its sleek, deep-green body had disappeared down the street.

"Another early day at the office for the boy wonder, I see," Paula said as she approached Andrea. "It looks as if the two of you have straightened out your differences."

The young woman smiled mysteriously. "You could say that." She looked closely at Paula. "He's a good man, you know. I hope you won't be too hard on him over the cliff-jumping incident."

"Well, you're the one he terrorized; so if you haven't already killed him, I guess I won't, either." She smiled at Andrea, who was breathing an obvious sigh of relief. "But you can bet I'll give him a good talking to."

"No doubt," Andrea laughed. "Just remember—things are not always what they seem."

Paula cast her a puzzled look. "Care to tell me what that's supposed to mean?"

"Nothing." She threw her arms around Paula. "Thanks for a wonderful weekend. It was heavenly to see everybody again, and little Lexi is adorable. I hope to see you again soon."

"Count on it," Paula said. "If things keep humming along between Mark and Kelsey, I expect we'll all be together for a wedding before many months go by."

"Something to look forward to," Sam said as he and Ruthie joined them. It was just after six-thirty A.M., and the eastern sky was ablaze with a firefall of brilliant colors—deep pinks, oranges, purples, and lingering traces of cobalt blue. The smog wasn't good for much, but its presence in the air certainly made for some spectacular sunrises.

Mark strolled out of the house just as everyone had said their good-byes, and one more round of hugs was exchanged. "I'm so proud of you," Paula breathed into his ear as he bent to kiss her.

"And I'm so happy for you," he said. "Ted and I spent some time together yesterday, and I'd say you picked a winner. He's a great guy. And someday, if Kelsey and I . . . if I ever have the privilege of being a father, I hope I can . . ." His voice softened and drifted off as he stared into the vibrant eastern sky.

"You'll be the best daddy on the planet," she said warmly, sensing the truth of her own words. "Just be careful, and stay close to the Lord. It's what your mother would have wanted more than anything else." They shared a final embrace.

Mark's car pulled out of the driveway, and Ruthie's humongous sigh reverberated through the cool morning air as she leaned against her father. "I can hardly wait till Andy gets home for the summer," she said mournfully. "I hate making cookies by myself." Then another thought occurred to her, lighting her eyes up like two huge shooting stars. "But Mark said he might bring his girlfriend home for a few days, and we can ride bikes and go to the movies 'n stuff. It'll be like having two sisters—cool!"

By the time Paula had sent Ted off to work after breakfast and taken Sam and Ruthie to the airport early in the afternoon, she was exhausted. "Why don't you go upstairs and have a little nap, dear?" Millie urged following a light lunch of leftovers from the open house. "You've had an awfully busy weekend, and you're still not completely recovered from your surgery. You need your rest." Her kind blue eyes took in the subtle lines of fatigue in her friend's face.

"You're right—and it sounds like a wonderful plan," Paula agreed. They were standing in the kitchen, and she felt a gentle pressure against her leg. Without looking down, she knew it was Rudy, and she instinctively bent over to pat his wide, golden head. When he moaned gratefully, she changed her mind. "You know, I think a little outing with my favorite golden retriever would hit the spot." She glanced down and saw the dog's soulful brown eyes watching her. "You agree, don't you, old boy?" The gentle wag of his tail clinched her decision, and she turned back to Millie. "We haven't really spent much time together lately, and it's a beautiful afternoon. You'll watch the munchkin, won't you?"

"You have to ask?" she laughed. "I never get to hold that little angel enough; seems like she's always in someone else's arms, being fed or coddled or played with. We'll have a perfectly lovely time together."

Paula smiled down at Rudy. "Then let's go for it, buddy. I'll get into my walking shoes, and I'll meet you at the door in a couple of minutes." The dog lowered and raised his head as though confirming the appointment, then turned and sauntered toward the entryway.

The air was fresh and mild as they strolled easily through the peaceful neighborhood, neither of them in much of a hurry, just glad to have a leisurely hour or two together. Rudy sniffed at trees and shrubs along the way, while Paula relished the feel of movement in her legs, the sounds of birds twittering from fences and rooftops, and the occasional micro-burst of gentle wind against her face. This was the first time since Lexi's birth, nearly three months earlier, that she'd taken such an excursion, and she felt rejuvenation surge through her body with nearly every step. By the time they reached their favorite small park about a mile and a half from home, her weariness had all but evaporated.

Spreading her lightweight fleece jacket beneath a friendly-looking willow tree, Paula sat down and patted the thick grass with one hand. Rudy took the hint and stretched out beside her, his massive golden shoulder pressing cozily against her thigh, his furry chin resting on her leg just above the knee. Feeling the warmth of his body brought a smile to her face, and she reached out to scratch the tops of his ears. His eyes closed, and a mellow sigh erupted from deep in his chest. "That's my good boy," she murmured, moving one finger up and down along the wide bridge of his nose while his eyelids fluttered with contentment. She couldn't help noticing that his muzzle, his forehead, and even the small tufts of fur above his eyes were no longer the deep, rich golden patina of his youth, but were now marbled with much lighter-colored hair, giving him a somewhat grizzled appearance. "Showing your age a bit, I see," she observed. "Well, it looks very handsome on you." He snuggled even closer to her leg. "Have I mentioned that Lexi loves the more mature look? She told me so herself."

Paula's thoughts sallied back over the past few weeks. Because of possible health risks inherent to any premature infant, Rudy and Alexis had not been introduced for nearly two months. Even then, it had been a rather formal meeting, with Rudy keeping a respectful distance, standing in the nursery doorway, watching intently from across the room as Paula changed and nursed the new little stranger. From that day on, the dog had taken up his watchful station at the nursery door every time someone entered the room, and he never failed to follow several paces behind when the baby was carried to other rooms. On several occasions, lying outside the nursery at night or very early in the morning, he had heard Lexi's quiet fussing and padded quickly into Ted and Paula's room, where he would nudge one of them awake with a cold nose pressed to any conveniently exposed body part. Usually it was Ted's arm or hand, dangling off the side of the bed. "Someday I'm going to teach you how to change a diaper," he would grump good-naturedly at Rudy as he stumbled toward the nursery.

Dog and baby finally met officially two weeks before the blessing. Paula had just finished feeding Lexi, with Rudy lying in his usual place at the nursery door, silently watching their every move. Lexi was alert and seemed in a playful mood, tugging at her mother's shirt, then vigorously waving her tiny arms and hands in the air, as though conducting some unseen symphony orchestra in a lively rendition of her father's favorite, Mozart's "Eine Kleine Nachtmusik." Most days she fell into a blissful sleep after eating, but this was not one of those days.

"Okay, wild child," Paula said, wiping a bit of dried milk from the baby's petal-like lips, "I think it's time you met the four-legged member of this family. He's been following you around for weeks, you know, just waiting to get a closer look, and he's been very patient. Besides which, he's just been freshly bathed and groomed, so now would be a very good time." She leaned slightly forward in the rocker. "Pssst, Rudy," she whispered loudly. The dog's ears sprang to attention first, then the rest of his body straightened and he sat up smartly. "Rudy," she repeated, crooking her finger, "come here." He hesitated, as though an invisible force field prevented him from crossing the room. "It's okay, boy," Paula said in reassuring tones. "Come here, pal. There you go; that's a good boy."

Rudy didn't have to be asked again. He moved gracefully across the room to the rocker, stopping just short of Paula's knee. She reached out and patted his head. "A little closer, buddy." He inched forward and pressed the side of his muzzle against Paula's leg so the top of his head was slightly higher than her lap. "That's better," she smiled. "Now, Master Rudy Retriever, it is my great pleasure to officially introduce you to the little lady of the house, Miss Alexis Hope Barstow. As you can see, she's looking lovely and feeling quite lively this morning."

Paula turned the baby slightly toward Rudy, but Lexi continued to wave her arms and didn't seem to notice the curious canine, whose dark eyes were riveted on her.

"Okay, so much for the formal introductions," Paula said. "Let's try something else." With infinite gentleness, she clasped one of the baby's wrists and guided her tiny hand, palm downward, toward the top of Rudy's head. The dog didn't move a muscle.

When Lexi's miniature palm and fingers brushed against Rudy's fine, silky fur, the child's body seemed to tense for a fraction of an instant, then it relaxed as though she had just encountered the most intensely pleasurable sensation of her very young life. Her lips pursed into a small sucking motion, and her free arm stopped its frenetic motion and settled against her mother's body. Where she touched Rudy, her hand burrowed into his coat as far as it could, then made a tiny fist around a few strands of soft hair. The infant did not seem inclined to let go any time soon, and the dog appeared mesmerized by her touch, his long, feathered tail waving in slow, satisfied circles in the air. Paula had never seen anything quite like it.

"No doubt about it—that was the beginning of a beautiful friendship," she murmured now as they reclined under the tree. It was true; everyone had noticed it. From their first connection, Lexi, while still too young to develop much of a bond with anyone besides her mother, and whose eyes could barely focus on specific objects, had never failed to respond to the feel of the dog's fur against her skin. And it was more than that; she seemed to know when he was in the room, seemed to sense his watchfulness, seemed to be more content when he was near.

As for Rudy, these days he walked with a more lively gait, downed his food with more gusto, even chased stray cats in the backyard with more purpose than he had since . . . well, since he'd lost his best friend almost three years earlier. "Hmm," Paula mused, brushing her hand along the dog's smooth flank, "I'll bet TJ arranged the whole thing from the other side. He knew you needed someone, didn't he? He knew you needed each other." Two thumps of Rudy's tail on the grass seemed to confirm her theory. She smiled, fingering the CTR ring on her hand as a few bars of the old crooner's favorite, "Someone to Watch Over Me," ran through her mind. "Wherever you are, TJ," she whispered, glancing heavenward, "keep up the good work."

That evening at dinner, Paula looked up from her meal to see Ted staring distractedly out the window. "Anything interesting going on at the office?" she questioned. Usually she didn't have to ask; but then, she reasoned, they were probably both weary after their hectic, guest-intensive weekend. An uninterrupted night's sleep would do them both good.

"Not much," he murmured, nudging a piece of meat across his plate with a fork, then once again staring past her to some invisible dimension beyond the kitchen window.

"The Northridge people giving you fits again?" she pressed.

"Hmm. Maybe not."

His detached response puzzled her. "Something I should know about?" she asked.

He seemed to shake himself back to the present and gave her a crooked smile. "Nothing. So, how was your day?" He reached over to squeeze her hand, then shoveled a forkful of baked potato into his mouth.

"Good. Rudy and I went for a lovely long walk. Have you noticed how gray he's getting lately?"

"Hmm." He was staring again, this time at a small discoloration on the back of his hand. It seemed to consume every shred of his attention.

"It's probably cancer," Paula said evenly.

"Uh-huh," he replied, his gaze moving to the window again.

"The TV room flooded," she ventured. "Three feet of water down there."

"Sounds good." He took a long, slow drink of his diet soda, then looked at her with perfect candor, his blue eyes still distant. "So, how does the rest of your week look?"

Paula stared at him intently. "Ted, are you all right?"

A slightly defensive glint rose in his eyes. "Why, don't I look all right?"

"Well, yes, you . . . you . . . well, no. You don't." Paula bit her lip. "You look like you're somewhere about a million galaxies away."

He regarded her quizzically for a moment, then shrugged and sank back against his chair. "That close, eh?"

Paula felt the tension drain from the knotted muscles in her midsection. He was back, but she had every intention of finding out where he'd been. "Want to talk about it?" she asked gently.

His crooked grin returned. "It's not like I have a choice, is it?"

"No," she smiled.

"And what if I said I wasn't ready to talk about it?"

She pursed her lips and considered her options, then glanced at her watch. "I'd say you have about an hour to *get* ready."

Ted's eyes moved to the clock on the kitchen wall. "Hmm . . . until eight. What makes you think I'll be ready by—"

"Easy," she interjected. "I happen to recall that it's your turn to do family home evening tonight. Have you planned anything yet?"

His face colored. "Gee, with all the company and everything, I haven't exactly . . . well, it kind of, uh, slipped my mind," he stammered.

"What's left of it." She grinned slyly. "Not to worry. Tell you what: I could go rent my favorite movie, *Beaches,* and we could watch it—"

"Ugh," he groaned. "The ultimate chick-flick."

"Or we could talk about what's bothering you." He gave her an exasperated look. "On second thought," she said indulgently, "let's just talk about what's bothering you."

"You really know how to cheer a guy up, you know that?" He grimaced. "But hey, why postpone the inevitable?"

"I knew you'd see it my way," she cooed. "Don't you just love all this communication in marriage stuff?" He rolled his eyes. "Now, I need to run up and feed Lexi, so why don't you just get comfortable and whip up a batch of cookies or something? I'll see you in the living room at eight. Deal?"

"Deal," Ted muttered as she pressed a quick kiss to his cheek and hurried upstairs.

They had the house to themselves; Scott hadn't returned from work, and Millie had gone to a friend's home for the evening. Following an opening prayer, they sat close together at one end of the long sofa, holding hands. "This is lovely, isn't it?" Paula said when the moment had stretched into a rather lengthy silence.

"Mmm," Ted responded, brushing his lips against her hair. "You know, sweetness, we really ought to take advantage of this magical evening together."

Paula swallowed a giggle. "All in good time, my love," she said. "But first, you promised we could talk about what's bothering you."

He sighed and rested his head against the back of the sofa. "You've got me there, boss. And I get the feeling you're not going to let it go."

"How perceptive of you," she smiled. "I'm all ears."

"That's what I was afraid of." He stretched out his legs, then rested his right ankle on his left knee. Then switched his left ankle to his right knee. Then planted both feet on the floor and leaned forward, balancing his elbows on his thighs. Then sank back against the sofa again and closed his eyes.

"Comfy now, are we?" Paula inquired solicitously while the fingers of one hand beat a subtle pattern against her thigh.

"I suppose." He pressed his palms against his eyelids. "Do you really want to do this?"

"Only if you want to," she replied sweetly. "No pressure—I'm sure the video rental store is still open, and they usually have several copies of *Beaches.* The night is still young; maybe we could watch it twice, and—"

"Okay, okay," he squeaked, raising both hands in surrender. "I'll talk." He glanced at her sideways. "You didn't by any chance ever work in a prisoner of war camp, did you?"

"No," she conceded, "but I'm rather good with prisoners of *love,* don't you think?" She tugged on his earlobe. "So, what's the story?"

Ted cleared his throat. "All right, here it is. But after all my distraction and avoidance, I'm warning you that once you hear this, it'll probably sound like pretty small potatoes."

"I'll be the judge of that," she said. They sat in amiable silence for a few minutes, then she spoke again. This time her tone was more serious. "I'm listening, sweetheart."

"And I guess I'm ready to talk about it now," he said in a voice matching hers. "The thing is, I think I'm having a . . . a . . . well, for lack of a better description, I'll call it a family crisis."

Paula's dark brows knit together in puzzlement. "A family crisis? I thought we were doing just fine."

Ted grabbed her hand. "Oh, no, it's not that—not us. Definitely not us. We're perfect." Seeing relief flood her countenance, he hurried on. "It's just that this weekend, when I saw how you lit up when you saw Mark and Andrea, then Sam and Ruthie, then your mom, and what a great time you had introducing each of them to Lexi, then laughing and talking and reminiscing with them, having a great old time, I guess I—I felt kind of left out."

She rested a hand lightly on his leg. "But you know you're a member of the family, just as surely as if—"

"I know that. And believe me, I appreciate it. They're all great people, even if Marjorie appears to be a little distracted these days."

"I called her this morning," Paula reported. "She seemed fine."

"Terrific," Ted smiled. "But that's just the point—you *called* her." He paused and Paula waited, eyeing him curiously. "Do you know how long it's been since I've called *my* mother? Since I knew where she lived, or even if she was still alive? Over half my life." He ran the fingers of one hand through his short blonde hair. "Way too long."

Paula's mouth fell open slightly. "I thought you didn't care if you ever saw any of your family again."

His shoulders sagged. "So did I—but I've been doing some reconsidering. And if you want to know, I've been thinking about very little else all weekend. Who knows? My mom, my brothers, my sister—I suppose they've all made lives for themselves to some degree, and I can't help being just a little bit curious to see how they've turned out."

"And your father?" Paula's voice was low and infinitely gentle.

A muscle tightened in his jaw, then relaxed. "Maybe . . . someday. But I'd rather start with the others. The question is"—a shadow flickered briefly across his eyes—"do any of them *want* to be found?"

"Well, now," Paula smiled, "I guess that's for them to know and you to find out. Want to give it a try?"

He bit down on his lip. "I'm definitely leaning in that direction. It might not come to much—but on the other hand, it could add a few more Barstows to our family reunions."

"The more the merrier. Maybe we should see an architect about getting that new house built," Paula suggested.

"I like that idea," Ted beamed.

He was leaning over to kiss her when the front door opened and closed with a tiny click and squeak, and they heard a few careful footsteps followed by someone sprinting up the stairs.

"That would be Scotty," Paula whispered, glancing at her watch. "He hopes we're in bed by now, or that we didn't hear him. He and I still have some unfinished business, you know."

"Ah, yes—the cliff-jumping incident," Ted observed.

"Exactly. I really need to talk to him." She smoothed her palm against the back of his neck. "Would you mind if I took care of it now? If you'd rather talk some more, I could always catch him in the morning, and—"

"Hey, don't even think about it," he said with a kiss to her forehead. "Your work here is done. Although I could use some more encouragement later."

"That would be my pleasure," she said. "Just give me about an hour."

"I'll be waiting," he called as she moved around the corner and out of sight.

Scott's door was closed, as usual, and her initial tapping brought no response. She waited several seconds and knocked again, this time louder and more insistently.

"Keep it down, would you?" a booming whisper said behind her. "All that banging will probably set Chiclet off for the night. I've just been checking on her."

Paula whirled around to find Scott towering over her, still dressed in his martial arts uniform, its black belt firmly knotted around his slim waist. His fisted hands on his hips attested to the frustration he was feeling. "Geez, Mom, can't you be more like Rudy? He *never* makes any noise."

Her glance moved to the big dog lying quietly outside the nursery door. "I—I guess I wasn't thinking," she said numbly. "Sorry."

"Yeah, okay," he muttered, motioning her into his room. He lay back on his bed, and she sat on a brown suede ottoman nearby. "I guess we're all pretty wacked after that killer weekend," he sighed. "Man, I've never seen so many bodies in this house before. They were all over each other." He crooked his elbows and put his hands behind his head, then stretched his neck as though doing some kind of relaxation exercise.

"As if you were ever here," Paula said through tight lips. Her cutting reply had sprung to the surface before she could intercept it.

He looked at her coolly. "I was here enough." Following a tense silence, he spoke again, this time in a softer voice. "I don't suppose you came to tuck me in. I found your note the other night."

Suddenly the reason for her visit came back to her in a rush of tangled emotions. How could someone who was so warm and protective toward his tiny sister be guilty of causing Andrea so much pain? Didn't he care? She had to find out. Rising from the ottoman, she moved to the bed and sat down beside him. "Speaking of killer weekends," she began, "I wonder if you have any idea how terrified Andrea was when you took her up to your secret hideaway, then pulled that little cliff-jumping stunt. She thought you'd fallen to your death, and then to have you pop up in front of her again like that was just about more than she could take. Poor girl . . . when you dropped her off at the house afterwards, she was pale as vanilla ice cream and shaking so hard she could barely say a word. She finally told me what happened, and I was so angry that if you'd been anywhere within striking distance, I would've . . . I could've . . . well, young man, that was just a thoroughly rotten thing to do. You should be ashamed of yourself." She clamped her mouth shut and sat still, waiting for his defenses to rise. Good thing she hadn't tracked him down earlier, while she was *really* mad, or she might have—

"You're right. It was just about the lamest thing I've ever done, and I'm totally ashamed of myself. I'm really sorry, Mom. Really." Scott's tone was utterly, heartbreakingly sincere, and she felt a rush of compassion for this sometimes troubled, often troublesome, more than a little reckless son who was finally coming to terms with life's realities. At least a little. *He would never have admitted this a year ago, much less apologized,* she mused silently. The thought satisfied her.

She reached out to touch his arm. "I believe you, Scotty, and I'm glad to see you taking some responsibility for your actions. I'm sure it's taught you something important. I just hope you've apologized to Andrea; she's the one who—"

"We've talked it all out, Mom. She gave me a pretty hard time at first, but now she's okay with it. She even invited me up to the farm for a few days this summer. I think I can swing the vacation time."

Paula smiled. "That's wonderful, dear. And if Andrea has forgiven you, I guess I can, too. Just don't go jumping off any more cliffs, real or otherwise, okay?"

"You got it," Scott grinned. "Now, if you don't mind, I'd like to do a little reading before I turn in, so—"

"Reading, huh?" Paula's eyebrows arched. She had never known him to sit still with a book for any length of time, and there was only one subject she could think of that might capture his attention for more than thirty seconds at a stretch. "Some new car magazine with step-by-step instructions for snazzing up your Viper, I'll bet."

"Something like that," he drawled. "Kind of an instruction manual, I guess. Andy recommended it, so I'm giving it a shot."

"Hmm . . . I didn't think she was into cars," Paula murmured. "Anyway, I'll leave you to it." She stood, then leaned over to smooth an unruly lock of his dark hair and press a light kiss to his forehead. "Good night, Scotty."

"'Night, Mom. See you tomorrow."

When she had closed the door behind her, Scott switched on the wall-mounted lamp directly above his head. Then he reached beneath his pillow and pulled out a small, dark-blue book. "Okay, Andy," he whispered, rubbing his thumb across the gold lettering on its cover, "this one's for you."

Across the hall, Paula folded herself into her husband's arms and sighed contentedly. "I take it this means things went well with Scotty," he murmured against her ear.

"Oh, yes," she replied. "He apologized for his little misadventure, and he's straightened everything out with Andrea. She's even developed an interest in the Viper—gave him a magazine or manual or something to help with the restoration work. Everything's perfect." She turned in his embrace until their noses were just touching. "Now, what did you say was bothering you?"

He smiled as he felt her fragrant breath against his face. "Not a thing, sweetness. Not a single blessed thing."

Chapter 12

In the weeks following Lexi's blessing, the Barstows' life settled into a comfortable routine. Paula's den became her home office, from where she remained involved with the operation of her business for a few hours each day. Ted was doing an exceptional job as partner and acting president, and she trusted him implicitly. But Donroe was in her blood; she could never let it go completely. And why should she? In today's high-tech world, anything was possible. Still, she had sensed a definite shift in her priorities since the baby's birth. She wasn't ready to admit it just yet, but it was quite possible that her real contentment now lay within the walls of her own home.

She moved Lexi's green-and-white cradle to a quiet corner of the den, nursed and played with her between conference calls, ate lunch and went for a leisurely stroll with baby and dog around noon, took a short nap at three, and occasionally checked in with Carmine for a briefing before closing time. The report was invariably good, and she had no trouble greeting Ted with a wide smile when he arrived home. After dinner, their evenings were often taken up with Church responsibilities as Ted directed elders quorum activities and Paula went visiting teaching with Meg O'Brien or coordinated assignments in her new Relief Society calling: chairperson of the Enrichment Night committee. ("Don't know—I guess I'll make it up as I go along," she had assured Ted when he asked what the job entailed.) Life, on the whole, was busy and satisfying.

On a morning in early June, Mark called with official news of his engagement to Kelsey Taggart. "Last night she actually said yes," he reported, his voice vibrating with elation. "Can you believe that?"

"Gee, I don't know," Paula said, her tongue anchored firmly against the inside of her cheek. "Did you record it?"

"I should have," he laughed. "Then I'd have proof, and she wouldn't be able to back out on me. But we're going to do it soon, so hopefully she won't have much of a chance to change her mind. We want to tie the knot and be able to fit in a reception in Illinois, an open house in Idaho, and a short honeymoon before school starts in the fall. So we're planning it for August fifteenth, in the Chicago Temple. It's pretty close to her home in Oak Brook—only about a half-hour drive."

"Whoa, that's soon," Paula whistled. "Do you think her mother is up to getting a reception together that quickly?"

There was a long silence, and she could almost hear Mark grinding his teeth. "If it was up to Mrs. Taggart," he finally said, "there wouldn't *be* a reception. She's a strange one, that lady—has nothing good to say about the Church, and you can bet she's enraged about the whole temple marriage thing. When Kelsey and I called to tell her the news, she was about as warm to me as one of those wax museum people. I doubt if she'll even show up at the reception."

"Then why not just get married in Idaho Falls, and save all the time and expense of going to Illinois?" Paula offered.

Mark chuckled a little. "That's exactly what I suggested, but my beautiful fiancée had other ideas. She has a lot of close LDS friends back there—including her music teacher, dear Sister Norton, who's basically been a mother figure to her for several years. The people in her ward are like her family; the way she talks about them, I can tell she loves them more than anything, and I'm sure the feelings are mutual. There's going to be standing room only at our sealing!"

He said the words with such pride and anticipation that Paula felt a lump rise in her throat. "Then by all means, Chicago it should be," she said.

"Kelsey will organize and coordinate the reception," Mark continued. "And of course the whole ward will help put it all together."

"Sounds like everything's under control," Paula said. "I'm thrilled for you, Mark, and I wish you and Kelsey every happiness. I hope your wedding day will be absolutely perfect."

"Well, there is one thing that would make it that way," he said earnestly. "Paula, I—we'd love it if you and Ted could be there. I know it's a lot to ask, flying all the way out to Chicago and everything, but all of us consider you a dear member of the family. And Mom would have been the first to insist that you come." His voice caught, and he paused for a moment. "I hope she'll be with us, too," he said quietly. "I'll be praying for that."

A vivid, heart-wrenching image of Karti Richland's exquisite features and vibrant smile came to Paula's mind. "Are you kidding?" she said. "Your precious mother might be on the other side, unseen to us for the moment, but this is one wedding she'd move heaven and earth to attend." Her voice softened. "And so would I." She wiped a small tear from the corner of one eye. "Count on us."

She heard a ragged sigh escape his lips. "Thank you so much, Paula," he breathed. "You can't imagine how much this means to me. To all of us."

"And you can't imagine what an honor it is to be asked," she said warmly. "It's kind of like everything is coming full circle, you know?"

"I know," he agreed. "I've thought about that. It'll totally be a day to remember."

"Totally," she smiled.

Less than thirty seconds after they said good-bye, Paula dialed Marjorie Enfield's number. She had made a point to call her mother every few days since Lexi's blessing, and Marjorie, while often sounding weary and distracted, had never failed to ask about Mark.

"Mother?" she said cheerily when the older woman picked up the phone after several rings. "Mother, I have some wonderful news!"

"Who is this?" Marjorie's voice had an irritable edge. "Are you calling about the pruning? I can't get the hose started."

"Mother, it's me—your daughter," Paula said evenly. "Sorry, but I don't know anything about the pruning—or the hose, for that matter." She shook her head, feeling slightly deflated at Marjorie's irascible tone. "How are you, Mother?"

"Is this Mother? I thought you'd gone to town for the chicken feed. Roosters squawking out back. And the hose won't work." Marjorie was sounding more frustrated by the moment. "Can't talk now. Roses won't wait till morning." Paula heard a firm click, and the line went dead. She immediately dialed the number again and waited patiently for at least a dozen rings, but there was no answer.

A colicky baby diverted her attention, and more than three hours passed before she dialed Marjorie's number again. "Hello?" a pleasant voice said after only two or three rings.

"Uh, hi . . . Mother . . . is that you?" Paula asked uncertainly.

"Why, yes, Paula," the woman replied agreeably. "Who else would it be? Don't you recognize your own mother's voice, dear?"

A tiny surge of indignation rose in Paula's throat, but she quickly swallowed it. "Yes, of course I do, Mother. It's just that when I called earlier, you—"

"Oh, you mean last week," Marjorie broke in. "I'd had a little cold—probably didn't sound much like myself."

Paula bit her lip. "Then . . . you don't remember about the pruning, or the hose, or your mother . . ."

"What about my mother?" She chuckled softly. "Have you been doing some of that Mormon genealogy again? I've already given you all the information I have about my parents."

"Excuse me?" Paula squinted into the phone, then rolled her eyes. "Oh, no . . . it's nothing, Mother. Never mind. How are you feeling?"

"Quite well, thank you. A little tired, though . . . prone to longer naps than usual. It seems the days slip by so quickly, and there are too many stairs in this old house. I'm keeping up the best I can. Thank goodness for Maria, who comes in twice a week to clean. She brings groceries, too."

"That's nice, Mother," Paula said. "But don't you think you really should have someone there with you all the time? You could get a full-time housekeeper and cook, like you had when I was growing up, and—"

"Nonsense," Marjorie declared firmly. "I'm perfectly fine on my own—healthy as a horse, and there's no need to hire someone when I can do for myself." Her tone put an end to any further discussion.

Paula shrugged, sensing the futility of arguing with this strong-willed woman. "Well, okay; maybe we can talk about it later," she said. "Besides, that's not why I called. Mother, I have some fabulous news!"

They spent the next few minutes chatting amiably. Marjorie was thrilled to learn of Mark's engagement, and seemed interested in every minute detail of the wedding plans. "You must send pictures," she insisted.

"You know, you could come if you wanted to," Paula suggested. "Of course you wouldn't be able to see the actual wedding, but I'm sure the reception will be lovely. Ted and I could meet you at the airport, and—"

"I think not," Marjorie decreed abruptly. "But I will appreciate the photographs."

"Right . . . whatever." Paula shrugged again. "Listen, the baby's fussing and it's time for me to feed her. You'll call if you need anything, won't you, Mother?"

"And why would I need anything?" There was an austere inflection to Marjorie's voice. *Almost as if she's purposely keeping me at arm's length,* Paula thought. *It's the story of our lives: don't ever, ever get too close.*

"You have my number," Paula said, forcing a trace of warmth into her voice. "I'll call next week. Give my best to Maria."

"Very well," Marjorie murmured. "And thank you for telling me about . . . about . . ." She hesitated, and Paula could almost hear her mother's chin jut into the air. "About everything. Good-bye, then." A small click, and she was gone.

Ted worked late, then had a meeting at the church, and it was close to midnight before Paula was able to share the day's news with him. "Why do you suppose it is," she wondered out loud, after describing her conversations with Marjorie, "that parents and children so often push each other away? My mother's done it to me all her life; and now, when I get the feeling she might really need me, I can't get close enough to find out what's going on. Kelsey's mother has obviously been through some difficult times in her past, too; but instead of working through the issues, she's pretty much turned her back on her daughter at what should be one of the most joyful times of her life. And I . . . ," she hesitated for a moment before going on, "I pushed TJ away when he wanted to join the Church, and I shut Scotty out when he seemed to turn on me, but all the time he was really just blaming himself for his brother's death. It seems like it takes a huge disaster or something to bring people back together, if it ever happens at all. I don't get it."

Ted nodded as he turned back the bedcovers. "Yeah, I know what you mean. I've played that game myself." His voice was deeply edged with regret. "I left home at eighteen and never looked back. I walked out on my entire family because my father betrayed us and my mother seemed to lose all interest in whether we lived or died. There was a heckuva lot of pushing and pulling going on in those days, let me tell you. And more than two decades later, what do I have to show for it? A father who has never been a part of my life. A mother who may still be living, but is certainly lost to me. Siblings who—well, who knows? And sometimes I wonder who even cares." He slipped into bed beside Paula, pulled the covers up under his chin, and turned to look at her. She was smiling. "What?"

"Well, aren't we quite the pair," she replied with an endearing smirk. "Good grief, I haven't been to such an all-out pity-party for years. But we're pretty darn good at it, don't you think? We could make a fortune doing 'Poor Me' seminars."

He rubbed his stubbled chin, then returned her smile. "You're absolutely right. There's nothing like a little wallowing to get the kinks out. Maybe we could do this, say, every Friday evening or something. Kind of like a weekly date, only with"—he lowered his voice to a mysterious growl—"*deep psychological implications.*" He reached over to tickle her. "Then we could write a book about it and be on Oprah."

"Amen," she giggled, scooting away from his teasing fingers. They laughed like children until they could hardly breathe, then lay side by side, holding hands, until the calm night took over and their hearts beat in quiet harmony. As his grip on her hand began to relax, Paula ventured a final observation. "You could still find them, you know," she whispered.

"Hmm?" If there was a pleasantly drowsy sound, this was it.

Paula could tell he was rapidly losing the battle for wakefulness, but she persisted. "Your mom and the rest of the family. They're out there somewhere, and a few weeks ago you told me yourself that you sometimes wonder about them. I say we start looking."

"Okay, be my guest, Sherlock," Ted mumbled from somewhere on the outer edges of alertness. "Just not tonight. 'Sides, wouldn't know where to . . ." A soft snore eclipsed the sentence, and he drifted beyond her reach.

She laid her head against his shoulder and smiled into the darkness. *Okay then. We'll start looking. How hard can it be?*

* * * * * * * *

"So I said to myself, 'How hard can it be?' Then I woke up the next morning and hit a brick wall." Paula was trying to explain her predicament to Meg O'Brien over a lunch of taco salads and non-alcoholic piña colada smoothies. "I have Ted's parents' names and his mother's approximate age, but so far every Internet source I've checked has come up with zip. You'd think I would've made some progress in two days, but I guess I'm not much of a sleuth—probably don't even know what I'm looking for. I called the Church's membership department in Salt Lake City, but they couldn't find her. They told me that if she'd been excommunicated, or if she'd moved around a lot and purposely dropped out of sight, she either wouldn't appear in current Church records, or the information they had wouldn't be accurate."

"Uh-huh," Meg said between bites of cheese-and-sour-cream-drenched beef. "Sounds like you need BigHugs."

Paula sighed with mild exasperation. "Of course I do; everybody needs big hugs now and then to get through what life throws at them, and I certainly wouldn't mind one right about now. But frankly, that won't get me any closer to solving this mystery, and I—"

"Oh, no-no-no-no," Meg interjected, vigorously shaking her head of thick, wheat-colored hair. Her blue eyes were twinkling as she reached across the table to squeeze Paula's arm. "What I meant, my dear friend, is BigHugs—really! It's a company in Florida that specializes in finding missing people—friends, relatives, deadbeat parents, abducted children, almost anyone you could imagine. A few months ago, I was watching a TV talk show where they reunited people who'd lost track of each other and hadn't been together for ages; I bawled my eyes out for the whole hour. At the end of the show, they introduced the founder and president of BigHugs—he's a huge, affable guy with big hair who looks like an enormous teddy bear—and he explained how they found these people. It was fascinating to hear how they did it—sometimes pretty miraculous, too. And here's the kicker: I was talking with a friend in the ward about it later, and she told me the president and chief hugger is a member of the Church. Seemed to make the whole thing even sweeter somehow."

"Really?" Paula's interest was piqued. "Maybe they could help me."

"Sounds like a good bet," Meg grinned. "I don't know all the details, but their Internet site is BigHugs.com. I say go for it, girl!"

That was all Paula needed. By mid-afternoon a telephone connection had been made, and BigHugs was on the trail. It could be weeks, possibly a few months before they found who they were looking for, but the researcher she spoke with sounded hopeful, even confident. Paula decided not to tell Ted about BigHugs, but instead planned to surprise him with the good news when it came. He occasionally inquired about her progress with the search, but she simply shrugged and reminded him that with all of her other responsibilities, she didn't have much time to devote to the project. He never pushed, although once in a while the longing in his eyes would tempt her to spill the secret. She resisted, hoping it wouldn't be too much longer. In her heart, she couldn't help wondering if this story would, indeed, have a happy ending. For her part, she could only wait—and pray that all of her good intentions wouldn't blow up in their faces.

Toward the end of June, on a breezeless Saturday morning when the air was warm and fragrant with the smell of newly mown grass, Paula had just been out for a stroll with Rudy. Dressed in a lightweight plum-colored cotton jogging suit, she was sitting at the kitchen table, sipping a tall glass of pineapple-grapefruit juice over ice, when the doorbell rang. "Got it!" a voice boomed from the entryway, telling her that Scott was on his way to work. The front door opened, and she heard her son speak again, this time with cheerful energy. "Hey, there! How's my girl? C'mon in!" Someone stepped into the entryway, and there was a brief silence punctuated by what sounded like . . . well, like a hug. Paula couldn't help smiling a little at her own vivid imagination. What exactly did a hug sound like, anyway?

She cast a furtive glance at Millie, who was loading the dishwasher. "My girl?" The older woman shrugged.

A moment later, Paula's son sauntered into the kitchen, his arm slung casually across the shoulders of a full-figured young woman with flame-red hair. Her arm was curled affectionately around Scott's waist.

Paula and Millie did a double take at the same instant. "Carmine!" they blurted out in unison.

"The very same," Carmine grinned. She tugged playfully on the white sleeve of Scott's martial arts uniform. "Don't you think he looks adorable in his pajamas?"

Paula could barely speak. "Well," she finally managed, "this is a surprise. I certainly had no idea . . . didn't know you were . . . how long have you two been . . ." She couldn't quite say it.

"How long have we been what, Mom?" Scott asked. He winked at Carmine, his hazel eyes dancing with mirth.

"Well, uh . . . dating," Paula choked out.

Scott leaned against the wall and folded his arms smugly across his chest. Paula thought she had never seen such an amused expression on his face. Carmine smiled beguilingly in Scott's direction, then turned to face Paula with both hands on her hips. "Dating? What a novel concept," she declared. "I mean, he's an awesome-looking guy and all, but I prefer my men a little meatier." She reached over to pinch the muscled flesh over his ribs. "Nothing to hang on to there." He made a face and swatted her hand away.

Paula looked from Scott to Carmine, then back to Scott. "But I heard you in the entryway. You called her 'my girl,' and I—"

"Come on, Mom," he cut in breezily. "She's a girl, and she's my friend. You figure it out."

Paula wasn't convinced, but decided to give him the benefit of the doubt. "Well, I didn't think you even knew each other," she said with a childish pout.

"We didn't—until that awful wait at the hospital while you were under the knife," Carmine explained. "I was totally bummed out about what had happened to you, and he was trying to reassure me, so we talked a little. One thing led to another, and he ended up inviting me to visit his karate class sometime—offered to teach me a few moves. 'Hey,' he said, 'you never know when a pretty lady like yourself might get hit on by some dirtbag, or when you might need to help somebody else. It pays to be prepared.'" Her smile was tentative, almost shy. "I've been taking classes for a couple of months now."

"I see," Paula said, running a finger up and down her drizzling juice glass, at the same time recalling what Carmine had recently told her about a certain bargain she had struck with a higher power. "It would seem that you had quite an interesting day at the hospital.

I'm sorry I slept through it all." She paused. "Is there anything else I should know?"

"Hey, everything's cool. It all worked out," Scott grinned. He bent over to whisper a few words into Carmine's ear, then glanced at his watch. "I've got to go, so I'll leave you chicks to your, uh, chicking. See you later, Red." Carmine gave him a little wave, and he disappeared into the entryway. A few seconds later, they watched him lope across the lawn and inject himself into the driver's seat of the Viper.

When the screech of the car's tires was out of earshot, the three women stared at each other for a few moments. Carmine was the first to speak as she shifted from one foot to the other. "So, I guess you're wondering why I've called this meeting."

"You didn't come to see Scotty?" Paula questioned.

"Oh, no," the young woman said quickly. "I came to see you. I have news."

For the first time since her arrival, Paula took note of the not-so-subtle changes in Carmine's appearance and demeanor. Had she lost weight? No, it wasn't that; but just about everything else about her was different. The color of her hair could still set off a fire alarm, but her formerly wild locks were now trimmed to perfection, framing her wide, heart-shaped face in a flattering style. A dainty application of makeup and translucent powder complemented her flawless skin instead of hiding it under a thick layer of foundation, and her eyes were completely free of their usual heavy liner and crusty mascara. One simple gold stud adorned each of her earlobes—a far cry from the myriad chains and baubles that had decorated the perimeters of her ears since Paula had first known her.

The rest of the package had taken on a new look, too. Carmine's fingernails, usually painted a garish orange-red color and long enough to be used as tools or dangerous weapons, had been neatly trimmed to within a quarter-inch of her fingertips and subtly lacquered with clear polish. A single classic gold-braided band on the little finger of her right hand and a small topaz stone on her left ring finger had replaced the collection of large, chunky jewelry she had previously worn. And the silky blue-green fabric of her stylish pantsuit flowed loosely and gracefully across her expansive figure instead of competing with it. Even her shoes—simple navy pumps as opposed to the faddish thick-heeled, open-toed plastic models she generally wore—reflected an altered sense of fashion. In a word, this new, improved version of Carmine Brough was stunning. Paula couldn't take her eyes off the woman. But what had precipitated such a drastic change?

"You're staring, Paula. So are you, Millie," Carmine declared in a slightly impish voice.

Paula cleared her throat, then looked directly into her friend's sparkling green eyes. There was something different about those eyes, too. Were they deeper, clearer, more engaging than before? "It's just that you're so . . . beautiful," she said softly. "I mean, you were always attractive in a breezy sort of way, but now . . ." Her voice trailed off.

Carmine smiled broadly, obviously delighted at Paula's observation. "What a difference a couple of months makes, eh?" She smoothed one of the arms of her suit. "That's my news."

While Millie and Paula waited expectantly, she seated herself elegantly at the table. "Okay," she said at the end of a dramatic pause. "I think you knew this was coming, Paula, but today I'm making the official announcement. I'm getting baptized." Her eyes weren't sparkling now. They were glowing.

So that was it. *The refining influence of the gospel.* Words from the book of Revelation flooded Paula's heart: "Behold, I make all things new." It had happened in her own life, and in Ted's; and now it had literally transformed Carmine from the inside out, like a magical shift in currents guiding a castaway ship into safe port. This moment was miraculous beyond comprehension. Paula sat without moving as tears filled her eyes and coursed down her cheeks.

"I take it those aren't tears of disappointment," Carmine smiled. When Paula shook her head and wiped at her eyes, she continued. "I guess the last time I saw you was at the open house after your little girl's blessing." Paula nodded. "Well, a couple of weeks later I just sat down with myself and said, 'Self, there's no beating around the bush any longer. You gotta be either in or out of the Church, so make up your mind. And getting a testimony would be nice.'"

"That's my Carmine," Paula sniffed, giving her a watery smile. "The no-nonsense approach to getting things done."

"And that's exactly what I did," Carmine said grandly. "I got it done. I got down on my knees right then and there, and I didn't get up until I knew. I *knew.*" Tears shimmered in her eyes, but she tossed her head and went on. "'Course, I still had to clean up my life, but the sister missionaries were a big help, and I worked hard at it if I say so myself. Tithing and Word of Wisdom all the way, tons of prayer and scripture study, no more sleazy movies and trashy romance novels—or trashy boyfriends, for that matter. It was a turnaround, I'll tell you. But it finally paid off." Her gaze met Paula's as she wiped a stray tear from her cheek. "The top-dog elder interviewed me last night, and he said I was ready. So I guess all that's left to say is . . . will you come to my baptism?" She glanced toward Millie. "Will both of you come? And Ted, of course. I'd like to do it a week from today—the Fourth of July. Kind of my own personal Independence Day, if you know what I mean. Spiritually speaking, anyhow."

"I know exactly what you mean," Paula smiled. "And we'll be honored to attend your baptism." The three women rose and exchanged warm embraces.

They chatted for a few minutes longer, then a beaming Carmine took her leave. "I still can't quite believe it," Paula said, pouring a fresh glass of juice. "But then, you never know; we've seen it happen time and time again. The Lord—"

"Works in mysterious ways," Millie interjected with a curious smile. "I wonder what He'll think of next."

Chapter 13

Carmine's Independence Day baptism, conducted at a stake center near the UCLA campus, went off without a hitch—if not without a few personal fireworks in Paula's corner. "Am I hallucinating," she whispered, nudging Ted as they sat together a few minutes before the service was to begin, "or does a certain young man behind us bear a striking resemblance to someone we know and love? I noticed him a minute ago, in my compact mirror." While focusing her gaze on the baptismal font in front of her, she made a subtle motion with her head in the direction of a rear corner on the opposite side of the room. "Don't look!" she warned as he craned his neck to see.

Ted's head snapped back to the face-forward position. "All righty . . . but may I ask how you expect me to see anything if I don't *look?*" The words were spoken sideways out of the corner of his mouth.

"Okay, go ahead and look," she relented. "But make it fast. And be discreet about it."

"Hey, discreet is my middle name," he grinned. "That is, it would be if I *had* a middle name. Although I would have preferred Xavier." He slid far forward on his metal chair, ducked his head, slowly swiveled his body around as far as he could, raised his head again, and peered cautiously between the heads of several couples in rows behind him. Within seconds he found what he was looking for, watched for a few moments, then suddenly whirled back to face the front. "Omigosh, you're right!" he wheezed in exaggerated tones. "It's Scotty, looking for all the world like a regular church-going fellow, complete with a suit and tie and everything." He slapped a hand against his cheek. "I declare, whatever is this world coming to?"

Paula giggled in spite of herself. "Quit kidding around, Barstow. What do you think he's doing here? I mean, he stood way at the back of the chapel during Lexi's blessing, but other than that, he hasn't set foot inside a church for at least a couple of years." Could this be a sign, she wondered, that something was changing?

Ted folded his arms across his chest, still staring straight ahead. "Well, from what you told me last week, he and Carmine have gotten to know each other pretty well. It only makes sense that he'd want to support her on this occasion"—he glanced around the crowded room—"along with two or three hundred of her other closest friends." He shook his head in puzzlement. "I didn't know she knew this many people in the whole L.A. area. Especially this many well-groomed people."

"You're probably right," Paula conceded warily. "I'm sure it's a gesture of friendship and support . . . nothing more."

"Oh, and what 'more' did you think it might be?" Ted asked pointedly, his shoulder pressed against hers. "As far as the Church is concerned, it seems to me the boy has made it abundantly clear that he's not going to latch on to the iron rod—or let anyone beat him over the head with it—in the foreseeable future. When I was his age I felt exactly the same way. What he needs now is some space."

Paula was considering her response when an ardent young elder stood to begin the service, and a reverent hush settled over the room. The next hour was devoted to inspirational talks, musical numbers, and testimonies, including a tearful one from Carmine, whose simple white gown seemed to glisten as she spoke. When the time came, Paula, Ted, and Millie, along with several other witnesses, gathered around the font to see the ordinance performed. Afterwards, as they returned to their seats, Paula wiped the mist from her eyes and searched the back of the room for her son. There was no sign of him. "He's gone," she whispered to Ted. "He must have left early."

"I could have told you that," he chuckled. "Without even looking."

Paula knocked softly at Scott's bedroom door, feeling a small prickle of guilt as she glanced at her watch and realized it was near midnight. Still, she'd seen a light under the door, so she was fairly certain she wouldn't be wrenching him from a deep sleep.

"It's open," a deep voice called out. He didn't even sound drowsy. As she entered, Scott tucked something beneath his pillow and stretched out full-length on his bed. "Hiya," he drawled, motioning for her to take a seat on the familiar old brown ottoman. "What's up?"

"I was hoping you could tell me that," she said, lowering herself gracefully to the sagging piece of furniture and balancing herself atop one of its larger lumps. "Ted said I shouldn't ask, but you know me—too curious for my own good." She was watching his face, and she saw his eyes narrow slightly.

"So you're going to go ahead and ask anyway, aren't you?" he returned, flashing her a guarded smile.

"You know me so well," she grinned. "The question is, how well do I know you?"

Scott's brow furrowed, and he rubbed a large hand across his forehead. "Geez, Mom, isn't it kind of late to get into one of your deep philosophical discussions?" He stretched his mouth into a prolonged yawn.

"Nothing like that," she assured him. "But I was wondering about something. It'll only take a minute."

He extended his arms perpendicular to his body and flexed the hard muscles from his shoulders to his wrists until they bulged beneath his long-sleeved yellow T-shirt. "Okay, shoot. But not to kill."

"Deal." She leaned forward until her face was close enough to his arm to almost touch it. "I just wondered how you happened to show up at Carmine's baptism this morning."

The boy's muscles froze in mid-flex, and a deep crimson blush flooded his face from neck to hairline. "H—how did you know?" he stammered. "I saw you guys from the back of the room, but I kept an eye on you so I could duck or something if you turned around. Then I even left early. How'd you figure it out?"

Paula kept a straight face as she raised an eyebrow. "Trust me, a mother knows these things." She said it tongue-in-cheek, then continued in soothing tones. "I just think it was *awfully* sweet of you to support Carmine that way . . . especially when you don't care anything about the Church, and there are so *many* better things to do on a Saturday—the Fourth of July, no less—besides getting all spiffed up and going to a meaningless religious ritual." She leaned closer and rested a hand on his leg. The muscles twitched beneath his jeans. "Or am I missing something here?" She fell silent, determined to wait until he found his voice. One way or another, she was going to ferret out what was going on.

The long moments wore on through several coughs, wheezes, and deep sighs, followed by a final conciliatory groan. "You win," he muttered, one long arm slung carelessly over the edge of the bed. "Not that I'm admitting anything, you understand, but I suppose you'll find out sooner or later. Looks like it's gonna be sooner."

"I'm listening." Paula held her breath, not daring to second-guess his revelation.

"The thing is," he began, propping himself up on one elbow, "it's me and Carmine. I know we said there was nothing going on, but that's not exactly true. For a while now, we've been . . . well, we have this thing going, and well, we kind of . . . geez, this is so hard." He slumped back against his pillow and stared vacantly at the ceiling. After a few long, awkward moments, his voice seemed to come out of nowhere. "We've kind of been going to church."

The words filtered into Paula's mind one by one, like tentative snowflakes fluttering to the ground on a late autumn afternoon, melting immediately but still leaving their impressions—small, damp marks on the sidewalk or grass or porch steps, reminding passersby that something had happened. At this moment, Paula knew that indeed, something had happened—something important. But she couldn't quite comprehend its meaning.

When the tension became unbearable, Scott swung his long legs over the edge of the bed, sat up, and reached over to tug gently on his mother's sleeve. "Hello, Mom?" he began carefully. "Mom, I said Carmine and I have been—"

"Going to church. Yes, I know." Paula lifted her head and looked into his eyes, her mouth set in a firm line, her expression completely inscrutable. "The question is, which one?"

Scott's face went soft with relief, though his laugh had a slightly nervous edge. "What do you mean, which one? Carmine went and got herself dunked, didn't she? And you've been telling me for at least a hundred years that the Mormons have"—he curled his fingers like quotation marks—"'the only true church on the face of the—'"

"No, no . . . I'm serious," Paula interrupted, a curious light rising in her eyes. "Which one?" Seeing his perplexed stare, she hurried on. "I've never seen you anywhere near our chapel; besides, you're always either still asleep or working on the Viper when we leave for church on Sunday mornings. Which *ward* have you been going to? That's what I meant."

"Oh, right," he said a little sheepishly.

"And I want the whole story," she added. "Don't leave anything out." She was beginning to enjoy this turn of the conversation—or was it too good to be true?

"It's not all that complicated," Scott began, rubbing his large hands up and down his thighs. "When Carmine started taking martial arts classes, we'd talk a little on some of our breaks. She told me about the deal she made with the Man upstairs when you got hurt, and pretty soon she said she was having the lady missionaries over for dinner." He leaned back against the wall behind him as he continued. "Before I knew it, she was practically *begging* me to go to church with her—said she felt uncomfortable going alone or hanging with the sisters. I figured why not, so we went. Meetings didn't start till noon, and I still had some time to do what I wanted in the mornings. It was a student ward at UCLA, not a lot of old people or anything, and there were some pretty nice-looking girls, too. It didn't suck as much as I thought it would."

"What a relief," Paula murmured, resisting an impulse to roll her eyes. "Please, go on."

"Anyway, after a while Carmine started getting serious about the Church. Big time."

"And how did you feel about that?" Paula asked calmly.

"I told her I'd be there for her, whatever she wanted to do. That's basically why I was there today—because I wanted to support her decision." He snorted softly. "Not that it mattered a whole heck of a lot, I suppose. Pretty much the whole ward was there. These days she's got more friends than she knows what to do with." He shrugged and picked at a piece of lint on his shirt.

"She's a nice girl," Paula said. "And how about you, Scotty? What do you think?"

"I think she's a nice girl, too," he said, rolling the lint into a little ball and flicking it off his finger.

"No, not about that." *Are we ever going to get on the same page here?* "I mean, what do you think about the gospel? Now that you've been to church, gotten acquainted with some LDS young people, and watched a friend go through the conversion process, what's your take on the whole 'Mormon thing,' as you call it?"

Scott was quiet for a long time. "Seems like there are a lot of really smart kids who believe it," he finally said in a monotone. "But I'm not taking their word on it. That wouldn't be right."

Paula didn't know quite how to respond. The boy wasn't openly hostile, as he had been in the past, but he obviously hadn't followed Carmine's lead either. What would it take to tip the scales in the Church's favor? "I understand why you wouldn't want to just follow blindly," she ventured. "Still, there's something to be said for leaning on the testimonies of others until you—"

"I'm doing my own research." He pulled something from beneath his pillow and held it out to her. "Getting it right from the horse's mouth, so to speak." He grinned slyly. "Or right from the angel's mouth, if that's what it turns out to be."

She gazed down at the Book of Mormon in his hand, then back at him with narrowed eyes. "Did Millie give you this?"

He laughed out loud. "Naw. She might've given me one a couple of years ago, but I think I used it in my hamster cage. This one came from Andrea—it's autographed and everything, see?" He opened the cover, and Paula read a few words scrawled on the title page:

To the Scottster—This is the best book ever! Don't leave home without it. Love, Andy.

"She gave it to me the day of Lexi's blessing," he explained. "Made me promise to read the whole thing by the end of the year." He gave her a wily chuckle. "Too bad for her she didn't say *which* year."

"The Scottster?"

"Yeah—just a little nickname," he said, coloring slightly. "So I told her I'd do it. I'm figuring out all the weird names and stuff as I go along." He made a grisly face. "I get the feeling she'll rip into me if I don't keep at it." Paula noticed there was a marker toward the front of the book. "Gotta keep the lady happy," he said with a plaintive sigh.

"Yes, I suppose that's a good idea," Paula smiled. "Definitely better than, say, jumping off a cliff."

"Yeah . . . she mentions that quite often," he admitted. "Every time she calls or picks up the phone and hears my voice, it's 'Hiya! Fallen off any mountains lately?'" He grunted good-naturedly. "I swear, she won't let me forget it for the rest of my life."

"Smart girl," Paula said, pleased to hear that the young people were staying in touch. She decided to get back to the subject at hand. "Are you enjoying the book?"

He shrugged. "Enough to keep reading it, I suppose. That Lehi and his crazy kids, always beating on each other . . . talk about a dysfunctional family. And you'd think Nephi would've gone with a hunger strike or a sit-in or something, instead of chopping off that guy Laban's head." Paula cringed inwardly but maintained a placid, attentive expression. "Carmine says you kind of learn to go with the flow after a while," he added. "Some of the battles are pretty cool, but I'm not much into the religious stuff."

Paula reached out to pat his knee. "Well, you just keep plugging away at it, sweetie. I'm sure it'll all come together eventually." *Isn't that what Thomas Edison's mother kept telling him when he was trying to invent the lightbulb? Hang in there, Scotty. Good things come to those who wait—and sometimes to their mothers, too. Just please don't make me wait too long; Mama Edison couldn't have enjoyed all that suspense, and I'm not exactly a model of patience myself.* "Besides," she added, "look at all the nice friends you're making in that new ward. Do you ever go to their parties or firesides or anything?"

"Nope. Carmine gets off on all that, and I think she's dating a couple of guys right now. One of them is the returned missionary who baptized her. But me? I don't really fit in, not being a student or a member, or even an investigator at this point. I just do my reading, and I show up at church most Sundays. That's enough, don't you think? I mean, I've got my own life, too. There's work, and the Viper, and afternoons on the mountain, and . . . lots of work, and . . ." He looked at her with just a hint of defiance in his eyes.

"Absolutely," Paula assured him quickly, realizing that at this moment, her response could make all the difference. *He might not be polishing up his missionary name tag just yet, but he's a lot closer than you ever thought possible ten minutes ago. Don't shut him down now.* "I think you're doing great, Scotty. Just great." His relieved expression told her she'd struck a happy medium.

"Okay then," he announced, "I guess I'll do another page. Well, maybe half a page." He grinned at her, and—was that a wink? "I was only a little sleepy when I first got down to it, but I figure a few more verses will put me out like a light."

Paula stretched elaborately and rose, her muscles stiff from clinging to the edge of the ottoman. "That's my boy," she clucked, bending over to ruffle his dark hair. "Rest well, and I'll see you tomorrow."

Minutes later, Ted made a small moaning sound when she slipped between the cool sheets next to him. He was lying with his back toward her, just beginning to relax into welcome oblivion. "Sweetheart," she whispered close to his ear, "do you remember at Carmine's baptism this morning, when you said we should give Scotty some space?"

"Mmm."

"Well, he and I just had a little heart-to-heart, and after what he told me, I agree with you completely. Time, space, tolerance, free room and board—whatever it takes, however long it takes. But I honestly don't believe it'll be that long. I have a really good feeling about this, Ted. I think he's going to be all right, don't you?"

"Mmm."

"I mean, he's reading the Book of Mormon, going to church, even has his own personal cheerleader up in Idaho. I don't see how he can go wrong, do you?"

Ted inhaled shallowly, then let out a reluctant snore that sounded like the gurgle of a sprinkler system being shut down for the winter.

"Me neither," she murmured tranquilly, settling herself comfortably against his back. "Sweet dreams, my love."

July passed in its usual blur of smoggy mornings, sweltering afternoons, and sultry evenings, but Paula rarely noticed the weather except when she took Alexis and Rudy out for a stroll in the neighborhood or an excursion to the park. Most of her time was spent indoors, sometimes working at her computer, but more often nurturing the close bond she had developed with her young daughter. "I know, I know—you can't quite pronounce 'Rumpelstiltskin' just yet," she would murmur as she cradled the baby on her lap and read to her from the colorful pages of a book of fairy tales, "but you'll see. One day you'll figure it out—along with walking, eating macaroni and cheese, and playing T-ball." Invariably, she would feel a rush of anticipation. "And you can count on your old mom; I'll be there for every single one of those fabulous firsts."

At least twice a week, she and Lexi would visit the hospital's newborn intensive care unit. While Lexi played with her toys in a corner of the large room, Paula would do her best to cheer and comfort parents who kept long and anxious vigils at their tiny infants' bedsides. Occasionally she held a grief-stricken mother in her arms moments after her child's passing, and their tears would mingle as Paula quietly reflected on the death of her own son a few years earlier. Nothing, she knew, was harder than saying good-bye, and her heart ached for these women. When it seemed appropriate, she would share a brief, simple testimony of the eternal nature of life and of a loving Father's tender care for His children. After such an experience, she would never fail to breathe a silent prayer of thanksgiving for the gospel. If that were to be her only legacy to her precious daughter, she knew it would be enough.

One evening at dinner, Ted smiled at her over their plates of chicken and steamed vegetables. "I have a terrific idea," he announced.

She speared a baby carrot with her fork. "I'm listening."

His eyes danced. "Well, I was thinking that since we'll be flying out to Chicago for Mark's wedding, why don't we take a couple of extra days and have ourselves a little mini-vacation? I've never been to your mother's place in Connecticut, you know, and we'll already be more than two-thirds of the way across the country. I know you've been concerned about her, and this would give you a chance to check things out for yourself. What do you think?"

The suggestion took her by surprise. "I—I don't know," she responded, a wave of hesitation washing over her. "As it is, I'm feeling terrible about leaving the baby overnight while we're in Chicago. She's barely weaned, and—"

"The child will be eight months old. Practically in law school," he interjected. "Besides, we both know that Millie lives to take care of her, and no one does it better—present company excepted, of course. And we're only talking about another day or two away. We could fly to New York, maybe take in a Broadway show, then the next day drive on up to Connecticut and spend a few hours with Marge. We'll be back in L.A. before Lexi has finished her strained peas." He made a comical face.

Paula laughed. "You have a point . . . but I still don't know. Let me think on it, will you?"

"By all means. You may think on it, around it, through it, and all over it for as long as you like. Just promise me you'll say yes."

"Maybe," she smiled.

"Good enough for now. I'll make the plane reservations—just in case." He chomped down cheerfully on a piece of chicken.

For the next few days, Paula mulled over Ted's suggestion. It would be best, she finally decided, to make the trip—especially in view of the increasingly strange and disordered things that had been coming out of Marjorie's mouth during their phone conversations. Actually being there would give her a chance to really assess the situation firsthand and make sure her mother was all right—a relative term, she thought, since Marjorie herself insisted that nothing was amiss. Besides, it would be lovely to see the estate again—to show Ted around the elegant mansion, watching his eyes grow wide at the opulence of it all; to stroll with him around its expertly tended grounds and magical gardens; to sit with him, holding hands, in the quaint little gazebo where she had spent so many tranquil hours as a child. The prospect of sharing this gracious part of her past with him filled her with delicious anticipation, and she was also convinced that their visit could only have a positive effect on her relationship with her mother. Marjorie, on the other hand, seemed somewhat less captivated by the idea when Paula brought it up, but in the end she raised no strenuous objection to their coming.

Late one muggy Friday morning, Paula was flipping her desk calendar over to the eighth of August when Millie knocked at the open office door. "I have the mail," she announced cheerfully, holding out a small bundle of envelopes. "Lexi's awake; why don't I just trundle her for a few minutes while you take a look at your letters?" Favoring her arthritic hip, she hobbled to the far corner of the small room and bent over to lift the baby from her cradle. "There's an interesting envelope from Florida," she reported as Lexi gurgled playfully and the two settled into an overstuffed chair. "Something about hugs. Probably just junk mail, but it's a cute name. And speaking of hugs . . ." She wrapped her arms around the baby and squeezed firmly, her mouth and nose buried in the little girl's dark, fragrant hair. Lexi seemed to relish the closeness, and snuggled comfortably against the older woman's round body.

Paula had seen the letter at the same instant Millie mentioned it, and now her heartbeat quickened as she stared at the BigHugs logo in one corner of the envelope. She had not heard from the company's researcher since she'd made the first contact nearly two months earlier; and since then, preoccupied with mothering, work, Church responsibilities, and getting ready for their trip, she hadn't thought much about the matter. What use was it to fuss and fume and worry about the search, anyway? If there was news, she'd have it soon enough; if there was no news, she'd deal with it later. Besides, Ted hadn't mentioned it for weeks, so he couldn't be all that concerned, could he? Still, there might be something inside this envelope that would be useful, that might give them a clue about whatever happened to Alma Barstow, the mysterious vanishing mother. But what?

She decided to read it later, after her work was finished, in the privacy of her own room. Setting the unopened envelope aside on her desk, she turned back to her computer. *And Ted thinks I'm too curious for my own good,* she gloated silently. *If he could see me now—cool as a strawberry daiquiri (non-alcoholic, of course), completely under control, focused on my priorities, getting so much work done. I didn't get where I am today, after all, without a whole lot of determination and self-discipline. Now, where was I?* Clicking on the appropriate icon, she pulled up a quarterly revenue analysis and began to do some mental calculations.

Two minutes later, Paula pushed her chair back from the desk and stretched her arms in a wide, lazy arc. "You know," she sighed, flashing Millie a casual grin, "I've been shut up in this office since early morning, and I'm *exhausted.*" She rubbed her temples as if shooing away a pesky headache, then glanced at a small clock on the desk. "It's nearly noon, but I'm not all that hungry—think I'll just go upstairs and sneak a little nap. If you're okay with watching little cutie-pie, that is."

"My pleasure," Millie smiled, gazing down at Lexi, who was nodding off. "I'll call you when lunch is ready—say, about one?"

"Perfect," Paula replied with a little smirk. "I'll see you in a bit, then." She calmly scooped up several unopened envelopes from her desk, tiptoed over to brush a kiss across the baby's forehead, then sauntered leisurely from the room. Confident that no one could hear her slippered feet in the entryway, she picked up speed and sprinted toward the stairs. Seconds later, the door of her bedroom opened and closed.

By the time Paula reached her bed, she had tossed every envelope but one to the floor. "Okay, BigHugs, let's see what you've got," she murmured as her fingernails slipped efficiently beneath the envelope's flap. Carefully removing the letter, she unfolded it and pressed the sheet flat against her lap, then raised it so she could see the typing clearly. "It's probably nothing, but I might as well—"

Her eyes stopped partway down the single page. A name, a date, an address, another name, another address, then another. It was all there, printed out in self-assured black letters that looked like rows of little soldiers lined up to salute an inescapable truth. And suddenly it made perfect, heart-stopping sense. "Oboy . . . I never dreamed it might turn out like this," Paula breathed. "Never in a million years. These kinds of things don't happen to real people, do they?" And what would Ted make of it? How would he handle the news? Only one thing was clear at this point: he had to know. Right away. This would make a difference in their lives, no doubt about it. Maybe a big difference. "I'll tell him tonight," she vowed, feeling a little shiver of anticipation despite her uncertainty about what his reaction might be. She blew out a long, thin stream of air and relaxed against her pillows. "Teddy, my boy, this is going to knock your socks off."

"Wow, that was incredible stroganoff," Ted sighed as he pushed one remaining noodle across his plate and into a small pool of rich brown gravy. "Maybe we should have saved some for Millie; she made it, after all." His voice held no trace of guilt as he scoured the serving platter for any leftover morsels.

"I'm sure she'll survive," Paula replied. "She and Caroline Wintersweet went out to eat tonight—and knowing Caroline's penchant for fine dining, they're probably nibbling hors d'oeuvres at the uppitiest place in town." She smiled as she pictured the elegant and eccentric but endlessly good-hearted widow, an elderly woman in the ward whom she and Meg O'Brien had grown to love and admire. They had been her visiting teachers for almost three years now, and she never failed to delight and entertain them with her grand stories of days gone by.

"It couldn't be any nicer than this," he said, gesturing toward their surroundings. Knowing this would be a special occasion, Paula had added her own touches to Millie's flavorful meal—a lovely cream-colored linen tablecloth with matching napkins in teakwood rings, fresh white and peach roses floating in a small glass bowl, swirled burgundy tapers in brass candlesticks, and crystal wine goblets filled with—what else?—sparkling grape juice.

"Well, maybe—with one possible exception," she observed, her eyes twinkling as she inclined her head toward the breakfast bar, where a baby monitor stood like a tiny sentinel, occasionally emitting a brief pulse of static. "But it's a rather homey touch, don't you think?"

"I think," he said, reaching across the table to take her hand, "it's been a perfect evening. Great food, wonderful company, a peacefully sleeping baby, and—"

"And the night has only just begun," Paula interjected.

"Oh?" He considered her statement for a long moment. "Do you want to go to a movie or something? We could get one of the girls in the ward to baby-sit, and—"

"I don't think so." Paula's voice was firm. "We need to talk, Ted."

He leaned back and blew out a small puff of air. "Uh-oh—a *conversation,"* he said in resigned tones. "I don't suppose it's something we can talk about and eat ice cream at the same time, is it?"

"I'd rather talk first," she said. "Let's go into the living room. There's something I need to show you."

"All righty," he said cheerfully, then followed her across the entryway. On their way to the sofa, she retrieved something from a nearby end table.

When they were comfortably settled, he leaned over to kiss her lightly on the cheek. "So let's get to it," he said.

Paula hesitated for a moment, then held up one of two white envelopes. "Okay." She gulped audibly. "Here goes."

Ted took the envelope and gazed at it impassively. "BigHugs? Catchy name—what is it, a computer dating service or something?" He smirked endearingly and tugged on her earlobe. "I'd say we're way past that, wouldn't you?" When she didn't return either his smile or his banter, he took notice and sat up straight. "Is this something important—you know, something like always remembering to wear clean underwear in case I get in an accident? My mother already told me that, thank you very much."

"My point exactly," Paula said evenly.

He stared at her without comprehension, finally rubbing his forehead. "And that point would be . . ."

"BigHugs is a group of professional researchers, Ted." Paula's eyes were riveted on his face, his eyes, his jawline showing an end-of-day stubble. "They specialize in finding lost people." His expression was still vacant. "Family members."

She saw the muscles in his jaw tense as he considered this new information. When he spoke, it was in a low, intense voice. "As in . . . *family?*"

"That's right," she said, anxious now to share the news. "Meg told me about them a couple of months ago, when I mentioned that you might be interested in locating your mother. So I gave them a call, and they said they'd see what they could do. It's taken a while, but I got this"—she nodded toward the envelope in his hand—"in the mail today." She took in a breath and exhaled slowly.

"Well, . . . well." Ted turned the envelope over and over in his hands, studying its exterior from every angle, running his finger along its edges, tentatively lifting its open flap and closing it again. Finally, he glanced up at her like he was getting ready to make a dash across the interstate. "I suppose you know what it says."

"Yes, I do," she confirmed gently. "The information is a bit . . . unusual, but it's something you need to know. I think you'll find it interesting." *To say the least,* she added silently, her heart thudding against her ribs.

He chuckled nervously. "Hey, with an introduction like that, how can I resist?" Giving her a stoic smile and a feeble thumbs-up sign, he lifted the envelope's loose flap, pulled out the single sheet inside, and unfolded it carefully.

Three minutes passed, then five, then a few more as he studied the words on the page, moving his finger down the lines of type, desperate to make sense of the names and numbers. When his finger paused on a line near the bottom, Paula picked up the second white envelope and skillfully nudged it into his hand. One look at its upper lefthand corner and a quick glance inside told him what he needed to know.

A bemused smile hovered at the corners of Ted's mouth as he turned to Paula. "Well, well, well," he said, slowly taking one of her hands into both of his, "who would ever have imagined this?" He glanced down at the calendar on his watch, then back at her. "If what I've just seen is what I think it is, then exactly one week from today, your son will be marrying my sister."

Chapter 14

They sat huddled together on the sofa for the next hour, poring minutely over the BigHugs report. "There's no way it could be wrong," Ted murmured. "But it's just so bizarre."

"Read it again," Paula suggested.

"Okay." He repeated the information line by line, beginning at the top.

"'Alma Lenore Dunford.' They have her correct birthdate. 'Born in Athens, Georgia. Married Jeffery Terrence Barstow in Salt Lake City, Utah. Children: Theodore,' that would be yours truly, 'James, Michelle, Troy. Divorced.'"

He paused before continuing. "'Moved to Spring City, Nevada. Married Franklin D. Taggart. Moved to Decatur, Illinois. Children: Kelsey Lenore, David Franklin. Husband deceased.'"

Ted cleared his throat before reading the last line. "'Current Address: 257 Rocklin Avenue, Oak Brook, Illinois.'"

"The same address as the one on Mark and Kelsey's wedding invitation," Paula added, picking up the second white envelope for another look. She pulled out the engraved announcement. "Same names, too—'Kelsey Lenore Taggart, daughter of Mrs. Franklin D. Taggart,' etc., etc."

"How old did you say Kelsey was?" he asked.

"Almost twenty."

"Then she would have been born about two years after I left. My half-sister." Ted ran the fingers of one hand through his short blonde hair. "So," he said after a long pause, "let me get this straight. That strange, angry, disagreeable, embittered old woman, who at this moment is stewing in her own juices back in Illinois because of her daughter's upcoming temple marriage, is in fact my own mother. *My mother.*"

"Kind of looks that way," Paula said, her voice tinged with gentleness.

He chuckled derisively. "Sort of brings new meaning to that cheery little Disney tune, doesn't it? 'It's a small world, after all.'" A low moan rose from deep in his chest.

They sat in silence until the last silver threads of sunlight had disappeared from the room, leaving them suspended in a blue-gray twilight. "What happens now?" Paula whispered against his shoulder. When he didn't respond, she ventured another comment. "I feel like something horrible has happened here, and it's all my fault." She shivered as a formless chill seemed to creep over her body. "If I hadn't been so anxious to find her, we—"

"We could have had the amazing warm-fuzzy experience of just running into her at the wedding luncheon, out of the blue, with no warning. Can you even imagine?" Now it was Ted's turn to shiver. "No, I'd say you have just saved us from . . . from whatever happens when long-lost relatives bump into each other's lives like ships in the night. I'm quite sure it wouldn't have been pretty—especially with one of them being a grumpy old lady who never had any intention of being found. At least now I'll have a few days to psych myself up for it."

Paula sighed with relief. "Do you think we should tell any of them about this before the wedding?" she asked, perfectly willing to go along with whatever he suggested. "I'm not sure how Alma might react, especially given her apparent distaste for all things Mormon, not to mention all things Barstow. But on a brighter note, Kelsey might be interested to know that she has an exceptionally handsome, accomplished, and thoroughly charming half-brother who just happens to be married to her fiancé's birth mother, and—"

"Whoa, you almost lost me there!" Ted laughed. "I think I've had just about all the family history I can take for one evening." His tone was lighthearted, but Paula sensed an undercurrent of confusion. Even fear.

"You're absolutely right," she soothed. "We don't have to make any decisions tonight—or even tomorrow, for that matter. Let's sleep on it, pray about it, try to figure out what would be best for everyone concerned." She snuggled close to him and laid her head on his chest, where she could feel the strong, steady pumping of his heart. "I have perfect confidence in your ability to handle this."

He snorted softly. "Easy for you to say . . . it's not *your* mother who's out there impersonating the wicked witch of the West."

"No, *my* mother is out there impersonating a crazy lady."

"Same difference," Ted observed. "Except that yours knows who and where you are."

"Most days," Paula clarified with a pensive sigh. After a moment, she went on. "At least we've found Alma. I suppose that's some kind of a beginning."

"Yeah," he agreed. "And now we're on track not only for a wedding, but for an impromptu family reunion as well. Two for the price of one." He stroked her hair in the rapidly fading light. "I just hope there won't be any dangerous ice sculptures or sharp pieces of cutlery involved."

It was Sunday evening before they spoke about the matter again, although Paula could tell by the vulnerable, distracted look in Ted's eyes that he had been thinking of nothing else. When he refused food or drink from Saturday morning until after church the next day, in addition to spending a few hours away from home on Saturday afternoon with his cell phone turned off, she knew he was fasting and supplicating a higher power for guidance. It was heart-wrenching to see him agonize over this new and unnerving development in their lives, and she silently prayed he would receive the help he needed. She had her own opinions about what should happen, but Alma Barstow Taggart was his mother, and this was his decision to make.

They were getting ready for bed after a busy Sabbath, during which they had hardly seen each other, and Ted was unusually quiet. Paula was more than a little curious as she watched him meticulously pull on a pair of crisp blue-and-white-striped cotton pajamas, brush his teeth, and hang his clothes for the next morning on the back of the closet door, all in unbroken silence. Then he knelt by the bed and bowed his head for a long while. "Are you all right, sweetheart?" she finally asked as he whispered "amen," sat on the edge of the bed, and began to pull off his socks. "I know you've had a lot on your mind."

He looked up as though seeing her for the first time, but his blue eyes quickly found hers and he smiled—a little wearily, she thought, but with a certain determination she hadn't seen earlier in the day. "I'm all right," he said. "In fact, I think I'm good."

I *know* you're good," she smiled back at him. "Good at everything you do. Does this mean you've sorted things out about your mom?"

"I believe I have," he replied, sliding beneath the covers and relaxing against his pillow. "And I hope you'll go along with me on this."

Paula brushed her fingers across his cheek. "You know I'll do anything I can to help." She looked at him expectantly.

"Then here's the plan," he said. "Please feel free to jump in and tell me I'm out of line if it sounds too crazy."

"You know me—open mouth, insert Nike," she chuckled. "I'm listening."

"Okay." He turned to face her and leaned up on one elbow. "First of all, I'd prefer that no one knew about this, at least until after the wedding." She nodded her compliance. "Now, do we know where Alma will be during the temple ceremony?"

"I think so," Paula said. "Last week, Mark told me that he and Kelsey, as well as other members of the wedding party, will be going through a morning endowment session. I told him that you and I would like to join them. The sealing's scheduled for eleven, so we'll meet at the temple around eight. Kelsey's mother is just going to stay at home; Mark was quite sure she wouldn't go to the wedding luncheon, and she might not even show up at the reception that evening. I guess hostile emotions are running pretty high at the moment."

"Thank you for sharing that," he said, smiling grimly. "But back to the plan. When we arrive in Chicago on Thursday night, we'll rent separate cars and meet at our hotel. The next morning you'll go to the temple session as planned; if anyone asks, tell them I had a previous appointment, but I'll be there for the sealing." He paused and looked at her resolutely. "I'd like to use that time to go visit my mother."

His words seemed to catch Paula by surprise, and she pressed a hand over her heart. "Are you sure?" she asked quietly.

Ted nodded. "Sure? Yes. Sure of myself? Not really. But it's the only thing to do. Believe me, I've spent a lot of hours trying to figure out how to avoid the whole thing. But, as it turns out, the Lord has other plans. He *wants* me to do it; He couldn't have made it clearer if He'd hit me over the head with a two-by-four—no, make that a sledge hammer. There are no guarantees, of course; there's a good chance she might toss me out on my ear." He grasped her shoulder and squeezed it gently. "But whether it turns out to be a miracle or mayhem, I need to see her, make some kind of a connection, find out whatever I can about her life, tell her a little about mine. Maybe even share my testimony with her, if she'll listen. If not, then at least I'll have done my part. The rest is up to Someone else." He leaned back against his pillow and rubbed his eyes. "Darn hard way to start off a wedding day, though."

Paula reached for one of his hands and kissed it tenderly. "It'll all work out," she whispered. "I know it will. It'll be a glorious day."

"Uh-huh," he groaned. "Just remember—if I don't make it to the temple in time for the wedding, you can send someone with a spatula out later to scrape me off the pavement."

"I'll keep that in mind," she giggled.

* * * * * * * *

Chicago in the summer was almost as smoggy as Los Angeles. At least it looked that way as Ted gazed out the side window of their fourteenth-floor hotel suite. He could barely see the street below, and from his vantage point the tops of several trees lining a spacious park on one side of the hotel resembled large broccoli florets suspended in a yellowish, viscous steam. *If my mother doesn't kill me, the air probably will,* he thought miserably as he straightened a blue-gray tie beneath the neat collar of his navy-and-white-striped oxford shirt. Despite the cool temperature of the air-conditioned room, he felt a few beads of perspiration trickle down his back.

"All ready?" Paula said behind him. Her voice sounded altogether too cheerful. "You didn't eat much breakfast, sweetie."

He glanced toward the room service cart, where one of the two plates sat virtually untouched. "Not so much to lose later," he replied grimly.

"You're that nervous, are you?" she asked. "You seemed okay on the plane, and even through most of the night. But then when you started pacing at four A.M., I figured something was up."

"Sorry if I kept you awake," he said absently. "I guess it isn't every day a guy knocks on his mother's door after not seeing her for two decades."

She brushed a small piece of lint from the sleeve of his dark-blue suit, thinking how utterly adorable he looked. Any woman in her right mind would be thrilled to find such a son standing on her front porch. The operative term here, of course, was "right mind . . ." Paula felt a knot of turbulence forming in her own stomach at the thought. Mentally pushing it aside, she reached up to massage the tops of his shoulders. "Do you think you can find her place?"

"I'm afraid so," he sighed. "The map makes it look pretty easy; it should take me less than half an hour to get there. I'll leave around nine-thirty." He glanced at his watch and shrugged off her hands. "You'd better get a move-on yourself, or you'll be late. Give the bride and groom my best, and I'll see you at the sealing ceremony." He smiled down at her.

"That's the spirit," she grinned, giving him a playful punch on the jaw. Then she kissed him warmly and hugged him close, as though to infuse him with an extra portion of courage. "You'll be wonderful," she declared, pulling back to wipe a trace of lipstick from the corner of his mouth. "The angels will be with you."

"They were with Daniel in the lions' den, too," Ted joked nervously. "Just the same, I'll bet he wasn't an awfully happy camper when they first opened those doors and shoved him through." He gulped audibly.

"Well, it all turned out," she smiled. "The kitties didn't even get a little taste."

"What a deal," he murmured, straightening his tie again.

Paula opened the door. "I love you," she said with a final kiss. Then she was gone.

Rocklin Avenue was part of a nondescript neighborhood in Oak Brook, a middle-class suburb of Chicago. Its small, older stucco tract houses were built close together, but most were neatly landscaped and painted in soft tones of beige or yellow or green. A few minutes after ten on a hot, muggy summer morning, the street was just beginning to come to life with a scattering of youngsters on scooters or rollerblades, an elderly gentleman mowing his lawn, and a workman tinkering with a small satellite dish in the corner of one yard. A rather peaceful setting, Ted mused as he steered his rented white Ford Mustang toward the end of one block.

He had no trouble locating number 257, its wide black metal lettering hung diagonally beside the heavy screen door. The house itself, painted a pasty turquoise color, was similar to all the others, except that it had a small front porch, shaded by overhanging wooden eaves that drooped like tired arms over a tiny two-person swing at one end. A green metal chair sat primly next to the swing, giving the porch a slightly congested appearance. Out on the lawn, a small imitation wood wishing well sat balanced beside a pile of smooth, oval-shaped rocks, and off to one side of the yard sat a single well-tended rose bush, teeming with the most glorious yellow blossoms Ted had ever seen. Seeing the bush, he couldn't restrain his mind from leapfrogging back to his childhood in West Jordan, Utah. There had always been a rose bush in the front yard. With roses so big and so yellow that they almost didn't seem real. The memory brought an instant lump—was it of fear or longing?—to his throat. "This must be . . . the right place, as a famous man once said," he murmured.

He swallowed hard as he opened the car door and stepped out into the blistering, oppressive air. The short walk to the porch made his lungs burn and his throat constrict, and he half wished the well in the yard had real water in it. *Good thing it doesn't,* he told himself as he trudged up the three front steps and paused in front of the door. *I'd be tempted to jump in and never look back.* He straightened his tie and considered his reflection in one of the screen's glass panels. *If you looked any more scared, Barstow, your eyes would pop out of your head like two giant blue ping-pong balls.* He set his jaw firmly, took a deep breath, and pressed his thumb against the round, tin-framed black doorbell. The sound it emitted was halfway between a loud buzz and an obnoxious grinding noise. *No chance of escape now; anyone could hear that thing a mile away.* Seeing a movement on the periphery of his vision, he turned to see a large, potbellied yellow cat scurry under the porch swing. *The lion's den,* he thought with a little smirk.

If there was someone home, they weren't in any hurry to open up. A minute later Ted rang again, feeling beads of sweat trickle down the back of his neck. Then, on a sudden impulse of terror, he decided he'd had enough and turned his back to the door. Only a few steps and he'd be away from here, blessedly out of the war zone, on his way back to—

"Awright already!" a voice screeched behind him as the main door scraped open. The tone was high enough to be a woman's, but gruff enough to be a man's. "If you're selling something, I definitely don't want it. That's right, mister, just keep on moving."

Now he recognized the voice, and it spun him around like a powerful magnetic force. He couldn't see the woman clearly behind the glass-and-screen door, but he straightened his shoulders and stared hard at a place where he thought her face might be. "Alma Barstow?" he asked, surprising himself at the firmness of his tone. Too late, he remembered that her name was no longer Alma Barstow.

Her dimly outlined figure moved back a pace as she seemed to catch her breath. "Maybe, maybe not," she barked, "but it's certainly none of your business. Who are you, anyway? The sun is right in my eyes, and I can't see through this . . ." She pushed open the screen door a crack and shaded her eyes with one hand, then looked up at him. "There, now at least I can tell who I'm—" Her words suddenly broke off as her gaze traveled slowly, meticulously from his polished navy wingtips to his broad shoulders, quickly up to his short blonde hair, and back down to his face. Then their eyes met, both pairs bright blue and wide with astonishment. The syllables fell from her barely moving lips like gold-plated question marks. "Ted . . . Teddy Barstow, is that you?"

A smile would be appropriate at this point, he reminded himself. *Anything to ease the tension.* "One and the same," he grinned, again surprised, this time by the genuine warmth in his voice. "How are you doing, Mom? May I . . ." There was a tiny gasp behind the screen, followed by a solid thud as a body hit the floor.

". . . come in? Why, thanks, I'd love to." He yanked the screen open wide, stepped across the form lying just inside the doorway, and quickly knelt beside it. His mother was moaning softly, her eyelids fluttering like hummingbird wings as he clasped one of her hands in both of his. "Just take it easy for a minute now," he soothed. "No use getting up until you're ready." He stared down at her colorless features. "Are you okay?"

A sardonic grin barely curled one corner of her mouth, and her voice was paper-thin. "Stupid question."

"I reckon it was," Ted admitted. They lapsed into silence for a minute or two, then she tried to sit up. He carefully helped her to her feet, then guided her to a recliner across from the living room's small picture window. She slumped into the chair and closed her eyes while Ted took a seat on the nearby floral-upholstered couch.

While he waited for her to move or say something, he surveyed the room. It was short and narrow, carpeted in a dark-beige berber and sparsely furnished with the couch and recliner, an end table supporting a miniature grandfather clock built into the base of a metallic lamp, and an older-model television squeezed into one corner of the room. A gold-framed landscape painting hung above the couch. There was no other ornamentation, except for a small wood-framed photograph perched on the TV, showing two blonde teenagers, a boy and a girl, grinning at the entrance of some kind of amusement park. A window-mounted air-conditioning unit pumped a thin stream of tepid air into the space. If Ted remembered correctly, this room reminded him a little of his family's home in West Jordan—not much in the way of luxury, but clean and serviceable. Not a speck of dust on the furniture or a smudge on any of the windows. That was one thing about his mother: any doctor could have performed surgery on her kitchen table and not found a germ within twenty miles. After Ted's father moved out she didn't seem to care quite so much, but she was always tidy. Except for that one day when, right in the middle of their queen-sized bed, she had inexplicably smeared catsup, mustard, and motor oil all over a shirt he'd left behind . . .

A deep sigh drew Ted's attention to the recliner, where Alma was . . . well, reclining. "Can I get you anything?" he whispered. "A glass of water, or . . ." Her eyes remained closed and she didn't respond. He took the moment to study her features—the face and form of a woman, now much older and worn-looking, who had brought him into the world, but who had been lost to him for over half his life. *And whose fault is that, anyhow?* He winced at the thought, recalling how two weeks after his eighteenth birthday he had crept silently out of the house in the middle of the night, thumbed his nose at her bedroom window, and never looked back. Now, perhaps, it was payback time. *On the other hand, she never tried to find me, either.*

His eyes moved from her thinning gray-blonde hair, puffy eyes, and leathery cheeks down to her round, thick-waisted body, clad in a dun-colored polyester blouse and brown slacks, and finally to her ankles, which were surprisingly slim and youthful-looking. *Her legs and ankles were always her best features. Still are,* he thought. Her narrow feet were encircled by open-toed sandals, and he smiled a little when he noticed that her toenails had recently been painted a bright coral color.

"If I'd known you were coming, I would've painted them blue. That's still your favorite color, isn't it?" The voice sounded hollow and parched, as though it had just been disinterred from a mausoleum. When Ted lifted his gaze to meet Alma's, he saw a hard, steely glint in her eyes.

He quickly glanced down at his navy shoes and socks, navy suit, blue-gray tie, blue-and-white shirt. "How could you tell?" he joked, flashing her a tiny self-conscious grin.

"Why are you here?" Her question was not an idle pleasantry, and the icy edge to her voice sent a chill rippling down his spine despite the room's oppressive warmth.

So much for the prodigal son's welcome return. "I—I'm in town on some . . . personal business," he stammered. "I thought it might be nice if I, uh, dropped by."

"How did you find me?" Her tone sounded like fingernails being scraped down a chalkboard. Slowly, without mercy.

"Well, my wife, Paula—you'd like her, she's very nice—heard about this company that finds people, and she knew I hadn't seen you for a long time, so she got in touch with them, and what do you know? They—"

"Stuck their nose in somebody's else's affairs. You and your snoopy wife." This was not going well. "What kind of personal business? I'm sure Chicago is a long way from wherever you live." She glared at him.

Ted shrugged, willing himself to be courteous. "A wedding, actually. Paula's son is getting married, and we wanted to be here for it."

"A fine day for weddings." Alma spat out the words as if she had just tasted rotten eggs.

Suddenly, in a rush of painful understanding, Ted knew it was over—knew he couldn't ignore the reality any longer. It was true; his mother was a bitter, disagreeable old woman, with hardly a passing interest in life and no inclination toward common civility. He had found her; but at this moment, he wanted nothing more than to lose her again. Why had he even come here in the first place? Life was too short to spend it in the company of nasty people. He would explain the circumstances of his visit, but then he'd walk right through that door, out of her life. And this time he would never, ever be back. Never let himself be hurt like this again.

A sarcastic comment rose to his tongue, but he bit it back and forced his lips into a reserved smile. "It certainly is a fine day for weddings," he said with as much warmth as he could muster. "Especially temple weddings."

Her eyes bored into his for an instant, then she tittered derisively. "You—and a temple wedding?" She laughed again, and he hated the jeering sound. "I thought you were about as far away from something like that as a person could get. Your father was such a fine, upstanding example of Mormonism at its best, after all. That's what a temple marriage got me—a no-good philanderer who didn't care one whit if he destroyed his whole family." She snorted bitterly. "I assumed you'd followed in his footsteps."

"People change, Mom," Ted replied without visibly reacting to her insinuations. "I wasn't active in the Church until a few years ago, when Paula—well, it's a long story. But the bottom line is that her oldest son is getting married here, in the Chicago Temple, the House of the Lord, this very morning." He paused and looked directly into her glacial blue eyes. Had they always been so cold? "And he's marrying your daughter."

Alma stared at him blankly for several seconds. When the realization dawned, she leaned back against the pillowed headrest of the recliner, shot him a haughty look, and began clapping her hands slowly, mockingly. "Well, then, I guess congratulations are in order," she said, her voice dripping with contempt. "Mark Richland gets what he wants—a cute little Mormon trophy wife who *thinks* a few vows spoken over an altar will guarantee her eternal happiness. And Kelsey gets what she wants—a card-carrying returned missionary who *thinks* he's going to save the world with that awesome priesthood power of his. Not to mention his good looks. A match made in heaven, I'd say."

Ted felt blood rise to his cheeks, but kept his voice even. "It's not like that, and you know it."

"Oh I do, do I?" Resentment oozed from her eyes. "Then look back into your own history and tell me how wonderfully it turned out for the Barstow family. *I* was one of those starry-eyed young girls, remember. We did everything right—and it all went wrong. After your father left, I had a devil of a time raising four kids and keeping body and soul together."

"That I remember," Ted murmured. "If you'd asked, the Church would have helped."

She shook her head sharply. "I'd already groveled enough, begging Jeffery to stay. When that didn't work, I took matters into my own hands. Eventually, after the kids were mostly grown, I had my name taken off the Church records, and I moved around until those home-teacher people didn't come looking for me anymore. By the time I remarried and Kelsey and David came along, no one knew I'd ever had a connection with the Mormons, and that was just fine with me. I was trying to protect them, you understand—didn't want them to get all caught up in religion like I had. I knew they'd only get hurt." She rolled her eyes disparagingly. "Then along came miss goody-goody Mormon harp teacher, and I knew Kelsey didn't stand a chance. She lapped it all up, then convinced her brother to go along with it. David even wants to go on a *mission,* for goodness' sake. Waste of time."

"A mission is a good thing," Ted interjected quietly. "I wish I'd gone on one."

Alma's harsh laugh dealt another blow. "You! You didn't care anything about the Church—or your family, for that matter. You couldn't wait to get out of Utah, and I doubt if a mission ever crossed your mind. There would have been too much *structure* to it, not to mention bleeding your heart out on thousands of people's doorsteps. Why, knowing you, I'd say that even if you'd gone, you wouldn't have lasted a—"

"You don't know me! You don't know *anything* about me!" Ted hissed, coming to his feet as a wave of fury engulfed him. He had had enough. Clenching both fists at his sides, he approached the recliner. Alma saw his dark expression and clamped her mouth shut abruptly. For a few interminable moments, the air pulsed with rancorous silence.

Ted stuffed his hands deep into his pockets, dug one knee into the side of the chair, and glared down at his mother, fighting an impulse to grab her fleshy shoulders and shake her senseless. *Remember who you are, what you represent,* he warned himself. *Don't make it any worse. You lose control and nobody wins.* When his anger only escalated, he turned to the last resort. *Father, help me. Please.*

He took a deep breath and spoke, hardly trusting his own voice, barely hearing it above the pounding of his heart. "I came here today," he began in low, steady tones, "because I thought we might be able to make a connection—something that would bring us back together after all these years. Catching up, remembering some of the good times, Kelsey's wedding, the gospel . . . I had great hopes that somehow we'd at least end up on the same page, and we could go on from there. Put everything else behind us and start building a relationship. Better late than never, I reasoned. Life would go on, and it would be wonderful." He paused, and the muscles in his jaw tightened. "Clearly, I was mistaken."

Alma shifted uncomfortably in the recliner and moved her gaze to the window.

"But you know what?" he continued. "There was one thing I *wasn't* mistaken about. Life *does* go on. The thing is, whether it's wonderful or not depends on how one goes about living it. Happiness is a *choice,* Mom. Everybody has garbage in their lives; the key is knowing when to bag it up and take it out to the curb. Otherwise, it just piles up and makes a big mess out of everything, don't you think?" He looked at her intently, but her eyes seemed to be riveted on a small crack at one corner of the window.

Ted thought he felt a gentle nudge at his back, and before he knew it he was kneeling beside the recliner, his hands resting a few inches from his mother's arm, his heart inexplicably swelling to fill his chest. "I know it hasn't been easy," he heard himself say in a firm but gentler tone. "No one ever expects to lose a husband the way you did—to another woman, and after a temple marriage, too."

"But that's exactly what happened, isn't it?" Alma's voice vibrated with bitterness as she continued to stare out the window.

"Yes, it is," he agreed. "And no one can possibly calculate how much our family has suffered because of it. But don't you see?" He leaned closer. "The Church wasn't to blame for what happened; it was human error, pure and simple. You've spent your whole life condemning the very thing that could have healed you, made you whole. It could have gotten rid of all the garbage. The gospel could have"—his voice caught—"could have made it *not hurt anymore,* Mom."

She slowly turned her head to look at him, her cool glance taking in the custom cut of his suit, his diamond-studded wedding band, the expensive platinum watch on his wrist. "And what would you know about hurting?"

"More than you think," he replied, grateful that at least she was listening. "In fact, I did more than my share of it for nearly twenty years, including two failed marriages and buckets of hatred and resentment toward Dad, the Church, and even you. Nothing made any sense, because I was so *angry*. Then someone I cared about very much lost her son in a terrible accident. The pain nearly destroyed her; but over time I saw the Lord's hand in her life, watched her embrace the gospel, even envied the new peace I saw in her eyes. Gradually, I began to understand how the healing comes. It's invited; you have to get down on your knees and ask for it, plead for it, open your heart to it. I know firsthand how it works . . . I've done it . . . and that dear friend showed me the way. To my everlasting blessing, she is now my wife."

"Happily ever after," Alma remarked snidely.

Ted ignored her comment, feeling the warmth of his emotions begin to intensify. "And speaking of hurting, if you can't admit to your own pain, at least you have to know that at this very moment, a beautiful young woman who loves the gospel, and loves you more than anything, is trying to come to terms with being alone on the most important day of her life. She's marrying the man she loves, but her own mother won't be there to share this most joyous occasion. Talk about a world of hurt." He touched Alma's arm lightly. "And I suspect that Kelsey isn't the only one who's feeling it."

The woman jerked her arm away as if she had been burned, then wriggled as far to the other side of the recliner as she could and turned her head toward one of the empty, colorless walls leading to a short hallway.

Ted closed his eyes for a moment, expecting a rush of indignation at her affront. Instead, the words of a scripture, recently discussed in Sunday School class, flowed through his consciousness: "*. . . showing forth afterwards an increase of love.*" Accompanying it was an outpouring of warmth and tenderness that took him by surprise. He decided to go with the feeling.

"I didn't come here to start an argument or to make you angry," he said gently, "although I seem to have done a pretty good job of that, and I'm sorry. I just . . . I just wanted to see you again, to share with you what I've learned about being happy. It *is* possible, you know, if you just let Heavenly Father take care of you. And He will . . . I know that. You just have to ask. It took me most of a lifetime to figure it out, but once I did, it's been a night-and-day difference. It's never too late, no matter how much or what kind of garbage somebody's piled up. The gospel has worked in my life, and it can work in anyone's. I know it's true. That's all."

Ted waited patiently for her response, clenching his teeth against the tears that threatened to overflow onto his cheeks. Alma didn't move a muscle, didn't make a sound.

"And one more thing," he finally said, again yielding to a power beyond his own. "I love you, Mom. I love you."

It could have been half a minute or half an hour. The silence was so profound that it seemed to smother time, stop it in its tracks. Alma was still facing the wall, her eyes closed, when her lips began to move. "You'd better go now," she murmured in a toneless voice. "You'll miss the wedding."

An overwhelming sadness flooded Ted's heart as he rose, glanced at the miniature grandfather clock across the room, and looked down at his mother one last time. "I already have," he said quietly. "And so have you, Mom. So have you."

The clock chimed eleven as he opened the door and stepped out into the blazing August sunlight, then closed the screen soundlessly behind him.

Chapter 15

Paula glanced around the sealing room—the largest one in the Chicago Temple, she had been told, and they'd still had to bring in extra seating. She saw Sam Richland at one end of the room, sitting with his son Alex, waiting to witness the ordinance, and gave him a little wave in greeting. He smiled warmly, but she could see the deep melancholy in his eyes, and instantly she perceived his thoughts. If only his beloved wife, Karti, had lived to see this day, had been here to clasp his hand, to whisper loving words into his ear as they watched their eldest son kneel at the altar across from his bride. *Of course she's with us in spirit; nothing could keep her away,* Paula mused silently, thinking of the joy undoubtedly brimming in her dear friend's luminous eyes at this very moment. *Still, it isn't quite the same as if she were here. You can't reach out and hug a spirit.*

A worrisome thought tugged at her mind. *And speaking of the dearly departed . . . where in the world is Ted?* She had saved a seat for him as long as she could, but now, with the ceremony about to begin, she had no choice but to motion another guest into the empty chair beside her. As the doors of the sealing room closed, her heart sank. Had something gone wrong? Was he stranded somewhere with a flat tire—or worse, had there been an accident?

Don't be ridiculous! she chided herself, refocusing on a more heartening scenario. *It just took a little longer than expected with Alma, that's all. Of course he won her over; they're probably sitting together on her living room couch right now, oblivious to the time, sipping lemonade and catching up on each other's lives, laughing and reminiscing and wondering why they hadn't done this years ago. No one can resist the Ted*

Barstow charm—and once he pulls out his wallet full of Lexi pictures, she'll be a goner. Why, it wouldn't even surprise me if he sweet-talks her into coming to the luncheon, or the reception. Or both. It'll be the perfect ending to a perfect day. The prospect cheered her heart, and she watched the sealing ceremony with new relish. Had there ever been a more beautiful bride, or a more handsome groom? Or so many people, their faces shining with love, who had come to share their joy? She could hardly wait to regale Ted with every detail of this exquisite occasion. *And it'll all be that much sweeter now that Alma has come to her senses,* she reasoned.

"So, where's this mystery husband of yours?" Kelsey asked as they were sitting down to lunch with twenty other guests in a private dining room at Applebee's restaurant. The bride had changed into a deep-blue silk pantsuit that seemed to set off sparks of radiance in her striking blue eyes and lustrous shoulder-length blonde hair.

"I'm not quite sure," Paula said lightly, "but I know he'll be here as soon as he can. I should have kept him on his leash." Everyone laughed, and she relaxed a little as the conversation turned to other things. Chatting with Kelsey, she quickly understood why Mark had fallen so completely in love with her. Though she was not yet twenty, there was a substance and maturity about this young woman that drew others to her and put them instantly at ease. She was bright, witty, compassionate, and, even while being at the center of attention on this grand occasion, she seemed to go out of her way to touch a hand here, hug a child there, and do everything she could to make this day enjoyable for her guests. Paula sensed that Kelsey's difficult upbringing had not embittered her, but instead had made her more loving and responsive to people of all kinds, and to life in general. No wonder Mark adored her.

As one hour stretched into two, and finally dessert was cleared away and the rounds of toasts concluded, a knot of worry formed in Paula's stomach that couldn't be ignored. Excusing herself from the table, she leaned over to whisper in Mark's ear. "I've got to go find Ted," she explained. "I gave him directions to the restaurant, but I swear sometimes he can't find his way out of a paper bag. And he'll never ask for help—it's a guy thing, I guess. We'll see you at the reception, okay?"

Mark grabbed her hand and kissed it warmly, then looked up at her, his chocolate-brown eyes reflecting more happiness than she had ever seen in one man's face. "Sure thing," he said with an affectionate grin. "Seven sharp. Don't be late."

"I'll drive," she smiled. Kissing him quickly on the cheek, she turned and hurried from the room.

It took Paula twenty minutes to reach the hotel, another five to take the elevator to the fourteenth floor and make her way down the long corridor to their suite. Once there, she inserted the key card into its slot, rotated the steel handle downward, and pushed the door open. Willing her feet to move forward, she ventured into total darkness. Even the drapes were pulled tightly shut against the glaring afternoon sun.

"Ted?" she called out tentatively, trying to adjust her eyes to the blackness around her.

No answer.

"Ted, honey, are you here?" she repeated, this time a bit louder.

Still no answer.

Paula's hand moved to a switch near the door. She flipped it up, and a dim light came on above her head, barely illuminating the spacious sitting room before her. No sign of anyone there. The door to their adjoining bedroom was closed. Tossing her purse onto one of two large overstuffed chairs near the window, she opened the heavy brocade curtains and sighed with relief. Everything looked so much better in the light of day.

Then she noticed Ted's keys on a small lamp table near the television.

"That's good; he's here," she assured herself firmly. "You can calm down now." Apparently her stomach did not hear the comment, as it remained tightly lodged near her throat. Her hand trembled ever so slightly as she reached for the heavy brass knob on the bedroom door. Turning it, she pushed cautiously into the room. It was dark and oppressively warm.

A thin stream of light from the sitting room showed her what she was looking for. Someone was lying on the king-sized bed—no, *in* the bed, completely covered by the heavy mauve-colored comforter. There was no hint of breath or motion.

"Ted?" she whispered warily. "Is that you, sweetheart?" When there was no answer, she moved closer to the bed and raised her voice a little. "Ted, you're scaring me. Are you all right?" Silence reigned. Finally, she lowered herself carefully to the bed until she was sitting beside the covered figure, then she reached out and touched what she thought might be a shoulder. She felt a tiny ripple of movement beneath the comforter. Switching on a small bedside lamp, she leaned close to the still form and spoke again. "Ted, it's me, Paula. Is something wrong? Are you ill? Do we need to call a doctor, or—"

"No," a muffled voice rasped from beneath the comforter. "Don't. Please, just . . ." A hand snaked out and grasped her wrist. It was ice cold.

"Good grief!" Paula exclaimed. "It's a hundred degrees outside, the room's air-conditioning is turned off, and you're freezing. What in the world is going on?" She curled her fingers around the top edge of the comforter and pulled it down in a single no-nonsense movement. "There," she said, seeing the top of his head appear, then the side of his face, then his torso. "Now, please tell me what—" Her words evaporated when he turned his face toward her and opened his eyes. "Oboy," she murmured after several seconds. "This can't be good."

Ted was staring up at her through swollen, heavy-lidded eyes that were no longer blue—more like dark-purple pockmarks floating on twin oceans of deep-pink saline solution. He blinked in the dim lamplight, and it appeared to cause him pain. Covering his eyes with one arm, he turned onto his back and groaned. "What time is it?" he asked through parched lips.

"Nearly three-thirty." She paused, and the room was so still that she could almost hear both of their hearts pounding. A quick glance told her that Ted was still fully dressed, except for his shoes, which had been tossed beside the bed. "Do you want to tell me about it?" Her voice was low and intense, urging him to speak. She grabbed his clammy hand and rubbed it between both of hers to generate some warmth.

"Not much to tell," he said thickly, rolling his tongue around in his mouth to stir up a little moisture. "I went to see her. She was unresponsive, unfeeling, unreceptive. Un-nice. We talked for a while, but mostly it was just her slinging mud at me and the Mormons. Finally I tried to bear my testimony, and she looked the other way. So I left, and went out and sat in my car and bawled like a baby." He was silent for a moment, then Paula saw a tear trickle down his cheek. "This was a really bad idea . . . I'll never go back there. Never." Moving his arm, he looked up at her, his eyes watering. "I even told her I loved her, you know? She just sat there—wouldn't even look at me." The tears began in earnest again, and Paula pulled his head onto her lap. He sobbed helplessly as she rocked him, her own tears falling on his thick blonde hair. "Shhh," she whispered. "Just rest now. It'll be all right."

"I don't think so," he moaned.

Half an hour later, she bent over to kiss his brow. He had fallen asleep, his head resting against her stomach, and she had spent the time considering what she could do to help. "Are you awake?" she said, her lips moving to his ear.

"Mmm?" he mumbled, stirring a little.

"That's good," she said, gently nudging his head off her lap. "We need to start getting ready for the reception. For starters, I'll need to make a quick trip to the hotel dry cleaners." She fingered his rumpled suit. "They should be able to fix this up just fine in a couple of hours. I'm sure you brought another shirt and tie."

He looked at her in disbelief, his swollen eyes twitching in the dim light of the lamp. "I—I'm not sure I'm up to doing the reception. Nobody'd want to see me in this condition."

"Maybe not," Paula replied, "but I'd be willing to bet you could be almost back to normal by seven. A hot shower will do wonders, and I just happen to have some miracle eye drops in my purse that will get the red out before you know it. I'll stop and get some ice on my way back from the cleaners; it should help with the swelling."

"I don't know," he said, rubbing his eyes gingerly.

"Well, I do," she declared without hesitation. "If nothing else, I'd like to have the pleasure of introducing Mark's stunning new bride to her gorgeous half-brother. There's a striking family resemblance, you know."

Ted shrugged. "Small comfort, when her own mother won't even be there. Did Kelsey say anything about it today?"

"We visited at the luncheon," Paula reported. "I could tell she was quite disappointed that Alma wouldn't have any part in her wedding day, but she's trying to reconcile herself to the estrangement. Having Mark in her life is a great comfort—and meeting you will help, too,

I'm sure. In fact, let's go a little early so we'll have time to make the proper introductions before the reception gets underway." She looked at Ted with a tiny glimmer of hope in her eyes. "Any possibility your mother might show up tonight?"

He chuckled cryptically. "Not a snowball's chance in Tahiti."

Paula shook her head. "That's what I was afraid of."

Ted couldn't help smiling a little. "You'd be more afraid if she *did* show up."

She tossed a pillow at him. "Hit the showers, young man."

"Sounds like a plan," he said, shedding his suit jacket. There was a bone-deep weariness in his voice that tore at Paula's heart.

They arrived at the ward meetinghouse just before six-thirty. It was a small older chapel, built perhaps fifty years earlier of lustrous red brick with impeccable white wooden trim, surrounded by wide beds of vibrant summer flowers and nestled on a corner lot with a carefully trimmed side lawn that sloped gently upward into a generous stand of lush foliage. This church had real character.

"You look mahvelous," Paula smiled, squeezing Ted's arm as they walked toward the building. He squinted into the late-afternoon sun as though his eyes were still tender, but the ice and drops had magically returned them to a near-normal appearance. Now only a hint of puffiness remained around their edges.

"Never as mahvelous as you, my dear," he returned, glancing down at her shimmering royal-blue evening dress, then at her dark hair, swept dramatically back from her face, leaving a few curly tendrils at her temples, cheeks, and neckline. "I'm glad I came."

They found Mark and Kelsey in the cultural hall. Mark was overseeing a bit of last-minute decorating with small bouquets of pink and yellow roses on each of several guest tables placed around the room. Kelsey, dressed in a simple but stunning white silk wedding gown, stood off to one side chatting with Isabel Norton, her friend and mentor, who would be providing harp music during the reception. Ted quickly commandeered Mark's attention, while Paula approached Kelsey. "Could I talk to you for a minute?" she asked casually. Within seconds, the four had come together somewhere near the middle of the hall.

Paula slipped her arm through Kelsey's and smiled up at Ted. "Kelsey Taggart—no, excuse me, now it's Kelsey *Richland*—I'd like to introduce you to my husband, Ted Barstow. He's been looking forward to meeting you."

"Yes, indeed," Ted grinned as he extended his hand. "It's a great pleasure."

Kelsey clasped his hand warmly, then stared up at him with a quizzical expression, taking in his clipped blonde hair, vivid blue eyes, and chiseled jawline. "It's good to meet you," she said in a puzzled tone. "But . . . have we met before? I really don't think so; it's just that you look so—so familiar." She bit her lip, trying to make a connection.

"Nope . . . we've never met," Ted replied, then winked at Paula and continued. "But we should have—a long time ago. That's where the 'familiar' part comes in."

Now Kelsey was totally lost. "Excuse me?" she said blankly.

Instead of responding, Ted motioned to a nearby table. "Would you and your husband do us the honor of sitting with us for just a few minutes? I have something to tell you, and after such an exciting day, it might be best if you're sitting down when you hear this." He paused as they took their seats, then added, "I can only apologize for doing this right now, in the middle of getting things ready for the reception and all. I'd meant to speak to you at the luncheon earlier, but"—he glanced at Paula—"something came up."

Kelsey turned to Paula. "Does he always talk in riddles?"

"Only when he's nervous," she laughed. "But stay with him; I think you'll be interested in what he has to say."

The four of them huddled together then, and Ted quickly spilled out, in very abbreviated fashion, the story of his life, ending with the BigHugs report of a week earlier and his encounter with Alma that morning. "So you see," he finally said, leaning back in his chair, "it's completely normal that I should look familiar to you. We share a mother."

Clearly in shock, Kelsey stared at him wide-eyed, her own sculptured jaw slack with astonishment. "I had no idea," she breathed after a long silence. "She was always very secretive about her past, but this . . ." Her azure eyes filled with tears. "Why couldn't she have just *told* me?"

Ted reached out to clasp her hand. "Resentment does weird things to people, and I'm afraid our mother is the queen of bitterness. I'd hoped to make some kind of a connection with her today, but . . ." His voice broke as the awful memories came rushing back, and his jaw muscles tightened. "Now it looks like that'll never happen."

"Maybe," Kelsey said, "but I'd like to think that things will eventually work out. I guess all we can do now is stay in touch, try to make a family for ourselves, keep the faith. Even if our mother won't have anything to do with us." She paused to delicately wipe a tear from the corner of her eye. "I do love her, you know. In spite of everything. And I wish she'd come back." She pressed a hand to her heart.

"I know," Ted responded. "So do I."

Mark curled an arm around his new bride's waist and they stood up. "Well," he smiled, "I hate to interrupt this unexpected and truly delightful little family reunion, but I believe our guests will be arriving shortly." He looked at Ted, his eyes twinkling. "Let's see now . . . this would make you my stepfather once-removed, as well as my long-lost half-brother-in-law. Welcome to the family, daddy-bro!" He laughed heartily and slapped Ted on the back. Ted pushed back his chair, stood, and wrapped his arms around Kelsey and Mark in a brief embrace. "Big hugs is right," Kelsey said, then pulled back to look at him with a tremulous smile. But they were out of time, and Mark grabbed Kelsey's hand to lead her toward the waiting reception line.

Ted sat back down beside Paula, who was smiling broadly. "What?" he questioned.

"See? I told you it would all work out," she beamed. "Isn't this fun?"

"Compared to the way my day started out, it's the celestial kingdom," he conceded.

They sat together, holding hands, enjoying the lush harp music in the background, savoring the festive atmosphere, reminiscing about their own wedding. "That's a mighty handsome reception line," Ted observed as a pretty teenaged girl from the ward served them punch and strawberry cheesecake drizzled with chocolate. "Didn't the BigHugs people say something about a brother to Kelsey? I don't see anyone who looks like her." *Not even her own mother,* he said to himself wryly. *Maybe if I hadn't gone to see her, she might have decided to come after all.* The possibility caused him a sharp twinge of regret.

"That would be David," Paula said, interrupting his guilty thoughts. "Someone asked about him at the luncheon; apparently he's in the military, taking a very elite and intensive pilot training course in Texas for the next several months. He couldn't get away."

Ted nodded. "At least Sam and Alex are here to represent the Richland side of the family."

"And I'll bet Andrea and Ruthie are having a blast back in Idaho, getting ready for the open house there," Paula added. "Sam put them in charge."

Not ten minutes had passed when Ted heard a light rustling sound beside him and looked up into Kelsey's sparkling blue eyes. "Whoa," he said with a wide smile, "this is almost like looking into a mirror—only the reflection is so much prettier than what I usually see." His brows furrowed. "What's up?"

"You two, I hope," she beamed, resting a hand on each of their shoulders. "As my newest and dearly loved relatives, I would be deeply honored if you would stand beside me in the reception line for the rest of this magical evening. I should have asked before, but"—she blushed slightly—"it took a few minutes for the reality to sink in. It's not every day one meets a long-lost brother and his wife roaming the cultural hall."

Ted's gaze met Paula's, and they both rose at the same moment. "The honor is all ours," he said with a deep bow and a kiss to the bride's hand. Arm in arm, the three walked to the head of the line.

* * * * * * * *

Paula relaxed against the soft upholstery of the restaurant booth. After sleeping in until nearly noon, she and Ted were now lingering over a late lunch before heading for the airport to catch their flight to New York. They sat in silence for a time, and she found her thoughts wandering from coast to coast. How was little Lexi doing back home in Los Angeles, without her mother to see to her every need and want? Probably better than ever, she reasoned; with fairy-godmother Millie and fairy-dogfather Rudy watching over her, no harm could possibly come. And what of Marjorie Enfield, mysteriously cloistered on her aristocratic Connecticut estate, seemingly beholden to no one but at the same time prey to whatever demons her aging faculties were presently conjuring up to beset her? The thought stirred up a small eddy of concern in Paula's mind. Thank goodness they'd be able to see for themselves what was happening within the next day or two. This little vacation, she felt, had come just in time.

A small scraping noise diverted her attention to Ted's plate, where his fork was pushing and pummeling a small clump of mashed potatoes from side to side. The tender veal cutlet and steamed vegetables had not been touched. "No dessert until you eat your peas and carrots," she joked. When he didn't respond, she reached across the table to touch his hand. "Want to talk about it?"

He shrugged, sighed, then offered her a slightly forlorn smile. "That was a pretty great reception, wasn't it? And meeting Kelsey—that was the best."

"But you wish things had gone differently with your mother." Paula's voice was low and filled with tenderness.

He laid the fork down and began to rub his temple, where a reddish scar was still visible from the accident several months earlier. A dry, humorless chuckle escaped his lips. "I just thought it would all work out, you know? Maybe a little tense when I first saw her, but a happy reunion in the end. Forgive and forget, that sort of thing. I really thought I could make a difference." His shoulders sagged under the weight of some unseen burden.

She squeezed his hand firmly. "I believe you *did* make a difference, Ted. You followed the promptings of the Spirit, and you did exactly what the Lord asked of you; nobody could have done more. From what you've told me about your conversation with her, I'm sure you planted some seeds—gave her a lot to think about. It may not happen overnight, but we can always keep hoping and praying that she'll eventually turn around. What's that scripture in the Doctrine and Covenants? Oh, yes—'After much tribulation come the blessings.'"

"I suppose," he conceded. "But it still would have been nice if she'd shown up for the reception."

"Or not," Paula suggested. "Given her frame of mind, she might have made a scene. As it was, everything went smoothly and it was a glorious, memorable occasion. Mark and Kelsey couldn't have asked for a nicer wedding day." She winked at him. "Besides, they got a couple of great new relatives in the bargain."

"And so did we," he smiled, finally warming to the pleasant memories. He could almost feel his sister's arms wrapped tightly around him as they said good-bye at the chapel door.

"Don't be a stranger," Kelsey had whispered close to his ear. "We're family now." The words had sent ripples of joy coursing through his veins, and now he felt the happy warmth filling his heart again.

He nibbled on a few vegetables and took two or three bites of meat. "Could we please have dessert now?" he asked, regarding Paula with childlike anticipation.

"I thought you'd never ask," she laughed.

They were enjoying fresh banana cream pie when a muted sound like a miniature calliope brought them both to attention. Paula's gaze shot to her handbag, lying beside her in the booth. "Lexi," they both said at once as she burrowed her hand into the purse.

"We're so paranoid," she huffed as she put the small Nokia phone to her ear. "Yes? Oh, hi, Millie." She glanced at Ted and decided to get right to the point. "Is the baby all right? I'm sure you and Rudy are taking good care of her, but she must miss her ol' mom and dad. Is she sleeping well? That ear infection hasn't come back, has it? I told the doctor we needed another prescription, just in case. If you can't get in touch with him, try . . ." There was a brief pause while Paula listened. "Oh, I see. Of course; hold on just a minute." She quickly dug a pen and a scrap of paper from her purse, then turned back to the phone. "Okay, I'm ready." She scribbled a number, then repeated it to Millie. "Got it. Yes, right away. What's this about, anyway?" Propping her elbow on the table, she listened intently for several seconds. "Beats me," she finally said, "but I'll give him a call. Yes, I'll let you know. Kiss the wild child for me, will you? Thanks, Millie. Talk to you soon." She pressed the disconnect button and laid the phone on the table, staring at it as though it was a foreign object.

"What is it?" Ted questioned. "I couldn't exactly follow."

Paula raised her eyes to meet his. "Someone called from the New Haven Police Department. He gave Millie his name, but wouldn't talk to her. Wanted me to call him ASAP instead. She gave me his number." A cold chill settled across her shoulders.

"Would you like me to dial?" Ted offered, reaching for the phone.

"No," she said, intercepting his grasp, "I'll do it. I have to do it."

She placed the call quickly, then waited while it rang two, three, four times. When someone picked up, it was a gruff male voice. "Hello, New Haven P.D. Can I help you?"

Paula cleared her throat and attempted to speak normally. "Yes, sir. This is Paula Barstow. I was asked to call this number and speak to an Officer Stillman. Could you connect me with him, please?"

She counted to ten before the voice responded, this time in a gentler tone. "Mrs. Paula Barstow, currently residing at 10410 Valley View Drive in Woodland Hills, California? Daughter of Marjorie Enfield, 102 Mapleton Crossing?"

"That's correct," Paula said, dispensing with any thought of polite conversation.

"This is Officer Stillman," the voice clarified. "I'm afraid I have some . . . unfortunate news for you, Mrs. Barstow."

Paula snapped her eyes closed and set her jaw. "I'm listening, Officer."

"Very well." The voice was deadly calm. "On behalf of the New Haven Police Department, I'm sorry to inform you that the Enfield estate burned to the ground this morning. We have spent most of the day investigating the scene. It appears that there were no survivors."

Chapter 16

"I'd like to go out to the estate first," Paula said as they unpacked. "Then we can talk to the police. There'll be plenty of time to arrange for . . ." Her voice caught, then trailed off.

Ted opened a drawer in the heavy oak armoire. "I understand," he said, his voice warm with compassion. "We'll go first thing in the morning."

They were settling into their room at the Westbury Inn in New Haven, one of Connecticut's most charming bed-and-breakfasts. Paula had found the Inn when she had come to Yale University as a guest speaker nearly three years earlier, so it was natural that she should think of the place now, when they were suddenly summoned to New Haven in this moment of crisis. After receiving the ominous phone call, they had caught the first available flight to Hartford. By midnight, exhausted from the day's news and frantic travel, they lay side by side in the darkened room, unmoving, sleepless, numb with shock.

"She was reading the Book of Mormon," Paula said after a long silence. "I don't know if she ever took the time to find out if it was true. With her mind the way it was, she probably died not knowing." A cold knot of anguish formed in her throat, and the entire bottom half of her face trembled beyond control.

"Well, there's one thing I'm pretty sure of," Ted offered, curling an arm around her shoulders. "If TJ had anything at all to say about it, he would've been right there on the other side of the veil, the first one to meet her when she passed—maybe even the one who was sent to bring her home—with his missionary name tag pinned proudly on his chest, ready to give her the biggest hug of her life." He chuckled softly. "Her new life, that is. You can bet he hasn't left her alone for a minute; she's probably had all the missionary discussions and been personally introduced to every one of the major players in the Book of Mormon by now. There's no way she *can't* know it's true."

Paula nestled against him and twisted the CTR ring on her little finger. "That's a comforting thought, my love. I doubt that death ever occurs in a vacuum, and it makes sense that there would be a personage of light sent to accompany a spirit through the veil. If that personage happened to be my darling son, Mother couldn't have asked for a happier transition from this life to the next." She wiped at a tear on her cheek. "What a blessing to understand that even if there were no mortal friends or family around at the time, she wasn't alone."

"You're right," Ted agreed. "We can certainly be grateful for—"

The sound of Paula's phone sliced through the calm air. "Who in the world . . ." She quickly switched on a light above the bed and reached toward a nightstand. "It's one o'clock in the morning. This can't be good." Lifting the small instrument to her ear, she spoke warily. "Yes?"

"Mrs. Barstow," a man's voice said, but she couldn't quite place it.

"Speaking," she replied.

"Officer Stillman here. New Haven P.D. Sorry to bother you at such an hour."

"Oh, yes, Officer. No bother; we weren't asleep anyway. With everything that's happened, we're just—"

"I understand," he broke in. "That's why I thought you wouldn't want to wait for this news. I tried to call your cell phone several times earlier, but I never got through."

"I couldn't use it on the plane, and had it turned off until just a few minutes ago," she explained. "Sorry." She paused. "You have news?" *Strange,* she thought. *What couldn't wait until morning?*

"Yes, ma'am," he said. "We've found your mother."

A sudden wave of grief flooded Paula's chest, as if she were feeling it for the first time. Perhaps the numbness was beginning to wear off. And now it was really over; they had located Marjorie's body. "I see," she said evenly, though she could feel her heart pounding behind her eyes. "Were you able to determine how . . . how she died?"

The officer cleared his throat after a brief silence. "Oh, no, ma'am. That's why I'm calling. Marjorie Enfield didn't die in that fire—although it appears that she's the one who started it. She's safe and sound." He hesitated. "In a manner of speaking."

This was a bit too much information for Paula to assimilate all at once. "Are you telling me," she said, pressing a hand to her chest, "that my mother is still alive?"

"I am," he confirmed. "We found her a few hours ago at a small community hospital about ten miles north of here; she'd been wandering along the road, and some lady picked her up and took her there. She had no identification and was extremely disoriented—didn't even know her own name. But one of the nurses started putting two and two together when she heard about the fire on the news. Later, Mrs. Enfield was lucid for a few minutes and able to identify herself. So they called me, and . . . well, I got hold of you as soon as I could."

Relief and gratitude surged into Paula's throat. "Thank you so much, Officer. What happens now?"

"Well, I'd suggest you folks get a good night's sleep," he said. "No use running out to the hospital now; they're keeping Mrs. Enfield sedated, and her doctor won't be there. Let's meet out at the estate in the morning, and I'll give you all the information I have. Then you'll probably want to see your mother, and I'll show you how to get to the hospital. Of course I'll do whatever I can to help."

"That's very kind of you," Paula said warmly. A few seconds later, she punched the "off" button and turned toward Ted. "I guess you got the gist of our conversation."

"I certainly did," he smiled. "And all of a sudden, it looks like tomorrow is going to be a little better day than we thought."

Just after nine o'clock the next morning, Ted pulled their rented sedan into the thin stream of traffic heading west. By the time they reached the outskirts of the city, they had the two-way country road to themselves, and for the next twenty miles the big car seemed to glide through deep-green meadows and vigorous stands of birch overlooking cool, bubbling streams. The verdant natural landscape seemed to relax them, and Paula leaned back against her seat. "I used to ride my bike along this road every day in the summer," she reminisced. "The air was so warm and moist that it felt like a huge blanket wrapped around me, but I never minded. If I got too hot or tired, I'd just stop by a little brook, spread that imaginary blanket down on the grass beneath me, and take a long, lovely nap. As long as I was home by dinnertime, I had the days to myself. It was wonderful. I remember one day, after my nap, I woke up to find a mother deer and her fawn, drinking from the stream less than ten feet from me. I was totally mesmerized, and I watched them for a very long time, until finally they—"

She broke off as a sudden curve in the road warned her of a sharp bend just ahead, and she squeezed Ted's knee. "You'll need to slow down a little," she warned. "We're almost there, and the road turns unexpectedly."

He eased his foot off the gas pedal, and the car slowed to a nominal speed as it approached Mapleton Crossing. They turned a wide corner, and suddenly the estate came into full view. "Oh, my heavens," Paula breathed.

It was all there, spread before them like a scene from *Gone with the Wind.* Nothing about it had changed; everything about it had changed. Acres of lovingly manicured lawn, bordered by meticulously trimmed shrubs and lush flower gardens, sloped gently up toward the house. Except that there was no house. What had just one day earlier been an imposing two-story Colonial mansion, situated grandly on a low rise flanked by centuries-old evergreens, its front pillars and second-story porticoes glistening white in the hot August sun, was now an unrecognizable heap of charred debris, scattered across its ash-covered concrete foundation like Rome in the wake of Nero's pyromaniacal frenzy. A few blackened timbers still stood along the periphery of the site, but the first modest breeze would topple them like matchsticks. Eddies of super-heated air were still rising in some places, creating a shimmering, rippling effect in the atmosphere above the ruins. There could be no hope of repair or restoration; the devastation was complete.

Seeing the reality firsthand, Paula felt her mind and emotions retreat into stunned disbelief. Nothing about this picture seemed real, and she squeezed her eyes shut, hoping to dispel the unsettling image. But when she opened them again, the identical scene assaulted her senses. Slowly she began to comprehend the enormity of it, and her throat constricted until she could hardly breathe.

Ted steered the car up the long circular drive and stopped in front of the four wide cement steps leading to the porch, which now appeared to be eerily suspended in air. He shut off the motor and turned to Paula. "Want to get out and look around?" She nodded, and he walked around to the passenger door and opened it, offering her his hand. Swinging her legs out of the car in slow motion, she stood and leaned heavily against him. His arm circled her waist, and they shuffled in silence to one end of the house's foundation, where they stared numbly at the steaming ruins. "It was a large house," he observed quietly after a time. "Very impressive."

"It was more impressive with walls," Paula joked grimly. Her gaze darted beyond the bright yellow "Do Not Cross" police tape to what had once been the formal dining room. Not a single item was recognizable—no carved cherry wood table, no polished high-backed chairs, no elegant china hutch. Nothing but huge clumps of wet ashes. So much destruction; it was barely comprehensible. She closed her eyes, clutching Ted's arm for support.

"What say we take a load off?" he said kindly. "Look—there's somewhere we can sit for a while." She opened her eyes as he motioned to an area at the far perimeter of the yard, then she lifted her gaze toward the spot. The gazebo! Situated far enough away from the house to have survived the blaze, it now stood as a solitary beacon of hope and normalcy in Paula's life—the secluded, welcoming place she had retreated to so often as a child to read or dream away a long summer afternoon. She felt a mild surge of strength flowing into her limbs, and eagerly grabbed Ted's hand as they moved across the wide expanse of lawn between the house and the gazebo. "I love this place," she murmured as they stepped onto its polished wooden floor. "So many memories here; I couldn't even begin to tell you."

Ted used his handkerchief to wipe a thin covering of pale ash from two of the latticed structure's cushioned window seats, and they sat together in the canopied shade, holding hands, gazing away from the house and toward the lushly wooded landscape bordering the Enfield property. It was just the way Paula had envisioned it as they were planning their trip—except, of course, that this was the only part of the vision that bore any resemblance to reality. All the rest of it lay behind them in smoldering ruins. There were no words to express the feeling of the moment.

"Excuse me . . . you must be Mr. and Mrs. Barstow."

The words came from directly behind them, spoken by a deep and rather gravelly male voice. Ted and Paula spun around on their seats and peered through the latticework at a large, solid form dressed in a dark-blue law enforcement uniform. "And you must be Officer Stillman," Paula ventured.

The man sauntered halfway around the gazebo to its doorless entry and leaned inside. "Morning," he said with an easy smile. They all shook hands, and he took a seat on the bench across from them. "You must be anxious to see Mrs. Enfield."

"Of course," Paula said. "It was so kind of you to call last night. All of this," she gestured toward the burned-out mansion, "is pretty hard to take, but at least my mother survived." A bewildered expression shadowed her face, and she shook her head. "I just don't understand how something like this could have happened."

"Unfortunately, I've seen it before—especially with these old Colonial places," Stillman explained. "Most of them were built by master craftsmen in the late 1700s and are still structurally sound, but the fact is they're made of wood, and over the years it just dries out, deteriorates, and is more susceptible to a fire situation than newer buildings. Even a little spark can do it, and there's not much left afterwards. In this county alone we've had two other estates like this go up in smoke during the past year."

"A real tragedy to lose these historic treasures," Ted observed. "Mind if I ask a question about what happened here?"

"Not at all. I'll tell you whatever I know," the officer replied.

Ted slid forward on the bench. "Okay, thanks. Paula told me that last night, when you were talking with her, you mentioned something about Marjorie starting the fire. Could you clarify that for us?"

"You bet." Stillman spoke in a low, almost apologetic voice. "We have investigators who come right out to the scene of a fire and try to pinpoint the cause. Even when it looks like there's only a pile of wet charcoal left, these guys are awfully good at figuring things out. They find stuff that you and I would never even notice. In this case, they poked around in what was left of the kitchen. All three of them came to the same conclusion—someone had left a pan on the stove with the gas burner still on. It could have taken an hour or two for the fire to start, but once it got going, the whole place went up in a matter of minutes. Fortunately, Mrs. Enfield had left by then, or this story would have had a much different ending." He shrugged and shook his head. "Still, it's an awful thing."

"And you're sure it was my mother who left that pan on the stove?" Paula would admit that Marjorie was becoming a little forgetful, but burning down a house where one had lived for nearly half a century was beyond comprehension. On the other hand, given the older woman's declining mental state, perhaps comprehension had nothing to do with it.

"Was there anyone else living in the house with her?" Stillman asked.

"No; she preferred to live alone, at least the past year or two. But wait! Her housekeeper, Maria, comes in a couple of days a week—Mondays and Thursdays. She always does some cooking while she's here—makes little one-serving meals and puts them in the freezer for Mother to eat later. Maybe she just forgot to turn off the stove before she went home last time." Paula looked at him expectantly. "I think you should give her a call, and—"

Ted's hand on her shoulder stopped her in mid-sentence. "Paula," he said gently, "Maria came on Thursday. The fire started on Saturday."

"Oh." Paula's chest suddenly felt deflated, like a balloon that had unexpectedly lost its air. She smiled thinly. "Well, then, I guess we should get to the hospital. Officer, could you please tell us how to get there?"

"Absolutely," he said, giving them simple directions. They could be there inside of twenty minutes. "This is a real mess," he added, motioning toward the scorched remains of the house. "I hope she'll be okay."

"We'll manage," Paula declared with a terse smile, wondering how in the world she could say such a thing with any degree of certainty. How *would* they manage?

Marjorie Enfield lay on her side facing the window, her usually straight, proud body curled like a child's beneath the peach-colored hospital sheet. At Paula's touch, she turned her head and squinted up at her daughter. "Madeline?" she asked in a parched voice. "Maddy, is it time yet? Teacher won't let us go until it's recess." She had been sedated, and her gray-blue eyes seemed barely able to focus.

"No, it's not . . . recess," Paula murmured, deciding at the last second not to stir the already-muddied waters. "Not yet. I'll come and get you when it's time." Marjorie nodded and closed her eyes. Moments later, her even breathing told Paula she was asleep.

"My own mother doesn't even know me," Paula sniffed as she and Ted sat together in the waiting room.

"I'm sure she'll be back," he soothed. "She's probably just taking a little mental vacation until she feels like it's safe to be herself again. Or something." He sighed, and Paula knew he was as puzzled as she was.

"Mr. and Mrs. Barstow?" They looked up to see a rather tall, slender, early-middle-aged man in a white lab jacket smiling down at them. His bushy brown hair, wire-rimmed glasses, button-down oxford shirt and striped tie made him look studious and trustworthy, while the jeans and Air Jordan sneakers showing beneath his lab coat suggested that he might have just breezed in from the basketball court. "I'm Dr. Gray—an appropriate name for a gerontologist, don't you think?—and I've been asked to oversee Marjorie Enfield's case. My practice is in New Haven, but I make rounds here twice a week." He looked from Ted to Paula with dark, twinkling eyes. "Who does she belong to?"

"She's my mother," Paula smiled. She liked this doctor immediately, and she hoped he could give them some answers. Or at least help them figure out what the questions were.

"Nice to meet you," he said, and sat across from them on a small, vinyl-covered green couch.

For the next hour, huddled in the deserted waiting room, Paula and Ted listened to Dr. Gray's assessment of Marjorie's future. There would need to be a battery of diagnostic tests and procedures, of course; however, based on his preliminary observation and interviews with the patient, backed up by more than fifteen years of experience and research in the field of geriatric medicine, he would be willing to bet his vintage 1957 Chevy Bel Air that Marjorie was in the throes of early to mid-stage Alzheimer's. Her physical health was good, he said; but as her mind failed, her body would eventually wear down under the strain. There was no way of telling how long the mental deterioration would take, or what course it would follow. Only one thing was sure: beginning the moment she left the hospital, she would need constant supervision. "We can keep her here for another day or two," he said, "but you'll need to made some decisions very soon."

Paula and Ted nodded mutely, their hands clasped so tightly that their fingers had lost all color. "Thank you, Dr. Gray," Paula managed after a long silence. "We appreciate your being so candid. We'd like to take her home to California with us." She glanced sideways at Ted, who nodded his support. "We'll take her to see a specialist there." She took a deep breath. "My mother will have everything she needs."

"That's good to hear," the doctor said. "We'll discontinue her sedation this afternoon; as she gets further away from yesterday's trauma, she'll probably recognize you and get back to a fairly normal state quite soon. In the meantime, I'll make some notes on her case and have a file ready for you when she's discharged. You can take it to her physician in California." He stood, and they followed his lead. "I'm sorry," he said, his dark, expressive eyes filling with compassion as he shook their hands. "I know it's never easy to get news like this; I heard it myself not so long ago. My own mother died of Alzheimer's last year. In spite of all my work and research, she still . . ." He cleared his throat, then looked directly into their eyes. "You'll learn to take it as it comes, one day, one hour, one minute at a time. Just be sure you do what's best for everyone concerned—including yourselves. No one wins against this disease if you let it tear you apart."

"Thank you so much . . . we'll remember that," Paula said.

Seeing the desolate look in his eyes, she impulsively reached out to embrace him. He returned the hug, and as he pulled away his genuine smile warmed her. "You take care now," he murmured, then turned and quickly disappeared down a long corridor, the rubber soles of his shoes squeaking against the vinyl tile.

"Nice guy," Ted observed when they were alone. "Makes me proud that Mark Richland is going into medicine. I could see him being that kind of a doctor one day—gracious, sympathetic, caring. Huggable."

She nudged him in the ribs, grateful for his attempt at humor. "Not to mention brilliant, dedicated, and genuinely concerned for the welfare of his patients. A harp-playing angel of a wife couldn't hurt, either."

"Uh-huh," Ted chuckled grimly. "I just hope their honeymoon is going better than our vacation."

* * * * * * * *

"Actually, it wasn't all that hard getting Mother here," Paula explained over a thick slice of whole wheat toast spread with butter and strawberry preserves. A gray memory of her childhood home reduced to tinder rose in her mind, but she quickly banished the image. "It wasn't like we had a lot of sorting or packing to do."

"Well, I'm glad you're all home safely," Millie purred. "I think Marjorie's enjoying her new room."

"Must be," Scott drawled, popping an entire strip of bacon into his mouth. "She sure spends a lot of time in there."

"That's because you did such a spectacular job of putting it together," Paula smiled.

They had been home just over a week, and thus far the adjustment had gone off with only a few minor hitches. While Ted and Paula had met with Marjorie's attorney in Connecticut to arrange the cleanup and maintenance of her property, Scott and a few of his buddies from the Ninja Academy had virtually transformed Paula's home office into a small but appealing bedroom/sitting room for Marjorie. A comfortable reclining easy chair and a large wall-mounted TV had replaced the desk and computer table; cheerful pink-and-white floral wallpaper instead of shelves and bookcases made the room more spacious and inviting; and a new full-sized bed behind an attractive portable screen in the far corner would provide rest and seclusion when she needed it. A small adjoining washroom had been re-plumbed and fitted with shower facilities. By the time Marjorie arrived a few days after the fire, Millie's decorative touches to the room—a small painting hung here, an intriguing knicknack placed there, a peaceful mauve-and-green comforter with ivory throw pillows on the bed—had made it home.

"This is lovely," Marjorie had said upon being ushered into her new quarters after the long flight from Connecticut. Then she had turned toward Paula, a gentle smile playing across her patrician lips. "In fact, it's so charming that I might never want to go back home after my visit." Ted and Paula had exchanged bewildered glances. Hadn't they explained it all to her a dozen times or more already, and hadn't she nodded politely every time, as though she understood perfectly? Apparently something had been lost in the translation, and they would need to try again—but not now. It was enough that for this moment, at least, she knew their names and recognized the dog.

"We'll bring your bags in from the car," Paula had said cheerfully. "You must be awfully tired; why don't you just have a little nap now, and Millie will fix you something to eat later."

"That would be fine, dear," Marjorie had replied. "I really am feeling quite"—she paused, as though hunting for a word—"weary these days, and I'm sure a little rest would make me more chipper."

Later, in their upstairs bedroom, Ted and Paula had talked far into the night. "I don't think this is going to be so bad," she had reasoned, her voice warm with optimism. "I must admit, I had some second and third and fourth thoughts after we agreed to bring her back with us; she and I weren't exactly best buddies when I was growing up, you know. I'd be the first to admit that a lot of baggage came with her when she walked into our home this afternoon—and I'm not talking suitcases. But you know what? The gospel teaches us to love one another, to forgive and forget. Maybe this is one way I can show her that things are okay between us. One way of bridging some of the time we lost."

"She's sick, Paula," he reminded her gently. "She'll never be the mother you once knew."

Paula felt a mischievous grin rise to her lips. "And who's to say that's all bad? We might actually be dealing with a new, improved version here."

"Shame on you, sweetness," he growled, his throat quivering with mirth.

"Okay, okay," she conceded with a tiny giggle. "I know this disease is serious business, but I think we can deal with it. Millie will be here to help, and we can both keep a close eye on Mother. Besides, maybe it isn't even Alzheimer's; maybe the specialist will find some other problem and just prescribe some good vitamins or something. She might be as good as new in a few months."

"Maybe," Ted sighed. "But for now, I say we just follow Dr. Gray's advice—take it one day at a time. We'll know what we're facing soon enough."

Paula caught a glimpse of "soon enough" two days later, as she was passing Marjorie's room on her way to the kitchen. The door was slightly ajar, and a dainty sniffling sound was coming from the room's far corner. Pushing the door farther open, Paula slipped in and moved noiselessly across the thick, deep-green carpeting, stopping just short of the teakwood screen that separated Marjorie's sleeping area from the rest of the room. The sniffling noises continued, so she peeked around the side of the screen. "Mother?" she called out softly. "Are you all right?"

Marjorie, dressed in a teal-colored casual pantsuit (one of several Paula had purchased for her in Connecticut), sat on the edge of her carefully made bed, her shoulders hunched forward, a white linen handkerchief pressed to her nose. Hearing her daughter's voice, she raised her head and looked at Paula with wide, tear-filled eyes. "Something terrible has happened, hasn't it?" she blurted out in a rush of anguish.

Paula sat down beside Marjorie. "What do you think has happened, Mother?" she asked in a soothing voice. "What is it?"

"I—I don't know exactly," the older woman replied, rubbing the handkerchief between her hands. "There was an explosion or fire of some kind, and I was walking . . . a long way. I thought I saw Howard, but he wouldn't come to me." She looked at Paula pleadingly. "Of course he wouldn't . . . he's dead, isn't he?" Marjorie looked utterly, hopelessly confused.

She's finally remembering—at least bits and pieces, with a slightly bizarre twist, Paula thought. Her heart swelled with pity for this lost, suddenly fragile-looking woman. *How much should I tell her?* She sent up a silent prayer for assistance.

"Yes, there was a fire," she finally began in calm, reassuring tones. "But it was an accident, and no one was hurt. It turned out all right."

"A fire—at Mapleton Crossing?" Marjorie pressed. "On the estate?" When Paula nodded reluctantly, she pressed a hand to her forehead, and for an instant her eyes cleared. "I did it, didn't I? I burned it down! God's mercy take me, a foolish old woman. I burned it down!" Past consolation, she buried her face in the handkerchief.

Paula put her arm around Marjorie's shoulders and waited until the sobs died away. "Mother," she said, her voice barely a whisper, "no one knows for sure. It was an accident; that's all anyone can say. But you're here with us now, and everything's going to be just fine. You'll see." She gave Marjorie's shoulders a reassuring squeeze.

A few minutes elapsed in silence, then Marjorie lifted her head. "I thank you for taking me in," she said tonelessly. "Would you kindly leave me alone now? I need to . . . collect my thoughts. I'd be grateful if you'd close the door behind you."

"Of course." Paula rose from the bed. "We'll see you at dinner, then." Marjorie nodded once without speaking as Paula let herself out of the room, pulling the door shut with a soft click.

But Marjorie didn't appear at dinner, or at breakfast the next morning. One, then two food trays left outside her door remained untouched. Shortly before noon, Paula knocked softly and entered the room. Marjorie was sitting in her recliner, staring blankly at the TV on the opposite wall. It was not turned on.

Paula approached the chair and sat down on a small ottoman beside it. "We missed you last night and this morning," she began in a casual, cheerful voice. "Would you like me to bring you something to eat? Millie made some of her scrumptious curried chicken salad, and I know you love her homemade rolls. You wouldn't even have to come out to the kitchen if you're not up to it; I could just fix a plate and—"

"There's something wrong with me." Marjorie spoke the words slowly and deliberately, her gaze never leaving the darkened television screen. "I've known for months, but told myself it would pass." Her eyes met Paula's. "That's why you've brought me here, isn't it? Because now you know, too."

Paula decided to hedge. *No point in alarming her. We haven't even seen a specialist yet.* "We're just concerned, that's all," she said. "You were living all alone in that big, drafty old house clear on the other side of the country, and you seemed to be getting a bit forgetful, so—"

"Forgetful?" Marjorie let out a short, sardonic little laugh. "My dear girl, not remembering where you put your keys is being forgetful. Not remembering what to do with your keys when you have them is something else altogether. Sometimes I couldn't even recognize the numbers on a telephone." She looked at Paula wistfully. "Those were the days when I meant to call you, but I simply couldn't remember how it was done."

Paula gulped. *It's worse than I thought—a miracle she's been able to keep it together this long.* She forced a smile to her lips. "Well, now that you're here, we'll get everything taken care of. I promise. We'll get whatever help you need."

"What I need," Marjorie said, her eyes flashing with determination, "is to know what's happening inside my head, or my body, or wherever the culprit is currently residing. I need to plan for the future, whatever it might hold." She lifted her chin to emphasize her point. "No one lives forever."

Paula laughed uneasily, at the same time feeling relief that her mother had, in a way, come to terms with her own mortality and was willing to get on with it. "Hey," she said lightly, "let's not get the cart before the horse, shall we? The doctor in Connecticut had his suspicions about the problem, but we've made an appointment here for you to see a specialist next week. After that, we'll talk about the future."

"That will be acceptable," Marjorie said in her most formal voice, signaling that their conversation had come to an end. She clicked a button on the TV remote, and a year-old episode of *Survivor* flashed onto the screen.

Feeling the need to prepare her mother for what could be a dismal prognosis, Paula made one final observation as gently as she could. "You know, Mother," she said, "even with all the miracles of medicine in your corner, there may not be any easy answers. We could be facing quite a challenge here."

The formal voice came again as Marjorie continued to stare straight ahead at the TV screen. "I am not a stranger to challenges, my dear." She turned her head ever so slightly toward Paula, a tiny glimmer of amusement flickering in her eyes. "I lived with your father for nearly forty years." Without another word, she turned her attention back to the screen and revved up the volume.

Resisting an urge to simultaneously laugh out loud and hug her mother, Paula simply rose and patted her respectfully on the shoulder. "All right, then," she smiled, "we'll take it as it comes." *At least she hasn't lost that lovable droll wit that surfaces every decade or so.* She was just opening the door to leave when she remembered her reason for coming. "By the way, lunch is at one . . . will you join us?" she asked. When Marjorie nodded, she hurried to the kitchen to request that Millie prepare one of her mother's favorites.

The following Wednesday, Paula and Marjorie spent the entire day at the UCLA Medical Center, where the older woman was meticulously examined, exhaustively interviewed, and subjected to an encyclopedic array of diagnostic tests. "If I wasn't crazy this morning, I shall be a raving lunatic by the end of this day," she huffed as they lunched on tuna and egg salad sandwiches in the cafeteria. "When the poet Robert Browning wrote 'Grow old along with me! The best is yet to be,' he clearly hadn't yet experienced the indescribable delight of being asked by a dewy-faced medical student young enough to be his grandson if he remembered what he had for breakfast this morning." She paused, and her voice took on a whimsical quality. "The worst part of it is, I couldn't remember."

By Friday the results were in, and Dr. Evan Corey, one of the country's most prominent specialists in diseases of the elderly, summoned Ted and Paula to his cluttered office at the Medical Center. Marjorie insisted on going with them, and the doctor broke into a boyish grin when he saw her. "Come to take control of your own life, eh?" he said, peering at her with merry blue eyes over his reading glasses. "That's a good sign."

"Let's get on with this, young man," she directed as they took their seats.

"Yes, ma'am," the congenial physician said, drawing a sheaf of papers from a file on his desk. When it was time to spell out the situation, he pulled no punches. "Everything points to Alzheimer's, or possibly some other type of closely-related dementia. We don't know exactly how long ago it started, but it's," he glanced at Marjorie with an inscrutable expression, "moving along. There are medications that may help to slow the progress of the disease, and we'll try them all. Every individual is different, of course; but if there's one thing I've learned over the past twenty years, it's that patients who take an active part in their own care, for as long as they can, tend to do better and live longer." He smiled at Marjorie, then at Ted and Paula. "And it goes without saying that an involved, supportive group of family and friends doesn't hurt, either."

Paula reached for Ted's hand. "We'll do our best," she promised.

"I'm sure you will," Dr. Corey responded. Paula didn't miss the barely perceptible note of irony in his voice.

They spent an hour discussing the ramifications of Marjorie's condition, even working out a "therapy" regimen designed to keep her mentally alert and physically active as long as possible. Included on the list were Scrabble and other word games, crossword puzzles, reading, keeping a journal, gardening, regular walks in the open air, deep-breathing exercises, even water aerobics. ("What, no racquetball?" Ted asked in mock amazement. Paula rolled her eyes.) When an urgent call from the hospital summoned the doctor, he concluded the consultation by handing Paula a small blue booklet titled *Managing Alzheimer's: A Caregiver's Guide*. "It'll give you additional ideas," he said. Marjorie insisted on having a copy of her own, and he obliged. All four of them stood, and as Ted and Marjorie left the office, Dr. Corey grasped Paula's elbow and leaned close to her. "You should know this is only the beginning," he whispered. "I'll see her every month, but there will be days when . . . well, call me if you need someone."

She smiled confidently, shaking off any hint of uncertainty. "Thank you so much, Doctor. I'm sure we'll manage."

They walked quickly out of the building and into the blistering August heat. As an icy numbness closed around her heart, Paula wished she had brought a sweater.

Chapter 17

August slipped into September, then October, with no drastic changes in Marjorie's condition. Occasionally she mistook Ted for her gardener, or baby Alexis for her childhood doll, or Paula for her long-departed mother, and she could never find her latest crossword puzzle book; but on the whole she was a pleasant and innocuous addition to the family circle. Her favorite pastime was accompanying Paula, Alexis, and Rudy on walks to the park, where they would spread a blanket and enjoy a sack lunch, then spend an hour or two relaxing in the shade of a willow tree. Marjorie never tired of watching her granddaughter play with Rudy, and the park was the best place. The adorable dark-haired, blue-eyed baby, now in her tenth month and crawling with abandon, found endless delight in tickling, teasing, and tugging on the ears of the big dog, who lay serenely on the blanket and drank in her gleeful attentions like a thirsty sponge. If she wandered off, he would wait for a minute or two, then rise slowly to his feet and go after her, corralling her sturdy body like an attentive sheepdog, nudging her tenderly with his nose until she was back on the blanket. Then he would curl up beside her, and before long she would nuzzle against the soft fur of his body and fall soundly asleep, one tiny hand resting delicately on his shoulder. He wouldn't move a muscle until she had finished her nap; then, when he felt her stirring, he would tap one paw carefully against her back to help her wake up. Paula and Marjorie had watched this endearing scenario play out over and over again, and it had become a highlight of their days together.

On the tenth of October, a clear and golden Saturday morning, Paula felt a muscled arm snake around her waist as she lay on her side in bed. Next came the tingly feel of a bristled cheek against her neck. She moaned luxuriously. If this was a dream, she didn't want to wake up anytime soon.

"Good morning, my dear," a male voice crooned in her ear. "And happy birthday."

The moan turned to a groan. So much for the Elysian fields of dreamland; no one over there ever had to worry about getting old.

"So, what is it—forty-three now?" the voice added with impish glee.

Paula turned slowly onto her back and looked up into Ted's sunny blue eyes. To her surprise, he was already dressed. "Well, that may be your take on it, cowboy," she drawled, "but I prefer to think of this as the fourteenth anniversary of my twenty-ninth birthday. So treat me with a little respect."

"We aim to please," he grinned. "Let's see: I could go whip you up a nice, soft batch of mashed potatoes, or—"

"Go away," she said with an adorable little pout, then glanced at the small crystal clock on her nightstand. Nine-thirty. "Why are you waking me up at the crack of dawn, anyway? Let me age in peace." She pulled a blanket up over her head.

"Ah, but my dear lady," he said grandly, "we have places to go, things to do, magical visions to see. In other words," he tugged the covers away from her face, "it's party time!"

"Ugh," she grunted. "Couldn't this at least wait for a couple of hours?"

"Nope . . . time's a-wastin'," he said firmly. "You've got thirty minutes to shower, do your nails, have liposuction, and meet us downstairs. Alexis has something she'd like to show you."

"If it's a new dance step, tell her I can wait," Paula muttered as she sat up and swung her legs over the side of the bed. Her face broke into a wide yawn as she tried to stretch herself awake, then collapsed back against the pillows. "I'm too old to get up."

Ted bent to kiss her quickly on the forehead, then strode toward the bedroom door. "See you in a jiffy, Your Elderlyness," he called over his shoulder as the door closed behind him.

Just over half an hour later she shuffled into the kitchen, her hair still damp and her skin rosy from the hot shower. With no makeup and dressed in her favorite jogging suit and sneakers, she looked like a high school cheerleader ready to go to Saturday morning practice.

"Happy birthday!" an assortment of voices rang out. Every member of Paula's family was seated around the table, each with a colorful helium balloon tied to his or her chair. Even Rudy had a small red balloon attached to his collar. Lexi was having the most fun, batting her balloon from her highchair and squealing ecstatically whenever it bobbed against her face.

"First, nourishment," Ted declared, escorting her to a seat at the head of the table, where a huge yellow balloon sporting the number 43 hovered above her chair. She rolled her eyes and pretended to stab at the balloon with a fork. Millie served all of her down-home favorites: streusel-topped blueberry muffins, cheese-and-mushroom omelettes, crisp bacon and plump sausages, iced orange juice, and steaming hot chocolate topped with whipped cream and marshmallows. As breakfasts went, this was the highest degree of glory.

"Next, presents," Ted announced after everyone had had their fill and Scott had finished off the rest. Miraculously, several brightly wrapped packages appeared on the table. Paula opened them, exclaiming over the thoughtful gifts inside: a tasteful silk scarf from Marjorie, a pair of small silver earrings from Scott, a Church book from Millie, a gift certificate for dinner for two at Delaney's from Lexi. Not to be outdone, Rudy sauntered up to the table with a heart-shaped box of chocolates clenched carefully between his teeth.

When all the presents had been opened and admired, Paula leaned back in her chair and smiled serenely. "Thank you all so much," she said. "If I had to have a birthday, I couldn't have asked for a better one."

"Oh, but the best is yet to come," Ted countered with a mysterious smirk. "There's still a little something from *moi.*"

Paula shrugged. "Really? I thought maybe you and Lexi had gone in together on that expensive gift certificate from Delaney's. Either that, or the child must have a job she's not telling me about."

"Trust me, Mom," Scott interjected, "it's better than all the other stuff put together. Even *I* like it . . . well, in a cheesy sort of way."

Now her interest was officially piqued. She sat silently for several seconds, waiting, watching everyone else do the same. Finally, her curiosity bubbled into overdrive. "So, is this present animal, vegetable, or mineral, and am I going to see it sometime before my forty-fourth birthday?"

Ted and Scott smiled at each other across the table. "None of the above," Ted explained, "and now would be a very good time. Close your eyes, sweetness."

"Oh, really, Ted," she protested, "I don't see why—"

A long, thick strip of cloth was summarily pressed against her eyes, drawn around to the back of her head, and tied in a firm knot. "On the other hand," she said in a small voice, "I don't see why not." She allowed herself to be stood up, turned around in place a few times until she was slightly dizzy, then led by the hand through what seemed a labyrinth of unfamiliar territory. At last she heard a sliding door open, and she was escorted through it. Feeling the fresh morning air on her face, breathing in the fragrance of late-blooming roses, she knew immediately where she was—the backyard. Now she was more intrigued than ever.

Ted gripped her elbow and guided her to the edge of the patio, then paused and wrapped his arms around her. "The others are still inside," he said close to her ear. "I wanted this moment to be just for us. Just for you."

For some inexplicable reason, standing there with a blindfold obscuring her vision, having no clue what lay before her, Paula felt her throat constrict with emotion. Something in Ted's voice, in the way he held her close, told her this was no ordinary birthday present. She waited patiently while he tugged at the knot behind her head. Finally it was undone, and the cloth fell away from her eyes.

Suddenly Paula understood, and from some deep well in her chest the tears overflowed and coursed unrestrained down her cheeks. "Oh, Ted," she breathed, leaning heavily against him as though her knees would not support her own weight. "Oh, Ted."

"I'll take that to mean this is a pleasant surprise," he murmured into her still-damp hair.

She didn't answer, but continued to stare out into the backyard, where a small white gazebo, sole survivor of the Enfield estate fire, stood in a corner near the back fence, glistening in the morning sun. Her wide-eyed gaze took in every detail, from its smooth, rounded base to its latticed sides to its quaintly tiled roof. It was perfect—the cherished symbol of her most endearing childhood memories. Nothing could have moved her more deeply.

She reached up to touch Ted's cheek. "How did you—" she began, but words failed her, and she could only look at him with a thousand questions in her tear-filled eyes.

"It was kind of a group effort, starting last August," he said, picking up where she had left off. "When we discovered it hadn't burned, the second I saw your face I knew it belonged with you." His face lit up with the boyish grin she loved so much. "The truth of it is, some things in life, like some people, are definitely keepers. So I made arrangements with Marjorie's lawyer to have it dismantled and shipped out here. It was delivered to the O'Briens' house a couple of weeks later, and they've been storing it in their garage ever since. Last night, after you were asleep, a bunch of guys from the elders quorum helped me put it on a big truck—still in pieces—and bring it over here. Then we put it together. Took most of the night." His voice was warm with pride and exhilaration.

"I'm sure it did," she observed. "But how in the world did you assemble it without making a lot of noise? I'm a pretty light sleeper these days, always keeping one ear open to listen for Lexi, but last night I didn't hear the sound of a single hammer." She moved toward the gazebo, eager to relax in its comfortable shade.

He quickly grabbed her arm and pulled her back to his side. "Not so fast, young lady. Before you go dancing around in there like some teenager from *The Sound of Music,* you should know that it's not quite, well, finished yet. We knew if we made any noise, you'd be the first one downstairs. So we, uh, made do."

"With what?" she asked, clearly intrigued by this news.

He flashed her a sheepish but self-satisfied grin. "Let's hear it for duct tape."

"You mean you fastened my gazebo together with . . ." She burst into a gale of laughter. "Well, now, I guess one should never underestimate the ingenuity of a posse of weekend carpenters."

"Exactly," he crowed importantly. "Scott and I will get busy on the hammer-and-nail part right away, then we'll do a little touch-up painting and such to make it just like new. By this afternoon, it should be sturdy enough for the next generation of Enfield women."

The thought warmed Paula to her center. "Alexis will love it," she said. "And I love you for doing this. Thank you so much. *So much.*"

She kissed him deeply, then rested her head against his chest. This was a moment too exquisite for words, and she wanted to savor it for as long as she could.

After a few minutes, the rest of the family filed out onto the patio, Scott carrying two hammers and a pouch of nails, Millie balancing Alexis on her good hip, Rudy waving his tail in slow, contented circles. Marjorie was the last to appear. When she saw the gazebo, a distracted expression clouded her face. She sat down at a glass-topped table near the edge of the patio and stared at the structure for a long time, saying nothing, running her fingers nervously back and forth along the rounded edges of the table.

"Donroe's Pound, Paint, 'N Putty at your service, ma'am," Scott grinned, bending over to kiss Paula lightly on the cheek. "See? I *told* you it was a great present!"

"The best," she affirmed, suddenly feeling the elements of her past and present coming together in a tingling rush of joy.

"It's so lovely," Millie sighed, pointing to the gazebo so Lexi would notice it. She turned to Paula. "Ted told me about it, but his description didn't do it justice. With the tragedy of the fire and all, you can be so grateful it was saved. And now, to have it here as a permanent memory of your growing-up years, why, that's just the icing on—"

A small choking sound cut her off, and everyone spun around to see Marjorie clutching the edges of the glass table with both hands, her face chalk-white, her gaze riveted on the gazebo. She seemed to be barely breathing.

Paula hurried to her side. "Mother, what's happened? Are you ill? Can I get you a glass of water or something?"

Marjorie shook her head, and within a few moments had relaxed somewhat. "No, thank you," she said in a tone devoid of emotion. "I am a bit tired, however. If you'll excuse me, I think I'll go to my room now." She rose uncertainly, but steadied herself against the table and shrugged off any assistance. As she moved slowly toward the house, she paused and turned back toward Paula. "Happy birthday, dear," she murmured with a tiny plastic smile, then turned around and disappeared through the sliding glass doors.

"We'll save you some ice cream and cake," Scott called after her. When she was out of sight, he shrugged and shook his head. "That was weird."

"I'll check on her in a little while," Paula said, shaking off a vaguely bleak sensation. "In the meantime," she motioned toward Ted and Scott, "I fully intend to enjoy every minute of watching you two gorgeous creatures pounding and puffing and sweating to put the finishing touches on my wonderful birthday present." She held out her arms for the baby. "Alexis, my sweet, would you care to join me? It's not every day we get to observe the duct-tape masters at work."

* * * * * * * *

The first day of November dawned crisp and invigorating. Paula was up earlier than usual to go for a short jog before beginning her day. Downstairs, she found Millie sitting at the kitchen table, her shoulders hunched inside a light chenille robe, her head bent over a book of scripture. "Morning, Millie!" she sang out cheerfully. "I didn't expect to see anyone else up and about at this time of—"

Her words died in a gasp as the older woman slowly raised her head and tried to move her lips in greeting. No sound came out, and her red-rimmed eyes blinked rapidly, framed by heavy dark circles. Her skin was a pasty gray color.

Paula hurried to the table and sat down beside her friend. "Millie, what's wrong? You look awful—not well at all. Is it your arthritis? I was so hoping that new prescription the doctor gave you would help, but it looks like it's made things worse. You really shouldn't be trying to move around in this condition . . . can I help you back to bed?" She reached for Millie's arm.

"No . . . it's not that," Millie said in a parched voice. "That's not all of it." She rubbed her forehead with a gnarled hand, and a single tear made its way down one of her furrowed cheeks.

"What, then?" Paula questioned gently, carefully rubbing Millie's arm in an attempt to comfort her. "You know I'd do anything to help."

Millie smiled feebly. "I know, dear. It's just that I was hoping I could . . . I could . . ." She hesitated, then sighed from somewhere deep in her center. "Hoping I could do it all."

Paula stared at her. "I don't understand. You do everything for us, Millie—probably more than you should. I can't imagine—"

"It's your mother, Paula. I—I've done everything I could, but . . ." Her voice faded, and more tears trickled from her eyes.

A knot of uneasiness formed in Paula's stomach. "Tell me," she urged.

Millie sniffed and nodded, then began to speak slowly, reluctantly. "Things went so well for those first weeks after you brought her home from Connecticut. She was no trouble—no trouble at all, and I loved doing lots of little things for her. We got to be friends."

"More like sisters," Paula said. "You made the transition easy." She regarded Millie closely. "But that's not the whole story, is it?"

"I'm afraid not." Millie's hands twisted in her lap. "Do you remember three weeks ago on your birthday, when Ted and his friends put up that precious little gazebo in the backyard?"

"How could I forget?" Paula smiled, remembering the occasion with a rush of warmth. Since that day, she and Lexi had spent countless happy hours there. But there was something else. "I also remember that when Mother saw the gazebo, she acted quite strangely—almost as though she'd had the wind knocked out of her. She seemed all right when I checked on her later, though."

"I thought she was all right, too," Millie continued. "But a day or two later, things started happening."

"Things?" Paula looked at her curiously.

"Nothing, really," Millie said quickly. "I shouldn't have mentioned it." She wrung her hands again, refusing to lift her gaze from the table.

Paula was quiet for a time, then gently laid her hand on Millie's shoulder and began to speak in soft tones. "If you're trying to worry me, you're doing a pretty good job of it, my friend. There's something going on, isn't there? Something I should know about." Millie nodded forlornly, her gray head still bowed. "Tell me about it, Millie. Please. We can work it out together." Paula's hand moved in wide, comforting circles on the older woman's back.

"All right." Millie raised her head and wiped at her eyes, then met Paula's gaze. "I never meant to complain, but I . . . it's just that . . . well, the nights have been bad."

"The nights?"

She nodded. "I've been looking after her. Little things at first, like the night a noise in the kitchen woke me at two in the morning. It was Marjorie rummaging around in the freezer, sure she'd left an earring under one of the frozen hamburger patties. I got her back to bed just fine, and she didn't seem to remember it the next day. A one-time thing, I told myself. Then two nights later, I heard this shuffling and low moaning in the hall outside my room; she was roaming from one end of the house to the other, looking for her lost umbrella. 'I can't go out in the rain without protection,' she kept saying over and over. Finally I got an umbrella from the hall closet and put her to bed with it, then sang her lullabies until she fell asleep. Other nights she wants to go outside, or she just keeps flushing her toilet again and again. I've taken to sleeping with my bedroom door open and a flashlight under my pillow in case I need to hurry and round her up."

"I had no idea," Paula murmured, guilt rising like bile in her throat.

"Last night . . . last night we were up for hours on end, and I couldn't get her back to bed until just before dawn. She'll probably sleep until noon or later, but I . . . I have . . . things to do. People I love to take care of." She paused. "I thought she'd settle down and get over it, but something happens almost every night now. The problem is, I'm just worn out." Her shoulders slumped, as though she had just confessed a grievous sin. "I guess I'm getting too old to be of much use anymore."

Hot tears sprang to Paula's eyes as she wrapped her arms around Millie. "Don't you ever, *ever* say that," she insisted. "Even if you were deaf and blind and bedridden and unable to lift a finger, you'd still be a keeper. There will always be a place for you in our family, Millie. And I'm *so sorry* this has happened. While the rest of us were all cozy and asleep upstairs in our rooms, you were down here walking the floor with Mother every night. This is unforgivable . . . what can I do to make it up to you?" She pulled back and wiped at the moisture on her face.

"There's nothing to be made up, my dear," Millie said earnestly. "After what you and your little one have been through these past few months, what with the accident and the fire and all, I just wanted to help out. Maybe Marjorie will settle down yet, and I can—"

"No, you can't," Paula broke in firmly. "Whatever you're thinking, you can't do this anymore." She gingerly squeezed Millie's hand. "Now, you go back to bed right this minute, and don't even *think* of getting up until you darn well please. I'll take care of everything today. And as of this moment, you are officially off the graveyard shift."

"But—"

"No arguments." Paula leaned over to kiss Millie's pale cheek, then looked at her with a mix of steely determination and absolute compassion. "I'm not going to have to pull rank on you here, am I?"

The old woman smiled a little and shook her head. "I just wanted to help, that's all."

"And you have, Millie. More than you know. More than you should have. And it's long past time for you to rest. Don't you think another thing about it." She pointed decisively down the hall toward Millie's room. "Now go. Sweet dreams. We'll talk later."

Millie coaxed her aching body from her chair and reached for her scriptures. "Bless you," she said, smiling gratefully at Paula, then turned and shuffled from the kitchen. A few moments later, her bedroom door closed softly.

Paula sat quietly for a long while, gazing out the window at an exploding orange sunrise, overwhelmed by what she had just learned. "How? How could I not have known?" she finally whimpered, releasing a ragged, mournful breath into the early-morning stillness. A sudden wave of remorse and loneliness engulfed her, and she buried her face in her hands as great tears swept across her cheeks. "I'm so sorry, Millie," she sobbed. "Things will be different from now on. We'll make it up to you. I promise."

"What's this—are we expecting company?"

Ted's voice took Paula by surprise, and she looked up to see him standing at the top of the stairs leading down to the TV room, his attaché case in hand. She had just made up the queen-sized sofa sleeper at one end of the room, and was arranging a few brightly colored throw pillows on its thick floral comforter. "You're home early," she said, bounding up the stairs to greet him with a warm kiss on the cheek. "But never fear; dinner will be arriving any minute. One of your favorites—Mexican." She grinned slyly. "I ordered it myself."

"Then it must be Millie's day off," he laughed. "And who's coming to visit?"

"No one," Paula said with a hint of mystery in her voice. "Let's just say there's been a slight modification of, shall we say, . . . sleeping arrangements."

He eyed her warily. "Whose?"

She wiped a trace of lipstick from his cheek. "Mine."

Ted studied her face intently for a moment, then sighed deeply. "It's my snoring, isn't it?"

Now it was Paula's turn to laugh. "Good heavens, no. I love every little snuff and snort you make, and it never bothers me. But something else has come up. I'll explain over dinner; you go on upstairs and change, and I'll meet you in the kitchen in twenty minutes, okay?"

"Well, okay," he said with a perplexed scowl. "But this better be good."

Their meal went largely untouched as Paula related her conversation with Millie that morning, then expressed her firm resolve to take over the greatest part of Marjorie's care herself. For the time being, until they could get her mother settled into a more consistent routine, Paula would spend her nights on the sofa sleeper, where she could easily hear and tend to Marjorie's nocturnal wanderings. "Millie, bless her dear soul, has done way too much already," she said, sniffling as she remembered her friend's haggard appearance. "Now it's my turn. I told her to keep her bedroom door closed and wear earplugs."

Ted leaned back in his chair, a deep crease showing between his brows. "Maybe I should be the one to sleep downstairs," he suggested. "That way, you could be closer to the baby in case she needs you, and—"

"Lexi is *our* baby, Ted," she reminded him. "Either one of us—or even Scotty, for that matter—can take care of her just fine. Marjorie, on the other hand, is *my* mother, and I feel that at this point in her life she needs another woman to look after her. I should do the honors." She paused while he bit his lower lip and nodded gravely. "However," she continued, a teasing glint rising in her eye, "I don't see any reason why you couldn't come down to visit once in a while."

He jutted out his jaw in playful defiance. "It won't be the same," he grumped.

"I know," Paula conceded, "but we'll adjust. And before you know it, we'll have everything under control and back to normal. Mother's just going through a phase; I'm sure of it. Besides, I'm younger and stronger than Millie; and if I do say so myself, everything went quite smoothly today. Mother slept until one o'clock, which gave me plenty of quality time with Lexi. Then I fixed lunch, and later the three of us took Rudy for an excursion to the park. Mother's been in her room, watching TV, ever since we got back. I really don't think it'll be so bad. Millie will still help, of course, but only if and when she's up to it. She's been resting most of today." Paula looked at him earnestly. "I think we'll make it through this, Ted. I really do."

He offered her a plaintive little smile. "Would it be premature of me to say that I miss you?"

"One day at a time, my love," she soothed. "One day at a time."

Chapter 18

Paula swirled her jumbo shrimp in a shallow bowl of deep-red cocktail sauce. It was the middle of December, and she was lunching with Meg O'Brien at a quaint Chinese restaurant in the heart of Woodland Hills. This was one of the few times she had ventured away from home—away from her mother—in several weeks.

"I just can't figure it out, Meg," she sighed. "No one can—not even Dr. Corey. He says that seeing the gazebo again might have triggered something horrible in Mother's subconscious that caused a short-circuit somewhere in her brain, but he's only guessing. The reality is that she still has good days, but on the whole she's gone downhill so fast it's boggled our minds. None of the medicines seem to help, either. And it's very disconcerting. One morning she'll seem perfectly fine, and by afternoon she won't know any of us. Not to mention her constant wandering at night. I don't actually *sleep* anymore; I just take short naps in between tending her. Two weeks ago, she managed to find an open door and slipped outside. I must have dozed off, because the next thing I knew, Rudy was scratching at the front door, whimpering to beat the band. We found her at the end of the street, almost ready to turn the corner and walk right across an eight-lane highway." Paula chuckled bitterly. "I guess now it's my job to save her from herself—for the rest of her life."

Meg looked at her sympathetically. "How's the rest of the family holding up?"

"Like the leaning tower of Pisa. We want everything to be normal, try to pretend it's that way, but we're always just a little off balance. Or a lot." Paula rubbed the space between her eyebrows. "Ted is constantly in a bad mood about my sleeping downstairs, and between taking care of Lexi and Mother, I'm too tired to even have a decent conversation with him these days. When we do talk, we find ourselves snapping at each other. Millie does what she can to help, but I won't let her risk her health. Surprisingly, Scotty has been awfully good with Mother, and he spends quite a bit of his spare time with her in the evenings; she loves it when he reads to her. Still, he can feel the tension, and he doesn't like it, so he spends more time than usual in his room or away from home. Even Lexi has picked up on the strain; she fusses more at night, and Ted has to get up with her. Sometimes it feels like we're all connected to each other by a huge rubber band that's already stretched to its limit, and each of us is leaning backward. If the band breaks, we'll fall apart and out of each other's lives."

Meg sighed and shook her head. "I hate to say it, but the stress is showing. You look exhausted, my friend."

"It's taking its toll; no doubt about that," Paula conceded. "Strange . . . for a long time I thought everything was going so well. Mother spent a lot of time in her room, but she always seemed to be busy, even happy, and every week she'd ask me to bring her a new pile of crossword puzzle books and magazines. As soon as she got them, she'd start working furiously; I could hardly even get her to stop to eat. I took it as a good sign; she was keeping her mind active, after all, and she was working through the puzzles at record speed. Then one afternoon, while she was watching Lexi and Rudy play in the backyard, I decided to throw away some of the piles of old puzzle books in her room. You know what I found?" She bit into an egg roll.

"I'm not sure I want to know," Meg said.

"I flipped through a few of the puzzles. She'd finished them, all right—but she hadn't filled in even one correct word! They were all just a jumbled mass of letters. Just letters." Her shoulders sagged, and she let the unfinished egg roll drop to her plate. "Then, when I questioned her gently about it, she was convinced that she'd completed every puzzle with one hundred percent accuracy. She was quite proud of herself, in fact—said she figured she was beating this thing, in spite of all the odds."

"Whoa," Meg breathed.

"But that's not the worst part," Paula said, lowering her voice. "For a woman who's been a poster girl for fastidiousness all her life, Mother's personal habits these days are . . . well, it isn't pretty, and that's all I'll say. I'm thinking of hiring someone to come in every morning to get her cleaned up and ready for the day. I can't ask Millie to do that, and I'm not comfortable with . . . those sorts of things."

Meg was quiet for a few moments, seemingly intent on capturing a clump of noodles between the chopsticks held awkwardly in her hand. "You know," she said after several unsuccessful lunges, "she seems to be losing ground pretty quickly, and . . . I hate to say it, but the time may be coming when you'll need to consider . . . other alternatives."

Paula looked at her sharply. "Such as?"

Meg quickly reached across the table to squeeze her hand. "Now, don't freak out on me here. We'e been friends for nearly three years, and you know I'm not one to beat around the mulberry bush."

"I know. I'm sorry," Paula said meekly.

"You're also worn out and discouraged and half-crazed with worry." Meg pointed to Paula's half-eaten lunch. "Look at this. You have the appetite of a hummingbird. This is not the Paula I know. You're going to have to figure out how to handle this before it rips you and your family into little pieces."

The creases in Paula's forehead deepened. "You're right, Meg. Most days I'm reminded constantly of what Dr. Gray said when he gave us his preliminary diagnosis: 'No one wins against this disease if you let it tear you apart.' It's just that this is completely new territory for me—trying to come to terms with my responsibility as a daughter without sacrificing my own family in the process. In a way, knowing what the Church teaches about the importance of families makes it even harder. My mother was hardly the ideal parent, but does that relieve me of the responsibility to take care of her when she's sick and unable to care for herself? I don't think so. On the other hand, my husband and children could become casualties if I allow Mother's illness to take over our lives. I feel like I'm caught in the middle, and it's virtually impossible to choose between the two."

Meg looked at her intently. "Maybe you don't have to choose. Maybe there's another way."

"I'm listening," Paula said, but regarded her friend suspiciously.

"Just hear me out," Meg urged. When Paula nodded, she went on. "I get the feeling that the idea of putting your mother in a nursing home or care facility is pretty much repugnant to you. After all, she spent her whole life as a wealthy, privileged socialite, and anything less than concierge-type treatment would be indignity personified." Paula nodded again, cringing at the suggestion. "I understand—and I'd feel exactly the same way, especially given the uncertain quality of care such an institution might offer. We've both heard enough nursing-home horror stories to last a lifetime." Another nod, and she continued. "But what if you knew—absolutely *knew*—that a place could be trusted? That your loved one would be at least as well off there as in your own home, and maybe even better off?"

Paula chewed on her bottom lip. "I suppose that would make a difference."

"Of course it would," Meg declared. "That's why I'm bringing it up."

"Bringing what up?"

"Something I heard last week," Meg said with an eager lilt to her voice. "Believe me, I wasn't going to mention it today, but what you've told me makes it seem appropriate at this point. The thing is, Eloise Martin told me that some new members of our ward, Brother and Sister Tremayne, have bought a large, beautiful old Spanish villa-type home over on Cristobal Drive. They've just finished converting it into a residential care center for people with Alzheimer's and other types of dementia. From what Eloise says, it's more like a five-star hotel with all the amenities than a rest home. Alicia Tremayne is a registered nurse with a specialty in geriatric medicine, and her husband Bart has a business background, so they both know what they're doing. I understand the place will be open for business in a month or so." She paused and looked at Paula expectantly. "What do you think?"

"I don't know," Paula answered dubiously. "It still sounds pretty institutional. I mean, even with a competent staff, how do you manage a lot of elderly people whose minds are—"

"That's the best part," Meg interjected. "My understanding is that Mira Vista Manor—that's what they're calling it—will never have more than a total of eight residents, and every single patient will have at least two staff members to look after them twenty-four/seven. Personal care with all the TLC they can handle, gourmet meals, constant medical supervision, special activities, even a gym for those who remember what a treadmill is used for. Like I said, all of the amenities with none of the scary stories."

"Hmm . . . sounds expensive," Paula mused.

"You're darn tootin'!" Meg laughed. "Let me tell you, one month in that place would probably send the O'Briens into bankruptcy. But then, that's the difference between our Taurus income and your Jaguar lifestyle. Hey, I say if you've got it, use it where it'll do the most good." She leaned far forward in her seat. "Honestly, Paula, it could make all the difference. Will you at least talk to the Tremaynes? When they start advertising, the Manor could fill up overnight."

"I'll think about it," Paula said, "although I'm still hoping things will get better at home." She rubbed her forehead. "I'm just a little tired today, that's all; the baby was up half the night with an ear infection, and Mother was up the other half, trying to talk me into taking her for a wagon ride into town." She smiled tightly and reached for a fortune cookie.

"What does it say?" Meg asked.

Paula cracked open the cookie and pulled out a small white strip of paper. "'Smart cookies don't read fortunes. They make them.'" She chuckled. "What about yours?"

Meg broke her cookie and retrieved the paper. "'Good friends are like fine wine; they age well and are to be savored with gratitude.'" She grinned at Paula. "Okay, so the writer wasn't a Mormon . . . but he or she definitely had the right idea."

"Besides which," Paula added, returning her smile, "it wouldn't have had quite the same ring if he'd said 'Good friends are like green Jell-O.' Or 'Good friends are like caffeine-free diet Coke.'" They laughed heartily, relieved to feel some of the tension drain away.

As they waited for the check, Meg looked at her friend affectionately. "I'm awfully glad we did this; it's been a long time," she said, then paused for a moment. "And will you humor me now, my good-friend-like-fine-wine? Will you think about the Manor—just a little?"

"Well, okay—just a little," Paula promised lightly.

Later that evening, she recounted the conversation to Ted. "I can't imagine we'd ever have to put Mother someplace like that," she concluded. Noting his long, intense silence and the muscle twitching in his cheek, she looked at him carefully. "Can you?"

"It's something to think about," he said coolly. His distant tone told her that their conversation was over, so she firmly tucked the subject away in a remote corner of her mind.

* * * * * * * *

"Hey, Mom, you got a minute?" Paula looked up to see Scott making his way slowly downstairs into the TV room, where she was reading the paper. His face was pale and his dark hair disheveled, as though he had been running his fingers through it. His shoulders were in a major slump, and he wouldn't look directly at her.

She put the paper aside. "Scotty, you look terrible. What's up?"

He sank heavily into a burgundy-colored leather chair. "It's Gran. She—she . . . I can't believe it." He stared at the floor, shaking his head, looking miserable.

Paula's eyes grew wide with concern. "Has something happened to your grandmother? She seemed perfectly well this afternoon, and I know you've spent most of the evening with her. Do we need to call the doctor, or—"

"No, Mom, it's not that. Nothing's happened to Gran. She's fine." He shook his head again.

Paula relaxed. "Well, that's a relief." She noticed his wan, gloomy expression. "But what's got you so upset—and what does it have to do with my mother?"

He closed his eyes and leaned back against the chair. "What is it, sweetie?" she asked. "We can deal with it if you'll just let me know what's going on."

Scott took a deep breath and let it out in short little bursts. "Okay, here's the skinny." He looked at her gravely. "You know I've been spending quite a bit of time with Gran over the past couple of months."

"Yes, I'm aware of that," Paula said gratefully. "I know how much she enjoys having you read to her."

He shifted his position in the chair. "Yeah, well, we haven't been reading just any old thing, you know. It's been her choice."

Paula winked and flashed him a sly smile. "My goodness, I hope you haven't been wading through some of those trashy romance novels."

Her humor seemed lost on him. "Um, I don't think so."

"What, then? You don't sound all that thrilled about her taste in reading materials."

He shrugged. "It isn't that, exactly. It's more like we've, uh, been reading the . . . the Book of Mormon."

She lowered her head a bit, raised not one but both eyebrows, and stared directly at him. "Really."

Scott let out the longest, deepest sigh she had ever heard. "Yeah. Turns out she believes it. She told me so last night."

Inexplicably, tears sprang to Paula's eyes. "Why, that's wonderful," she said. "But does she even understand it?"

"Mostly, I think. Sometimes more than others." A gleam of humor rose in his eyes. "A few times she's thought I was Nephi or Captain Moroni or somebody—understandable mistakes, since those guys were cool and buff like me. But every time she can't quite get the drift, I make sure to read the same thing over again the next night. We even talk about it sometimes. When she has her head on straight, she's a smart lady. I like her a lot." He sighed again. "I—I just never figured she'd go and . . ." This time, his pause was long and disconcerting.

"And what, Scotty? What did she do?"

He looked at her with a dazed expression. "A few minutes ago, she told me she wants to join the Church."

"I see." A jumble of thoughts raced through Paula's mind as she considered the implications of this news. Would it even be possible? Marjorie would need to listen to and understand all of the missionary discussions, of course, then commit to baptism with a clear mind, then actually receive the ordinance. The question was, did she have that many good days left? "Well, it would be quite a big step," Paula said, resolving to speak with her mother about it right away. "But if she feels like she really wants to do this—and I'd be delighted if she could—then I think we should do everything we can to help her. We've been taking her to church whenever she's able, although I've never been quite sure if anything was sinking in."

Scott stared through her as though she hadn't spoken. "And there's one more thing," he said, his mouth as dry as cotton. "She wants me to baptize her."

Paula felt her jaw drop. "Come again?" she asked, stalling for time to collect her thoughts.

Scott shook his head, his face paling another degree. "She says she won't do it unless I do the dunking."

"That's what I thought you said," she murmured, her mind racing. "And how do you feel about that, son?" She was beginning to see some possibilities here.

He laughed sardonically. "What, you think they'd give me a temporary membership or something, just to get the job done?"

"Obviously not," she returned, warming to the subject. "But as I recall, several months ago you told me you were reading the book, attending church, and doing your own independent 'research.' Maybe now it's time for you to put it all together. Time to take a stand."

"You mean . . . *join?"* He gulped loudly.

"That's something only you can decide, son. A testimony is very personal." She smiled and reached over to squeeze his arm, her eyes twinkling. "But just remember—there's a little old lady who's counting on you to do the right thing."

"Yeah, terrific . . . no pressure," he muttered, rolling his eyes and sliding farther down in his chair.

"I'll go speak to her," Paula offered. "If this is really what she wants, we should start making plans."

"No hurry," Scott said. "You guys can figure it out. I'm going to bed." He stretched his long, muscular legs out in front of him.

She stood, then bent over to kiss the top of his head. "Good night, sweetie," she whispered, and couldn't resist adding one little thing. "Don't forget to say your prayers."

"Geez, Mom!" he blustered.

She grinned. "Just a thought. See you in the morning."

A moment later she had disappeared up the stairs, and he could hear her knocking softly on Marjorie's door. "You've really done it this time, Gran," he moaned.

"So, Scotty tells me you'd like to become a Mormon," Paula began when she had settled herself on the ottoman next to her mother's recliner. "I didn't know you were even interested."

Marjorie switched off the television. "It's been weighing on my mind—what's left of it." She let out a soft chuckle. "A body doesn't get to this stage in life without stopping to consider what's just around the corner. In my case," she turned toward Paula with a stoic expression, "since I might not recognize the corner when I get there, it pays to take steps while I'm able. 'This life is the time for men to prepare to meet God'—isn't that what the book says?"

"The prophet Alma, I believe," Paula smiled.

"Amulek," Marjorie corrected with a little smile of her own. Then her expression sobered. "The point is, at my age I have little enough time left; but with this, this *disease,* I feel like I'm losing a little piece of myself every day. And who knows when all the pieces will be gone? If the Book of Mormon is the word of God, and I believe it is, then I'd best not be making any bones about the rest of it. Baptism into the Church seems the only responsible way to prepare to meet my Maker." She clasped her hands tightly together and gazed at her daughter with emotion-filled eyes. "Once I'm safely in the fold, you see, it really won't matter what happens to this old mind or body during the rest of my mortal life. I'll be clean, and that's what will count in the end, when I'm finally taken home. I'll be clean." She closed her eyes briefly, as though imagining the joyful event.

"It's a wonderful feeling to be clean, Mother," Paula said softly, recalling the experience of her own baptism three years earlier. "I can't think of anything I'd rather share with you. There are some things that need to happen before they start filling the font, however. The missionaries will need to teach you the gospel, then you'll be interviewed, and—"

"And I bear my testimony and we go shopping for a white dress." She rubbed her hands against her knees. "When do we start, and how long will it take?"

"I'm not quite sure," Paula laughed, enjoying her mother's enthusiasm, "but, depending on how you're, uh, feeling—"

"You mean if the lights stay on," Marjorie interjected.

"Yes, I guess that's it," Paula conceded. "And judging from my own experience, if all goes well, I'd say everything could happen within the next month."

The older woman leaned back against her recliner with a beatific smile. "Perfect," she breathed. "That will be plenty of time."

"Plenty of time?" Paula repeated.

"For that stubborn, proud-hearted son of yours to get his act together and find out the truth for himself." She gave Paula a sharp glance. "He did tell you what I've asked of him, didn't he?"

"Oh, yes—and I can tell you he was pretty shaken by it. I don't know if he's ready to make a commitment yet."

"He's ready, all right," Marjorie stated unequivocally. "At least he will be when he gets down off his high horse and onto his knees. He's already halfway there; if you'd heard him reading the book to me with such feeling, answering my questions like he'd thought it all out on his own, telling me about what he learned in Sunday School class last week, you'd know it, too. Truth be told, I'm quite aware that I might never make it to the font on this side of the grave; I may be just too far gone, although I'll give it my best effort. But your young Scotty has his whole life to live the gospel, and I'll be darned if I won't fight until my last breath to see that he does it. That's why I insisted that he be the one to take me into the water—not for myself, but to nudge him along toward that iron rod until he gets the bright idea to grab hold of it all by himself." She lifted her chin and looked squarely into Paula's eyes. "I may be losing my mind, but I'm not an imbecile."

"No, you most certainly are not," Paula beamed. "In fact, I think you have definitely made all the difference in your grandson's life. Thank you for that, Mother."

Feeling her heart swell with love for this woman whose indomitable spirit was, for this moment at least, shining so brightly, she moved to the recliner and bent to put her arms around Marjorie. Leaning together, cheek to cheek, they shared a moment together that seemed to transcend a lifetime of flawed dreams and fractured encounters. Perhaps, finally, the healing had begun.

Chapter 19

"She's better today, Elder Staples."

"She's worse today, Elder Boynton."

"She's not even *here* today, Elders."

Christmas came and went, and Marjorie's "better" days seemed to occur with maddening infrequency—perhaps twice a week, and they were never quite as good as the previous "better" days. But when they did come, the elders were ready. Slowly and surely, with infinite patience, they taught her the gospel. She insisted that Scott sit in on every one of the discussions; and in the evenings, when she was up to it, he and Marjorie continued to read the Book of Mormon behind closed doors. Sometimes he brought Rudy, Alexis, and an armload of toys along with him, and the baby played quietly on the carpeted floor while they visited.

"I wish I could be a fly on the wall and hear what they're talking about," Paula commented one Saturday morning over an early breakfast. It had been an easier week than most, and both she and Ted were feeling relaxed and agreeable. "I hate to admit it, but I'm actually a little bit jealous. She's my mother, after all."

Ted speared a chunk of cantaloupe with his fork. "Aye, there's the rub. On any given morning I know that, you know that, and Scott knows that. But does *she* know that?"

She shot him an exasperated glance, to which he responded by adding, "Hey, if this all works out, we'll have two new Mormons in the house. You can't argue with a fifty percent increase. Or slightly less, depending on the day and Marjorie's unique take on things."

Paula was aiming a large melon ball in his direction when they heard footsteps in the entryway. Soon Scott appeared, dressed in corduroy Dockers, a navy-blue T-shirt, and a down jacket. He carried his old high school backpack.

"Going somewhere cold?" Ted asked casually. "It may be the day after New Year's, but it's almost seventy degrees outside."

"There's something I need to do . . . up the canyon," he said, zipping his jacket closed.

"Then at least have something warm to eat before you go," Paula urged. "There's hot cocoa on the stove, and Millie's made some scrumptious cinnamon—"

"Thanks, I think I'll pass. Maybe later." He gave her a small, lopsided grin. "Back in a while . . . see ya." He turned back toward the entryway, and in a moment the front door opened and closed. Within a minute or two the Viper's engine sputtered to life, and its lively clatter could be heard until it rounded a corner at the end of the street.

"Now, where were we?" Paula smirked, retrieving the melon ball from her plate. When Ted put up his hands in a defensive gesture, she popped the fruit into her mouth. "Oh, yes . . . we were discussing the relative merits of having an Ivory household."

"Excuse me?" he blinked.

"Ninety-nine and forty-four one hundredths percent pure—Mormon, that is. On Mother's good days, it could actually be a hundred percent."

"Could be," he agreed. "Seriously, though, do you really think she'll make it? She drifts in and out so often, it's anybody's guess when she might know what she's doing."

"I think," Paula said, using her fork to swirl a bit of frosting on her cinnamon roll, "she's determined to see that Scott accepts the gospel. She cares a lot about him. It took her a while, but she's already done everything she needs to, including finishing the discussions and having her baptismal interview. Now she's just waiting for him—and I wouldn't be surprised if she's already told him so in no uncertain terms."

Ted nodded. "Let's just hope her condition doesn't get in the way."

"Oh ye of little faith," Paula returned with a winsome smile. "Things will work out; I can feel it in my bones. In the meantime, don't you have to help somebody move or something today?"

He glanced at his watch. "You're right—and I'll be late if I don't leave ten minutes ago." Standing, he bent over to pick a large red grape out of the fruit bowl between them, tossed it into the air, caught it in his mouth, then winked at her. "Thanks for a grape breakfast, my dear." He kissed her quickly, then bounded toward the garage door.

Paula leaned back in her chair and sighed with satisfaction. She had accomplished more in the past two hours than she had during the entire past week. With Millie upstairs tending to the baby, Marjorie still secluded in her room, and Ted off on his mission to help the elders quorum move Brother and Sister Coverly and their nine children into a new home across town, she had taken advantage of this peaceful morning to cloister herself in the far corner of the TV room. This was where she had moved her desk, computer, and other office equipment to make room for her mother, and it was from here that she kept tabs on Donroe & Associates. This morning she had updated some important account files, crunched a few budget figures, and written an outline for a new ad campaign. The work was exhilarating, and now she admitted to herself that she had missed it during these last weeks when caring for Marjorie had consumed so much of her time and energy. A fleeting thought of the Mira Vista Manor surfaced in her mind, but she quickly dismissed it and turned her attention to the computer screen in front of her. Immersing herself in year-end revenue reports, she barely heard the front door open and close.

The rustle of Scott's down jacket was her first clue that he had entered the room; his low whistle behind her was the second. "Whoa, it looks like your company is in the deep green stuff," he murmured, staring at the figures on the screen.

"Something like that," she chuckled, keeping her back to him so he wouldn't see how pleased she was that he had noticed. "Did you have a nice time in the canyon?"

She could feel him hesitate. "Yeah. Yeah . . . I guess you could say that," he replied after a moment.

His unusual tone prompted her to swivel her chair around toward him. "I don't know what you found to do up there," she began. "At this time of year, you could easily catch your death of . . ." Her words trailed off when she saw his face.

Scott's expression instantly brought to mind the title of a book Paula had read many years before. It was C.S. Lewis, she thought, though at the moment she couldn't remember what it was about. But it didn't make any difference; the title said it all. *Surprised by Joy.* That was exactly how Scott looked; she couldn't have described it any other way, didn't even want to try. All she knew was that this was not the same young man who had zipped up his jacket and hurried out the door less than three hours earlier.

"What's happened?" she asked, her voice hardly more than a whisper.

Without a word, he shrugged off his jacket and tossed it on a nearby chair. Then he retrieved a small dark-blue volume from his backpack and knelt on the floor so he was at eye-level with Paula. As their gazes locked, he reaching tenderly for her hand, turned it palm up, and carefully laid the book across it. Without even looking, she knew what it was, and she rested her other hand on the cover's gold lettering.

"It's true, Mom," he said meekly. "All of it." His lips trembled with emotion as he wrapped both of his large, sinewy hands around hers.

"And how do you know this?" Paula's heart was pounding like a sledge hammer in her chest.

"I asked," he replied simply. "Went up on the mountain and hiked to my cave. The same one where Andrea and I went last year, and I—"

"Yes, I remember," she smiled. "The cliff-jumping incident."

"That's it. Anyway, I went there because I needed to feel close to . . . well, close to the universe or something, you know? It's always been a good place for thinking, or reading, or sketching, or just settling myself down. Today, it was a good place for praying."

"Then I take it you got some answers." Her voice was calm, but the sudden anticipation of joy felt like fire in her veins.

"Yes. *Yes!* It was just like Andy said it would be; but I had to find out for myself. Now it all makes sense—everything I've heard in church and Sunday School, all the prayers and testimonies, those smart kids telling me I'd know for sure one day, Gran's unique brand of encouragement. But you know what? I could have found out months ago; I just should've asked." He flashed her a sheepish grin.

"Carmine's going to love ribbing me about this. I can hear her now: 'I told you so, I told you so, I told you so!'"

"Come here," Paula said, spreading her arms wide. He came into them eagerly, and she cradled his head on her shoulder, much as she had done when he was a toddler, smoothing his dark hair, whispering words of affection and encouragement in his ear. "I'm so proud of you," she murmured over and over. "So proud. And I love you so much."

He pulled back a little so he could see her face, touch her cheek. "That's exactly what I heard today on the mountain," he said, his eyes brimming. "Only it was Heavenly Father doing the talking. It's awfully good to know that both of you are on my side."

"Always." She was smiling through her own tears. "And you see? Once you were ready to ask, it didn't take long to get an answer, now did it?"

"Heck, that's a no-brainer," he grinned. "The Man upstairs knew He didn't have a lot of time to mess around. It was *cold* up there on that mountain! Not to mention the fact that I was *starving,* since I was right in the middle of a big ol' fast. He had to get right to it."

"Well, I'm glad the two of you worked it out." She pressed a kiss to his cheek.

"Me too." He jumped to his feet. "Now I need to go tell Gran; if she's 'in' today, she'll be happy to know I've finally come around. There are some phone calls I need to make, too. And a triple-decker sandwich with my name on it in the fridge."

"Absolutely," she agreed, watching him sprint up the stairs. "And Scotty?" she called out at the last moment.

He spun around on the top stair. "Yeah, Mom?"

"I told you so."

He laughed and gave her an exuberant thumbs-up signal before disappearing into the entryway.

"Well, what do you know," she mused as she switched her computer off. "We're going to be an Ivory household after all."

Once Scott had made up his mind, he moved quickly. Before the day was over, his and Marjorie's baptisms had been scheduled for the following Saturday, and the next day the news was announced in his UCLA ward. "Carmine nearly hugged me to death," he reported to Paula after church, "and a lot of people said they'd be there. One of the guys said he was coming just to witness a real live modern-day miracle taking place. I took a little ribbing, but it's okay, since everyone in that ward is awesome. They're my friends, you know?" He smiled, and there was a light in his eyes she hadn't seen before.

"I know," Paula said, offering a silent prayer of gratitude for faithful young men and women who saw the best in her son. "And speaking of friends, have you called Andrea yet? I think she'd like to know."

He tugged at his tie, loosening it and then pulling it off altogether. "I'm way ahead of you there, Mom. I called her last night." The glimmer in his eyes died down a little. "She and Kelsey are doing their harp-and-flute thing at a wedding reception next weekend, so she won't be able to make it to the baptism. It's pretty far to come all the way out here from BYU, anyway, especially when she's just getting started on a new semester. But she was jazzed . . . I could hear it in her voice. She said she'll be thinking of me."

"I'm sure she will," Paula agreed, noticing the subtle disappointment in his tone. "You'll have a lot to talk about when you see each other again."

He shrugged. "Yeah. She said we'll have to get together this summer, visit all the old Idaho haunts. Maybe she'll come out here."

"I'd love that," Paula said. "Now, what can we do to help you get ready for the big event?"

"Nothing," he grinned. "The kids in the ward insisted on putting the whole thing together. They're even having a little lunch for us afterward in the cultural hall. I've already talked to Ted; he actually got a little teary when I asked him to baptize me—can you believe that? It nearly blew him away when I also asked him to confirm me, then ordain me a priest right afterward so I can baptize Gran. I could've pushed him over with a Twinkie. You've got it a little easier, Mom; all you have to do is show up and bring Gran, then help her get ready. It should be a piece o' cake."

"It'll be wonderful, sweetie," she smiled. "I'm sure of it."

* * * * * * * *

"What was that somebody said about the 'best-laid plans'?" Paula murmured, slumping against the passenger-side door of Ted's Jeep Cherokee.

"Ah, I think I know that," Ted offered as he steered the vehicle onto the freeway. "The best-laid plans just lie there until something more interesting comes along."

She managed a small laugh. "That would explain it."

They were driving in the Cherokee, Millie sitting quietly in the backseat, headed for the stake center where they had attended Carmine's baptism six months earlier, and where, in less than an hour, they would participate in Scott's baptismal service on this gleaming January morning. Scott had gone ahead earlier to help set up the luncheon tables, and was unaware of recent developments. They would have to tell him when they arrived.

"I hated leaving her," Paula said forlornly.

Ted reached over to clasp her hand, closing some of the emotional distance between them. "She'll never even know we're gone, and Mrs. Spencer from the Senior Center will take good care of her. She works with Alzheimer's patients all the time. Besides, Marge will probably sleep the morning away."

Paula nodded silently, trying to banish her mother's distracted stare from her memory. Only last night, Marjorie had played a lively game of Scrabble with the family—and she'd won! She hadn't been this alert for weeks, and she'd spent the evening chattering about her upcoming baptism, wondering out loud about how she would spend her first day as "full-blown, true-blue Mormon." When Scott volunteered to take her for a stroll around the grounds of the Los Angeles Temple, her gray-blue eyes had sparkled merrily.

But there was just one problem: only two hours ago, those same gray-blue eyes had shown no recognition, no anticipation, absolutely no understanding of what this day held for her. It was as if, in the night, some giant vacuum tube had snaked into her room and sucked her mind away from the moment, and she had utterly lost herself by morning. Locked in a despair of silence, she had been unable to comprehend or answer even the simplest questions. Clearly, this was no day for a life-altering ordinance to be performed. Her baptism would have to wait.

They rode in silence for several minutes, then Ted spoke in reassuring tones. "It'll happen; you'll see. We'll keep a close eye on her, and the second she's back we'll pull together an impromptu service.

Do you know Keith Lubeck in the ward?" Paula nodded. "Well, he told me that on his mission in Ecuador, there was this little old man who was dying of cancer but begged to be baptized before the end came. He slipped into a coma, but came out of it long enough for them to carry him down to the river and get the job done. Two days later, he died a happy man." He paused. "Which all goes to show that it's never too late."

"I suppose," Paula conceded. "At least Scotty will have his day to shine, then he'll be ready when Mother needs him."

"Exactly. Now, let's enjoy this day, shall we? You've waited a long time for it."

She had to smile. "And who would have thought it—my own mother serving as the catalyst for this occasion. It's like . . . like healing all the old family wounds in one big splash. Literally. She might not have been a June Cleaver role model in my previous life, but she's certainly piling up mountains of brownie points with this one. I can't help thinking the Lord is pretty pleased with the way it's coming together."

"Things do have a way of working out," Ted smiled as they pulled into the church parking lot. It was half an hour before the service was to begin, but there were only a few empty spaces on the side of the building where the font was located.

Inside, two accordion-type curtains had been opened and the multi-purpose room expanded as far as possible to accommodate Scott's large entourage of friends. Carmine, the official greeter, saw his family coming and rushed to throw her arms around them. She steered Ted toward the men's dressing room, then escorted Paula and Millie to a row of reserved chairs next to the font. As Paula took her seat, Carmine's brow furrowed. "Wait a minute . . . I thought your mom was being baptized today. Scott said he was being ordained a priest so he could do it, and you'd be helping her get ready." Her face brightened. "Oh, she must be coming later. I can show you where the ladies' dressing room is, and—"

"Thanks," Paula interrupted, "that won't be necessary."

"Oh . . . okay." The young woman didn't seem to know what to do next.

"Mother wasn't feeling very well this morning," Paula explained, "so we decided to wait and do it another time. Ted will let Scotty know what's going on." She smiled up at Carmine, thinking how vibrant and attractive—even beautiful—she looked this morning. "So I guess this is my son's big day."

"And it's about time!" Carmine beamed. "Some of the ward members were thinking of starting up monthly meetings of the Scott Donroe Support Group, just to nudge him along. But I always knew he'd come around, and I told him so."

"Yes," Paula chuckled, "I expect you did."

She and Millie sat quietly, listening to the pianist play a medley of hymns, until Scott and Ted joined them on the front row, one on either side, minutes before the proceedings were to begin. "My two favorite men look extraordinarily handsome this morning," she whispered, noticing the smartly tailored white shirts, ties, and trousers they wore. "Talk about white knights." Their eyes shone at the compliment.

In a graceful, self-assured movement, Scott circled his mother's shoulders with one long arm. "Ted told me about Gran," he said close to her ear, and she felt a small lump of regret form in her throat. "It's all right, Mom. I'm here today because of her, and now I'll help her get where she wants to be. I promise. Whenever she's ready." She smiled and nodded gratefully, then reached out to pat his knee.

When the bishop of Scott's ward stood to begin the service, a congenial hush fell over the group. After nearly an hour of lively talks, testimonies, and musical numbers, Ted leaned close to Paula and spoke so softly that no one else could hear. "Can't help myself," he murmured in a voice laced with barely controlled humor. "Leave it to the younger generation . . . this sounds more like a roast than a baptism. Whoever heard of 'The Fourteenth Article of Faith, as penned by Scott "the Turtle" Donroe'?"

"I guess we all have now," Paula giggled.

"I heard that," Scott whispered loudly. "Awesome, isn't it?"

The final talk was delivered by the bishop, a middle-aged gentleman who reined in the playfulness in a kindly way, then focused on the deeply spiritual nature of Scott's baptismal covenant. After sharing a few moving personal experiences and bearing a powerful testimony, he announced that it was time for the ordinance to take place.

"I guess this is it," Scott breathed, standing up to smooth his trousers and straighten his tie. He nodded at Ted, who was also standing, and the two moved toward the side of the room and the entrance to the font. Paula watched them, her eyes radiating pride and affection, until they were out of sight.

At that moment, she felt a light pressure on her shoulder. Looking up, she stared into the most luminous green eyes she had ever seen. "Oh, you're here!" she exclaimed softly, her face breaking into a wide, welcoming smile. "Come and sit beside me." The person declined, pointing to the font's entrance, and Paula nodded. "We'll see you afterwards, then." She relaxed into her seat and relished the feeling of pure joy bubbling up inside her. When several people began filing up to the railing, she joined them and waited expectantly for her son and husband to appear.

"Okay, big guy, you go first," Ted declared as he and Scott stood at the top of the steps leading into the font. "I'll be right behind you."

The boy grinned nervously. "Cutting off all escape routes, eh?"

"You'll do great," Ted returned, nudging him down the first two steps with a firm hand at his back. After that, feeling the warm, undulating water lapping at his feet and ankles, Scott seemed to gain confidence and moved easily into the center of the font. Standing waist-deep in the blue-green water, he smiled shyly as Ted joined him and raised his right arm to the square.

The requisite words were spoken, then Scott closed his eyes, bent his knees, and slipped beneath the surface. For a second or two that seemed to stretch into the eternities, he relaxed as he felt the cleansing liquid swirl about his long body in perfect, weightless silence, creating a sensation of peace that he had not really expected. When he felt Ted's hand tugging at his arm, he secured his feet against the tiled bottom of the font and broke through the water to a warm buzz of approval and delight from those gathered at the railing.

At that instant, he noticed a shadowy movement at the top of the steps he had descended only minutes earlier. Wiping the water from his eyes with both hands, he stared at the figure until it came into clear, unmistakable, glorious focus. When it did, his whole face erupted into the smile of the century. "Andrea!"

She was balancing on the top step, as though she was considering taking a dip herself, just to be near him. Her thick, shoulder-length chestnut hair seemed to smolder in the dim light of the stairwell, and tears coursed from her green eyes across her porcelain cheeks, making small damp marks where they fell on her emerald-colored silk dress. Without actually smiling, the gracious upward curve of her generous lips conveyed more than words could express.

Scott plunged through the water, splashed up the steps, and gathered her into his arms, crushing her slender body against his in a jubilant embrace. "So it's not just a dream," he murmured, unwilling to let her go, stroking her luxuriant hair until it glistened with dampness from his wet hand. "You're here . . . you came!"

"Of course, silly boy," she chuckled, enjoying the feel of his cold, dripping shirt against her cheek. "Did you really think I'd let a little thing like a wedding reception keep me from showing up at my best friend's baptism? I just wanted to surprise you, that's all. I told Kelsey that she and her harp were on their own; I had better things to do. The only available flight got to LAX about an hour ago, then I rented a car and broke every speed limit to get here. It was a beautiful service, Scott. Tell me . . . how do you feel?"

He pulled back just far enough to gaze deeply into those extraordinary green eyes. "Like I just jumped off a cliff—and sprouted wings!"

"I haven't heard it described exactly that way before," she laughed. "But for some reason, coming from you, it sounds absolutely appropriate." She winked at him, then kissed his cheek.

"Ahem," a voice said from the font, "I believe we have a confirmation to attend to."

Scott glanced around and quickly ascertained that there was room for only one person—or two, standing *very* close together—on the steps, and Ted had been waiting patiently below. "Oh, uh . . . sorry," he said with a self-deprecating little grin.

"No problem." Ted started up the steps, and the three were soon standing outside the dressing room, where he gave Andrea a welcoming hug before turning to Scott. "You coming?" he questioned, reaching for the door handle.

"In a second," Scott promised, his eyes never leaving Andrea's face. The door opened and closed, and they were alone. A few bars of "I Need Thee Every Hour" drifted in from the multi-purpose room. "I still can't believe you're here," he said, grasping both of her hands, his smile reflected in her eyes.

"Well, believe it," she declared. "You would have done the same for me if I'd been the one getting baptized."

He nodded. "You know I would. It's just that . . . there's something I've never realized before. You're so . . . so very . . ." His gaze traveled deliberately from her forehead down to her ankles, and he took in a deep breath. "So very *soaking wet!*"

"Oh, right," she giggled, reaching down to wring out the hem of her dress. "I guess that's what you get when you hug someone who's just gone for a little swim."

Without warning, the dressing room door opened a few inches, and a hand appeared clutching a large while towel. "Compliments of the house," a teasing voice said from the other side.

"Why, thank you, Brother House," Andrea smiled, gratefully snatching the towel as the hand disappeared behind the door. "This will be perfect." She glanced up at Scott as she pressed the warm, dry fabric against the front of her dress. "You'd better go change; and I believe your mother is saving a seat for me." She balanced on tiptoe to kiss his cheek. "See you in a few minutes." Casting him a dazzling smile, she turned and moved toward a set of double doors leading to the multi-purpose room.

He stared after her for a moment before turning away. "So beautiful," he breathed, then pushed through the dressing room door.

After the confirmation, ordination, and luncheon, Scott and Andrea dropped off her rental car at the airport and drove home in the Viper. "Just as noisy as I remembered it," she commented as they rattled down the freeway. "But now that a Saint is driving, I'm less inclined to worry."

Scott grunted. "What—that it'll fall apart, or that I'll give in to my less-than-Saintly impulses and burn a little rubber?"

"Both," she replied sweetly.

He looked at her sideways, and thought she had never seemed more appealing. "Want to go up to the mountain?" he asked on impulse.

Instead of answering, she bent over and tugged off one of the delicate sling-backed leather pumps on her feet, then tapped his shoulder with its toe. "Does this look like a hiking boot to you?" she inquired. "A hundred bucks says you'd have to carry me up to the cave."

"So I would." He raised an eyebrow. "Worse things have happened."

She punched him playfully on the shoulder. "Actually, I would like to revisit the scene of your crime. Tell you what: let's go back to your place, change into something a bit less dry-clean-only, then see where the rest of the weekend takes us. I don't fly back to Utah until tomorrow afternoon."

"Deal," he said evenly while his heart bludgeoned his ribs.

They pulled up to the house and parked in the driveway. The garage door was open, so Scott decided to escort Andrea in through the kitchen. He stepped out of the car, strode around to the passenger side, and opened the door. "Shall we?" he said, offering his hand. When she took it, he felt a warm, evocative sensation flowing upward from his fingers to his shoulder. Once she had alighted from the vehicle, he was in no hurry to let go of her hand. And she didn't seem to mind. They walked slowly through the garage and paused briefly while he opened the door leading to the kitchen.

Inside, there was no sound. But it was not just an absence of noise; it felt like an airless vacuum, a dark silence that made even breathing unbearable. It was not overly warm in the short hall, but suddenly Scott felt himself perspiring and shivering at the same time. "That's strange," he whispered in a tight voice, "I thought everyone would be—"

Andrea's fingers against his lips cut him off. She pointed, and they both looked toward the entryway just in time to hear it.

A high-pitched, nearly hysterical woman's voice was pleading, begging, warning, cajoling—all in the space of three words. "Mother, please. Don't!"

"I'm not your mother, and I can do what I want!" a hoarse, angry voice responded.

Still gripping Andrea's hand, but now more tightly, Scott led her noiselessly through the kitchen until they were standing just inside the entryway. His jaw clenched as he took in the sight. "Oh, no," he moaned.

Ted, Millie, and Paula were huddled together near the stairwell, staring upward with wide, glassy eyes. Rudy stood nearby, whining softly, his large paws shuffling nervously in place, his nails making tiny clicking sounds against the tiled floor. Above them, on a small landing halfway up the stairs, Marjorie was leaning against the banister, clad in a long, turquoise-colored chenille bathrobe, her usually impeccable hair now uncombed and sticking out from her head in small, gray-white tufts. She was balancing something against the railing.

"Chiclet!" Scott gasped as he saw the baby's arms flailing the air a few feet above him—almost, but not quite within his reach. She wasn't making a sound, but was straddling the railing and wiggling energetically in her grandmother's arms. One playful kick from her sturdy little foot, and . . .

"What happened?" Scott whispered, moving closer to Ted.

"She's out of her mind—thinks she's a little girl," he murmured out of one side of his mouth while keeping an eye on Marjorie. "She was standing up there, arguing with Mrs. Spencer, when we got home about half an hour ago. Mrs. Spencer came down to make her some tea, trying to get her calmed down, but while she was in the kitchen, Marge went and got the baby. Keeps calling her a 'bad little dolly.' If anyone moves toward the stairs, she gets real fidgety. Anything could happen." He rubbed a hand across his eyes.

Scott knew he had to do something. "Let me try," he said. "We have a connection, and I might be able to talk her through it." Ted nodded tersely.

Like a cat on the prowl, Scott moved slowly, cautiously in the direction of the stairs while Ted spoke to Marjorie in low, conciliatory tones. When he was in position, his foot on the bottom step, he raised his head and looked up at her. "Gran?" he began tentatively. "Gran, it's me, Scotty. I've been looking for you . . . don't you want to come down and read with me?"

"I don't know you," she spat out. "Where is Mama? She told me she'd be back after Christmas with a new dolly. This one is bad . . . won't do a thing I say." She tightened her grip on Lexi's arm. The baby began to whimper softly, struggling a little harder to get free.

Scott moved up a step. "Your mama . . . couldn't come right away, so she sent me to tell you . . . to tell you she's hurrying as fast as she can. She wants you to take good care of the dolly you have. Can you do that, Marjorie?" He swallowed hard and moved up another step. *Only a few more,* he told himself. *Hold on, Chiclet.* "Can you do that?"

The old woman's voice faltered. "But . . . but I wanted a new one." She shifted the baby so that both of her small legs were now hanging over the banister. Below her, there was a collective gasp. "This dolly only causes me trouble."

"I know, Missy," Scott said, using the childhood nickname that Marjorie had told him about months earlier. "Your mama is bringing you an awesome surprise, but you have to look after this dolly till she gets here." He extended one long leg and put two more stairs behind him. "I can help you, Missy. We can take care of her together. That way, she won't be such a bother."

"I don't know." Marjorie's face scrunched into a gnarled little frown. "It better be a good surprise."

"Oh, it is. It absolutely is. I promise," Scott said in the warmest, most affectionate voice he could muster as he carefully took one more step. *Almost within grabbing distance now. Please, Father . . . watch over my little sister.* "What's your dolly's name, Missy?"

"I—I forgot. She's just . . . just too wiggly."

"I understand," he soothed. "Maybe I could hold her for a little while, so you can get some rest before your mama comes." Holding his breath, he put another stair behind him. When she held up a trembling hand, he stopped abruptly.

She leaned against the railing and squinted down at him. "Howie . . . Howie, is that you?"

Scott recognized the name she had always used for her late husband, Howard, when recalling the early years of their marriage—the happier times they had once shared. Praying that her reaction would be positive, he nodded. "I'm here, Marge. I'm here for you."

"Oh, Howie, I've missed you!" she cried, one hand gripping the railing, the other still holding Lexi tightly. "Come to me, my sweet love," she pleaded, her voice transparent with longing.

"On my way," Scott said under his breath, smiling and opening his arms wide as he cleared the last stair. *Yes! Thank You!* Below him, Paula was moving toward the staircase, ready to dash up and reclaim her precious child, while Ted, Andrea, and Millie dared to breathe a little as they watched the conclusion of this heart-stopping drama from the entryway.

Scott reached the landing and strode quickly toward Marjorie, his arms still extended to draw her and the baby into a firm circle of safety. As his fingers touched her chenille sleeve, she tore her free hand from the railing and reached for him. At the same instant, her hold on Lexi slipped and the baby wriggled free.

A fraction of a second later, a sickening thud rocked the entryway.

Chapter 20

Paula gaped in sheer horror at the scene before her. Rudy lay sprawled on his side at the bottom of the stairwell, too stunned to move. The impact of Lexi's body had knocked him over, and now the baby was sliding slowly, limply down his flank toward the floor. She did not appear to be breathing, and her face was rapidly turning a bluish-purple color.

Someone shouted "Call 911!" as Ted rushed forward to scoop the child into his arms. "No!" he shouted back. "There's a community hospital less than five minutes from here. We can get her there faster on our own. He looked up the stairs, where Marjorie was still locked in Scott's arms, a dazed expression clouding her face. "Scott, we'll need you to drive. Millie and Andrea will stay with Marge." The boy quickly disentangled himself from his grandmother's embrace, took a second to whisper "Sorry, Gran" into her ear, and bounded downstairs.

"But Howie, you just got here," she protested with a thin, confused wail. Sobbing, she sank to the floor and slumped against the banister spindles. "Oh, Howie, must you go away again? We were so happy, walks by the sea, every night a sky full of stars, such a future to . . ." Her voice faded into a desolate sigh.

Paula gripped Ted's hand with white-knuckle intensity when the doctor pushed through a set of double doors and strode into the emergency room waiting area. More than an hour earlier they had seen their barely conscious daughter whisked away through those same doors, and there had been no guarantees of a miraculous recovery. Only silence, and the relentless movement of a sterile black-and-white clock on a wall near the entrance. Now, the doctor's expression was grim as he approached them. Was that simply a reflection of his personality, or did it have something to do with the news he was about to convey? Paula hardly dared look him in the eye as she and Ted came to their feet. Scott was right beside them.

"Your daughter took a nasty fall," he began without preface. "It could have killed her."

Ted blew out a short, puffy breath. "Then she's alive." Paula leaned heavily against him. They could face anything, as long as she was alive.

"Yes," he confirmed, and his face relaxed a little. "In fact, she'll be fine. She had every bit of wind knocked out of her and blacked out from the lack of oxygen; she also sustained some bruises to her back from the impact, and she'll be sore for a few days. Other than that, she's in good shape; the x-rays showed no broken bones or internal injuries. We've given her a mild sedative, so she'll be drowsy for a time." He looked at them over his small, silver-rimmed glasses. "I don't think I need to tell you that the outcome would have been very different if she'd landed on your tile floor." His mouth curved into a half-smile. "If I were you, I'd give that dog of yours a big, juicy bone every day for the rest of his life."

"And whatever else he wants," Paula assured him. "Can we take Lexi home now?"

"Of course. I'll do the final paperwork and bring her out to you in a few minutes." The doctor turned and walked back through the double doors while Ted, Paula, and Scott fell together in a grateful, relieved embrace.

The short ride home was quiet and somber as each of them reflected on what might have been. As they turned onto Valley View Drive, Scott leaned forward from the backseat. "What about Gran?" he asked in subdued tones. "She's never done anything like this before, and even when she wasn't quite all there, we weren't really worried about what she might . . . about what might happen. But now . . ." He reached over the seat to touch the sleeping baby's loosely curled fingers. "I mean, I love Gran and all . . . it's just that, well, Chiclet's too little to protect herself."

"We'll figure something out," Ted responded tonelessly. Paula could see the muscles in his jaw tighten.

"I'd still like to baptize her," Scott said as they turned into the driveway.

"We'll see," Ted murmured.

Inside, Paula took the sleeping baby upstairs while Ted stayed in the kitchen to share the good news with Millie and Andrea. "Praise the Lord," Millie said. "We were sure something terrible had happened to that sweet child."

Andrea wrapped her arms around Scott's waist and hugged him tightly. "We're all pretty shaken up. I know how much you love that little girl," she said warmly.

For the first time since this heart-stopping ordeal had begun, Scott felt his calm facade begin to crumble. "We—we almost lost her," he stammered, a large knot of emotion choking off his words.

"But thanks to you, we didn't," Andrea murmured against his chest.

He regained a little of his composure. "Hmm," he said, "I like the sound of that."

She raised her head and regarded him curiously. "The sound of what?"

"'We.' I like the sound of 'we.' He pulled her head back to his chest and buried his lips in her abundant, sweet-smelling hair.

"Where's Marge?" Ted asked. His tone was casual, but there was an anxious edge to it.

"In her room," Millie reported. "I got her to take one of the capsules Dr. Corey prescribed for her bad spells, and she was almost asleep before we got her down the stairs. I don't think she'll be up and around again before morning. Maybe she'll feel better by then." She sighed and shook her head. "Poor thing."

Minutes later Paula entered the kitchen, looking drawn and pensive. "Lexi's down for the count," she announced. "She woke up and actually giggled when I was changing her and getting her ready for bed. The little imp doesn't seem any worse for the wear—which is more than I can say for her mother." She sank into one of the chairs by the table and let out a ragged breath. "As they say in the wild, wild West, I feel like I've been rode hard and put away wet."

Ted moved behind her and began to massage the knotted muscles in her neck and shoulders. "Your mother's asleep, too," he said. "Millie gave her some medication, and she'll sleep through the night."

"That's good. I'm not sure I could face her tonight." Paula turned, and her eyes met Ted's as she reached up to smooth a few tangled locks of dark hair back from her pale forehead. "After this day, I'd certainly like to spend a night in my own bed."

Ted touched her cheek with more tenderness than she'd felt in weeks. "I'd like that, too," he said.

"Everything will look better in the morning," Millie declared. "You and Rudy and the baby will go for a nice, long walk, and—"

"Rudy!" Paula exclaimed, as if suddenly remembering a forgotten treasure. "Where is my super-hero, anyway?"

"I let him out back after the accident," Millie said. "He was moving pretty slowly, and it seemed like he wanted to be left alone."

"I guess I'd be moving pretty slowly too, if I'd just taken a hit like that," Paula observed. "Eighteen pounds of plummeting baby had to smart." She stood, and Ted stepped aside. "Thanks for the scrunching," she said warmly. "All those tight muscles feel much better now."

"Hey, what's a husband for?" he grinned. "Maybe I could do the same for Rudy. In fact, I think we should set him up with a full-time massage therapist. He's definitely got it coming." He pushed open the sliding glass door and followed her into the backyard.

Paula whistled and called the dog's name, but there was no response. She tried again, then again, and finally they heard a thin whimper from a far corner of the yard in back of the gazebo. Hurrying to the spot, they found Rudy lying on his side, panting softly, as though every breath was an ordeal. They knelt beside him and he tried to raise his head in greeting, but it was no use. He thumped his large tail twice on the grass, and the effort seemed to exhaust him.

"Hey, buddy," Paula said, carefully stroking the dog's head and neck. "We've been looking for you—wanted to thank you for being Lexi's guardian angel. She'll be just fine. You did good, pal." Her voice caught as she gazed down at Rudy, understanding in some profound way that his devotion to the little girl had saved her from . . . from . . . She couldn't even think it.

Ted laid a hand on her shoulder. "I'll stay here with him; you go call the vet. And when you come back, bring a blanket, would you? I think Rudy's cold." His hand rested on the dog's quivering flank.

"Here you go," Scott's voice said behind them. "We followed you guys partway out here, and when we saw you find him, we went back and got this. Figured it might come in handy." He and Andrea knelt on Rudy's other side and spread a lightweight beige thermal blanket over him. "There you go, boy," Scott murmured, scratching behind the retriever's ears. "You just hold on now. Help is on the way." Rudy's eyes closed, and he lay perfectly still except for one of his big front paws, which was twitching a little.

Paula raced into the house and to the kitchen wall phone, where she punched in the home number of her veterinarian, Dr. Thomas MacKenzie. They had been friends for years, and he had looked after Rudy since the dog had been a frisky six-week-old puppy. "Mac," she said as soon as he answered, "it's Paula. There's been an accident, and Rudy—" Her voice faltered and she swallowed hard, then managed to blurt out the story. "I think he's hurt, Mac," she said at the end. "He can barely move."

She listened for a few minutes while he gave her instructions, then hung up and dashed outside to the little group huddled on the lawn. "Mac wants us to bring him in," she reported. "He'll meet us at his clinic as soon as we can get there, and he told me how we should move Rudy."

They followed Mac's directions to the letter. Ted found two thin pieces of pegboard in the garage; taped together, one on top of the other, they made a perfect stretcher. They carefully slipped the board beneath Rudy's body, then secured him to it with several long strips of fabric torn from a sheet. Finally, as the dog whimpered weakly, Ted and Scott painstakingly lifted the makeshift litter and carried it to the Cherokee. Paula and Andrea climbed into the back with Rudy while the men took the front seats. Twenty minutes later, the vehicle pulled up in front of the Creature Comforts Animal Clinic. Mac's Chevy Blazer sat in the parking lot, and the building's lights cast heartening beams of reassurance into the deepening gloom of the winter evening. "You did a fine job of getting him here," Mac insisted as he hurried out to help carry Rudy inside.

"Just give us some good news," Paula pleaded. "It's been a long day." *Has it really only been one day?* she asked herself. *I've had* months *that have seen less action.* She set her jaw grimly. *If tomorrow's the Sabbath, it should be a day of rest. We can hope for that.* The group silently took their seats in the waiting room.

It was nearly half an hour before Mac, a well-built man with thinning gray hair, dressed in jeans and a purple sweatshirt, emerged from the examining room. He was scratching his head. Before anyone could ask, he launched into an explanation of sorts. "I don't know; the preliminary x-rays are inconclusive at this point. It could be bad; at his age, he's developed quite a bit of osteoporosis, and the baby's falling on him could have done some real damage. On the other hand, he might just be badly bruised, stiff and sore, maybe some torn muscles, and when the swelling along his back goes down, he could be fine. In either case, he shouldn't be moving around right now. I'll keep him overnight, then do some more extensive x-rays and other tests tomorrow, when my assistant can come in to help. I called her tonight, but she was gone for the evening."

"Will he be okay here alone . . . all night?" Andrea asked, her voice heavy with concern.

Mac smiled, and his kind brown eyes met hers. "I'll stay and keep an eye on him. We don't exactly have a doctors' lounge here, but the old sofa sleeper in my office comes in handy every so often." His smile dimmed a bit, and he stuffed his hands into the pockets of his jeans. "Besides, Rudy's been my pal for almost ten years now, and I'd never leave him alone at a time like this." He turned to Paula. "I'll give him some meds for the pain, and he should sleep through the night. When there's any news, I'll give you a call."

In a rush of gratitude, Paula gave the vet a warm embrace. "Thanks so much, Mac. We'll wait to hear from you, then." After exchanging a few pleasantries, the four filed out of the clinic and headed for home. The Cherokee's dashboard dial read eleven-thirty by the time they pulled into the driveway.

Millie had changed the bedding on the sofa sleeper for Andrea, and Scott followed her downstairs to say good night. "Sorry we didn't get up to the cave," he murmured as she tossed her handbag and sweater jacket onto a nearby chair. They were both still wearing the clothes they'd worn to his baptism.

"What—and miss all the excitement?" Her smile was subdued as she fingered the lapel of his rumpled suit jacket. "It's not every day this Idaho farm girl gets to watch a genuine hero at work."

"I hear you," he grinned. "That Rudy's a pretty amazing dog, isn't he? Heck, if he hadn't been right there when Chiclet fell, I hate to think what would've happened."

"Well, that too," she replied, looking up at him with a gaze that was at once as vivid as a spring morning and as misty as a fog-shrouded San Francisco dawn. "But I was thinking more of a certain young man showing the courage of his convictions by making sacred covenants with the Lord and receiving His priesthood. Then going to the nth degree to calm his grandmother down when no one else could. Then comforting his mother in a cold, unforgiving hospital waiting room. Then getting down on his hands and knees in the grass to minister to a poor, sick, frightened animal. All of it definitely adds up to a hero in my book." She touched his cheek. "I've learned more about you in the last twelve hours than I have in all the years we've known each other. And I don't mind telling you I like what I've learned. You're a good man, Scott Donroe. An awfully good man. I'm so proud to know you." She wrapped her arms around his waist and rested her head against his chest, as if she might enjoy spending the rest of her life there.

Above her glistening hair, he squeezed his eyes shut as his lips silently formed the word *Yes!* With a deep sigh, he lowered his chin to the top of her head in perfect contentment.

Paula glanced sideways at the luminous dial of her alarm clock: three-thirty A.M. "Are you awake?" she whispered without moving a muscle.

"I wondered when you'd get around to asking that," Ted replied, also without moving. "Long night, eh?"

"The longest," she sighed. "You'd think after such a big day, I'd be exhausted and out like a light. But it's just the opposite; with so much on my mind, I may never sleep again."

He turned on his side to face her. "Let me guess. You're pleased and proud and excited that Scott has finally taken the plunge. You're wondering what—if anything—is going on in your mother's mind, and you're scared to death of what might happen today or tomorrow or next week. You're worried that the accident this afternoon might have some long-term effects on Lexi's development, physically or emotionally or both. You're thankful beyond measure that Rudy was there when he needed to be, and you're terrified that it might mean losing him." He reached through the darkness to smooth her hair. "Have I missed anything?"

"No . . . but I have." Paula's voice was heavy with weariness and regret. Long moments later, she spoke again. "I've missed you, Ted."

A heavy sigh escaped his lips. "Not half as much as I've missed you. Seems like we've lived on different planets these past few months."

"And it's all my fault," they both said in unison.

"I've been grumpy, selfish, and insensitive," he confessed.

"I've been distracted, unrealistic, and pathetically self-centered," she admitted.

"Can you ever forgive me?" he asked.

"Only if you return the favor."

"Then let's start from here, and try to pull together instead of apart." He took her into his arms and kissed the top of her head. "I'm so sorry, Paula. I love you."

It was the sweetest sound she had heard in a long, long time. They fell asleep holding hands, each praying silently for the blessings of heaven upon their home.

The next morning, after Ted had left for an early meeting, Paula insisted that Millie go to church while she stayed home with Marjorie and the baby. "It's my turn to take care of things here," she reminded the older woman. "We'll be fine. Besides, I'd like to see Andrea off; she'll go to church with Scott, then he'll drive her directly to the airport. And I definitely want to be here in case Mac calls with any news about Rudy."

Millie's face broke into a grateful smile. "I would like to go," she admitted. "Brother and Sister Turpin have been called on a mission to Kenya, and their farewell is today. Ida and I have been close ever since I joined the Church."

"Then you should definitely be there," Paula said.

"Marjorie is doing pretty well this morning," Millie reported. "I went to check on her earlier, and she let me help her shower and get into a fresh nightgown. She's still quite groggy from the medicine we gave her yesterday, and she asked to be left alone, so she may sleep into the afternoon. I set some juice and crackers by her bed in case she gets hungry. The baby's been fed and bathed."

Paula impulsively drew Millie to her in a grateful embrace. "You're the best, my friend," she murmured. "Thank you so much . . . you're more appreciated than you will ever know."

"Oh, pooh," Millie said with a self-conscious chuckle. "I'm the lucky one. Now I'd best run and get my church duds on—don't want to be late." She pressed a loving kiss to Paula's cheek, then turned and hurried toward her room.

By ten-fifteen, Scott and Andrea were ready to leave for church. Seeing the two young people talking, laughing, and interacting in a way she had not observed before, Paula couldn't help thinking that something between them had changed significantly over the past twenty-four hours. While Andrea was finishing her breakfast and Scott was upstairs donning his tie and suit jacket, Paula had to ask. Pouring a second mug of steaming cocoa, she sat down at the kitchen table and looked deeply into the young woman's extraordinary green eyes, now more vibrant than she had ever seen them. "So, are you going to tell me?" she asked, her voice a study in nonchalance.

Andrea returned her gaze with a wide-eyed, innocent expression. "Tell you what?"

"What's going on with you and Scotty," Paula replied, sure she was on the right track.

"Oh, that." A deep blush flooded Andrea's cheeks. "You noticed," she added with an endearing lilt of shyness in her voice.

"Of course I noticed. A mother can't help seeing these things." She reached out to squeeze Andrea's graceful hand. "Especially when she loves them both so much."

Andrea's face lit up. "That means a lot to me, Paula; it really does. You know I've thought of you as a second mother ever since my own died."

"I know," Paula responded warmly. "And I've thought of you and Ruthie as the daughters I never had. Welcoming Alexis into our lives has only tripled the joy." She paused. "Now, what gives between you and Scotty?"

Andrea laughed—a low, musical sound that reminded Paula so much of the girl's mother, her dear friend Karti. "You don't give up, do you?"

"Never," Paula smiled.

"Well, okay." Andrea took a final long, slow swallow of orange juice, then dabbed at her lips with a napkin. "Last night, after we got home from the vet's and things had calmed down a little, I told Scott how impressed I was by the way he'd handled everything—how much I admired a man who could be so kind and courageous and empathic and," she blushed again, "all that stuff. Not to mention finally seeing the truth of the gospel and acting on it. And I meant what I said . . . meant it with all my heart."

"I can see you did—and do," Paula remarked, noticing the sheen of affection in Andrea's eyes.

"Anyway, when I said that to him, it was like peeling back one layer of our relationship and finding a whole new one underneath. He kind of relaxed after that, really opened up to me, and we talked way far into the morning. I swear, it was like having a four-hour-long spiritual experience. And then he . . . he . . ." She hesitated, and began twisting a lock of her luxuriant hair around one finger, as she had done the very first time Paula had met her.

"It's okay," Paula prompted sweetly. "I can take it."

"He kissed me. On the lips. For the very first time." She ran the fingers of one hand quickly across her mouth, as though checking to make sure it was still intact.

"I see," Paula said evenly, willing herself to remain calm but feeling tears of joy spring to her eyes. *Oh, my sweet girl,* she thought. *I don't know exactly what this means, but it's quite possible that Scott Donroe could be the luckiest young man alive.* "And how was it?"

"Magic," Andrea beamed. "I'll never forget it as long as I live."

"What's that you'll never forget?" Scott's voice said behind them. He had just come in from taking Andrea's luggage out to the Viper.

Paula cleared her throat as she turned in her chair to face him. "Uh, the weekend. She was just saying how she'll never forget this weekend as long as she lives."

He glanced toward Andrea with barely concealed adoration. "Yeah, I know the feeling. After everything that's happened, our lives will never be quite the same again. So Andy, it's getting late. Are you ready to go?"

"I think so," she said, rising from her chair. She hugged Paula tightly, then Scott grabbed her hand and urged her toward the door. With a faintly whimsical smile, Paula watched them dash across the lawn and climb into the Viper. Moments later, they had disappeared in a plume of blue exhaust smoke.

She was upstairs in the nursery, playing with Lexi, when the phone rang sometime after noon. Hefting the giggling baby under one arm, she hurried across the hall to her room. A glance at the caller ID—*Creature Comforts*—raised a flutter of apprehension in her chest as she lowered her daughter to the bed and lifted the receiver. "Mac?" she said. "How's Rudy?"

Hearing the dog's name, Lexi eagerly repeated it in her baby chatter. "Woo-woo! Woo-woo!" It was the first word she had learned, and she loved to say it. Rudy, too, adored hearing it; when this energetic little person spoke, then tugged playfully on his huge, floppy ears, his brown eyes sparkled with delight.

"Hello, Paula," Mac said. He sounded defeated and exhausted, almost unable to utter even another syllable.

Paula closed her eyes and pressed the fingers of one hand to her temple. "Tell me, Mac."

She could hear him take in a long breath and let it out slowly. "It's bad," he finally said. "Much worse than the first x-rays suggested."

"How much worse?" She pressed her lips together and impulsively reached for the baby.

"His age has worked against him, I'm afraid; with so much osteoporosis, those old bones just didn't stand a chance when the baby hit him. His back is fractured in a dozen places; two ribs broken, one punctured a lung. Massive nerve damage; his legs are useless. He can move his neck and turn his head, but that's about all. Anything else is too painful." He paused, and she heard him swallow with difficulty. "It won't get any better, Paula."

She forced the words out between trembling lips. "And what is your recommendation?"

"I think," he replied, his own voice cracking with emotion, "we need to let him go. Rudy has been my very favorite patient since the day I gave him his first puppy shots, and if there was anything else to be done, you know I'd try. But . . ." As his words trailed off, in her mind's eye Paula could see this gentle man's face, contorted with grief.

"I know," she said, wiping at her cheeks. "When . . . how . . ." She couldn't think of what to ask.

"A simple injection," he managed after a few moments. "Once it's done, he'll be gone in seconds. No discomfort."

"A good death," she observed.

"And a kind one. He's in a lot of pain, Paula—even with the medication I've given him. I can see it in his eyes. It's time to let him rest."

"I'll be there for him," she sniffed. "We'll all want to say good-bye."

"Of course," Mac said. "Just tell me when. I hate to say it, but the sooner the better. Watching him suffer is . . . hard. I'll stay with him until you come."

She studied the clock on her nightstand, squinting until her eyes cleared enough to make out the time. Twelve forty-five. "Then let's say five o'clock. Can it wait that long? My son Scott is taking someone to the airport after church, and I'm sure he'll want to—"

"Five will be fine. I'll have everything ready."

They hung up, and Paula gathered Lexi into her arms. "Well, my little princess," she murmured as her tears fell against the baby's dark curls, "I guess it's time to tell your old pal Rudy good-bye. He saved your life, you know. Someday I'll tell you all about it."

"Woo-woo!" the little girl sang out with a high-pitched squeal of glee. "Woo-woo!"

"I can't believe he's gone," Paula sobbed against Ted's shoulder late in the evening. "Even when he could barely lift his head, that beautiful big sweetheart spent the last five minutes of his life licking the tears off my face, like he was giving me a gigantic good-bye kiss. It was absolutely the noblest thing I've ever seen." She looked up at him, her eyes streaming. "Next to what he did for Lexi yesterday."

Ted dried her tears with a fresh tissue, then stroked her hair, her arm, her back. "We'll all miss him," he said tenderly. "A little while ago, as I was walking past Scott's room, his door was open and I heard him on the phone with Andrea. He's brokenhearted over losing Rudy."

Paula nodded, recalling the desolate look on her son's face as he had stroked the dog's silky golden flank for the last time. "Take care, good buddy," he had whispered close to Rudy's ear before leaving Paula and Mac alone to administer the lethal drug. As the moment arrived, the only way Paula could bear the separation was to rest her cheek lightly against Rudy's muzzle, press her hand over his heart, close her eyes, and envision a certain energetic, sandy-haired twelve-year-old boy kneeling just on the other side, his arms open wide, a huge grin splitting his freckled face. "C'mere, big boy," TJ was calling out to Rudy, his dark eyes positively glowing with anticipation. "I've missed ya so much, pal . . . are we ever gonna have fun today!" At the very instant the beating ceased beneath her hand, she saw the dog leap buoyantly into the youngster's arms, covering his face with wet kisses, his magnificent feathered tail wagging his entire body in shivers of delight. At this moment of unspeakable pain on one side of eternity, it was a vision of transcendent joy on the other. And it would have to last her until she saw them both again.

Chapter 21

Monday morning dawned cold and rainy. Thankfully, Marjorie had again slept through the night, and Paula stayed in bed until well after Ted and Scott left for work. Only Lexi's playful gurgling noises could draw her from beneath the covers of her sofa bed. Pulling on a thick terry robe, she shuffled upstairs to the nursery. The baby had pulled herself to a standing position in the crib, and was alternately chewing and jiggling its plastic-coated wood railing, babbling to herself in cozy little one-syllable words of undetermined origin. When her mother appeared in the doorway, she opened her blue eyes to their widest circumference, stretched out her chubby arms, and began chanting "ma-ma, ma-ma" like a golden mantra that would surely deliver the key to all of life's most delicious treasures. Paula found it irresistible, and hurried to the crib to scoop Lexi into her arms. "Mama's little angel," she murmured, burying her face in the child's neck and breathing in the fresh baby scent of her. Perhaps this day would be bearable after all.

At breakfast, Paula nibbled on a piece of French toast while Lexi, who had been bathed and fed earlier, sat in her highchair and tossed Cheerios onto the floor. When she began to chant "Woo-woo! Woo-woo!" over and over again, Paula realized with a sad start than on any other ordinary morning, Rudy's big tail would have been thumping the floor right about now as he caught one after another of these flavorful morsels on his wide, pink tongue, then licked up the strays and waited for more. Lexi had never tired of playing their little game, and this morning she seemed puzzled at the collection of Cheerios littering the floor with no Rudy to claim them. The sight tore at Paula's heart, and she felt a knot of grief pressing into her throat.

"It's going to take some getting used to," Millie said kindly, resting a comforting hand on Paula's shoulder. "He was a big part of this family."

"And he saved Lexi's life." Smiling up at her old friend, she noticed that Millie's eyes were puffy-looking and tinged with red. She reached up to her shoulder and rubbed the woman's hand.

They shared a moment of unspoken consolation before Millie pulled away and shuffled toward the refrigerator. "I'll just get some more orange juice," she said in a quavering voice. Later, she swept up the Cheerios from the floor.

Near noon, Paula lay stretched full-length on her bed downstairs, the baby curled serenely against her chest and stomach, sleeping peacefully. With the best of intentions, she had brought Lexi here with a small box of toys, hoping she would play quietly while her mother worked at the computer. And the plan would have been perfect, except that Paula was in no mood to crunch budget figures. What she really wanted and needed was to hold on to something or someone, to press it so closely against her that it would fill the raw, empty place in her heart. After more than an hour of staring blankly at her computer, casting frequent glances toward the cheerful little girl playing with a menagerie of stuffed animals, she gave up and joined her daughter on the floor. Within a few minutes they were on the bed, snuggled in each other's arms. As Lexi relaxed and made small, contented noises, Paula crooned a few words, almost forgotten now, that she had once sung to her two sons. "Hush, little baby, don't you cry; Mama's gonna sing you a lullaby . . ." The song eased them both into a tranquil state of lethargy, and Paula welcomed the sensation.

A light touch on her knee barely roused her, but the words brought her to reluctant attention. "Paula, dear, could you wake up for a minute?" The baby stirred briefly, then went back to sleep. "Paula, I don't mean to bother you, but . . ." The voice hesitated, and Paula screwed open one eyelid to see Millie staring down at her with an anxious, apologetic expression.

"No bother," Paula yawned. "What's up?" She was already enjoying thoughts of getting back to her nap.

"Marjorie is asking to see you."

She squinted up at Millie. "Excuse me?" she questioned, trying to buy a little time for her head to clear.

"Your mother. She's quite insistent—and quite in her right mind today, too, I believe. This is the first time since the accident that she's wanted to see anyone. She's up and dressed, and has even been watching TV."

Paula swung her legs slowly over the edge of the couch, careful not to wake Lexi as she sat up. "Okay," she whispered. "Would you mind doing the honors?" Millie smiled and lifted the baby gently from her arms. "Thanks—back in a minute."

The door to Marjorie's room was slightly ajar, and Paula knocked lightly before pushing it farther open. She could see her mother sitting in the recliner, dressed in a silver-blue fleece lounging suit and wearing heavy beige chenille house slippers. Her gray-white hair was neatly styled—a far cry from its unkempt appearance two days earlier. She seemed to be staring at the television, but the picture was very poor and the sound was turned off.

Paula ventured a few feet into the room. "Mother? Millie said you wanted to talk to me. Is now a good time?"

Instead of answering directly, Marjorie pointed a long, slender finger toward the TV screen. "That's what it's like having this disease," she said in a hollow voice. "Some days the reception is clear as can be. Other days, it sucks."

Paula's jaw dropped. "It sucks?"

"A little expression I learned from my grandson," she explained, her face showing no trace of emotion. "Granted, it's a bit on the colloquial side, but it seems to get the point across."

"I see," Paula said. *I'll bet he didn't get that one from the Book of Mormon.*

"No, I don't think you do see," Marjorie replied. She pressed a button on the TV remote, and the screen went dark. "Please, sit."

Feeling suddenly like a twelve-year-old girl in the shadow of a stern parent, Paula obediently took a seat on the ottoman next to her mother's recliner. She tentatively opened her mouth to speak, but Marjorie raised her hand and she thought better of it.

"I know what happened on Saturday," the older woman began, speaking slowly and distinctly.

Paula's face paled, but Marjorie went on. "That is, I don't exactly remember it, but Millie was kind enough to fill in some of the details when I asked. Left to my own devices, I can only recall scattered images—a doll I had as a child, my mother's long trip into town one day, and your father . . . your father as a much younger man. Strange. It's all very muddled and confusing." She shook her head and folded her blue-veined hands loosely in her lap. "Millie said there was an accident of some kind, and the baby took a fall, but she's fine." Marjorie's gaze was riveted on her daughter's face. "Can you tell me any more?"

Paula sighed. What was the use? Nothing could ever erase the horror of those heart-stopping moments or bring Rudy back, and knowing the truth might only accelerate Marjorie's descent into madness, or the abyss of Alzheimer's, or whatever it was. The challenge now was keeping her calm and safeguarding her lucid moments. She decided to play it close to the vest. "Everything's all right, Mother. You had one of your bad spells and Lexi took a tumble, that's all. Things are back to normal now."

Marjorie lowered the footrest on her recliner and leaned forward. "I don't believe you," she stated firmly, "and I wish you would tell me the truth. It's very important."

Paula's brow furrowed. "But why?" She couldn't think of a single reason her mother should be exposed to further emotional stress.

Like a flaky pie crust too tender to hold its filling, Marjorie's determined expression suddenly crumbled, leaving her face looking worn and deflated. Her chin trembled as she lifted her head and forced herself to look directly at Paula. "Because . . . because if I've done a terrible thing, I must repent." Her eyes closed briefly, then opened again. "Before I can be baptized, I must make my peace with God. I must be ready to receive the covenant."

"But Mother," Paula argued, "what happened wasn't your fault. It was the illness, and you had no control. Surely the Lord wouldn't hold you responsible for—"

"Responsible for what?" Marjorie cut in. "I knew there was something."

Paula knew she'd been caught. "Well, for . . . for anything that might have happened while you were, uh, confused."

"Ah, yes—confused," Marjorie repeated with a thin smile. "Such a benign way of saying I'd taken leave of my senses. But it doesn't make any difference. Don't you see? Whether or not God might hold me responsible, it's important to me that while I'm able, I try to make it right. Nothing else will do if I'm to become a member of the Church." She looked at Paula with hope and pleading in her eyes. "Please . . . will you help me?"

Paula studied her mother's countenance—the face of a woman who was struggling mightily against some unseen force of destruction, trying to make some sense of the catastrophe that had befallen her, determined to win this tiny battle even though she knew the war was already over. Compassion bubbled into her chest, and she nodded in resignation. "All right, Mother. I'll tell you."

For the next several minutes, as gently as she could, Paula related the events as they had unfolded. She began with Marjorie's encounter with Mrs. Spencer, then moved to the terrifying banister balancing act, to Scott's intervention, and finally to Lexi's fall from the stairwell and her miraculous rescue by Rudy. In a voice quivering with emotion, she concluded by reporting that the dog had not survived.

Throughout the account, Marjorie sat quietly in her chair, her eyes closed, her hands clasped tightly in her lap. While her body never moved, the skin and bones of her face seemed almost liquid as they quaked and rolled with each new bit of information Paula imparted. At the end, tears streamed from the corners of her lidded eyes.

When she was finished, Paula leaned over and touched Marjorie's arm. "It really was an accident, Mother. Your hand and arm just slipped; it certainly wasn't done on purpose. No one blames you." She retrieved a box of tissues from a nearby table and gently wiped her mother's cheeks before dabbing at her own.

After a few moments, Marjorie slowly opened her eyes and fixed them on Paula's face. "It may be true that I was not entirely responsible," she said, "but I should do what I can to make amends. The least I can do is apologize—to my granddaughter, to Millie, to Scott and Ted." Tears spilled from her eyes again as she continued in a small, forlorn voice. "I would hope that someday . . . someday you will be able to forgive me. I'm so terribly, terribly sorry." She pressed a trembling hand to her lips and bowed her head to her chest, unable to say more.

A rush of empathy and affection flooded Paula's heart, and without hesitation she bent over the recliner and pulled her mother into a warm embrace. "There's nothing to forgive," she whispered. "It's over now, Mother. It's over."

Marjorie returned the hug, then pulled back a little and sighed deeply. "Thank you, my dear. I only wish it were that simple."

Paula returned to her seat and gave her mother a puzzled look. "What do you mean?"

"I mean," Marjorie said, "that it's *not* over—never will be, at least in this life. I may not throw a baby over the banister again, but other things are bound to happen. And I think we need to face the facts and do something about it."

Paula could see that her mother was clear-eyed and determined, at least for the moment, so she decided to see where this conversation was leading. "What did you have in mind?" she asked.

Marjorie's back straightened and her chin lifted. She spoke precisely, as though she had rehearsed every word beforehand. "I believe it's time I found other living arrangements." She winced slightly. "A home of some kind."

Paula was stunned. "Why, Mother, whatever would make you want to—"

"It's not a question of wanting," Marjorie interrupted. "I'm very comfortable here, and I've appreciated your attentions more than you know. But before I lose my way completely and turn this household upside down, before I do harm to myself or anyone else, I'd prefer to be settled in a place where such things can be . . . taken care of." She rubbed her hands up and down her narrow thighs.

"You've really given this some thought," Paula observed. Her chest felt constricted with a feeling she couldn't quite describe. Was it relief, guilt, disappointment, resistance, gratitude? All of the above?

"Yes, I have," Marjorie admitted, "and I thank the Lord I've been alert enough to do it. I would, however, like to make one stipulation if my plan is to go forward."

"I'm listening." Paula was still dazed by this turn of events.

Marjorie sat up to her full height and looked at Paula, her eyes flashing with pride and tenacity. "I must insist that wherever I go, the care and service I receive will be the absolute best that money can buy." A half-smile made its way to her lips. "I can afford it, you know. A lifetime of wealth and privilege shouldn't be compromised just because one's mind has vacated the premises. With what your father left me, I could buy half the retirement homes in California and remodel the rest."

"I understand," Paula said, allowing her own bewildered smile to surface. "But . . . are you sure?"

"Today, I'm sure," Marjorie said with the hint of a chuckle. "Tomorrow, I might have completely forgotten this conversation." She reached into her pants pocket and pulled out a folded sheet of paper. "Which is why I've written it all out. Everything I want. It's signed and dated—something on the order of a living will. Just so there will be no question, even if I can't recall a bit of it." She handed the paper to Paula. "Of course, I hope I'll have at least a few good days left. There's still the matter of my baptism."

Paula unfolded the paper and scanned her mother's elegant handwriting. It was all there, spelled out to the last detail. She refolded the sheet and held it to her chest as a swell of emotion tightened her throat. "Very well, Mother. When should we . . . how soon do you want to . . . um, what would you like me to do now?"

"About the baptism or the change of address?" Now that she had stated her case, Marjorie's eyes were twinkling with a new vitality.

"Both, I guess."

"Then let's take first things first." Marjorie looked thoughtful. "What day is this?"

"Monday. It's Monday," Paula replied.

"I knew that," the older woman smiled. "Have you planned your family home evening yet?"

Paula shrugged. "Frankly, I haven't even thought about it, with everything else going on. I suppose we could—"

"Then if you don't mind," Marjorie cut in, "I'd like to take a few minutes to do what we talked about—set things right with the rest of the family. Then I'll make my announcement, and we'll see if anyone knows of a convenient but exclusive retirement manor where the rich and crazy go to be pampered for the remainder of their lives." She was actually enjoying this turn of the conversation.

"Yes," Paula said, "an exclusive retirement manor. I like the sound of that."

"Just promise me there won't be any pink flamingos out front," her mother insisted with a small, aristocratic giggle. "I detest pink flamingos."

"Your wish is my command," Paula laughed. "No flamingos—red, pink, or purple. I promise."

The family gathered in the TV room at seven o'clock. Scott had originally made plans to meet with a home evening group from his ward, but when Paula explained Marjorie's intentions he quickly rearranged his schedule. "How're you feeling, Gran?" he asked as she took a seat next to him.

"Well enough, thank you," she replied with a fond pat to his knee. "Congratulations on your baptism."

"I wish we could've made it a twosome," he said. "But at least I have the priesthood now, so you just say the word whenever you're ready."

"I'll do that," she smiled.

Following a song and opening prayer, Paula announced that Marjorie would like to say a few words. She did so with grace and eloquence, even humor, as she described the debilitating effects of her illness. "But what I never expected," she said after apologizing for the events of the weekend just past, "was that it would place the people I care about most in harm's way." She looked at them with a penitent expression, then apologized again. "Paula tells me it wasn't anyone's fault, and I would like to think that what she says is true. But you are my family, and I'm deeply, terribly sorry for the calamities you have suffered because of me. I pray that you'll find it in your hearts to forgive what I have done." She lowered her head and wiped at a stray tear.

Scott was the first to respond. "Heck, that's a no-brainer. It's forgotten. We're just glad you're okay." He reached over to put his long arms around her, and gave her a resounding smack on the cheek. Then, rising from their chairs, Ted and Paula did the same, each offering words of affection and support. *Thank you,* she mouthed, her eyes brimming.

When Millie approached carrying the baby, a split-second of tension ignited the air, but it was quickly replaced with delight. "Gan!" Lexi squealed, grinning widely and reaching out with her chubby hands. Millie released her into Marjorie's open arms, and the little girl snuggled eagerly against her grandmother's body. "My precious child," Marjorie murmured again and again, stroking Lexi's back, kissing her dark curls. "My own Alexis."

"She loves you," Millie smiled, bending to press a kiss of her own to Marjorie's face. "We all do." A small chorus of sniffles echoed her sentiment.

"What a blessing love is," Marjorie said through a volley of tears. "Even when it blossoms so late in life."

"It's never too late for love," Paula insisted. "You're a keeper, Mother. Definitely a keeper." And with every particle of her heart, she meant it.

Over dessert, Marjorie revealed her intention to move to "a retirement manor, where every little thing can be taken care of. Then, when you all come to visit, we can simply relax and enjoy one another's company without worrying about . . . banisters and such." She smiled demurely.

"Manor . . . did you say manor?" Ted asked. His eyes quickly sought Paula's, and they exchanged a hopeful glance.

"Why, yes, I did," Marjorie replied. "'Manor' sounds so much more inviting than 'home,' or 'facility,' or 'center,' or 'assisted living,' don't you think?" She sighed wistfully. "I do hope we can find such a place nearby, so you can visit often."

Ted winked at her. "Oh, I wouldn't be surprised if something came up that's exactly what you're looking for. I'll do a little checking around."

"That would be lovely, dear," she said. "Now, just one more thing." She turned to Scott. "About my baptism. As you can see, most of my marbles are in place at the moment. If this delightful state of affairs continues, do you suppose we could schedule the ordinance this week? I'd rather not postpone it."

"You name the day, time, and place. I'll be there," he grinned. "Ted, could you and Brother O'Brien do the confirmation?"

"It would be our pleasure," Ted replied.

Scott gave her a thumbs-up. "Then we're all set. Once I know the day, I can arrange my schedule at work."

"If I might make a suggestion," Millie said, "as you know, Lexi's first birthday is Saturday, and we were planning to have a little family celebration that evening. If we had Marjorie's baptism that same day and moved the party up a few hours, we could have a *double* celebration! I'll put together a little buffet, and we'll invite several ward members who know and love Marjorie. Then we'll polish it off with ice cream and cake, all in grand birthday and re-birthday style!"

By this time, Marjorie was beaming. "That's the nicest thing I've ever heard," she said.

"Then it's settled," Paula declared, clearly pleased with the idea. "This will be an occasion to remember."

"For as long as possible," Marjorie joked genteelly, adding an elaborate sigh. "Perhaps until Sunday, at any rate."

"We'll take pictures," Ted quipped. "Kodak moments preserved for all time."

Over the next few minutes, Marjorie seemed to lose much of her energy. Before long, she stood and smiled wearily at the group. "My goodness, this has been a rather long day; so if you'll excuse me, I believe I'm ready to retire." She looked around her at five pairs of eyes shining with affection. "I wish you a good night, and do thank you all so much for . . . for understanding."

Scott jumped to his feet. "No problem, Gran. Here, let me walk you to your room. Maybe we can read for a few minutes." He carefully took her arm, and they made their way slowly up the stairs. Several moments later, her door opened and closed softly.

"I hope she'll be okay on Saturday," Paula murmured.

"We'll all pray for that," Millie added.

"Right," Ted agreed. "Paula, what time is it?"

She checked her watch. "Eight-thirty."

"Uh-huh," he said. "So . . . you must have something important to do."

She regarded him quizzically. "Like what?" It was Monday night, after all—family time.

"A phone call to make," he persisted.

"To whom?" Everyone in the ward unplugged, switched off, or in other ways disabled their phones on Monday nights.

Ted rolled his eyes and cleared his throat loudly. "You know . . . that very *manor*-ly family over on Cristobal Drive." Out of the corner of his eye he watched Millie clearing away the dessert dishes.

The realization finally dawned. "Oh, *that* family," Paula said. "You're probably right; I'm sure they're waiting to hear from us. I'll get right on it."

Afer she left the room, Ted picked up a magazine from the lamp table and began to thumb through it. As Millie shuffled over to him and picked up his dessert plate, she let out a sly little snicker, and he looked up at her. "Marjorie will like it there," she said.

He closed the magazine. "Excuse me?"

"Mira Vista Manor . . . she'll like it there."

His mouth fell open. "How did you know about . . . about . . ."

"The Manor? Alicia Tremayne's mother is my visiting teaching supervisor. We have a nice little chat every month, and she's been telling me about this lovely place her daughter and son-in-law have just opened. It's on Cristobal, so when I heard you say it just now, I put two and two together. I've been to see it; one never knows when such information will come in handy. It's very elegant and refined—just the kind of environment Marjorie would enjoy. And so convenient, too."

Ted's eyes lit up. "I'm glad you like it, Millie. Paula and I have been concerned about how to . . . handle things."

"Handle what things?" Paula's voice called out from the entryway.

"Hey, pretty woman," he grinned as she sauntered down the stairs. "As it turns out, Millie already knows all about the Manor—says she thinks it'll be perfect for Marge."

"And the other perfect thing," Paula added, "is that I've just spoken with Alicia Tremayne, and they'll have a vacancy in the next week or two. If Mother wants the room, it's hers."

"So the news is all good," Ted breathed. "Everything is turning out just fine." For the first time in months, his smile was broad and genuine. Life was finally getting back to normal.

Chapter 22

Ted's alarm sounded early. He shut it off, then stole downstairs and sat beside Paula on her sofa bed. "Good morning, sweetness," he crooned close to her ear, "and happy Sunday. It's time to rise and shine. Or at least rise and flicker."

She stirred and stretched languidly. "Hmm . . . I was just having the most delicious dream."

"Those are the best kind," he said, stroking her arm.

Paula smiled and reached for his hand. "I dreamed that after only a couple of touch-and-go days, Mother's mind cleared and she was baptized on schedule by my extraordinarily cool and handsome son, who later thanked his grandmother for the privilege because it was giving him some good practice for all the folks he'd be baptizing on his mission. His *mission!* After the baptism, my uncommonly attractive and spiritual husband confirmed Mother a member of the Church, giving her the most comforting and sensitive blessing I've ever heard. We then returned to the house and a spectacular birthday celebration for our beautiful daughter, Alexis Hope, helper of mankind, who has already begun capturing the boys' hearts, starting with her daddy and big brother. Later in the evening, we all had family prayer and a group hug."

"That was quite a dream," he chuckled. "Sounds remarkably like . . . yesterday."

"That's because all the really good dreams come true—one way or another." She sat up and squeezed his hand. "Now, let's get a move on. It's time for this Ivory household to get ready for church."

"By all means," he returned. "I'll get myself and Lexi ready, and you can spiff Marge up for her first Sunday as a bona fide Latter-day Saint. Did she sleep well?"

Paula swung her legs over the edge of the bed. "Compared to a few nights last week, I'd say she slept like an angel. We were up a time or two, but on the whole she was fairly easy to manage." A hint of weariness shadowed her eyes as she looked up at Ted. "You know, even with all the long nights and stressful days we've endured over these past months, it's taken me a while to come to terms with the fact that Mother won't be living with us much longer. But I do think the Manor is better equipped to handle her condition than we are."

Ted nodded. "The vacancy is coming up soon, isn't it?"

"At the end of next week," she confirmed. "I've already driven Mother past the Manor several times and told her about it, just to get her used to the idea, and she seems perfectly fine with it. I've heard stories about older people resisting moves of this kind, but so far it doesn't appear to be a problem for her."

"That's probably because she's already made up her mind that it's the best thing for everyone concerned. You know how independent she is."

"Tell me about it," Paula laughed. Then her expression sobered. "But she's losing ground fast. I'm just grateful the missionaries were willing to stick with us until she was baptized."

"Yesterday," Ted observed, "Marge was as lucid as I've ever seen her. She understood exactly what was going on."

"I know—and those simple ordinances of baptism and confirmation meant everything to her. They affected Scott deeply, too. I've never been more proud of him."

"So . . . all's well that ends well," Ted declared as he stood and reached for her hand, pulling her up beside him. "Now, let's get this Sabbath show on the road, shall we?" With a breezy smile and a quick kiss to her forehead, he turned and strode up the stairs.

Paula rubbed the sleep from her eyes as she padded barefoot across the entryway and knocked at the closed door to Marjorie's room. "Good morning, Mother," she called out cheerfully. "Time to get ready for church." Her heart beat a little faster as she pictured her mother partaking of the sacrament for the very first time.

There was no answer, so she knocked again after a few moments. "Mother? I thought I could help you get dressed. Millie said she'd fix one of your favorites for breakfast, and then we can all go to . . ." Her voice trailed off, and she listened intently for any kind of response. All was silent. "Hmm . . . the festivities yesterday must have worn her out. I'll just slip in and wake her." She turned the knob and pushed the door slowly open.

The covers on Marjorie's bed were thrown back, and a hurried check of the rest of the room and the adjacent bathroom revealed that she was nowhere to be found. A cold knot of apprehension formed in Paula's stomach as her mind flirted with the possibilities. *She could be upstairs right now—with Lexi!* Mentally reliving the terrifying events of the previous weekend, Paula vaulted up the stairs and to her daughter's room, where she found the baby sleeping peacefully in her crib. Weak-kneed with relief, she leaned heavily against the wall until she could catch her breath, then tiptoed across the hall to her own bedroom. Ted was singing loudly in the shower, but there were no other signs or sounds of activity. Just to be sure, she checked every other room up and down the hall. No Marjorie.

Another deep breath calmed Paula's jangled nerves, and she returned to the main floor entryway. There weren't that many other places to look, but her thoughts traveled everywhere. *Front door . . . no, locked and bolted with a special key. Garage door . . . no, it always slams; I would have heard it. Sliding door to the patio . . . no, she'd have to come down to the TV room, then walk right past me to get to it, and I'm a light sleeper these days. Unless . . .* her mind flashed back to the few minutes when, after settling Marjorie in her room for the last time at about three A.M., she had taken a brief detour to the hall bathroom before returning to bed herself. *If that's it, Mother's been outside for more than three hours.* The realization cut her speculation short, and she flew down to the TV room, where she stopped at her sofa bed to quickly wrap herself in a terry cloth robe and thrust her feet into a pair of slippers. A few more steps took her quickly to the door. Pushing the floor-length drapes to one side, she urged the large, heavy pane of glass sideways along its track. A rush of cold air swirled about her as she stepped onto the patio, and she pulled her robe more tightly around her body.

Paula squinted as her eyes adjusted to the dim gray early-morning light. "Mother?" she called out tentatively, her gaze sweeping the patio with its colorful chaise lounge, padded chairs, and glass-topped table. Nothing—only a pair of ambitious robins off to one side near the roses, pecking hungrily for worms in the dewy grass.

She moved to the very edge of the patio, straining to see or hear any movement in the shadowy yard beyond. At the moment she opened her mouth to call for her mother again, she saw what she was looking for. She knew exactly where Marjorie was.

The gazebo.

Of course. They had spent time there on a mild afternoon a few days earlier. Marjorie had thought she was home in Connecticut. "As soon as I'm able," she'd said with a whimsical little smile, "I'd like to go out to California to visit your father."

"We'll see what we can do," Paula had assured her.

Now she sprinted out to the small wooden structure, noticing how chilly the air was on this mid-January morning. She found her mother huddled on one of the cushioned window seats, clad only in a thin cotton nightgown, her head bowed as if in prayer. She was shivering violently.

"Good grief, Mother, what are you *doing?*" Paula blurted out in frantic, staccato tones. "I've been looking all over for you! It's freezing out here, and you'll catch your death of cold, and we need to get ready for—"

Marjorie raised her head, and Paula's mouth snapped shut. Not even a glimmer of recognition was evident in her mother's eyes—only a wide, vacant, terrified stare that tore at Paula's heart like a cruel joke. The old woman's mouth opened and closed, but no sound escaped.

"Oh, Mama. Mama," Paula murmured through trembling lips, barely able to discern the quailing profile through her tears. She had not called her mother by that name since . . . well, she couldn't remember how long it had been. Sitting down close beside Marjorie, she shrugged off her terry robe and wrapped it firmly around her mother's quivering frame, then drew her close and hugged her fiercely against her own warm body. Marjorie clung to her like a lost child, her eyes squeezed tightly shut, and long minutes passed before either woman moved or spoke.

Finally, Marjorie lifted her head slightly. "I thought this was home," she said in a small, thin voice, "but it's too cold to be home." She looked imploringly into Paula's eyes, still without recognition. "Can you . . . can you help me find the way home?"

"Yes, I believe I can," Paula said, her head throbbing with grief and defeat. "We'll go home now. I'll take you." She gently helped Marjorie to her feet, then slowly walked her back to the house and tucked her into bed. Almost immediately, her mother fell asleep. Paula sat with her until long after the rest of the family had gone to church and come home again.

"Is she all right?" Ted asked later that evening. He had returned from a meeting with the bishop to find Paula sitting alone at one end of the living room sofa.

"Scotty's with her now," she said. "He's been reading to her, but I don't think she's understood a word." Her whole body slumped dejectedly.

Ted moved behind the sofa and began to massage the tense muscles in her shoulders and the back of her neck. "She'll pull out of it—bounce back like she's done so many times before. You'll see."

"Maybe; but I believe it's beyond our control now." She reached up to pat his hand. "I called Alicia Tremayne at the Manor earlier; she's spent most of her nursing career working with Alzheimer's patients. I told her what happened with Mother this morning and she said they could make room for her right away. The best way to do it, she says, is over the course of a few days; she's had a lot of experience, and she'll help with every step of the transition. At least we won't be alone."

"Thank the good Lord for that," Ted said quietly. "What can I do to help?"

She looked up at him, her eyes brimming. "You know, when it came right down to it, I really didn't think it would be all that hard to let her go, especially after all we've been through. But it is. Oh, it is. I know this sounds corny, but could you . . . could you just hold me for a little while?"

They sat close together, whispering softly, touching each other's face and hair, holding hands, until they heard Scott's weary voice in the entryway. "Gran's asleep," he said. "I don't even know if she understood, but I tried to let her know I was there. I read to her from the Book of Mormon for a while, but she couldn't follow along." He shook his head forlornly.

"Thank you, son," Paula sighed. It was all she could think of to say.

"No problem," he replied. "Guess I'll head on up to bed." He moved toward the stairs, then turned back. "Hey, I'd be glad to keep an ear open for little Chiclet, if you guys would both like to stay down here tonight."

"That's very thoughtful of you, Scott," Ted smiled. "We'd appreciate that." A sideways glance at Paula told him she agreed.

"Okay then. I'll see you in the morning." Scott quickly disappeared up the stairs.

"He's a good boy," Ted murmured as they made their way slowly, arm in arm, down to the TV room.

"The best," Paula concurred in her most adoring motherly tone. "Absolutely the best."

* * * * * * * *

Alicia Tremayne was a large woman in her mid-forties with kind, merry eyes and a no-nonsense approach to life. When she showed up on the Barstows' doorstep early Monday morning, dressed in blue jeans and an oversized denim shirt, her air of confidence and optimism quickly put Paula at ease. "We'll figure this out together," she said as they discussed Marjorie's condition over cups of steaming cocoa.

By ten o'clock the plan was in place, and Alicia asked to meet her newest patient. "I—I don't know if she's up to having visitors," Paula said dubiously.

"Well, I do," the woman replied firmly. "Actually, she probably isn't. But that has never stopped me from introducing myself." She smiled, and Paula could see even rows of large white teeth between her deep-red lips. "In my line of work, I don't count on these folks knowing me for more than a couple of minutes at a time, anyway. Everything else is gravy, and I just love them for who they are."

"I'll tell Mother you're here," Paula offered, moving toward the entryway.

Alicia laid a hand on her arm. "Why don't you just let me take it from here? I won't scare her away. I promise." Paula nodded, feeling instinctively that she could trust this unassuming, good-natured woman. As her sturdy frame disappeared into Marjorie's room, she hoped she was right.

Half an hour later, Alicia closed the door softly behind her and crossed the entryway to the kitchen, where Paula was seated at the table, absently stirring her third cup of cocoa. Hearing the squeak of rubber soles against the tile floor, she looked up, a hundred questions flickering in her eyes.

"Marjorie is all right," Alicia said, lowering herself into a chair. "She's a little distracted, but I believe she knows who and where she is. At the moment, her biggest worry is the fact that she missed church yesterday."

"It would have been her first time as a member," Paula sighed. "Now I don't suppose she'll ever be able to go."

To her surprise, Alicia let out a spirited chuckle. "Are you kidding? The Mira Vista Manor is nothing if not a full-service residence. About half of our guests are LDS, so we have a little sacrament meeting and Sunday School lesson every week for them, as well as a non-denominational service for the others. They might not remember it five minutes later, but we believe it's a comfort to them nevertheless. I think your mother will enjoy her Sundays with us."

"Yes . . . thank you . . . I'm sure she will," Paula breathed. "Did you speak with her about the move?"

"Not directly; it was more important to get her used to someone new, develop a little atmosphere of trust and familiarity." She winked with one of her large, compassionate brown eyes. "If I do say so myself, I think she liked me. Said I reminded her of someone she knew—a woman named Maria?"

"Her housekeeper in Connecticut," Paula clarified.

"I see." Alicia reached across the table to squeeze her hand. "Well, we're on our way. In a matter of days, Marjorie will be safe and sound in her own cozy little place at the Manor, hopefully with a minimum of stress and strain."

"I'll do anything I can to help," Paula said.

"It'll take all of us. But we'll make it work." Alicia stood abruptly. "Now I need to get back to my other guests. Call if you need me, and I'll be in touch this afternoon." With a final cheery smile, she was out the door.

The week was devoted to Marjorie's relocation. It began with brief visits to the Manor, where, under the watchful and indulgent eye of Alicia and her husband, she was gradually introduced to the staff, the other residents, and the layout of the charming, graciously appointed building. Twice, she and Paula stayed for a gourmet lunch, took a leisurely stroll through the fragrant rose gardens, then watched old movies in a comfortable sitting area that reminded Marjorie of her Connecticut living room. Paula was never quite sure how clearly her mother understood the reason for their visits, but her doubts were laid to rest on Wednesday evening as Marjorie was getting ready for bed. "It's all right, you know," the older woman said with a resigned smile. "I'll go quietly."

Paula studied the look in her mother's eyes, now clearer than they had been since the day of her baptism. "Excuse me?"

Marjorie pulled on a robe and sat down beside Paula on a small loveseat near her bed. "I rather like the people at the Manor—especially that lovely woman Alicia," she said, "and I've had enough good days this week to know that I'd be well taken care of there." She paused, then looked at Paula earnestly. "I may be a proud, stubborn old woman who's losing her mind piecemeal, but I still have enough sense left to recognize a good thing when I see one. Some days, at any rate." She lifted an eyebrow. "You've already made the arrangements, haven't you?"

"Yes, Mother, I have," Paula admitted in a small voice, not quite sure whether to feel guilty or relieved.

"That will be fine," Marjorie returned rather formally. Then her voice softened as she continued. "There is one thing, though . . ."

"Anything, Mother. Just name it."

Marjorie moved her arm in a broad sweep of the room. "I'd like to take some of these lovely furnishings with me for my quarters, if you don't mind. It would certainly help to make things seem more . . . familiar."

"Your room at the Manor will be even bigger than this one," Paula said. "In fact, I believe it's a suite of two or three rooms. You could take everything, if you like."

"Thank you, dear. And one more thing . . . I've so enjoyed our walks and visits to the park with Alexis and Rudy. Do you . . . do you suppose we could keep doing that?"

A huge lump formed in Paula's throat at the memory of her faithful pet, whose loss Marjorie had never been able to comprehend, even though it had been explained to her several times. "Absolutely, Mother. Absolutely. We'll go to the park whenever you want." She wiped at her eyes. "And Scotty will come to see you, too. He loves it when you read together."

"Then it's settled," she declared. "I'm ready." She smiled at Paula with a peculiar sheen in her eyes, then gave her an aristocratic wink. "Remind me of that tomorrow if I don't remember it."

By Thursday afternoon, the small moving van had come and gone, and Marjorie was settled in her new suite of rooms at the Manor. She seemed comfortable, but just to be sure, Paula spent the night on a small sofa next to her mother's bed. They had breakfast in the dining room the next morning, and Paula stayed through the day, anxiously shadowing Marjorie like a protective mother hen.

At six o'clock, Paula watched from the hall as her mother sat dozing in a comfortable chair by the sitting room fireplace. "I think we can take it from here," a warm voice said next to her, and she felt Alicia's ample arm circle her shoulders. "You've been fabulous, Paula; this has been as smooth a transition as I've ever seen. Now it's time for you to go home to the rest of your family."

Paula raised her chin to protest. "But she might need some help with her dinner, and I—"

"Ted called a few minutes ago. He's waiting for you—said something about a little surprise." Paula felt herself being gently pivoted around to face the foyer. "Marjorie will be just fine."

"Well, I, uh . . . I . . ." She tried to turn back toward the sitting room, but the firm hands on her shoulders kept her pointed toward the entrance. Finally she took a few small steps in the direction of the door, then looked up at Alicia with a sheepish expression. "I guess it's really time for me to go, isn't it? It's just that I've never left her like this before, and I—"

"We call it separation anxiety," Alicia explained patiently. "It happens all the time. Although," she broke into a little smile, "it's usually the new resident who has it."

Paula felt a warm flush rise to her cheeks as she moved closer to the door. "Well, I guess I'll be . . . on my way, then." The antique brass knob turned in her hand, and she glanced one more time at Alicia. "Take good care of her, will you?"

"Cross my heart," the woman promised with a small wave and a wide smile.

The short drive home cleared Paula's head, and her heart fluttered as she turned into the driveway to find her husband standing on the front lawn in the dusky light, his arms open wide, a broad grin splitting his tanned face. But there was something else about him . . . something different. What was he wearing?

He strode across the lawn and hurried to her side as she pulled into the garage. She thought she'd seen it, and now she was sure. "Ted, what in the world were you doing out front—dressed in a tuxedo?"

"A fitting prelude for this celebratory evening, I should think," he said, bowing deeply as he opened the car door for her.

She cocked her head to one side and regarded him curiously. "And just what, might I ask, are we celebrating?" She was dog-tired, but the possibilities intrigued her.

Ted's eyes shone as he reached for her hand. "Our happy home. A new beginning. The first night of the rest of our lives. Anything you like . . . as long as we do it together." He pressed his lips to her palm. "I've made reservations for eight o'clock at Delaney's—just time for you to shower and slip into something glamorous. It'll be an evening to remember." His gaze, so full of love and anticipation, told her she would not be disappointed.

They talked, laughed, reminisced, and dreamed over dinner, then danced until Delaney's ballroom had cleared out for the night. Together for this transcendent moment in time, their spirits soared higher than they had even dared to hope. Every breath seemed to carry them closer to renewal and refreshment, a recommitment to life and to each other. They had faced enormous struggles and challenges over the past year; some of them were not yet resolved, and there would doubtless be others to come. It was the nature of mortality. But as long as they had each other, as long as they were a family, it would all work out in the end.

As they climbed the stairs to their room long after midnight, Paula thought—no, *knew*—she had never been happier.

Epilogue

On a Wednesday morning near the middle of February, Paula stared bleakly out the kitchen window. The sun was shining, and a few birds twittered in the tree branches, but their cheerful melodies did nothing for her gloomy spirits. It was too late for baby blues, too early for menopause, too complicated for a chocolate cure. Life, it seemed, was temporarily on hold until she could figure things out.

In the weeks since Marjorie had moved to the Manor, Paula's days had settled into a predictable pattern of activity. Her mornings featured an early breakfast with Ted, a bit of work at her computer and some time playing with Lexi, followed by a mid-morning visit to the Manor, where her mother was "doing splendidly, thank you very much" (except on her off-days, more frequent now, when she couldn't quite remember how she was doing). Two or three times a week, she and Lexi dropped by the hospital's newborn intensive care unit. She worked for an hour or two in the afternoon while the baby napped, then often pushed the little girl to the park in her stroller. Paula enjoyed these outings and relished watching her active daughter toddle, jabbering, from bench to bench and chase a Nerf ball to her heart's content. But somehow, the heart-wrenching memory of a large, affectionate golden dog shepherding his tiny charge along these familiar grassy paths inevitably made each excursion a bittersweet reminder of the loyal and loving friend they had both lost. Today would be another one of those days—a carbon copy of yesterday and the day before—and Paula wasn't sure she was up to facing it.

"Big day today." Ted's voice startled her back to the moment. "The top guys at the Northridge group are coming in to discuss the next phase of their ad campaign. You've been keeping an eye on it from the beginning . . . want to join us?" He sat down at the table and poured himself a glass of cranapple juice.

For a moment, the idea intrigued her; she hadn't seen the inside of Donroe's offices for over a year. She opened her mouth to ask more about the meeting, but a wave of lethargy suddenly engulfed her, and she backed off. "I—I don't think so. Maybe another time, okay?"

He shrugged, then reached across the table to grasp her hand. "There will always be meetings. What I want most is to see you happy. These past few weeks haven't exactly been a month at Disneyland, have they?"

"Oh, Ted, it's nothing like that." She pressed a hand to her heart. "In here I'm happy, really I am. I love you to pieces, the baby is such a joy, and everything has turned out perfectly with Scott and Mother. It's just that I seem to be at loose ends lately . . . distracted, like something's missing and I can't quite put my finger on it." She choked out a dry, humorless laugh. "If Rudy were here, we'd go for a long, leisurely stroll in the park, and I'd spill out my soul to him. He'd look up at me with those wonderful deep-brown eyes of his, understanding perfectly, and we'd both come home feeling much better."

"We all miss the big guy," he said. "And don't forget, my love, that you've been through one heck of a year—one crisis after another until you absolutely didn't know if you could take any more. Now that things have finally calmed down and your adrenaline isn't pumping twenty-four hours a day, it's only natural that you'd feel a little scattered—kind of an emotional jet lag, I suppose—and it might take you a little while to get your energy back."

"You're probably right," she conceded with a full-body sigh. "Everything will get back to normal eventually. I just need to have a little patience." She looked at him pleadingly. "Can you bear with me?"

Ted smiled at her, tenderness bubbling into his eyes. "Until Niagara Falls freezes over or Lexi is elected president—whichever comes last. In the meantime, however, I'm thinking of something that just might speed the process along. Are you game?"

Paula was beginning to feel better already. "What did you have in mind?"

"A little family excursion, actually," he said. "Just slip into something casual and be ready to go at seven o'clock tonight. Lexi and Scott will be joining us, too."

After a twenty-minute drive on the interstate, Ted steered his Cherokee off the highway at the Santa Clarita exit. "Where we going?" Scott called out from the back, where he sat next to Lexi's car seat. "Chiclet's getting fussy."

"She's not the only one," Paula muttered from the passenger seat.

"Almost there," Ted called back. Looking around as they drove through several middle-class neighborhoods toward the edge of town, Paula saw nothing familiar or particularly interesting. In less an hour, it would be past the baby's bedtime.

"And here we are," he said as they turned onto a nondescript street with matching houses built close together on either side. "Help me find 1341, will you?"

She cast Ted a puzzled glance, then started looking for numbers. They were almost at the end of the street when Scott spotted it—a well-kept white frame house standing back a little on a large corner lot. The porch light was on.

As Ted pulled up to the curb, turned off the motor, and began to unclasp his seat belt, Paula had to say something. "Don't tell me—after your stellar experience with BigHugs, you've found a bunch of other long-lost relatives, and you just couldn't wait to introduce us." Her voice was edged with sarcasm.

To her surprise, he didn't deny it. Instead, he leaned over and kissed her cheek. "You're a pretty smart cookie," he declared. Her eyes rolled and she breathed out a small, exasperated puff of air. He jumped out of the vehicle, sprinted around to the passenger side, and pulled the door open. "Come on," he urged, grabbing her hand. "They're waiting for us."

"Terrific," she muttered. *And this is supposed to make me feel better?*

With Scott and Lexi in tow, they hurried up a hedge-lined walk to the front porch. Ted gave the bell an eager punch, then grinned indecently at Paula until the door swung open and a short, wiry middle-aged woman appeared. "Mrs. Swenson?" Ted inquired. "I'm Ted Barstow, and this is my wife, Paula. We brought the whole family."

"Oh, that's lovely," the woman responded, pushing open the screen door. "Please come in. Everyone's out back; it's such a mild evening, we've been having a barbecue. The little ones love the excitement of it all." She led them through a tidy living room and kitchen, then pointed to an open sliding glass door leading outside.

Paula bit her tongue as she reluctantly stepped out onto the patio at one side of a large, grassy area behind the house. *Just what I need—a yard full of shirttail relatives who . . .*

Her silent words evaporated in mid-thought as the largest, most beautiful golden retriever she had ever seen trotted slowly toward her from a far corner of the yard, its luxuriant coat shimmering in the dusky light of a few Chinese lanterns set by a nearby fence. In the distance, several smaller forms darted in and out of a large boxlike structure.

Lexi was the first to react. "Woo-woo! Woo-woo!" she squealed, pushing against Scott's chest, demanding to be set free.

"It's all right," Mrs. Swenson said with a kind smile. "This is Duchess; she wouldn't hurt a flea. Your little one is perfectly safe. I have three grandchildren of my own, and they come over to play with her every day." Scott waited for Paula's nod, then set the little girl down on the patio. She toddled toward the dog as fast as her wobbly legs would carry her, then proceeded to wrap her chubby arms firmly around the top of the animal's leg. Duchess gently rested her furry chin against the baby's dark hair as Lexi chanted "Woo-woo!" again and again. The sound tugged fiercely at Paula's heart.

Ted circled her shoulders with his arm. "That would be Duchess of Rudolph," he murmured against her ear. "A cousin of Woo-woo's. Now with babies of her own." When she pulled away and stared up at him in disbelief, he shrugged and flashed her a rakish grin. "See? You were right—a bunch of long-lost relatives."

"But when did you . . . how did you . . ."

"Elementary, my dear Watson. Remember just after we got married, when I was moving some things from your closet into storage to make room for my stuff?" She nodded blankly. "Well, I happened to come across Rudy's American Kennel Club registration papers in one of the boxes."

"Richard handled everything when we bought Rudy," she reflected. "He must have saved all the paperwork."

"Anyway," Ted continued, "the papers listed Rudy's mother's original owners and their address. I just put them back in the box, not thinking anything of it. But when Rudy died and you seemed so forlorn, I decided to do some checking, so I dug out the papers again. The owners had moved, but I was able to track them down, and voilá! When I first spoke with Mrs. Swenson, Duchess's brood of six pups were a month old; now they're eight weeks and ready to find good homes." He looked down at her, his eyes shining with hope and eagerness. "What do you think, sweetness? I know it's risky to assume that someone would want a certain kind of pet, and we can forget this if you want to, but—"

Paula's long kiss silenced him, and when their lips parted he could see tears on her cheeks. "This would be an appropriate time to tell you that I love you," she murmured in broken syllables.

His face shone with relief and elation. "Does this mean that—"

"Let's go look at the babies," she smiled.

Mr. Swenson threw a switch that flooded the entire yard with light, then he and his wife escorted the foursome to the "puppy house," as they called it, with Duchess following close behind. Seeing their mother approaching, all six pups raced to her side like flashes of liquid gold. Satisfying themselves that she was within reach, they began playing amongst themselves, tugging and wrestling, chasing each other in and out of the puppy house, then across the wide expanse of lawn until they were completely out of breath. Seeing their antics, Paula felt a wide smile rise to her lips, and the weight of a month of gloomy days seemed to lift from her shoulders.

"They're adorable—every one of them," she gushed. "How could anyone possibly choose?"

"I think I can answer that," Scott said behind her. "May I?"

"Be my guest," she offered.

"Cool. Then let the games begin." Without further explanation, Scott moved a few feet away from Duchess and her pups, then lowered Alexis to the grass. "There you go, Chiclet," he said, watching her toddle rapidly toward the dogs, her little arms open wide.

Alarm rose in Paula's throat. "I don't know if this is such a good idea, Scott," she said, moving anxiously toward the baby. "They could get rough with her, and—"

Scott quickly grabbed her arm and pulled her aside. "Trust me on this one, Mom," he insisted. "You know I wouldn't let anyone or anything hurt my little sister. After we lost Rudy, Andrea told me how they let Ruthie choose a new puppy once. It'll work out."

Paula held her breath and stepped between the puppies and Duchess, ready to intervene at any instant but curious enough to let the scene play out as long as her daughter was safe. When the puppies spotted Lexi they surrounded her, wagging their tails with abandon, and began to tug playfully at her coveralls. The press of so many wriggling bodies against her unsteady legs proved too much, and a few seconds later she thumped unceremoniously to the grass on her bottom. The sudden jolt startled her and she began to whimper, ignoring the puppies altogether. No longer the center of attention, they eventually strayed back to their mother. Except for one.

He was the smallest of the litter, a champagne-colored chunk of fur with enormous chocolate-brown eyes and long, floppy ears that seemed entirely disproportionate to his short legs and stubby tail. This was not so much a golden retriever, Paula reasoned, as a bunny rabbit in disguise. And the little imposter was making moves on her daughter.

While his brothers and sisters frolicked under Duchess's watchful eye, the diminutive creature stood stock-still a short distance from Alexis, just out of range of her flailing arms. When her jittery motions calmed and the whimpers subsided into small hiccups, his short tail began to wave in a flat, back-and-forth motion, and his rosy-brown nose quivered as he watched her sitting bowlegged on the grass, sucking petulantly on her thumb and staring off into the star-filled evening sky. Moments later, all four of his stumpy legs appeared to move at the same time, and he seemed to hop (the bunny thing again) toward Lexi in one calculated burst of energy. This intriguing process was repeated three times, then a fourth, until his right front leg was actually touching the baby's knee.

Feeling a light pressure against her body, Lexi looked down at the same moment the little dog looked up. Extending her arm, she wriggled her fingers close to his nose, and he responded by flicking his brownish-pink tongue across her hand. When she giggled, he did it again. This time she reached out to grab his nose, but he dodged her by ducking and bounding quickly—and quite gracefully for a bunny, Paula thought—into the small circle created by the curve of her legs. Without hesitation he pressed his small, furry body against the inside of her knee and rested his chin on top of her leg. His ears were almost touching the ground.

Paula gasped. It could have been a moment ripped from her own photo album—she had at least a dozen snapshots of TJ and Rudy in that identical pose. And a dozen more of what happened next: the baby bent over almost double to nuzzle the soft nape of the puppy's neck. If there was such a thing as déja vu, this was it. "Kismet," she murmured to no one in particular.

For the next quarter-hour, Paula, Ted, Scott, and the Swensons watched in bemused silence as the two infants—one with dark, curly hair and vivid blue eyes, one with a slightly longer tail—came to a mutual understanding. It was simple, really: they would never be separated from this moment on. Lexi proved her point by refusing to budge from the spot until her arms were securely wrapped around the puppy, who had fallen blissfully asleep to the sound of her wordless chatter a few minutes earlier. Instinctively she refused to make a sound for fear of waking him, and the determined set of her tiny jaw and pursed lips warned away any interference.

"So, what do you think?" Ted asked in a low voice as they stood shoulder to shoulder, taking in the amazing scene.

In a flash of intuition, Paula realized that for the past hour, since walking into this magical place of uncomplicated fun and playful affection, she had been relaxed and at peace, not the slightest bit fretful or distracted or moody. Despite a year of crisis and change, so much of her life was good and right and happy; Ted and Scott and Lexi and the gospel had seen to that. Now it was up to her to put the important things back into perspective. And if a new little brown-eyed, bunny-sized package of puppy love could give her an emotional boost and help her embrace the grand adventure of it all, so much the better.

She sighed contentedly, linking an arm through her husband's. "I think we've just acquired a new member of the family. He's kind of funny-looking, but in an irresistible way. And, judging from the look on our little helper's face, I'd say he's definitely—"

"A keeper?" Ted was smiling down at her, his eyes brimming with love.

"The perfect description," she replied. "I couldn't have said it better myself."

"Come with me," he said. They walked a few steps to where Lexi was still sitting on the grass, half asleep now, cradling the little dog's head in the crook of her elbow.

Ted knelt and gently scooped both of them into his arms, then stood and moved close to Paula. "We're very pleased to welcome your new best friend into the Barstow family, princess," he whispered against the baby's cheek. "His name is Keeper."

"I knew that," Paula smiled. She was already planning their first visit to the park.

About the Author

JoAnn Jolley, a graduate of Brigham Young University, has enjoyed a successful career as a writer and editor. She has worked as a publications manager for two international corporations, as an editor at the *Ensign*, as managing editor of Covenant Communications, Inc., and has published dozens of feature articles and essays in national and regional markets. *Keepers of the Heart* is her third novel.

Among JoAnn's favorite pastimes are music, animals, spending time with friends and family, basketball, reading, writing, and ironing. She lives in Orem, Utah, where she teaches the Gospel Doctrine class in her ward.

JoAnn welcomes readers' comments. You can write to her in care of Covenant Cmmunications, P.O. Box 416, American Fork, Utah 84003-0416, or at her email address: *joannj@trufriends.com.*